Mohammed Umar was born in Azare in Nigeria's Bauchi State. He studied journalism in Moscow (1991) and political economy in London (1995). Mohammed Umar served as a judge for the Caine Prize for African Writing in 2009 and he was the winner of the Muslim News Award for Excellence in Arts in 2010. His first novel *Amina* has been translated into over thirty languages. He lives in London.

ALSO BY MOHAMMED UMAR

Amina
Samad in the Desert
Samad in the Forest
Samad in the Savannah
The Adventures of Jamil
The Hunter Becomes the Hunted

First published in Great Britain 2017
Salaam Publishing
London
www.salaampublishing.com
Salaampublishing@gmail.com

Copyright © Mohammed Umar 2017

ISBN 978-0-9572084-5-2 (Paperback)
ISBN 978-0-9572084-7-6   (ebook)

Designed in Baskerville by Judith Charlton
www. judithcharlton.graphics
Cover design by Andrew Corbett

MOHAMMED UMAR

THE ILLEGAL IMMIGRANT

Salaam Publishing
LONDON

For Salim, Karim & Nafisa

One

Into the Tunnel

It happened on a Wednesday during lunch break at the student's canteen in an institute in central London. I was working as a table cleaner, busy clearing racks of trays that had plates, cutlery, plastic cups and paper. I put the plates and cutlery in a trolley and the rubbish in the bin.

From the corner of my eye, I saw an African woman walking towards me with a tray in her hands. I could immediately tell that she was from the northern part of Nigeria. Her clothes were unique. She wore a wrap-around robe made of colourful cloth with matching blouse, headtie and shawl. Something stirred inside me. I glanced at her as she joined the queue of students in front of me. It was more than recognising the kindred spirit. I had never felt like that before. My gut knotted. My pulse was racing. I tried desperately not to keep looking at her but I felt a powerful urge to steal glances. I knew I must not smile at her or appear friendly. I was confused. Under normal circumstances, I would have smiled and greeted her cordially. My circumstances were not normal. One part of me hoped she would hand over the tray and walk away, another part of me wanted to talk to her.

I was in some kind of trouble. The Hausa woman had recognised me. Her smile was not the casual smile. It was a smile that indicated familiarity. I did not know what to do apart from lying to her should she start a conversation. I wanted to tell her to put the tray in one of the racks and go away but I could not bring myself to do it. She, too, did not put her tray away even though she could have done so. She waited and kept smiling at me.

When it was her turn, I collected the tray with a frown. When our eyes met, it felt like an electric shock ran through my body. There was a spark. I definitely felt it. She looked at me with her enchanting eyes. There was no make-up on her pleasant smiling face. The young Hausa woman with a small gap in her front teeth stood there, not too close and not directly facing me. Looking very relaxed, she adjusted her shawl and greeted me.

'Assalaam Alaikum Mustapha, yaya kake?' (How're you?)

I pretended not to hear and continued to work. She repeated the greeting. 'I'm sorry Ma, I don't understand what you're saying,' I finally answered with a frown, avoiding eye contact.

The Hausa woman was startled. 'I'm really sorry,' she stammered looking embarrassed. 'I thought you were Mustapha Abdullahi from Bauchi town in Nigeria.'

With a changed accent, I replied. 'Sorry Madam, my name is Michael Danquah. I'm from Accra, Ghana.'

'Allah Sarki,' (God Almighty) she exclaimed in a sympathetic voice. 'You look exactly like someone called Mustapha – a very popular television presenter from Bauchi town who is studying in London.'

'Madam,' I said nervously with a fake accent, 'I've never heard of Bauchi town.'

The young Hausa woman was not convinced. She looked at me twice. I was nervous but remained calm. 'In Ghana, we believe that every human being has a duplicate somewhere in this world so that person you are talking about is probably my twin stranger.'

Before she walked away, I heard her offer parting prayers in Hausa language.

Allah Ya sa mu gama lafiya
May our lives have a blessed end
Allah Ya sa mu dace
May God grant us success
Allah Ya saka da alheri
May you be blessed with what is good and nice.

I did not respond to her parting prayers with the customary Amin. I felt strange. The part of me that felt the spark wanted not only to acknowledge the prayers and thank her but to have a decent conversation with her. That part of me wanted to know her name, where she came from and what she was studying in the institute. I wanted to ask if she was in good health, a customary manner in which the Hausas start their greetings. But I had already lied. I also felt strange because it was the first time in my adult life that I had not responded to such prayers. I stole glances at her as she walked away, taking delicate steps into the crowd of students in the canteen.

The Hausa woman was right. I had been until a year before a popular television presenter on the state television station in Bauchi town. She was right to speak Hausa to me. It was my mother tongue. She was right to start her greetings with *Assalaam Alaikum*. I was a Muslim.

I felt sad because I had publicly rejected a kindred spirit. The Hausas say: *Dan'uwa zuma, dan'uwa rabin jiki.* (A kindred spirit is honey; a kindred spirit is half of you.) She was right; I was wrong. I felt different when our eyes met. It was the first time in my adult life that I had felt like that towards a woman. Everything about her, her attire, her face, her mannerisms but above all her fragrance reminded me of my past. There was something more than just nostalgia. There was something that connected me to her, more than just sharing the same language, culture and religion. There was a spark. I felt it. She probably felt it too. I had waited for years to have such a feeling that I had a connection to someone. I had met so many girls and had told some of them I had feelings towards them.

I continued to work. I hoped she would come again and I would have the opportunity to tell her the truth.

The truth was I had to lie – I had no choice. It was the only course of action left to me. I had lied out of necessity.

The initial sense of guilt and remorse gave way to an exhilarating sense of liberation. It was memorable because it was the moment that one personality seemed to have ended and another one began. From that moment, in the public at least, I was no longer Mustapha Abdullahi. I was now Michael Danquah.

The assistant manager walked up to me looking very angry. Miss Katsy Robertson started barking at me in her strong Scottish accent.

Pointing a finger at me – something I considered very rude from a woman hardly in her twenties – she said. 'Michael, I saw you talking to that African woman. I'll deduct thirty minutes from your timesheet. You came here to work, not to chat up women. If you talk to her again, I'll sack you. You are only a kitchen porter.'

'I'm sorry.' I apologised to her.

She repeated the last sentence loudly: 'You are only a kitchen porter.'

I was angry. How could someone obviously younger than me bark and threaten to sack me for a minor transgression like talking to someone for a couple of minutes?

Later that day, after work, as twilight descended over London, I took a bus to Camberwell. On the upper deck of the bus I had a strange sensation. I felt as though I was hearing the voice of the Hausa woman greeting me. I looked around. I felt I saw her gaze. Very briefly, sitting down in the crowded bus, I thought I could smell her fragrance. I looked around again but she was not on the bus. Remembering her voice and her face stirred something in me again. Everywhere I looked, I thought I saw her smiling face. Who was she? What was she studying? Was she upset? I asked myself several times. She must have recognised me from my days as a television presenter. It was quite possible that I had interviewed her on one of the many programmes I did. Or she may have seen me on the television, reading the news – something I did four days a week. As the bus travelled across the Thames and continued its journey south of the river, I found it difficult to forget our encounter that Wednesday afternoon.

It was drizzling when I alighted from the bus. I took hurried steps into the nearby supermarket called Bozo's Joint, a popular West African supermarket and bar in Camberwell.

'Good evening,' I greeted as I stepped into the store. Bozo welcomed me with a broad smile.

'Are you well?'

'I'm fine and you?'

'We thank God,' he replied.

'Is Jarvo around please?' I asked.

'Yes, but the politburo meeting is in progress. You can wait for him in the bar downstairs.'

I thanked him.

The politburo was the self-styled name for the executive committee of the West African Refugee Resource Centre. The main office of the centre was near Elephant and Castle Shopping Centre. From time to time, the politburo met at Bozo's Joint. I had many issues to discuss with Jarvo that evening.

There were about a dozen people in the bar. There was a sign on the only door in the bar.

POLITBURO MEETING IN SESSION: DO NOT DISTURB.

As I made my way to an empty chair, I heard the deep drunken voice of a Liberian war veteran. 'Hey! I thought you'd returned to Africa where you belong. Do you know what you're doing here?' he asked. Son-of-Adam as he was called moved his gaunt figure and staggered towards me. 'Only people like you can fight the devils terrorising our people by day but mainly by night. Go back to Africa and chase them away.'

I ignored him and sat close to the television set. I changed the channel to listen to the news.

Son-of-Adam interrupted. 'Young man, listen to me. The devil has two legs, two eyes, two hands and no heart.' I looked at him closely, not for the first time. He was struggling to light a cigarette. He was blind in his left eye and had a large scar on his forehead. He had a bullet wound on his chin and his right hand was broken in two places. An injury from a grenade had resulted in a limp.

'What's your real name?' I asked him.

He laughed revealing the fact that he had no upper front teeth. 'I don't know; just call me Lucky. I'm lucky to have escaped from the grip of the devil but now I'm suffering from my association with it.' He was always unsteady and looked like someone who had little life in him. He cast his haunted eyes at me again. I knew little about him. No one knew a lot about him or cared to find out. I was told he was traumatised by the civil war in Liberia. 'I'll never fight another war again,' he would say with regret and bitterness. 'We should not have taken up arms. Look at what the war has done to so many people. I've been to hell and back. Maybe I'm still there, I don't know. Does it really matter?' No one knew his real name. Bozo gave him the name Son-of-Adam. 'Can you hear me?' Son-of-Adam asked leaning over. I was afraid he would fall over but he somehow steadied himself. 'I was a useful idiot for a very cruel and greedy warlord. It doesn't really matter does it? At the end of the day, we are all useful idiots for somebody or something. We are all on a fool's errand. Do you agree with me that there's a useful idiot for every job?'

I nodded. 'Yes, I do.'

'Shakespeare is damn right. Hell is empty. All the devils are here.' Son-of-Adam struggled to stand. 'Did you read English literature?'

'No.'

'What did you read?'

I did not answer. I concentrated on the news. I was happy to see Niran walk into the bar. I knew he would sit next to me. He did not drink alcohol. Popularly known as *The Peacock*, Niran was tall and well built with a very loud voice. He liked showing off his expensive clothes, jewellery, watches and shoes. 'I drive a Mercedes Benz car, what about you?' was the way he started a conversation. That evening though, Niran was unusually quiet. He did not go around greeting people laughing and bragging. He came straight to the empty chair next to me and sat down. He was breathing heavily and from time to time would take a deep sigh. I could tell he was not listening to the news. He had a gold chain around his neck that carried a big cross. He wore a T-shirt emblazoned with 'Very Important Person' on it under a thick, brown, leather jacket.

'Do you know who I am?' Son-of-Adam asked him.

'You're the liberator of Liberia,' Niran joked half-heartedly.

Son-of-Adam laughed. He liked it. 'I'll get you a bottle of beer.'

'You know I don't drink.'

'Of course I do! You always say no to alcohol. I say no to alcohol too but it doesn't listen to me,' he said sitting down next to Niran. 'I can see you're sad,' he said looking at Niran. 'Don't worry, my brother. Tomorrow will be better than today. Next year 1992 will be better than this year 1991.'

'Why do you think so?'

'I'm an optimist.' He stood up. 'Tell your friend to stop watching television.'

'Why?' Niran asked.

'Because it's all lies. Listen to me,' Son-of-Adam shouted. 'Do you know what politicians and nappies have in common?'

I did not answer.

'They're both full of shit.'

The door in the bar opened. Niran sprang to his feet. He signalled to the politburo members to return to the room. He closed the door behind him. When the door opened half an hour later, it was clear something had happened to him. The expressions on the faces of the seven members had changed. They whispered to one another and looked concerned. It was not the usual convivial mood.

Niran and Taj left immediately.

I sat there waiting for Jarvo who waved at me as they continued their discussion. Jarvo was from Ghana and was nicknamed *The Philosopher.* He graduated from a university in Moscow and had claimed to be one of the very few Africans to have read the complete works of Karl Marx, Lenin, Engels, Mao and Stalin and other left-wing writers and thinkers. He freely quoted from these and other writers and philosophers all the time.

When I needed a second opinion on my application to the Home Office for the extension of my visa, it was he who had handled my case. Jarvo concluded a couple of months ago that my Pakistani solicitor had badly advised me. When the solicitor asked for more money, it was Jarvo I turned to. He raised the amount needed. When I was looking for work and was running out of money he advised me on how to get a job and gave me a national insurance number. As I waited for him, I remembered part of our conversation several months before. 'Now that your visa is about to expire, it's clear that the Home Office will not renew it. You have two choices: either you pack your bags and return to Nigeria or, you go underground and try your luck.'

'I'll go underground and try my luck,' I said without hesitation.

'In that case the earlier you go underground the better. To live under the radar successfully, you need a new identity.'

'I don't understand.'

'You must not be known as Mustapha Abdullahi from the day your case is rejected. Once your appeal to extend your visa is rejected, Home Office officials will be looking for you, Mustapha Abdullahi, *the over-stayer*. You certainly don't want to go around giving people your real name.'

'What sort of name?'

'Ideally something that will fit into the society. You need a simple Christian name, something that would make you belong.'

'For example.'

'Dave. John. Peter. Michael.'

'Okay. I choose Michael. What do you think?'

'It's up to you. Are you comfortable with it?'

'Yes I am. What about my surname?'

Jarvo thought for a while. 'You need an exotic name from Africa. Europeans still expect Africans to have Christian names as their first names and African names as surnames. If your name were to be Michael Straw, Michael Law, Michael Bridge then it would raise suspicion.'

I thought for a while. 'Nothing came into my head. Okay give me one.'

He thought for a moment too. 'What about Danquah?'

'Danquah,' I said laughing. 'Fine, at least I can pronounce it.'

'By implication it means you're a Ghanaian not Nigerian.'

There was a moment of silence.

'That's fine. I'll have to learn the accent just in case.'

'Always remember not to tell Ghanaians you're from Ghana.'

I nodded.

When moments later I told him I was not comfortable, Jarvo laughed and explained in a relaxed voice. 'First of all, you have to understand that to lie is to exist. It's simply out of necessity that we lie. For you Michael, you simply have no alternative but to tell blatant white lies. Sometimes Michael, you have to take a step back in order to move forward. Lying is normal. Lying is human. Actually many societies tell themselves elaborate lies about how they were founded and how great they are. A lot of what we call history of modern societies is pure fiction. It was Dostoevsky who once said: *I like it when people lie. Lying is a man's only privilege over other organisms. If you lie, you get to the truth. Lying is what makes me a man. Not one truth has been reached without first lying.*

He paused and continued. 'The bottom line here is to live successfully in the UK, you've got to lie. As an illegal immigrant, you have to lie to survive. Michael is a lie. Mustapha is the truth. Look at it this way. You are not what you think you are. You are what you hide away from the world. The real person is the one inside you not what you pretend to be. So from now on go out as Michael but you know you are not Michael. You are Mustapha. The real person inside you is Mustapha.'

Jarvo paused and looked at me and concluded. 'It was also Dostoevsky who also said: *Above all, don't lie to yourself. The man who lies to himself and listens to his own lie comes to a point that he cannot distinguish the truth within him, or around him, and so loses all respect for himself and for others. And having no respect he ceases to love.*

I had no choice but to agree with Jarvo. The conversation took place in the offices of the resource centre. Jarvo told me that day that 'technically the USSR collapsed today.' From time to time he would rush to the next room to watch live pictures from Moscow. He would come back looking very confused. I remembered he shouted, 'the Russian parliament has just killed the union. This is unbelievable! No more *sayoz*. The USSR is dead. Long live communism. Michael, you'll always remember this day. Your new identity was born on the day the Russian parliament voted to be an independent republic. The day things started falling apart in the USSR. The day the centre could no longer hold.'

Later that day Jarvo gave me a piece of paper with some numbers on it. 'Use this as your national insurance number. Go to any of these employment agencies on the high streets and register for work. Some of them might ask you for your national insurance number. Some don't. Just be bold and try your luck. Ask for low-paid jobs like cleaning, caring for the elderly or mentally ill, or working in the kitchen. If they have jobs these agencies don't usually care about valid documents.'

I left the offices confused.

The next day I went into an employment agency called TEMP-STAFF recruitment agency on Kilburn High Road.

'How can I help you?' a woman asked me as soon as I entered the office.

'I am looking for work.' I said, looking straight into her eyes.

'What sort of work?'

'I'm looking for anything really, kitchen porter?' I pointed to one of the posters on the windows.

'Have you got any experience?'

'No.'

'All right, are you a student?'

'Yes.'

'Please sit down.' She gave me a form to fill in. By now I knew her name was Sandra.

'When can you start?' she asked with a smile.

'Any time,' I replied.

'Come in on Monday, first thing in the morning.'

On Monday, I went and Sandra sent me to the London International Institute of Finance and Business Studies to work as a kitchen porter where I had met the young Hausa woman earlier in the day.

Jarvo, who was wearing a red T-shirt with the words: *Philosophers have only interpreted the world in various ways; the point is to change it, Marx,* inscribed on it walked to me smiling and holding an unlit cigarette. 'How are you coping?' he asked.

'I am fine,' I said and told him about my experiences at the employment agency and the institute.

He was happy. 'You've done well. You'll be all right with time. The first step is usually the most difficult one. A law of dialectics states that quantity change equals quality change.' He was very emphatic. 'The more you lie, the better you'll get at it.'

Other members of the Politburo sat around the table.

Son-of-Adam shouted from the next table. He was now sitting with another man known as *The Silent Man*. 'Listen guys. Life is cheap and African lives are the cheapest. Do you understand?'

No one answered.

'Could someone please explain to me how we allowed the devil to unleash all its evil forces on us? What happened to the goodness in us?'

'My friend, why didn't you buy your friend beer today?' Wassa asked him.

'Who's your friend? I'm your boss,' he stood up and staggered towards us. 'When you see a man that is silent, he's thinking. A silent man is a thinking man.'

'What about a silent woman?' Wassa asked.

'Aha! A silent woman is a mad woman,' he replied laughing. 'Women are made to talk.'

Ama was not happy. She smiled. 'I can forgive him.'

I walked out of Kilburn underground station later with so many things on my mind. My heart almost stopped when two uniformed policemen came out of an unmarked car and stopped a cyclist on the pavement. I panicked and felt like running. But I noticed that they did not even look at me. I walked past them in quick steps. I glanced over my shoulder from time to time. If they stopped and asked me who I was, what would I say, Michael or Mustapha? I had no idea. As I approached the flat on Fordwych Road, my attention turned to another problem I had been having for months – my landlady. It was because of my landlady that I had decided to return to the flat very late. I hoped she would be asleep by the time I returned or at least be in her bedroom. My routine within the last several months was simple. Get out of the flat as early as possible and return as late as possible. I was avoiding the landlady and her three dogs.

The dogs started barking as soon as I approached the door. I entered the flat, closed the door gently and locked it without excessive noise. My landlady would be very upset if the door made a noise. I went to the toilet and tiptoed into my room.

As I lay in bed that Wednesday evening trying to sleep, three things weighed heavily on my mind. I was worried about my new identity. When and where should I be Michael and Mustapha? For how long would this last? How should I behave as Michael? The more I thought about these issues the stronger and louder the voice inside me kept saying; 'You cannot live a double life like this. It's too complicated and risky. You can try but you will not achieve your goal of becoming a film director. Forget your dream and return and the earlier the better.'

No sooner had one voice stopped before another one grew louder and countered. 'You've left home for something, you must not return without it. If it takes changing your name to accomplish your goals, so be it. After all the Hausas say: *In kidi ya sauya, rawa ma ta sauya* (When the music changes, the dance, too, must change.)

Where in my life is Mustapha – the person I was until two weeks ago? Where is the successful journalist who came to the UK with a written script to be turned into a film? Where is he? Is this the end of Mustapha and his dream? Or is it the beginning of another Mustapha? Who is Michael Danquah? Is he a continuation of Mustapha or a different person? Will I in future be Mustapha or Michael? How on earth can I live with such contradictory identities?

I remembered what my mother told me so many times. *Karya fure take, ba ta 'ya'ya.* (Lying produces flowers only, it does not bear fruit.) My father had enjoined me many times too to make sure that, wherever I was, I told the truth. 'If you tell the truth, you'll have nothing to remember; if you are honest, you'll have nothing to worry about; if you are sincere, you'll have a good sleep.' He would often repeat a Hausa saying: *Marar gaskiya ko cikin ruwa ya yi jibi.* (A liar will sweat, even if he is in water.)

Finally my eyes closed. I started to sleep. I thought I saw a flash that brightened the room. I thought it was lightning and expected to hear the sound of thunder. Nothing happened. I opened my eyes and was shocked. I saw the gaze of the Hausa woman. I felt exactly how I had felt earlier when our eyes met. I felt that spark again. I had never experienced such strong feelings towards anybody before. Not for the first time that day, remembering her facial features and her voice made something inside me warm. Why was I having such feelings for someone whose name I did not know?

If I meet her again, I would apologise, I said to myself, trying to get back to sleep. It must have hurt her a lot to have been rejected in public I thought. The last thing I should do to a kindred spirit is to reject it; after all, it is half of me because the Hausas say: *Kowa ya ga na gida zai kasha ahu.* (Lavish hospitality on someone from the same place when you meet elsewhere.) The Hausas like to take their time to greet one another. After all, as the Hausa's say: *Sannu bata kare wuya.* (You lose nothing by greeting someone.) After all she asked me: *Yaya kake?* (How're you?) The least I could have done was to say I was fine but I didn't. It pained me that night that I had closed the door to any possible form of friendship or a relationship.

When eventually I drifted into that half-awake state I thought I could hear the supplications I knew my mother recited so many times. Since I had arrived in the UK, reciting some of these supplications had had a calming effect on me. They made me remember my mother, her voice, her fears, hopes, anxiety and wishes. I tried to follow her voice.

'Oh Allah! Give my son good health, wisdom and patience. Let him be in good company. May he not be lonely and may he not be in fear or in want. Oh Allah! The Almighty! Please protect my son from *shaitan* by day and by night. Guide him towards the right path and forgive him if he strays. Oh Allah! Give my son the inspiration to create and the energy to procreate. Let him be fearless in the face of dangers. Let him take the right decisions. Give him the strength to surmount his troubles!'

As I recited the supplications, I realised I was beginning to forget the lines and the words. I could still hear my mother's voice but I was beginning to forget the particular words and sentences.

I eventually drifted off to sleep.

In my sleep, I heard a voice call my name at the edge of a forest. I followed the sound and soon found myself walking down into a deep valley. I continued to follow the sound of my name. Soon I realised I was in a dark tunnel. I could hardly see where I was going. The voice said, 'Mustapha, welcome to the tunnel. You have a long way to go.' I continued to walk cautiously. The voice assured me that I was on the right track and that there would be light at the end of the tunnel. I began to enjoy the walk in the tunnel. From very far, I saw what appeared to be a light. Encouraged by this, I tried to run but I tripped on something and fell down. I was unconscious for some time. When I regained consciousness, I was shocked to see the heads of two big snakes: a python and a boa constrictor. The python had coiled itself around me while the boa was watching. The boa would give the python an order and the big snake would suffocate me when I tried to breathe out. It was like a game for them. After a while, the python uncoiled itself and the boa coiled itself around me and it waited for some time before it constricted me as I breathed out. They seemed to be enjoying the game. Meanwhile I was getting weaker and weaker. A human appeared with an instrument that discharged an electrical current. The snakes did not like the shock. They released me and disappeared. The person had a headlamp and I could not see their face. The person helped me back onto my feet and walked with me for a considerable distance. 'This is as far as I can go with you,' the person said and disappeared into the darkness. My walk in the dark resumed. I kept walking until I got to the point where I could see light at an exit. Then I saw what I thought was the figure of the Hausa woman urging me with her hands to walk faster. As I got closer and closer I thought I saw her run towards me in the tunnel but as soon as she held me I woke up.

I had been dreaming.

I woke up at dawn before Bruno, the German shepherd, started howling at the singing birds. Bruno had a particularly irritating howl at dawn. Occasionally Bruno would bark and run around in the hallway of the flat, from one end to the other. Pat, my landlady, said that the dog was either doing his morning exercise or was reacting to a passing dog.

It was only a matter of time before Bruno started barking and running from one end of the hallway to another. I was ashamed I remained in bed instead of saying my morning prayers. I had come to the UK with an inner clock that alerted me when it was time to say my prayers. It was like an itch. A muscle would pull somewhere in my body. Something in me told me it was time to pray. I even heard, during my first months in the UK, the prayer call by the *muezzin* floating into my ears, especially at dawn.

Assalatu khayrum minam naum
Assalatu khayrum minam naum

Prayer is better than sleep
Prayer is better than sleep.

In Bauchi predawn prayer calls pierced through the morning darkness enjoining the faithful to wake up and pray because prayer was better than sleep.

On that Thursday I tried to get up and pray but could not. It was as if someone or something was pressing me down onto the bed when I tried to get up. I looked at the time and decided to get up and get ready for work.

At the institute, I hoped and prayed I would meet the Hausa woman in a safe and convenient place and time so that I could apologise to her. When it was time for my short break, I chose to sit in the canteen instead of the staff room hoping to see her again.

When my fifteen-minute tea break was over and I stood up to continue my work, the Hausa woman walked calmly into the canteen. The newspaper in my hand fell. I didn't pick it up. She walked slowly, in calculated steps past me, without a smile or a glance. It was as if I were not there. She was wearing a wrap-around robe made of colourful cloth with marching blouse, head tie and shawl but in different colours. I was confused. I felt the spark again. I wanted to follow her and ask her for a minute to apologise and let her know that she was right after all; that I was the person she knew in Bauchi. I wanted to tell her and explain to her the circumstances that led me into lying about my identity. I wanted her to know that in my dream she represented light at the end of a long dark tunnel. I tried to take a few steps and follow her but felt as if I was fixed to the floor.

I looked round. Ms Katsy Robertson and Joe the chef were standing near the coffee machine looking at me. I went back to work clearing the trays and cleaning the tables.

'Niran is in real trouble,' Jarvo announced as I entered Bozo's Joint that evening. 'Home Office officials took him away this morning. He's in a detention centre awaiting deportation.'

'What happened?' I asked.

'Hmm, one of his women betrayed him. She called the Home Office and told them exactly who he was and where they could pick him up. They went there and took him away in his pyjamas. Imagine, *The Peacock* will be deported to Nigeria in his pyjamas. What sort of humiliation is this?'

Wassa laughed. 'He should have been arrested in that T-shirt that says Very Important Person.'

'Are they coming here?' I asked, frightened.

'Relax Michael,' Jarvo said. 'They don't usually visit locations like this.' He paused. 'I've just returned from the detention centre. *The Peacock* is disorientated. I learnt that he has four aliases.'

'What actually happened?' I asked.

Jarvo was reluctant to go into more detail. 'It's a bit complicated. He was very careless and to a certain extent very stupid. There was also an allegation that he assumed the identity of a dead person.'

'What? A dead person?' I screamed.

'Oh yes, people do assume the identities of dead people. While officially someone called Michael Stone might be dead, you'd find that some immigrants are working with his identity. But the most stupid thing he did was to refuse to take a paternity test. That was what got him into real trouble.'

The last sentence made us laugh.

'I didn't realise there was a baby involved,' Ama said laughing.

'As I said it's complicated. There are so many Nirans in this story that the authorities are not sure who they have in custody. The Niran we know was married to a fellow Nigerian and has two children. This Nigerian wife knows him as Isiaka. She lives in Woolwich with her two daughters. Three months ago, another Nigerian woman in Edmonton who knows him as Stephen claimed he was the father of her newborn baby. He disputed it. She wanted a paternity test but he refused. The woman threatened to get him deported if he refuses to take responsibility for the newborn. That was why he came to us yesterday. Taj tried to talk to her last night but she wouldn't listen.'

Jarvo paused and drank his Guinness. 'The woman in Edmonton told Taj that Niran was cheating on her. That he had been secretly seeing her friend, Lola. Niran claimed he was not the only man in her life and could not possibly be the father of the newborn. He said there was a minicab driver who was also seeing the woman. He thinks that the man called and informed the Home Office to get rid of him.'

'And he's going back to Nigeria in his pyjamas,' Wassa said laughing. 'It serves him right. He's very cocky.'

There was a moment of silence.

I was beginning to feel unease. It began to dawn on me that I had a bigger problem than I thought. 'A visit to the detention centre is always depressing,' a despondent Jarvo continued. 'You hear so many depressing stories ranging from officers verbally, physically and sexually abusing detainees to suicides. A young man from the Central African Republic hanged himself recently at the centre.'

'What?' I shouted.

Jarvo went on. 'This young man fled the war-torn country and came here many years ago. He had a son he really adored. For some reason he was arrested and was about to be deported, together with his son. The man decided to end his life because then the British authorities could not deport the boy alone to a country where he knows no one.' Jarvo paused. 'Life is terribly unfair. You flee a civil war and end up like this.'

Son-of-Adam's gaunt figure staggered towards our table. 'Could any of you please tell me why a group of squid is not called a squad but a group of footballers are a squad?'

No one paid any attention to him.

'I don't understand many things. What's the connection between being proud and a group of lions? Why do people say a pride of lions?'

There was a moment of silence. Wassa spoke first. 'It's tough man. A Nigerian man jumped out of his fifteenth-floor flat in a tower block in Wanstead last year.' Wassa looked at me and nodded several times. 'His suicide note read: *I want my daughter Blessing to have a chance in life.* No one exactly knows the full story. We understand that he was having a long-running dispute with relatives, one of whom was in the UK. It all had something to do with money, land and a house that was being built in his village. He was said to have had a row with his relative in the UK on the progress of this house. This relative wanted more money. He felt he was being duped. According to his neighbours, they had a big row and the man from Luton threatened to inform the council and Home Office of his real identity. Ignatius, as the man was called, felt blackmailed. He refused to give his relative more money. This relative then told him that he would receive a visit from the Home Office. Several days later, when the Home Office officials eventually visited his flat, he knew he would be deported with his daughter. He hurriedly wrote a note and jumped from his fifteenth-floor flat.'

There was a moment of short, tense silence.

'And what about Blessing's mother?'

'No one knows where she is. Anyway, social services took the child away.'

'There are so many tragic cases,' Jarvo said lighting another cigarette. As if he read my mind, after puffing out smoke, he remarked. 'You'll be alright. Whatever you do, don't get yourself into a desperate situation so as not to take desperate action.'

'Look at it this way,' Wassa added. 'You're lucky you're the only one here. You have no wife and kids to worry about. With a bit of luck you'll be okay. Just mind your own business and keep a low profile.'

I thanked him for the advice and went to the toilet again.

'This is for you,' Jarvo said with a broad smile pointing at a pint of beer when I returned.

'No thanks,' I said. 'You know I don't drink.'

'Of course I do. But Michael, you need something like this to help you cope with the anxiety and tensions, to make the transition smooth. It'll calm your nerves and you'll have a good sleep. A little bit of alcohol helps us through rough patches in life. Just one pint wouldn't harm you.'

I looked around and noticed they were all looking at me as if urging me to drink. I picked up the pint. Jarvo smiled, 'To your health, success and luck.'

'Thanks,' I said. For the first time in my life I tasted alcohol. I did not like it. I wondered why people drank such a bitter thing. I did not finish the pint.

That night, I slept very well.

Bruno's howling woke me up at dawn. It was a day I had been looking forward to with apprehension. I was due to meet my solicitor that morning to know the outcome of my appeal. The Home Office had written earlier to inform me that since my uncle who had taken care of my board and lodging was deceased and my scholarship had been stopped by the state government, I had no grounds to remain in the UK. However I had the right to appeal, which I did. I was nervous as I headed towards the Willesden Green area. I remembered the words of my late uncle. 'Imran is one of the best solicitors around. He's honest and very good. He knows the system very well and will take good care of you.' Imran had on several occasions assured me that he would make sure my visa was extended. 'Trust me brother Mustapha, everything would be fine *Insha'Allah*. When I am finished with your case, you will be able to study, work and have a family in the UK.'

I had no reason to doubt him. I trusted him and looked forward to being granted an extended stay. I waited for months. Imran promised and promised. When my visa eventually expired, Imran assured me that he would get it renewed easily. He did not. He claimed the Home Office had made new changes to the immigration laws. 'Trust me, there are sufficient grounds to appeal successfully.' I believed in him. 'There are always new rules and regulations from the Home Office and your application was caught in between the old and the new regulations,' Imran argued and asked for more money. I borrowed money to settle the legal fees before the appeal was heard. I entered his office and sat down. Imran was busy with a client in his cubicle. As I waited, I reviewed my past meetings with him and it became clearer how his story had changed over the months. I felt that the news I was about to receive would not be good. Imran had changed his stories so many times.

'NEXT' I heard him shout after the client had walked out.

I knocked and entered. Imran was busy writing something. 'Oh yes Henry from Nairobi, how can I help you?'

'*Assalaam Alaikum*,' I said.

'Ah! I'm sorry, Mohammed, the young man from Somalia.'

'No. Brother Imran, this is Mustapha from Nigeria.'

'Yes! Mustapha, sorry I've been quite busy. What can I do for you?'

I was shocked by the question. I reminded him that I had an appointment. 'I'm here to know the outcome of my appeal.'

'Oh! I see. Things are a bit hectic.' He stood up and walked to the drawers and pulled out a file. 'Mustapha Abdullahi,' he read out. 'Is that you?'

'Yes,' I replied. My heart began to race. I felt something was not right.

Imran sat down and started reading through the file. I was shocked by his behaviour. Some months ago, Imran had been one of the friendliest persons to me. When my uncle was alive, Imran recognised me from afar. He and I talked about almost everything -- prayers, fasting, cars, football and women. I found it hard to understand the sudden change.

When he finished reading, Imran looked at me with a frown. 'I'm sorry to inform you that your appeal was not successful. This letter states all the reasons why the Home Office had decided you have no ground to remain in the UK. You are therefore advised to leave the UK immediately.'

I could not breathe properly. I felt as if something was blocking my nose. My chest felt a bit tight. My mouth became dry. I blinked several times. Although I somehow expected it, the news hit me like a hard object. 'When am I supposed to leave?' I stammered.

'You should have left by yesterday,' Imran said indifferently. 'Technically, you are living illegally in the UK. By the way, the letter states that you must show the UK authorities proof that you have left the country.'

I looked at Imran in total disbelief. He avoided eye contact. 'As your solicitor I've done what was required of me. Your late uncle knows that it was a very difficult case. You should know this by now and should actually have made contingency plans. Have you got any other plans?'

I was too shocked to respond. He continued. 'So Mr Abdullahi, if you don't return to Nigeria immediately and choose to remain in the UK illegally, whatever happens to you is your responsibility. I cannot be held responsible for you being here illegally. Do you understand?'

I nodded.

'You're on your own now.'

'What should I do?' I asked.

'I've just told you,' he said laughing. 'You should return to Nigeria immediately. There's nothing else you can do. But as everyone knows, illegal Nigerians never voluntarily return; they get deported. You could live illegally but that's your choice, not my advice. You understand?'

I nodded.

'But the only way you could get a legal stay in the UK would be to marry a UK or EU citizen, a woman of course. I didn't tell you that okay?'

I nodded.

'I'm not encouraging illegal immigration. I'm only telling you some-thing in confidence.'

I nodded.

'Anything else I can do for you?'

'But Brother Imran, you promised me so many times …'

Imran interrupted. 'Listen young man from Africa. It's the law, not me. I can make promises but the law is supreme here. I intended to help you but the state made so many changes to the law. We are governed by laws and we all have to obey them. We have rule of law here, not like Nigeria.'

The phone rang. He picked it up. 'Sorry I've got a bad back and can't play golf.'

I looked at the books on his table. *Introduction to Money Laundering. Chasing Hot Money. Making Wise Investments.*

'Yes! I'm with you,' Imran continued speaking on the phone. 'No I can't. I'm going to Italy. Yes, I like Sardinia. I like the weather, the food but above all I like the people; they are lovely people. I want to be a trader in the city; yes, a hedge fund. I'm really sick and tired of wasting my time representing invalid immigrants for peanuts. I could be spending my time making real money. Okay then, see you later after *Juma'at* prayers, *Insha'Allah.* Don't forget the Swiss chocolates please. My nephews really like them, *Salaam Alaikum.'*

Imran stood up. Turned round and looked at me. 'You're still here?' he asked. 'I thought you were on your way to Nigeria.'

'My passport,' I managed to say looking straight at him.

'Of course you'll need it to get out of this country wouldn't you?'

Imran made a photocopy of the letter from the Home Office and gave it to me with my passport. He walked to the door and opened it. 'Good luck,' he said as I walked out of his small office.

'NEXT,' he shouted.

What was I going to do now? I asked myself several times on the stairs. Fear gripped me outside the building. I felt as if there were people waiting to arrest me, take me to the detention centre and then deport me. I looked around. There was no one. I walked slowly and sat on an empty bench in the courtyard behind the building. I was trying to make sense of what was happening to me. After all the promises, assurances and having spent thousands of pounds in legal fees, the person I trusted most had let me down. I tried not to believe he deliberately misadvised me. I began to think it was my fault. I should have packed my bags the moment I got the hint that renewing my visa would be a problem. I should have left the moment my scholarship was cancelled. Now I am in a mess, in debts and an illegal immigrant.

From that moment I was an over-stayer; someone residing in the UK illegally. I had partly prepared for this outcome. That was why Jarvo and I had created a new identity for myself. I felt dizzy and felt like throwing up in the courtyard in Willesden Green. Imran, the solicitor, was right. I was an invalid immigrant. I had no legs to stand on. I had no support. No balance, nothing. My eyelids became heavy. I tried to open my eyes but could not. I felt a chill all over my body. For a while I thought time stood still. It was a strange feeling. I had never felt like this before. I saw from the corner of the adjacent building that cars were passing by. I heard the trains running on the tracks nearby. But for me, time stood still. It was as if I froze for a while. I did not know for how long but I felt no connection to the world around me for some time. It was as if the light inside me had been switched off and then on. When that moment passed, I realised my mouth was wide open and dry. I shook my head gently. What next? I was finding it difficult to accept the reality of my situation. But I had to. I had no choice. I could not pretend any longer that the problem would resolve itself. I stood up to go to work. *Yes I'm on my own now* I said. I counted the money in my wallet. I had fifty-four pounds and some coins. That was all I had; everything. I had a huge debt to repay. There was a sudden realisation that fifty-four pounds was not enough to live on. I felt lucky I had a job. If I could keep the job I would earn some money.

To realise my dream I must have a legal permit to reside in the UK. To do that, I had only one option left. That was to marry a UK or EU citizen. To meet and marry someone required time and money -- I neither had time nor money. Fifty-four pounds would not make that dream come true I thought. The dream had to be put on hold. As I took slow steps toward the underground station, I knew my life in the

UK would never be the same again. The air I was breathing began to feel different. The people around me began to look different. I did not feel part of the world around me. I could not connect. I looked around and signs made no sense to me at all. I realised after a while that I was walking away from the station.

I was momentarily lost.

As I turned and walked toward Willesden Green underground station, I thought I heard someone whisper into my ears: 'Mustapha, welcome to life under the radar!'

Two

A Big Dream

15 August 1990

The immigration officer at Heathrow Airport asked me, when it was my turn. 'What's the purpose of your visit?'

'I'm here to study filmmaking and prepare my script for a film.'

'Really?' he asked with a smile.

'Yes.' I showed him a letter from the film college in central London confirming that they had read the script and would like to work on it and make it into a film. I also showed him a letter confirming that I had been offered a place in the college to study a specially designed course on filmmaking.

'I see,' he said, looking at me closely. 'Is that what you want to be?'

'Yes.' I showed him the manuscript. 'I'm here to prepare it for screen.'

'I don't have to see it. I believe you.'

There was a moment of silence. He looked at my passport again. I handed over a file containing all the relevant documents: a letter of admission from the college; a letter from the Bauchi state government confirming that I was on a government scholarship; a letter from my uncle, who was a UK citizen and resident in London, confirming that he would be taking care of my board and lodging. In the letter, my uncle made it clear that he had sufficient funds to take care of me and that I would not have any recourse to use public funds. The letter was endorsed by a solicitor, Imran.

The immigration officer took his time to read all the letters.

'How long are you going to be in the UK?'

'The course is for nine months. I don't see myself staying for more than a year.'

'Are you going to work?'

'Of course not.'

'Why not?'

'I have enough money to live on.' I showed him my wallet and a brown envelope full of cash.

'Should your circumstances change, are you going to work?'

'No. I'll return to Nigeria. I was working as a television presenter before I left and would have a job to return to.'

He smiled. 'You mean you would voluntarily return to Nigeria?'

'Of course, that's where I came from,' I said with confidence.

'Okay, I believe you,' he said with a dry smile. 'I'll give you the benefit of doubt. Mr Abdullahi, one final question. Should your circumstances change, are you going to marry a UK citizen so as to remain in the UK?'

'Absolutely not. I'm here for a very short time and for a particular purpose. I'm not here to live permanently. Once I rewrite my script and finished my course, I'll be off back to Nigeria. If however my circumstances do change I'll return immediately. I don't see myself settling down in this country.'

The immigration officer stamped my passport and handed over all the documents to me. 'Good luck with your film career.'

'Thank you very much,' I replied and walked through the immigration point.

While I was waiting for my bag at the carousel, a fellow passenger on that flight stepped closer, greeted me and asked with a toothy grin. 'First visit to the UK?'

'Yes and you?' I replied after greeting him.

'I live here. My name is Taj,' he said with a broad smile that revealed a gap in his upper teeth. Taj was wearing a blue, collarless, short-sleeved suit. We shook hands. He wanted to know where I was going. I showed him the address. 'I know the area very well. I'll explain how to get there on the train.'

We picked our bags. I followed him to the train. 'I don't have a business card on me,' he said sitting down on the train. 'Let me write my contact details for you somewhere.' I gave him the envelope that contained my draft script. He wrote down his contact details. He looked at the wordings on the envelope. *They Turned Day to Night* (Draft script by Mustapha Abdullahi) 'What's this? Are you a writer?' he asked.

I told him who I was and that the script had been accepted and hopefully the film will be on the World Best Film Series.

'Oh yes! I've heard of films on that series. Congratulations! That's one of the most prestigious film series in the UK. I'm really happy for you.' He shook my hand firmly. 'I'm really impressed. I hope you make it. Who knows you could be the next Ousmane Sembène. We certainly need filmmakers in the mould of Ousmane Sembène.'

At Acton Town underground station, Taj left the train. 'You've my contact details. Call me as soon as you've settled in,' he managed to say before the door closed.

I found my way to Maida Vale. I was nervous and excited. I had never met my uncle before. I had no mental recollection of what he looked like. The last photograph he sent home was taken about two decades before. I had spoken to him over the phone and had corresponded by post. I went into the corner shop and showed the man behind the counter the address. He confirmed that I was on the right street and that the flat was three doors away. I pressed the buzzer and waited. A middle-aged woman opened the door.

'Mustapha?' she asked with a polished West Indian accent.

'Yes,' I said with a smile.

'Please come in.'

'My name is Matilda and that's your uncle,' she said pointing to a middle aged man sitting in a black leather single sofa with several small pillows on its side. I removed my shoes and bowed.

The man laughed. 'You don't have to do that here. You don't have to greet me like that,' he said and stretched his hand. 'Please sit down and feel at home. I'm sorry I could not be at the airport. I've been ill for some time. I just came back from hospital some hours ago.'

Matilda gave me a glass of orange juice. 'You don't have to remove your shoes you know.' She showed me the toilet and my room. I could not help but think about how my uncle had changed over the years.

In the photographs I saw before I left, my uncle had Afro hair, thick sideburns. He wore shirts with wide collars and baggy trousers.

My uncle, Mohammed Aminu Dankobi was the first person from Bauchi town to study in the UK. He went to a missionary primary school and attended the famous Barewa College in Kaduna during the colonial period. He was exceptionally intelligent and the colonial administration sent him to the UK to study public administration and law. After his arrival in the UK in 1958, my uncle never went back to Nigeria. He was often referred to as the forgotten son of Kobi. Some people called him the man the white people took from us. No one knew why he never visited after he left.

A couple of years before I arrived, a journalist friend called Ibrahim visited the UK and tracked him down. It was Ibrahim who told him that I wanted to be a film director and had written a script. The state government was unwilling to pay the very high cost of the course, which would have included accommodation in the student hostel. My uncle contacted me immediately. I sent him the script and he got in touch with a well-known private college in central London. They agreed to work on the manuscript with me to make it into a film. The state government agreed to pay the tuition fee only. My uncle agreed to provide board and lodging.

'Welcome to London,' another middle-aged woman said when I returned to the sitting room. 'My name is Zoya. I live here too.' The woman sat next to my uncle looking at the medications on a trolley. 'Your uncle is very sick. He's got diabetes and a few other health issues.' Zoya confided when my uncle went to the toilet. I noticed he had difficulty walking on his swollen feet. He was partially blind and grimaced in pains as he walked.

I remained silent.

'Where's the direction of Makkah?' I asked my uncle the next day. 'I want to say my prayers but I don't know where to face,' I explained.

My uncle did not answer immediately. 'Go to the off-licence near the corner shop and ask them. They'll tell you. They're Muslims. You'll see the sign *Sunrise Food and Wine Store*. I honestly don't know where to face. I gave up all these rituals years ago. Life is too hard.'

I ventured out of the ground floor flat and wandered around the neighbourhood. I was shocked by my uncle's statement that life was too hard for prayers. I was also shocked to hear and see that Muslims owned off-licences. I was not comfortable with the idea of going into an off-licence to ask for the direction for Makkah. I returned to the flat.

My uncle sensed it. Without asking me, he picked the phone and spoke to someone. After replacing the receiver, he turned to me. 'A young boy called Samad will meet you in front of the flat. Go and wait for him. He's from Pakistan and he'll take you to the local mosque.'

I have observed that there was nothing in the flat that suggested my uncle was practising any religion. If he was my friend, I could have talked about it with him. My new circumstances dictated that I should mind my own business. I had a lot to think about and do. I remembered a Hausa saying: *Kowa ya daka ta wani zai rasa turmin daka tasa.* (Whoever minds someone else's business would not have the time to mind their own.) I resolved that I would mind my own business during the short time I was to live with him. I must not judge him, I reminded myself as I waited outside the flat.

'*Assalaam Alaikum,*' a teenager boy said and embraced me warmly. 'Your uncle Brother Mohammad told us you'll be coming. I'm really happy to meet you. Brother Mohammad said you're a practising Muslim.'

'Yes.'

'Good,' Samad said excited. He stood there, eyes ablaze in his strong expressive face with his hands on his hips. 'Your uncle wants me to show you our *masjid,*' he said proudly. 'Follow me. We've about thirty minutes before *Zuhr* (afternoon prayer).' Samad was wearing a white kaftan with a collar. His cap had the sickle moon and star of the Pakistani flag printed on it.

Samad and I walked down the street past the shops. We crossed two streets and turned into an alleyway. 'This is our *masjid,*' he said as he walked into a minicab office called SABAR CARS. I was puzzled. 'It's in the basement.' I followed him downstairs. 'Have you done your *wudu?*' he asked as we removed our shoes.

'No.'

'That's the washing area,' Samad pointed to a door. 'I'll wait for you inside the prayer hall.'

When I was ready, I entered the prayer hall. Samad was standing with another youngster. 'Meet Asghar. He's my cousin,' Samad whispered into my ears. I greeted Asghar in a low voice making sure we did not make noise in the prayer hall. When it was time for prayers, we all lined up behind an Imam and prayed. After the prayers, Samad suggested I introduced myself to Imam Murad. 'He knows your uncle very well. They are good friends.'

'I'm very happy to meet you,' Imam Murad said shaking my hand and hugging me. 'Brother Mohammad, your uncle told me you were coming. We're all happy to see you. How's he today?'

'He's okay.'

'Please take care of your uncle. He's very sick. Make *dua* (prayers) for him all the time.' He paused. Fingering his beard, Imam Murad continued. 'I've known him for a very long time. He's a very nice man.'

'Can I ask you a question?' I whispered.

'Of course Brother Mustapha, what's it?'

'Where is the direction of Ka'aba?'

Imam Murad laughed. 'We pronounce it differently here. You're not the first person to come and ask this question. *Qibla*,' he exclaimed. 'We all have this problem when we first arrive here.' The Imam asked Samad to get a compass from his office. Handing it over to me, Imam Murad added. 'London is 250°.'

I was puzzled. 'Do you understand?' Asghar asked.

'No.'

'Easy! Place it on a flat surface and when this arrow is on 250 then this arrow will be pointing toward the *Qibla* in Makkah. Understand?'

'Yes. Thank you.'

Samad gave me a schedule of prayer times.

'I'm very happy you came to pray,' Imam Murad started. 'Prayers are very important in human life. I don't know how long you'll be here but please say your prayers regularly. I do understand that life is not easy and that there are many distractions but saying prayers doesn't take a lot of time. Make it a habit to pray as regularly as possible. Please don't go for more than three days without saying your prayers. I understand from Brother Mohammad that you're here to make a film and I am very happy for you. But it's my responsibility to remind you that whatever you do must be *halal*. Think three times before you do anything to be sure it's *halal*. Remember that whatever message you want to convey in your film must be *halal*. Don't be tempted to poison people's minds because of the fame and fortune that the film might bring. Be honest and truthful. Remember that one day you'll be called to account for what you did in this *duniya* (world).'

I thanked them for the compass and prayer times and left.

A week later, my uncle said he would like me to meet some of his friends. 'As you can see I support Arsenal Football Club,' he said proudly. 'Arsenal will be playing today and some of my friends are coming over.'

I had noticed that there was an Arsenal jersey hanging near the cupboard in the sitting room. There was also a photograph of my uncle with two players under the banner WE ARE THE CHAMPIONS 1989. That Saturday I waited to meet his friends.

'A foolish driver almost knocked me off my bike. The bastard wasn't looking at where he was going,' I heard someone say in the sitting room.

'It's not your time yet, Frank B. When it's your time and if that's how you are destined to go, the driver would surely have knocked you off,' Zoya commented.

'My name is Frank, they call me Frank B here,' the man said shaking my hand. 'I don't know why I come second but everyone here calls me Frank B.' He tapped me on my shoulder. 'I'm really pleased to meet you. Mo told me you were coming and I read your wonderful script. It's an excellent piece of work. I'm really glad to meet you at last.'

Frank B gave Zoya a bottle of malt whisky. Sitting down next to me on the sofa, Frank B started. 'I like meeting young Africans fresh from the continent. They are different from the black people that were born and brought up here in the UK. There is a particular type of innocence about them. This old man here was once like you,' he said pointing at my uncle. 'He was once tall, handsome, healthy and innocent until he drank and met all these women. See what women and wine can do to a man?'

'Shut up Frank,' Matilda shouted from the kitchen.

'Oh dear! I didn't realise you could hear me.' He smiled. 'I'm sorry.'

Frank B told me about himself. He was from Guyana and studied in the US. 'I came here in search of love and adventure. I've been here for well over thirty years and I think I've had my fair share of both. I cannot complain. I've had some remarkable experiences and I made some wonderful friends.'

'Shut up Frank,' a man said as he opened the door and walked in. 'Never believe anything he says,' the tall man with grey hair and a grey moustache said to me laughing. 'My name is also Frank. Frank A. I'm first and he's second. I'm the real Frank and he's the fake one.' The man said with cool detachment. He was wearing a silver silk shirt under a vintage purple corduroy suit.

'Look at this man. Where have you been?' Frank B asked standing up to embrace him.

'I was in Trinidad for a long holiday.'

'I hope you brought some bottles of rum for me.'

'Of course I did.'

My uncle asked. 'Where's the most elegant Italian woman ever? I thought you said you were coming with Angela. She wants to meet Mustapha.'

'She's parking the car and will be with us shortly,' Frank A answered and gave Zoya two bottles of rum. Moments later an elegantly dressed woman walked in. She was wearing a brown leather jacket over tight jeans and high-heeled shoes. She went and embraced my uncle.

'How're you my dear?' she asked holding his hand tenderly. 'I was really worried about you. How're you feeling now?'

'So so! A lot better today thank you.'

'I was in Curacao for some months,' she explained in an Italian accent adjusting the sunglasses on top of her head. She pushed her dark shoulder length hair backwards. 'After Curacao, I went to Napoli to visit my beloved parents. When I came here I was busy with my charity work but I kept thinking about you and how you are feeling.'

'I'm fine,' he said smiling. 'You're still the most elegant Italian woman I've ever met.'

The lady stood up and walked towards me. '*Ciao* Mustapha, my name is Angela. I hear you're here to do a film.'

'Mustapha,' my uncle started when she sat down. 'I sought the advice of Angela when your script arrived. She's a film consultant and critic. She read it and talked to the film college. As soon as your script is rewritten, we'll talk to Angela again and seek her professional advice. She's also into film production.'

Angela looked at me smiling. 'Now we wait for you to deliver the script and we can take things forward.'

'Then you can take him to Curacao,' Frank B added.

'Yes, after the film, not before. *Allora*, he must work hard for it.'

'Do you know where Curacao is?' Frank A asked.

'No,' I said shaking my head.

'It's alright he'll know when he makes his film,' Angela said smiling.

'Now you have a good reason to sit down and rewrite your script. A beautiful woman like this taking you all the way to Curacao is more than an incentive,' Frank B added.

The men continued the discussion on football. 'My hero remains Michael Thomas. Can you imagine, his last minute goal, the last kick of the season at Anfield gave us the title last year. What a miracle,' my uncle said getting excited. 'I hope we whack the arses of Tottenham at today's North London derby. All these Tottenham supporters will be crying by the end of game.'

Just before kick-off, Zoya filled the glasses with drinks. My uncle raised his glass. 'To Arsenal FC,' he said proudly. 'I don't care if we don't win the title at the end of the season as long as we beat Tottenham today, I'll be happy. Good luck Arsenal.'

They drank and waited for the match to start.

'Oh blimey!' Frank B said looking at me. 'You mean you don't drink?'

'No. I don't.'

'Do you smoke?'

'No. I don't either.'

'And women?'

'None.'

'Jesus Christ!' he exclaimed. 'I didn't know that there are still young men like you.'

When it was time for *Asr* – the afternoon prayer, I sneaked into my room, laid out the towel I had been using as a prayer mat and placed the compass on the floor to be sure I was facing the right direction and said my prayers in silence.

After the game, my uncle said. 'Tell me more about yourself.'

'I don't know where to start.'

'Start anywhere,' he said smiling.

The moment I mentioned Christian Missionary School I noticed his eyes lit up. 'Is the primary school still outside Wunti Gate?'

'No. It's been knocked down and a stadium built in its place.'

'Is the Wunti Gate still there or have the barbarians knocked it down too?'

'It's still there but large parts of the historic city wall have been demolished.'

'It's so sad. These people don't know how to preserve their history.'

I continued my story.

'Is it true that you were very popular in the state and that girls really liked you a lot?'

'That's true.'

'Why are you still single then?'

'Things didn't work out the way I wanted them to. I met a girl called Hauwa. We were seeing each other for a while and just as we were about to announce our engagement, her father married her off to a very rich man.'

He laughed. 'They still do such things?' he asked and continued. 'In a way it's good you are not married. It gives you the freedom to pursue your career without worrying about a family back home. There are a lot of opportunities here for a young man like you. However, I would have preferred you were married before leaving the country. If you had a wife and maybe a child back home, then you wouldn't be tempted to stay here indefinitely. It's not easy I suppose.' He paused for a while. 'How's Ado?'

'Your brother is fine. He was ill last year but has recovered and is back in government as a Commissioner.'

'I know. He's always holding one big position or another in every administration.'

Zoya interrupted. 'Mo, it's time for your medication.'

After taking his medication, my uncle told me about himself. 'I came to the UK before independence. In some ways it was easy for us those days. Our respective governments took care of us. They gave us a lot of money. That was not the problem. We could also work if we wanted and some for us did work and earned lots of money. But it was really difficult in the sense that we suffered a lot of racism. I was posted to a university outside London. I was the only black student. I was lonely and isolated. I suffered, really, really suffered. When I couldn't take it anymore, I left the university and came to London where I could socialise with other foreigners and I felt at last like a human being. The rejection and loneliness outside London almost drove me mad.

'I still have nightmares about how I was treated. They treated us worse than a leper. It really affected me. I was openly spat at, verbally abused. People wouldn't talk to me because of the colour of my skin. Imagine. No one sat next to me on the buses. It was difficult to get somewhere to live. No landlord wanted to take in a black person. You often see signs in front of houses with rooms to let: No Irish. No Blacks. No Dogs!

'I really suffered during the first couple of years and I think those experiences changed my attitude to life completely. I never thought human beings would treat each other like that. I never ever thought that I would be treated worse than an animal. In the classrooms, I quarrelled with the teachers and students who were openly racists until I couldn't take it anymore.' He paused. 'That's life!' he said as he stood up and struggled to go to the toilet. When he returned to his sofa he looked at me with a delightful smile and continued. 'But we also had some good times too. When I came to London I got drawn to the nightlife. I enjoyed music and with time I played on drums and was later the front man of a popular band. I used to live across the road from here. When I eventually graduated from a university in London, I joined a very famous band made up of West Indians. We had a successful national tour and I bought this flat with the money we made. Everyone thought I was from the Caribbean. I even learned to speak like them, to walk like them and behave like them. I suppose no one heard about all the things I was doing. I was called Maddo. That was my nickname. Some just called me MAD.'

'What does it mean?'

'Take a guess,' he said smiling.

'Mohammed Aminu Dankobi.'

'That's correct. Very few people knew I was born a Muslim. Wherever we played the halls were packed full. We had girls jumping all over us. It was great. It was fun. That was the best time of my life. I thoroughly enjoyed myself,' he paused. 'I had many girlfriends and probably some kids out there. I refused to accept responsibility for two. Looking back, the bright lights were - to be honest, a distraction. I think I over did some things and I am in a way paying the price now. So Mustapha, don't fall for temptations the way I did. You're a lot older and more experienced than me when I first came here and hopefully wiser. London has lots to give a young man like you but it also can take a lot from you. Where there's heaven, there's hell. London has a dark side. I'm rather glad to see you don't drink alcohol. To be honest with you, it was alcohol that took me down this slippery slope. As I told you, I've other plans for you when you finish your course and have rewritten your script. I intend to send you to the US to work with one of the best African American film directors in Hollywood. He used to play in our band in those days. I've told him about you and he is looking forward to working on some projects with you. He's busy at the moment filming somewhere in Africa. If he's not ready when you complete your course, you could remain here and do more courses. I have enough money to take care of you. That's not the problem.'

The phone rang. I seized the opportunity to say *Isha* – the night time prayer.

Later he continued. 'Politically, the good old days were magical. You go into meetings and you learn a lot and you come out feeling that you can change the world. During the Vietnam War, I was very active campaigning against the war. We organised and had debates and demonstrations. We also followed closely the liberation struggles in Asia, Africa and Latin America. Looking back and to be very honest with myself, I wasted so many years and so many opportunities too. But we all have some things to regret in life. I really took some stupid decisions along the way. I hope you can learn from my experiences, make good decisions and have something better to show and fewer regrets when you reach my age.'

There was a long silence. I wanted to ask him why he never wanted to return to Nigeria. Why he chose to remain in the UK when it was difficult, even after he had graduated. I knew that had he returned my uncle would have been one of the most influential civil servants or a politician not only in the state but, in the whole country.

Just as I was about to open my mouth and ask him, my uncle rose to his feet slowly. 'Good night,' he said.

'Are you ready for the big day?' my uncle asked on Monday morning.

'Yes. I am,' I answered, smiling nervously. It was the day I was scheduled to meet my course tutor at the college.

As I made my way to the door, Zoya called me. 'One last thing my dear,' she said pointing to an umbrella. 'This is England and you must always have an umbrella with you. The forecast is for heavy rain this morning.'

I took the umbrella.

I was in the bus when it started to rain. At the film college in Regent Street, I waited at the reception. A woman walked into the building laughing and shaking her umbrella. 'I'm really sorry I'm late. What a terrible weather! You're Mustapha?'

'Yes I am.'

'I'm Hilary Rogers, your course tutor,' she said and extended her wet hand. 'Please follow me to my office.' I followed her. 'Here are three English proverbs for you to remember. The first one is, the sharper the storm, the sooner it's over. The second one is rain before seven, fine by eleven. But the one to bear in mind is this: The weather is never bad, we merely dress badly.'

Pulling the window blinds, Hilary exclaimed 'Ah! She is still on her eggs,' and showed me a pigeon on the window ledge. 'I thought they would have hatched by now. I obviously got the dates wrong. One thing is for sure, she's got two eggs there, one will be male and the other will be female.'

When we settled down, she explained why a tailor-made course was designed for me. 'When we received your draft script, we knew there was something in it. It came to us at the time we were looking for good material from Africa to include in the World Best Film Series. But as I explained in my letter to you, there are gaps and it is not well developed in some places. We thought a short course on campus would help you make it top-class. I've no doubt in my mind that at the end of the course you'll produce a magnificent manuscript then we can take things forward. We have sponsors for the film. That's not an issue. The only thing we want from you now is a very good script. You're very creative. You have the mind of a filmmaker and I've no doubt in my mind that you'll make a great film.' She gave me her contact details. 'Feel free to contact me at any time you have a problem. Your first lesson is in an hour's time.'

I thanked her and left her office feeling that I could do this. The meeting was refreshing and I learned a lot from her in a very short period. I was touched by her politeness and encouragement.

I went to the canteen for a cup of coffee.

After the class a German student asked what plans I had for the day. 'Nothing, I'm free.'

'Let's go to Buckingham Palace,' she said as a command. 'Have you ever been there?'

'No.'

'Then let's go,' she ordered. 'Wear your coat and let's go.' Anke was petite in stature and had short dark hair.

I reluctantly followed her. She brought out various maps of London. 'We're here,' she said showing me the map. 'Let's walk. It's not that far.'

Over the next few days, Anke and I visited tourist spots like the London Bridge, Kew Gardens, Covent Garden, Camden Town and Hampstead Heath.

Matilda asked me one Friday morning in late September. 'Are you free in the afternoon? I want you to go shopping with me between 12 and 2 pm.'

'I wanted to go to the central mosque for *Juma'at* prayers.'

'What's that?'

'It's the weekly congregation prayers.'

'Lord have mercy! You come to London and live with us and you don't help us? You leave your sick uncle and his partner to go and pray? You know very well that Mo doesn't pray.'

I could see Matilda was very upset. I apologised immediately and agreed to go shopping with her.

Matilda continued to complain loudly. 'How can you use our water and electricity for free then leave us and go somewhere to pray?'

I did not answer.

When she was ready, Matilda shouted. 'The man who thinks he is the master of the house. Let's go.'

I was upset but I followed her to the local supermarket.

'Why do you wake up so early?' Matilda asked when we returned from shopping.

'To say my first prayers,' I replied.

'You go somewhere to pray?'

'Yes. I go to the local mosque.'

'I see. This place is not clean enough to worship God?'

'It's not that. I prefer to pray in the mosque.'

'Also I notice that you don't eat my food. Is that what you are told in the mosque?'

'No.'

'You are not social. You eat in the Karachi restaurant down the road and what those Pakistani people give you but you don't eat my food.'

I was getting a bit irritated. I did not know what to do. I looked at my uncle but he was silent. He did not look happy. Matilda continued. 'It's very rude to reject my food you know. I feel hurt inside you know.'

I tried to explain calmly. 'I'm really sorry. I don't really eat a lot and I'm not rejecting your food.'

'But you don't stay at home during mealtimes,' she countered in annoyance. Her voice was rising. 'As soon as you see I am cooking you walk out.'

'No. It has nothing to do with your food. It's normally prayer time.'

'You're just looking for an excuse. I'm not saying you're lying but you're not telling me the truth.'

'That's enough Matilda,' my uncle intervened. 'Why are you upset? I told you that he should be allowed to eat what he wants and where he wants.'

Matilda was quiet for a while. I felt awkward. My presence was causing some tension in the flat and I did not like it.

'By the way, your friend Ibrahim called earlier, he wants you to call him back immediately.'

'Don't use our phone to call Nigeria,' Matilda shouted from the kitchen.

'It's alright,' I assured her. My uncle smiled and looked at me. I went to the nearest telephone booth.

'Your mother was very sick,' Ibrahim started. 'She's feeling a lot better now. She wants to talk to you another day.'

Ibrahim told me about changes in the state. Alhaji Tanko had been appointed as the new secretary of the scholarship board. Alhaji Sani Dutse was now the new managing director at the television station. The short conversation ended but I remained in the telephone booth worried about my mother's health and the appointment of Alhaji Tanko as the new secretary at the scholarship board. I felt something was not right and wanted to tell Ibrahim but I did not have enough coins.

I was anxious because I knew Alhaji Tanko very well. When I was working as a journalist, the former managing director asked me to do a multipart television series on corruption and nepotism and abuse of power in the state. I was given so many leads and secret documents. The managing director personally handed me a box full of documents. Alhaji Tanko was at the centre of my investigations. The man had, over three decades in various public offices, awarded himself and his children and relatives contracts for government projects. Most of these projects were never carried out. The most damaging allegations related to the award of contracts for the building of government low-cost houses throughout the state. Over fifty per cent of the houses were never built. Those built were substandard and many collapsed after the first heavy rains. A lot of people lost their lives. Alhaji Tanko never apologised for the shoddy jobs, never faced criminal charges and never refunded money for houses that were never built. Alhaji Tanko was accused of grabbing fertile land from peasants and selling them to developers. It was a long list of allegations. Alhaji Tanko was nicknamed *The Survivor* for his ability to remain in successive state administrations. After the programme was broadcast, Alhaji Tanko called me to his office. 'Mustapha you'll pay a heavy price. I'll get you where it will hurt you too. *Kowa ya ci tuwo da ni, miya ya sha.'* (Whoever crosses my path shall be the loser.)

I was not worried then. I had the backing of the managing director of the television station. I even laughed at him. I had just been offered a place in the film college and was preparing to leave the country. But that evening in Maida Vale, I was worried because Alhaji Tanko was now in charge of the scholarship board and I hoped he would have forgotten the case.

Anke invited me to a student's party. I reluctantly agreed. I was lonely and wanted to spend as much time as possible outside the flat. I was trying to avoid Matilda. At the student's bar, I bought a glass of soft drink and joined Anke who was sitting with two German boys. As soon as they saw me walking towards them, the boys started laughing loudly. Anke introduced me to them, Jurgen and Wolfgang. I noticed they did not want to shake my hand. It did not bother me anyway.

'Why don't you drink beer?' asked Jurgen. He was wearing a leather jacket. 'You don't have beer in Africa?'

'German beer is the best in the world,' Wolfgang boasted. He had blonde hair. 'God loves us and wants us to be happy all the time that's why we have the best beer in the world.'

I did not reply. I sat down.

'Is it true you have a script written already?' Wolfgang asked with amazement.

'Is it true you really wrote the script? Did you write it or somebody wrote it for you?' He paused, looking at me, bewildered. 'Anke said your tutor told them that your script is very good and soon will be made into a film.' He was scratching his blonde hair.

'Do you have films in Africa or is this the first film to be made by an African?' Jurgen asked after sipping his beer and adjusting his leather jacket.

'We've produced many films,' I replied smiling.

'But I've never heard about them in Germany.'

The boys drank more beer, spoke in German and laughed.

Looking straight into my eyes Wolfgang asked. 'How can a black man make a film?'

I was really upset but I did not reply. I looked at Anke and she looked away.

'It must be a film about monkeys and crocodiles,' Jurgen said laughing.

They both made monkey chants.

'Have you really seen a camera before?' Wolfgang asked.

'Have you actually seen a film in your life?' Jurgen asked. 'Is it true you people still live on trees?'

I was shocked. The two boys seem to be enjoying themselves.

Anke was quiet. 'Just ignore them. They're getting drunk,' she whispered into my ears. 'It's not their fault. They are nice boys. It's the beer. Maybe it's too strong for them.'

'Why do you think I cannot make a film?' I finally asked calmly.

The boys laughed again.

'You Africans are only good at sports like boxing, football and athletics,' Jurgen said with a sense of conviction. 'I see Africans a lot on television playing sports.'

I looked at him. I was getting angry.

'Africans cannot do intellectual things like writing a book or making a film.'

'Who told you that?'

'We Germans know that! We know everything. The great German philosopher Immanuel Kant once said something like black people are stupid.'

'Really, and I used to respect him.'

He looked shocked. 'You mean you've heard about the philosopher? Have you read his books?'

'Of course I have.'

'He's lying.'

'Yah Yah, and there was the great German missionary called Albert Schweitzer who once said that one must look at the negro not as an equal but as a child. The black man has the intelligence level of a 14-year-old white boy.'

'And you believe him?'

'Of course I do. He's a Christian missionary after all and he was in Africa.'

'Where was he in Africa?' I asked calmly.

'I don't know. There is only one Africa and Africa is a country isn't it?'

'He was a great missionary and he preached the words of God. And I believe everything he said was true.'

I was upset. I thought I had heard enough. I felt I should leave. I stood up, put on my winter coat.

'I told you it's the beer. Just ignore them,' Anke implored.

'Common, we're only joking. You see, you Africans don't understand jokes at all,' Wolfgang tried to shake my hand.

'Don't touch him. You'll get AIDS. Don't you know that German specialists believe that half of Africans have the HIV virus.' Looking very serious, he shouted, 'Don't touch him. Yah, Yah, German specialists have predicted that half the population of Africans will die of AIDS within twenty years.'

At this point I couldn't take it anymore and I left.

'I understand from Zoya that you and Matilda don't get along,' Frank B whispered as he settled down in one of the sofas on a Saturday afternoon.

'It's not really a problem,' my uncle said. 'I don't know why she's making such a fuss.'

'I suppose she finds it hard to understand you come from a different culture where people do things differently,' Frank B said. 'Some people are like that. You just have to bear it. In life you come across all kinds of people.'

Zoya give me a glass of orange juice and gave Frank B a glass of whisky.

'You still don't drink?' he asked. 'I envy you. I wish I could get myself off alcohol but then life would be boring. A day without a shot of whisky would be hell. Funny enough I believe whisky keeps me well and fit.'

'What were you doing in East London?' Zoya asked. 'I thought I saw someone that looks like you on the telly arguing with some white bald people.'

'I went to this meeting in East London last week organised by the National Front, these people who hate black people. During the meeting this white fella shouted that he wanted all black people to be deported back to what he called Bongo Bongo land. I raised my hand and I said that I agreed with the white fella. They were shocked to hear a black man say this. But I added that I wanted all white people in Africa deported back to Europe. They all said no.

The guy next to me argued that white people are civilising Africans in Africa. Bull shit!'

My uncle was unusually quiet. He sat in his sofa-eyes closed-shaking his head gently.

'What are you thinking about, old man?' Frank B asked him.

'I think I've suffered enough,' he replied and smiled slyly. 'Life to me seems like a long journey in suffering with only short periods of joy.'

'You just have to try and enjoy the short period of joy to the fullest. As they say, *make hay while the sun shines.'*

As the two men talked about life my mind flashed to where my father would be at that particular time of the day. He would be sitting under the tree he planted just before I was born. He enjoyed the shade. I could see him sitting on his favourite prayer mat reciting the verses of the Quran. It was something he preferred to do alone on Saturdays, at that particular time of the day. After that, he had a particular radio programme he would listen to. Later he would teach my siblings how to read and memorise verses of the Quran. As my uncle continued to complain about the difficulties of life, I could not help but appreciate the peace and tranquillity that surrounded my father. *Alhamdullilah* was the word that came out of my father's mouth most. He never complained about anything. Always smiling - showing his kola nut-stained teeth. His philosophy was simple. One must be grateful for everything and whatever we encountered was a test from the Almighty. *Insha'Allah,* everything would be fine.

When it was time to pray I went to mosque.

'My mother has just finished cooking your favourite dish -- chicken curry. We all know you liked it very much,' Samad whispered after the prayers. 'Let's go. Come and eat with us today. We have enough, don't worry! I'm not hungry anyway so you can eat my portion.'

I followed him to their house.

'Do you know how to use the compass?' Asghar asked.

'Yes I do.' I brought it out and demonstrated how to use it.

'That's correct. I told you it's very easy.'

Samad's sisters brought the food.

'Do you have sisters in Nigeria?' Safia asked. 'How many and are they coming to visit you?'

'I have four sisters but I'd don't think they'll be coming to visit me. They're all married and it's very expensive to visit.'

'That's a shame because I want to see them.'

'Samad said you're going to make a film,' Fajr asked.

'That's correct, *Insha'Allah.*'

'Is the film about Islam?' Safia asked.

'No.'

'Why not?'

'To do a good film about Islam, I've to travel to many Muslim countries. I don't have the resources. But *Insha'Allah* I hope to do something about Islam in the future.'

'*Insha'Allah,*' they all said in unison.

After dinner, I returned to the mosque. I found a place near the radiator and decided to recite verses from the Quran.

It was late when I returned to the flat. Matilda and my uncle were watching TV.

'Have you eaten?' Matilda asked.

'Yes. Samad invited me to their house for dinner.'

She looked at me with a frown. 'This is disrespect,' she blurted out. 'You keep rejecting my food day in day out. I'm really angry with you.'

'Matilda,' my uncle shouted, 'it's enough. I thought we had resolved this matter long ago. Leave him alone. You should be happy he's eating outside and don't be upset with him. What's the matter with you? What's your problem?'

'He saw that I was cooking and probably didn't like the smell and he goes to the restaurant or to his friend to eat.'

'You were not in the flat when I left and I didn't go to the restaurant. Samad invited me to their house.'

'How can we know that he invited you? You should have told him that I'll be cooking here. I hear you Muslims eat only something called *halal* food. You think my food is not clean right?'

My uncle was very upset. 'Please Matilda don't read meanings into everything. Mustapha has eaten your food, hasn't he? He didn't reject it. He knew when he first came here that you were not a Muslim but still ate your food. He probably went to the mosque and was invited to eat by Samad. That's normal. It's not disrespect towards you. Let him pray and eat with them. For many years before I met you, their neighbour Imam Murad fed me almost every day. Remember even when you moved into the flat he continued to give us food until you told him to stop. It's a different culture and you just have to understand and accept.'

'I see it differently. Maybe he should move out and stay with them,' Matilda argued still seething with anger.

'He's done nothing wrong,' he insisted.

I was confused. I could not understand how eating outside would make her so angry. I walked slowly into my room. I was beginning to be worried. I did not want my stay to cause problems between my uncle and his partner.

For the next three days, I avoided Matilda. I would tell her in the morning that I will be back very late and there was no need for her to cook for me. I would deliberately return late so that I only greeted them and went to bed. I could sense that the atmosphere was tense. I noticed that Matilda and my uncle were not talking as much as they used to.

'I've found a place for you to stay till the end of your course,' Matilda announced one evening. 'It's not far from here. It's in Kilburn. Mo will pay the rent for you. Here is the address,' she gave me a piece of paper. 'The lady is expecting you tomorrow.' My uncle was visibly upset. He did not say a word. I went and gathered my belongings.

The next day, when I was ready to leave, my uncle said. 'I'm really sorry for what happened. It's a temporary arrangement. The woman is Matilda's friend. You're welcome to visit me any time. I'm really sorry. Matilda can be unreasonable at times.'

'It's a temporary arrangement,' I repeated several times on the bus. 'Soon life would be normal again.' I had this belief that my uncle would convince her to take me back.

At the address in Kilburn, I noticed a sign: *Beware of the dogs* on the door.

'Please come in Mustapha,' said a middle-aged man. 'I've been waiting for you.'

I entered the flat.

'My name is Paul,' the man introduced himself. 'The landlady has gone out for a walk.'

Paul told me that he was born in Ireland and taught mathematics in a nearby secondary school. He showed me the room. 'I'm moving out today,' he disclosed. 'You're lucky the flat is very close to shops and public transport. But you are unlucky because the landlady is a real pain. She's a landlady from hell.' He paused. 'I just thought I should warn you. Pat is simply unbearable. So young man, welcome to hell. You'll need the patience of a saint and wings of an angel to survive the woman called Pat. In hell you'll have good company but here, dogs.'

Moments later the door opened. I could hear dogs barking. A big dog appeared in the sitting room and raced towards me barking loudly and jumping. I was terrified. It was the first time in my life that a dog had come so close to me. 'Stop that! Come back,' a female voice shouted from the hallway after the door had been closed. 'Come here!' she commanded. 'Who told you to go into the sitting room?' I thought she was talking to me. I stood up but Paul told me to sit down. 'She's talking to the dogs,' he whispered. The German shepherd ran back to the hallway still barking. 'Shut up. Don't you know how to behave? I told you I was expecting a tenant. That's not how to welcome him.'

Paul looked at me several times smiling. We both sat in silence.

'Sorry about that,' the landlady said entering the sitting room. 'The dogs are so excited to see you, especially Bruno, the German shepherd.' The dogs were now quiet and were wagging their tails. I was not comfortable in the company of the dogs. Bruno came closer to me sniffing around. Pat was holding a small hairy dog. Another dog called Apollo, a cross breed, joined Bruno in sniffing around me. 'Don't worry they are only trying to play with you. They are not dangerous dogs, just trying to register your smell. You know dogs have very strong sense of smell. Once they know your smell they will always recognise you.' Bruno started barking. 'Shut up,' Pat shouted. 'You know the rules very well. If you want me to talk to you, sit down.' She repeated the word several times. 'You must obey me,' she told Bruno pointing her finger. 'He's here to live with you and me so you better behave and bond with him. Can't you see he's a nice chap?' She turned to me. 'Don't be scared, that's his way of introducing himself. Bruno expects you to rub his ears or play with him. You see how he's wagging his tail? It means he likes you.'

I looked at Pat closely. She was a middle-aged woman with a wrinkled face. Her grey hair was unkempt. 'Be assured that the dogs, especially Bruno will not harm you. Dogs are humans' best friends.'

'I've never lived with dogs,' I disclosed.

'You've missed a lot -- one of the best things in life. The closest relationship we can have is not with another human being but with a dog. I cannot imagine my life without dogs.'

Paul stood up smiling and shaking his head. 'Nice to meet you,' he said and handed over the keys to the landlady. Shaking my hand again, he said, 'I wish you good luck.' He did not greet Pat. He simply walked out of the flat.

As soon as he closed the door Pat laughed. 'Thank God that crazy Irishman has gone for good. He was a nightmare.'

I settled down in my room. I knew I had a big problem to face in the new flat. The most important question was how could I, a practising Muslim, live and worship in a place inhabited by dogs? I had never lived with dogs before and I did not know how I was going to live with them now. This was new territory for me. My interpretation of Islam was that dogs were *haram*. I remembered that someone once told me that because dogs were considered impure, they were not supposed to be around where prayers were said. I could not remember exactly who told me but I had heard on more than one occasion that in Islam, dogs nullify prayers. The angels, it was once said, will not descend from the heavens and accept the prayers of the faithful when there are dogs around. I was confused.

I sat down trying to make sense of what to do. 'It's a temporary arrangement,' I repeated several times. Very soon my uncle will find a solution, I believed. I thought he would discuss with Matilda and in a matter of weeks I would return to the flat in Maida Vale. Given another opportunity, I would eat the food prepared by Matilda. I did not consciously reject her food and did not expect it to lead to this. Eating her food was more acceptable than living with dogs. I began to count the number of months I had left in the UK. 'It's a temporary arrangement,' I repeated several times again. 'Very soon I will complete my course, rewrite my script and either go to the US or return to Nigeria with the knowledge that my film would be made.'

I looked for the compass and found the direction of Makkah. 'As long as the dogs are not in the room when I am praying, it should be all right,' I convinced myself. The most important thing was I had the intention to pray.

On Saturday, I decided to visit my uncle. From afar, I saw an ambulance in front of the flat. As I walked closer, I noticed the door to the flat was open. I entered. I was nervous. There were paramedics attending to my uncle in the sitting room. I sat down quietly. After about half an hour, they decided to take him to the hospital. I could see that my uncle was in pains. Outside, Zoya whispered, 'Call me later. He'll be all right.' She did not look very concerned. 'We've been here before,' she said and entered ambulance.

'Should something happen to my uncle what am I going to do?' I asked myself as the ambulance drove off with its lights flashing and sirens blaring. There was only one place to go. And I was lucky it wasn't that far for me. I walked slowly to the mosque.

After the prayers, Imam Murad asked. 'Is Brother Mohammad alright?'

'I don't know. He's been taken to the hospital.'

'Yes I saw the ambulance.' He paused. 'Please make *dua* for him.'

'What am I going to do if something serious happened to my uncle? How can I survive should something serious happened to my uncle?'

I began to question my decision to leave my job and leave my country to come to the UK. I wondered whether I should have left in the first place. 'I think I've made a terrible decision.' But I told myself, it was once in a lifetime opportunity and I had to take it. It's too early to regret leaving. I could hear a voice tell me: 'Have faith in the Almighty. *Insha'Allah* your uncle would recover and continue to support you to the end of your course.'

I was beginning to have doubts. Something inside me was beginning to tell me that things would not be that straightforward.

Three

Life in the Doghouse

'Dogs first,' Pat said one Saturday afternoon as I was about to step out of the flat. She was ready to take the dogs out for a walk. Looking at me seriously, Pat explained, 'My dogs have been trained to go out of the flat first and to come in first.' I thought she was joking. I waited patiently. She was all set to go out. 'Oh bugger,' she cursed. 'I've forgotten the bags,' she said and went into the kitchen. 'It's called Sod's Law isn't it? Just when you don't want something to happen, it does. It's a day like this when I don't have bags with me that Bruno will do it on a crowded pavement. There could even be council wardens among them. Thank goodness I remembered in time.'

I waited patiently.

'Out you go,' Pat shouted as she opened the door. The dogs ran out excitedly. 'Stop,' she shouted several times. 'Not too far. There are many dangerous drivers around. Come here,' she chased them in front of the flat. 'Make sure you lock the door,' she told me as she tried to pull back Bruno. I went back and checked. It was locked.

In Maida Vale, I could hear my uncle's laughter as I approached the flat. I entered and greeted him and his guests.

'No man can say equivocally that he understands a woman,' Frank B was making a point. He waved at me and continued. 'We like them, enjoy them but don't understand them and cannot do without them.'

'I'm sorry I couldn't visit you at the hospital,' I apologised to my uncle.

'It's all right,' he said smiling. 'There was no need for you to come. I can understand you have other things to do. As you can see, I am fine. Meet Mr Michael Lau,' he said pointing to a Chinese man drinking herbal tea. 'He's my greengrocer friend.'

'Listen young man, I've got clothes for you,' Frank B said to me. 'I don't wear them any more. Some of them are new, some I wore only once or twice. Instead of giving them to charities I thought I would give them to you.' He laughed. 'By the way young fella, have you found a girlfriend yet?'

'Not yet,' I replied and thanked him for the clothes.

'Blimey, what are you waiting for? How can you live without a girlfriend? There are so many girls available and willing to be befriended by young fellows like you, not old men like us.'

'Leave him alone,' my uncle said laughing. 'The way they do things back home is different. He will marry when he finishes his course.'

'But we are in London and he should do as Londoners do. What has his course got to do with dating girls?' Frank B asked looking surprised. 'After all, these are two separate things but they compliment each other. He can have fun when he's not studying. Actually, having fun helps one to concentrate in class. Remember, you're only young once. Maybe this will help you,' Frank B said and looked through the bags of clothes he had just given me. He looked for a particular T-shirt. 'Here we are,' he brought out the blue T-shirt and showed it round laughing. 'I used to wear it when I was chasing girls. It worked for me and I hope it works for you too. See it says, *I'll Make Your Dreams Come True.*'

'You don't understand,' my uncle interjected laughing. 'The way they do things in Africa is different.'

'But the young fella is not in Africa. He's here in London and he should chase and mate like Londoners do. If he tries to chase girls as they do in Africa he'd never catch one. The way a lion feeds in the zoo is different from the way it feeds in the wild. In Africa you have to go through all those family shenanigans where you're expected to sit down and they arrange and bring the woman to you. Waste of time. Young man, go and chase and catch your game like a lion chasing an antelope in the wild. The joy is in the chasing and the catching. That's the fun. When it comes to women, the general rule in London is that everything is up for grabs. There are no complicated rules of engagement here. It's hit and go. You might as well have fun while you're here.'

'Frank, listen. What this young man needs is a homely, God-fearing and virtuous wife not any woman he picks up from the street. That's the way they do things back home. A wife is arranged for him with a heavy dose of parental input.'

'Nonsense,' Frank B said as he sipped his whisky.

'Frank, leave the young man alone,' Zoya said filling up his glass with whisky. He'll soon fall in love, true love and marry the woman. I can see it in his eyes.'

'What happens between now and when he falls in love?' Frank B asked.

Mr Lau who has been quiet asked. 'What's love?' He did not wait for a reply. 'I personally think that love is something that means two things – sex and money. Simple!'

They all laughed.

'Well that was my view many years ago. Now I think there's nothing like love; there's only friendship and companionship.' He paused. 'Young man,' Mr Lau continued looking at me. 'Don't rush into marriage. Take your time. Time is on your side. If you must, marry the woman that loves you more than you love her. In that way, you would have peace of mind. She'd tolerate your weaknesses. But if you love her more than she loves you, once you change a little bit she will make life difficult for you. Women are very complicated. We say in China that a girl changes eighteen times before she becomes a woman. All of you should remember that of the two sexes women are the stronger sex. Women always want their men to change into the person they want. Men, on the other hand, never want women to change. The truth of the matter is we all change!'

There was a moment of silence.

Mr Lau continued. 'Whatever happens never promise a woman what you cannot deliver.'

'Why not?' Mr Frank B asked looking surprised.

'Because they'll always remember and …'

'But hang on,' Frank B interjected. 'How can the young fella get a woman if he doesn't lie to her? How can a woman like him if doesn't promise her everything in the world?'

One after the other, the men and Zoya advised me on who was best to marry, when and how and why. 'Marry a divorcee,' Zoya advised. 'There are many of them out there you know. But you may have to join a dating agency.'

'What is a dating agency?' I asked her.

They all laughed at me. Frank B disagreed with Zoya. 'From my observations, divorcees are very difficult to handle. They often compare the man with their previous partners and forget that we are all different human beings. If the previous man cheated on her, there is a tendency for her to be very obsessive and jealous. It is hell but if you must, maybe Zoya has someone in mind. My advice here is you must know exactly why her husband left her.'

'Or why she kicked him out,' Zoya countered. 'Look for a single parent.'

'Have you got one for him?' Frank B asked laughing.

'That's a good idea,' my uncle said.

'At least she might not want another child and just want company. There are many out there you know?' Zoya said looking at me.

'I still think he should be free to choose. Let him have an adventure. A single parent would restrict him. He might be disturbed by a baby crying here, babysitting there. The father of the baby might be a nuisance. The young fella needs a single, wild, ready to love girl,' Frank B said. There was laughter. He continued. 'You don't have to remain in your racial lane, you know. You have a lot of races to choose from. That's one good thing about London – you can meet women from all walks of life. As the saying goes, variety is the spice of life!'

'I strongly suggest you marry an African, preferably from your country,' Mr Lau reasoned. 'Should something go wrong and things do go wrong in relationships, the kids don't have to travel from one part of the world to another to meet their relatives.'

There was a moment of silence.

'How's your lovely landlady?' Frank B asked with a sarcastic laughter.

'She's fine.'

'And her dogs?' Zoya asked doing her crosswords.

'They're still there.'

'She's crazy about them,' Zoya said laughing.

'Well that's the only company she's got. She cannot relate to human beings. She can relate only to dogs,' Frank B said. 'If I can come back to this world again and if I have the choice, I would like to return as a dog in the UK.'

'Definitely not in China,' Mr Lau said laughing.

'I'd end up in a pot of soup there.'

'Dog meat is a real delicacy you know,' Mr Lau added still laughing. 'I'd like to return somewhere in the posh areas of West London. Can you imagine the care and attention I'd receive? Ideally I would like a middle-class, middle-aged white woman to rescue me from the Battersea Dogs Home. These women like to talk about how they rescued the dogs and they enjoy spending so much money on them.'

'I want to return to this world as a horse,' Zoya said.

'Not in France though,' Frank B said. 'Otherwise you end up in a pot there.'

'Of course not and not as a racing horse but as one of those owned by some of these rich middle or upper-class families outside London. You see, these horses get the best of everything, food, shelter, medical care, exercise, clean countryside air. You get everything and you do nothing and get all the attention in the world. Just eat, sleep and run around.'

The phone rang. 'It's for you,' my uncle said and signalled at me. 'You can pick it up in the kitchen.'

It was Ibrahim on the line from Bauchi town. After greeting each other, Ibrahim told me. 'Your mother is in my office. She wants to talk to you.' There was a moment of silence. I could hear my heart racing. My hand began to tremble. I waited eagerly to hear the voice of my mother after several months. I could hear Ibrahim urging her to speak.

'Mama,' I shouted, '*Assalaam Alaikum.*'

'*Wa'alaikum Salaam,*' I could hear my mother's faint and nervous voice. My mother wanted to know how I was. I told her that I was fine and that I was looking forward to finishing the course in six months' time and then return to Bauchi.

'*Insha'Allah*,' she said in a weak voice. 'Do you say your prayers regularly?'

'Of course I do.'

'I'm worried because I understand so many of our children go there and forget the *deen* (faith).'

'Don't worry, I say my prayers regularly.'

'Are you going to marry a white woman?' she asked laughing.

'Of course not,' I replied laughing too.

'Thank you. That's one of the reasons why I wanted to talk to you. I wanted to remind you, please don't marry a white woman. I wouldn't know what to do if you brought one home. Please Mustapha, no matter how beautiful she is, don't be tempted. Think about me. How am I going to communicate with her? See what happened to your uncle? He married a white woman and completely forgot about us all. He never wrote or visited because the white woman prevented him from doing so. I hope she's taking care of you. I hope she allows him to talk to you.

'Please keep your prayers my son. It is important. Fast during the month of Ramadan. And please don't forget to give *zakat*. Finally, Mustapha,' she paused laughing, 'please don't marry a white woman. Promise me.'

I laughed. 'Mama, I promise I will not marry a white woman. *Insha'Allah*, you'll see me in six months' time alone without a white woman.'

'*Insha'Allah.*'

I spoke to Ibrahim. He informed me that he had resigned from the television station. 'I'm going to Abuja. It's terrible here since you left. I'm happy that you left before all these troubles and scandals. There have been quite a lot of changes in the government. A lot of witch-hunting taking place. I'm afraid things are not looking good at the scholarship board. Alhaji Tanko is really tearing the place apart.

He has ordered that some scholarships be scrapped. I'll tell you more when next we speak. Your mother is eager to leave.'

I thanked him.

I was happy that I had spoken to my mother. I was worried about the news at the scholarship board. If Alhaji Tanko decided to stop my scholarship, what would I do? I asked myself several times that day. There was nothing I could do but hope for the best. I had another thing to worry about: how was I going to observe fasting during the month of Ramadan in a place that was inhabited by dogs. I was worried about how I could wake up in the middle of the night to eat especially because my landlady did not like any noise at night. To properly observe fasting, I would have to perform the *Taraweeh* prayers, which usually finished very late at night. I was then supposed to wake up before dawn to eat something. But my landlady did not want to be disturbed. My landlady knew little about Islam and cared little about religion. She was an atheist. She told me so. She had on a couple of occasions made casual remarks about 'the insignificance of prayers.' When I first moved in, she made it clear that should I decide to cook in the flat I would pay extra for the gas bill. I decided that I would not cook in the flat.

As I wondered what to do about the month of Ramadan, I reminded myself that I had never missed a day of fasting during the holy month of Ramadan in my adult life. I stood in front of the flat and reflected on how best to deal with the problem. Even if she allowed me, I dreaded fasting alone. I always enjoyed fasting in the midst of others. For me the joy of fasting was seeing other people also abstaining in the same way as me, going through the pain and the pangs of hunger.

I entered the flat very confused and worried.

Bruno started barking. 'Come on stop that. He's no longer a stranger. Don't be a nuisance. Keep quiet,' she said patting and rubbing Bruno's ears. The three dogs gathered around me wagging their tails. 'You see they like you. See how they wag their tails? It means they're happy. There's nothing better than the sight of happy dogs. Why do dogs always make us happy?' Pat did not wait for an answer. 'Because they can read our minds,' she said smiling. 'Having said that, Bruno has not been well of late – he seems depressed. Something is affecting his well-being. I'm not sure what it is. It could be your presence.'

'What do you mean?'

'A new face does affect dogs especially in the way we treat or relate to them. It's possible that Bruno feels you don't like him. He feels rejected. Dogs can be very sensitive you know. I suggest you show you love him and let's see what happens. Try to bond with him. I'll teach you how to feed him, bath him and play with him. With time you could even take him out for a walk. They really like it when you take them out.'

'I don't think I'll be able to do that. I've never handled dogs in my life and have lots of work to do in the college.'

'Well, the dogs are very important to me you know. They're the most precious things I've got,' Pat said and went into the sitting room. She returned with some leaflets.

Bonding with your dog.
Understanding what your dog is thinking.
Never lie to your dog.
How to tell if your dog loves you.

Pat showed me a board in the kitchen. 'In this flat there is something called *Dogs' Time*. See, this is the time to eat. The time is fixed as you can see. Not too early and not too late. It affects their digestion. There is time to go out for a walk. It must not be too early and not too late because they are trained to ease themselves while on walks. As you know already, it's dog first. They go out first and come in first. My dogs have been trained to lead. Outside, they are always in front. And you follow.'

Pat showed me leashes of all the dogs. 'Your fluffy friend here Lilly likes to roll over. Here are balls and sticks for games in the park. Bruno is a big dog so you have to be very careful. Don't let other dogs near them. Always take at least five bags with you. It's a serious offence here in the UK not to clean up after a dog mess. It may not be an offence in Africa, but here someone can be reported to the council for fouling the pavement or any other public space.'

She went into the sitting room and came back with another leaflet. 'Here,' she gave me the leaflet: *Ten commandments of making your dog happy.*

I thought I should tell her that I would never take the dogs out or bond with them. Pat walked closer smiling. 'There's nothing more therapeutic than taking dogs for a walk. You feel loved by people just looking at you and your dog, you feel cherished by the dogs and you get a lot of confidence. People stop and admire the dogs and they are happy. You feel connected to people. Finally, for your information, my dogs would inherit whatever I have when I die. In my will, I made it categorically clear that whatever I have should go to my lovely dogs for they have kept me safe and sane.'

I picked up the courage and told her that I shall never take the dogs out. She was upset and she showed it immediately. I noticed her face changed. She walked away visibly angry.

I noticed that over the next few days she was still upset. If we met in the hallway, Pat would pretend I was not there.

A week later, Pat told me one morning. 'You woke me up in the middle of the night. You slammed the door so hard that I woke up. I told you not to do this when you first came. Bruno also woke up and was restless all night. Also, I noticed that you flush the toilet very hard and you use a lot of electricity before you sleep.'

I didn't know what to do and what to say. 'I'm sorry if I woke you up. It was windy and a window somewhere was open that was why the door slammed. I've been flushing the toilet in the same way as everybody does. I have not changed the way I flush the toilet since I moved in. There is nothing I can do about Bruno being restless. As for the electricity, I read a lot before going to bed. I promise not to read any more – is that okay with you?'

Pat did not answer.

Weeks later, I went to the St Mary's Hospital in Paddington where my uncle was hospitalised. In the ward a smiling Filipino nurse took me to his bedside and told me to wait. 'As you can see, the doctor is attending to him.' I sat next to a young man.

'Are you Mustapha?' the young clean-shaven Asian man asked. I was surprised.

'Yes.' I answered.

'Ah ha, you see we meet at last. My name is Imran and I am your uncle's solicitor and friend.'

'Nice to meet you. Yes, he's told me a lot about you.'

'I hope he said only good things about me. Don't tell me you support Arsenal too?'

'No I don't.'

'This is England mate; you have to support a football club.'

'Not yet anyway,' my uncle said from behind the curtains. 'There's only one team worthy of support. There's only one Arsenal.'

'Why would you support a loser? We're not the champions by chance.'

'Imran, Arsenal will be the champions at the end of the season,' my uncle predicted.

'Dream on mate,' Imran said smiling.

Later, when the doctors had left, my uncle said, 'Imran will sort you out. He'll help you with all the letters to the Home Office and any other queries. Don't worry about the money. He is very rich and spends all his money on expensive cars, Liverpool FC and holidays to Italy.'

'I know how to enjoy life,' Imran argued and gave me his business card. 'No problem Brother Mustapha, *Insha'Allah* everything will be sorted. Trust me. Don't worry. You're in good hands. Your uncle knows I'm a specialist in immigration affairs. I hope that you'll not support Arsenal when you have all your documents sorted.'

I noticed that the two men wanted to talk. I thanked them and left.

Hours later I entered the flat in Kilburn. Bruno was running and barking from one end of the hallway to the other. Pat looked unhappy. She hissed when she saw me enter. I had a feeling that I had done something wrong again. After making sure that the door did not slam,

I was glad when she said. 'That stupid woman is passing with her dog. That's why Bruno is agitated.' Pat went to the window. 'I'm right. Look at her. See what she's wearing; she walks around as if she has forgotten her skirt at home. I hate her. Look at her figure. I wish I could carry a camera and secretly photograph her filthy dog doing it on the pavement. I would love to report her to the council so that she can be fined. I really hate that woman.'

I did not say a word.

Moments later, I heard Pat shout. 'Who drank the milk?' I thought she was talking to the dogs. 'Mustapha, I'm asking you a question. I'm talking to you and you ignore me and walk away. That's very rude you know?'

'I thought you were talking to the dogs.'

'Who drank the milk?' she repeated still shouting.

'You know I don't drink milk. I don't touch anything in the fridge.'

Pat was upset again.

'I left home very early in the morning and have just returned.'

'I wasn't here either,' she argued. 'The bottle of milk was full yesterday and now it's half empty. Are you telling me that the dogs opened the fridge, drank part of the milk and closed the fridge? Listen to me Mustapha, we don't have ghosts in this flat. It's just you and me and if it's not me then it's you. Stop denying it. Just own up and apologise. I would understand if you said you were hungry or thirsty and I'll forgive you. From now on, don't ever argue with me.' She walked away in annoyance.

I stood there confused and shaken.

A couple of minutes later, Pat came back fuming. 'I noticed two drops of urine on the floor in the toilet. You're supposed to sit and pass urine, not stand. If you must stand and urinate, please be good at aiming. You men are worse than dogs. At least dogs know exactly where and how to pass urine. They carefully choose lampposts and other respectable places. You men just stand there and spray your urine everywhere.'

'The drops were not urine. I always sat on the toilet. They could have been from my wet hands. I don't stand to urinate.'

'You like arguments don't you? But there are hand towels in the bathroom. I hope you're not praying in this flat? Matilda told me some days ago that you spent so much time praying while staying in their flat. She said she once saw you washing your feet in the sink. Yuck! Disgusting! I hope you're not washing your feet in my sink. I don't want to smell your feet while I'm brushing my teeth, okay?'

I did not know what to do. Pat continued to talk and talk and talk. She was angry. I decided to go out. I called my uncle's flat. Matilda told me he was feeling poorly and would rather spend time in bed. I had nowhere else to go. I started walking around aimlessly. As I approached a bus stop, I saw an elderly man get out of a bus with many shopping bags. I could tell from his red cap and multicoloured gown under a thick jacket that he was a Nigerian. I volunteered to help him.

'I did something stupid,' he admitted. 'I bought more than I could carry.'

'I'll help you.'

'Thanks. That's very kind of you. Are you sure you have the time?'

'Yes I do.'

'Thank you very much young man. That's my early Christmas shopping.'

As we walked, the man introduced himself. 'My name is Dr Asibong. I teach history in one of the universities in London. I left Nigeria a few months before independence in 1960. I studied history in the United States, Canada and here in the UK. I have written a couple of books on missionary activities in West Africa, which is my area of specialisation. I have also written extensively on other political issues in various journals and magazines.'

We continued to walk. When we reached his flat on Sumatra Road, he asked, 'Do you want to come in for tea or coffee?'

I reluctantly agreed.

I noticed his flat was full of books and journals and newspapers.

'I'm very happy you read history,' he said after I told him about myself. 'It's important that we Africans know our past. It's one thing for us to look at the past, we should endeavour to understand and absorb it. One of the many tragedies that has befallen us in Africa is that we don't know our own history hence we tend to repeat it.'

Dr Asibong gave me some books to read.

'Feel free to visit any time. I'm around most of the time. I'm done with teaching for the time being. I do mainly research. You're welcome to come here and read as many books as possible. I want you to return to Nigeria a better-informed person. I'll be away for three weeks. I'm going to Nigeria for the Christmas and New Year holidays.'

I returned to the flat.

I was beginning to have layers of things to worry about. That night the one on top of the list was my laziness in saying my prayers. I had promised Imam Murad I would not go more than three days without praying. I had promised my mother that I will say my prayers. The truth of the matter was that I had forgotten when last I said my prayers five times a day. But it was not only my laziness that worried me. My landlady's open hostility worried me. I found it difficult that I could not even perform ablution openly. I had to hide and pretend that I was doing something else. I spent much more time making sure there wasn't a drop of water in the bathroom than paying attention to the rituals of ablution. Being alone made it difficult to motivate myself. I had never before been in a situation like this. I always enjoyed performing ablutions and praying with others. It made sense and had meaning. Initially I tried to get around this problem by praying twice a day-at dawn and late at night. I was sure my landlady would not know what I was doing. But, I was beginning to feel the guilt of letting the hours and the days pass without prayers.

Within the last few days, I decided to invoke the injunction of *Tayammum*, dry ablution. Islam allowed for dry ablution is extraordinary situations. I considered mine extraordinary. I waited for my landlady to take the dogs out for a walk before I performed the dry ablutions and said my prayers. Sometimes I would sit on the chair facing Makkah and pray hastily with an eye on the door. I did not want Pat to see me saying my prayers in the normal standing, bending and sitting positions. I did not know what her reaction would be. I prayed with fear and did not enjoy it. It was not what I was used to. I was used to being at peace with myself and with the environment while saying my prayers. I was used to praying in total devotion with my body and with my soul. I enjoyed praying when I managed to submerge myself into a state of subconsciousness and recite verses of the holy Quran either loudly or in total silence. I never thought I would be praying in a flat with dogs running around and barking. It was a strange situation for me. With time I decided it was better not to pray than to pray under such conditions.

'How's your father?' Mr Patel who owned a newspaper shop asked me one afternoon as I glanced through the headlines of newspapers. I knew he was referring to Dr Asibong.

'He's away for two more weeks,' I answered.

'I know because I deliver his papers and magazines. He's a lucky man. He's in a warm place. Look at the weather. It's snowing again.'

I did not answer.

'Is this your first experience of snow?'

'Yes.'

'Do you like it?'

'Yes I do.'

'Tell me something,' Mr Patel walked closer to me. 'Are you working?'

'No.'

'Do you have time to work for me? I want you to do a couple of hours a day. I'm short of one person to do paper rounds for me.' He said looking straight into my eyes. When I did not reply, he whispered into my ears, 'It's cash in hand.'

'What is paper round?' I asked.

Mr Patel explained what it was. 'You've to wake up very early, preferably at dawn, come here and take newspapers and deliver them to certain addresses in the area. I'll pay you twenty-five pounds a week. Cash in hand,' he emphasised.

I agreed not fully knowing what it was all about.

I told Pat as soon as I entered the flat about the job, especially that I would be waking up at dawn. She did not object.

I started immediately. I enjoyed the discipline of waking up at dawn.

I went to Mr Patel's shop, picked up the papers and delivered them. It gave me something to do and time to think.

At the college, Hilary Rogers, my course tutor was very pleased with the progress of my work.

I went back home satisfied.

'Mr Frank,' Pat shouted over the phone one day. 'How did you get my number? Who gave you my number?' She walked out of the sitting room. 'Mustapha, didn't I tell you not to give anyone my number? I don't want nuisance calls from pests like Frank.'

'Matilda could have given it to him.'

'Okay, he wants to talk to you,' she gave me the cordless phone.

'Hello Mr Frank.'

'How are you?' I noticed his voice was subdued.

'I'm fine thank you and you?'

He did not answer immediately. 'Can you come over immediately?'

'Where are you?'

'Maida Vale.'

'What's wrong? What happened?'

'Just come. You will know when you arrive.'

I could tell from his voice that something was wrong. I wore my winter coat and dashed to my uncle's flat.

I entered the flat. Four of my uncle's friends were in the sitting room, all standing in a sombre mood. I noticed that my uncle's sofa was empty. Zoya was in a corner sobbing.

'Lord have mercy on his soul.' I could hear her say in between sobs.

'Mo has passed away,' Frank B disclosed in a low voice, almost crying. 'I'm really sorry but such is life.' He looked disorientated.

I closed my eyes briefly. Frank B continued to speak but I did not hear what he was saying. I could pick out things like, massive heart attack, rushed to the hospital, doctors, emergency, life-saving machine. I was numb. I did not know what to do. I did not know how to react. I sat down. I repeated several times.

Inna lillahi wa inna ilaihi raji'un (Surely we belong to Allah and to Him we shall return).

I could hear conversations in low voices. I could pick up words like body in mortuary, autopsy and funeral arrangements. It was like a dream and I thought I would eventually wake up. The longer I sat listening to conversations about the burial arrangements the more I began to accept that it was not a dream.

A particular type of fear began to creep in. If they decided to send his body to Bauchi for burial, I would be the person to go with it. If I took the body home, I would have to stay there for a while … I began to fear that my uncle's death could mean the end of my dream. Going home would mean not coming back. His death could actually mean that I might not be able to pay the rent again. I began to worry seriously.

Imran came and sat next to me. 'Things are a bit complicated when a Muslim dies in the UK. Some administrative and medical procedures are contrary to Islamic teachings and make it a bit difficult for relatives. Let's see what Imam Murad says.' Imran spoke in Urdu over the phone for a long time with Imam Murad. When he finished, Imran sat next to me and whispered. 'The Imam said you should inform his parents immediately. Tell them that Brother Mohammad would be buried here in the UK according to Islamic customs.'

Imam Murad later told me. 'We shall liaise with the hospital and an ambulance. *Insha'Allah*, the body will be released on Thursday night or Friday morning. Leave all that to us. We'll do the *Janaiza* (funeral prayers) in the *masjid* after *Juma'at* prayers. An Islamic charity ambulance will bring the body and take it to a Muslim cemetery outside London. *Insha'Allah*, I'll perform the last rites and ensure that your late uncle and my very good friend is buried according to Islamic rites.'

I called Ibrahim in Nigeria and informed him.

'What are you going to do now?' Ibrahim asked.

'Honestly I don't know.'

'How's it going to affect your studies and your stay in London?'

'I don't know.'

'Are you going to return to Nigeria?'

'I don't know.'

'What are you going to do now?' Pat asked me as soon as I entered the flat in Kilburn. 'Who's going to pay your rent? You're not going to stay here for free you know?' Pat added with a sense of panic in her voice. 'You may have to find somewhere to stay. Matilda says she can only pay for a month or so but cannot pay till the end of your course.'

'I'll probably go back to their flat.'

'I don't think that's possible. Matilda plans to put the property up for sale in a couple of months.'

I withdrew into the room. There were too many things to worry about.

Matilda was still in shock when I met her the next day. She was tearful and reflective. 'I still can't believe Mo's gone. I still think he's going to walk out of his room and ask for one thing or the other. I still expect to hear him winding me up.' She paused for a while. Matilda stood up and made tea for me. 'Frank B and others are organising a memorial service at the Africa Centre. That would be in about a month's time. It would be for all those who knew him as Maddo during his days on the band called Reflection. You know that he was the face of the band. I understand you, Imran and the Imam are organising a Muslim part of the funeral.'

I nodded.

'Well, that's the best we can do. I hope we would all be able to give him a good send off. He was a good man. I loved him and will miss him. He had a style no one would ever capture. Once everything is done, I hope to go away to West Indies for a long break. I need some rest and sunshine.'

Matilda said nothing about my education. When I was about to leave, she gave me a letter from the college. I decided not to open the letter. In the flat, I put it on the table. I sat alone in my room. Tears started rolling down my cheeks. In Bauchi town, there was a popular saying: *you never mourn alone.* Whenever anyone heard of a death in the community, it was mandatory to visit the family of the deceased and offer prayers to the Almighty for the forgiveness of the departed soul. Then pray for those who were left behind to be able to bear the loss. There I was, alone in a room, mourning the death of my uncle. I could picture the family house of my uncle. It would be full of mourners for several days. People shared many things, including mourning. I was alone. Bruno was restless. He was barking incessantly. It was disturbing me and my thoughts. I looked at the time. It was the dog's time for a walk. When Pat and the dogs left the flat, I performed ablution and prayed.

'*Inna llahi wa inna ilaihi raji'un,*' Imam Murad said as soon as I entered his office on Friday. 'Everything is going according to plan, Brother Mustapha. The body of your uncle was released yesterday. Some Islamic charity workers have washed it in keeping with Islamic ritual and it has been wrapped in white cloth. The ambulance is on its way. I hope you can go to the Islamic cemetery with us. It's important for you to see the process in case your relatives ask you.'

'*Insha'Allah*, I'll go with you.'

After the *Juma'at* congregational prayers, it was announced that there would be a *Janaiza*. Most worshippers waited and offered the special funeral prayers. After the prayers, Imam Murad, Frank B, and I followed the ambulance in Imran's car.

'What else do you do back home?' Imam Murad asked.

'We normally have non-obligatory prayers eight days and then forty days after someone has passed away.'

'That's fine,' Imam Murad said. 'I'll do the forty days prayers for you but you have to remind me. I'm getting old.'

I felt numb and was in a daze for many days.

Exactly forty days after my uncle's death, about two dozen of us gathered in front of the minicab office at noon. Matilda and Zoya had their heads covered and Imam Murad ensured that the two women were seated separately in the mosque. When we were all seated, Imam welcomed us all. He started with a short prayer and then read part of *Surah Yassin*.

'Brother Mohammad was my friend, old friend and neighbour. I can say that he was very honest, sincere, humble and kind. We're not going to talk about the things he did that we did not approve of. We want to remember the good things he did and the good person he was.'

Imam Murad turned to me. 'The family members and loved ones left behind have a duty to pray for his departed soul.' Looking straight at me, Imam continued. 'Please be aware of the power of *shaitan*. The devil knows how to entice you from the *deen* and path of righteousness. Please Brother Mustapha, don't be tempted by the things that had negative influences on your uncle. I'm not going to mention them here and now but you know what I'm talking about. Please guard that which is in between your mouth and in between your legs. If you guard those places, *shaitan* will not be able to entice you away from the *deen*. Make sure what goes into your mouth does not hurt you, and what comes out of your mouth does not hurt anyone. Try to do things that would give you peace of mind. Remember that there's a day of judgement and we will all account for our deeds.

'Brother Mohammad, you'll agree with me, deviated from the *deen* over a period of time. We must not judge him. Allah knows best. About ten years ago I remember very well Brother Mohammad changed. He came here one evening and told me that he would like to return to practising his faith. I was very happy for him. He started to pray and came here once or twice a week. You probably don't know this but Brother Mohammad used his contacts to collect a lot of money for this *masjid*. One day he told me that his dream was to go on pilgrimage to Makkah and Madina. I honestly don't know what happened. After some time he stopped coming. May Almighty Allah bless his soul, forgive him for his sins and grant him eternal peace. Please Brother Mustapha, don't follow in his footsteps in the wrong direction. The biggest struggle in life is the struggle inside us. One of the easiest thing to waste is what is most dearest to us; our lives. Ramadan starts soon. Please say your prayers, fast during the month of Ramadan and give whatever you can afford as *Sadaqah*.'

Imam recited more verses from the Quran and concluded special prayers.

'What are you going to do now?' Samad asked showing his concerned face.

'I don't know. Only Allah knows what's going to happen next.'

'*Insha'Allah*, you'll be all right. May Almighty Allah make things easy for you.'

'*Amin*,' I said and hugged him.

When I was ready to go, Imran gave me a bag full of Arsenal memorabilia – the jersey, scarves, photographs and autographed season tickets and a letter from the state scholarship board in Bauchi. 'From now on you must support the Gunners. That's the best way to remember your uncle and keep his memory alive. He loved Arsenal right until the end.'

'We've done the best we could,' concluded Frank B. 'Life must go on. I shall miss him.'

Imran invited me into his car. It was a silver-coloured Mercedes Benz with a special personalised registration number IMR 786. 'It's the latest in the series,' he boasted. There were shiny grey prayer beads and a CD of the Quran in the rear mirror.

'Are you going to watch the best team in the world this weekend?'

'Who are they?'

'Liverpool of course.'

'No.'

'I know from now on you'll be supporting Arsenal but if you really want to see quality football, you have to watch the real champions. Nothing beats quality.'

'No thanks.'

That evening, I found it hard to relax. I looked at the two letters. What's inside? I wanted to open them at the end of the mourning period. The mourning period was over. Now I was afraid of opening them.

I visited Dr Asibong who had returned from Nigeria. I told him about my uncle. 'I know Maddie very well, as a musician I mean. He was well known and well loved. I didn't realise he was a Muslim and didn't even know he was a Nigerian. He used to hang around with lots of West Indians and we all thought he was one of them. I did notice that his accent was different. Come to think of it, nothing was ever written about his background. All the other members had articles written on their ancestors but I never read or heard anything about his background. He was really good on drums and later he was the front man. He knew how to dance. My God, he wowed the audience. I'm so sad to hear about his death. I read his obituary in *The Guardian* a few days ago. I went to so many of their performances. He was really *mad*, especially with the girls. They really liked him. He was known as the guy with the golden voice. Girls queued for hours to hear him sing. I still remember the iconic picture that made him famous. He had Afro hair, thick side burns and was wearing a white shirt with big collars and a baggy trouser.'

'Do you know what MAD stood for?'

'No.'

'Mohammed Aminu Dankobi.'

'*Abasi Kenyon* (Gracious God) I see. Thanks for telling me. You live to learn something every day.' He paused for a while. With a sympathetic face he looked at me and asked. 'What are you going to do now?'

'I don't know.'

'I'm really sorry about the death of your uncle. Things must be very hard for you right now. Listen you can always count on me.'

I returned to the flat to face the two letters and to try to find an answer to the question people had been asking me: *what are you going to do now?* I looked at the letters. I knew they contained important information. I felt it was time to open them. After my uncle's death and the period of mourning I was now ready to face an uncertain future. I did not care anymore how his passing away would change my life. Somehow I felt that the contents of the letter would actually make things better for me.

Four

Realm of Despair

I decided, after all not to open the envelopes that evening. I was afraid the contents would be too upsetting. I felt whatever was inside would make it difficult for me to sleep. I had been having difficulty sleeping and thought that I deserved a good night's sleep. Opening the envelopes in the morning and knowing what they contained would give me a long time to think and take possible action.

I had noticed that I was beginning to lose concentration and that any noise irritated me. I began to feel that I was losing control of my life. I could not answer this simple question: *what are you going to do now?* Where do you go from here? What happens next?

I called Samad from the nearest telephone booth. 'I'm sorry I cannot join you for Ramadan prayers as promised.' It was the first day of Ramadan. I could not share his excitement looking forward to thirty days of fasting. We had talked about saying the *Taraweeh* (extra prayers performed by Muslims at night during the month of Ramadan) prayers together. I had looked forward to following Imam Murad as he recited the entire verses of the Quran during the holy month. I had promised to break my fast as many days as possible with Samad's family. I felt bad calling him to tell him that I would not make it. I did not give him any reasons. There was silence. I hung up.

I knew I had to find money to live on from somewhere. What I was receiving from Mr Patel paid for the room. I asked Mr Patel if he had any other jobs. He gave me a three-hour-a-day job stacking shelves in the supermarket nearby and cleaning the floors.

One morning after the paper round, I picked up the courage to open the letter from the college. 'Dear Mr Abdullahi,' the letter started. 'We have received information from the Bauchi state scholarship board that your scholarship has been terminated. In view of this development, I am writing to inform you that you cannot continue with your course until you are able to pay the second and final instalment of your tuition fee. Please do contact me immediately. Yours sincerely, Hilary Rogers.'

I did not open the second letter. I knew it was from the scholarship board informing me that my scholarship had been stopped. I was not surprised. I brought out the photocopy of my passport. I looked at the visa page. 'Damn it,' I said to myself. 'My visa expires soon. I must take action. Imran is dragging his feet.'

After several attempts to talk to Imran over the phone failed, I decided to visit his offices in Willesden Green. I recognised his car with his personalised registration number plate, IMR 786 in the parking lot. The prayer beads and a CD-ROM were there hanging from the rear-view mirror.

'*Assalaam Alaikum*,' I announce my arrival.

'*Wa'alaikum Salaam*, Ramadan Kareem Brother Mustapha,' Imran replied.

He was standing in the middle of his office. I noticed he did not embrace me as he used to and did not even look at me properly. He looked tired and distracted. The phone rang. He picked it up. He looked stressed as he spoke. 'I'm on top of things, okay, but it's hectic. The guy really screwed me up this time you know.'

'Sorry Mustapha,' Imran said when he finished the phone call. 'I've been very busy and as you know Ramadan takes a lot of energy.'

'Oh yes I do.'

'Actually I have a letter for you.'

I was excited. I thought he had somehow extended my visa as promised.

'How's life treating you?' he asked.

'*Alhamdullilah.*'

I was disappointed when he handed over the letter. It was from Nigeria, from the Bauchi State Scholarship Board. It was identical to the one I had received earlier. I decided I might as well open it. 'I am writing to inform you that we have decided to cancel your scholarship with immediate effect. Your institution has been informed. As from

March 1991, the state government will no longer be responsibility for your education. You are advised to return to Nigeria immediately.' Signed Alhaji Tanko.

Imran asked. 'What's the good news? Matilda sent the letter to me.'

'Not good news I'm afraid.' I handed over the letter to him.

He read it quickly. 'Don't worry, there's always a way out. I'll sort you out somehow. There's another route I can use to extend your stay but it will cost you another five hundred pounds. You don't have to pay me now but as soon as I receive payment I'll write to the Home Office and *Insha'Allah* everything would be fine.'

Back in the flat Pat asked me. 'Have you noticed that Bruno is ill? I hope it's not infectious. I don't want the other dogs to be ill. What am I going to do?' she asked me looking very agitated.

'I don't know.'

'You don't look as if you care, do you?'

'I do but I'm not a vet. What else can I do?'

'You don't look sympathetic.'

'I've lots of problems.'

'Did you give him something to eat?'

'No. Why should I?'

'Maybe you decided to feed him. I just want to rule that out.'

'I've never fed your dogs.'

I went into my room. 'Oh by the way, Frank called. He wants you to visit him on Saturday during lunchtime.'

'Thank you,' I said lying down in bed.

'How are you keeping young fella?' Frank B asked as soon as I entered his flat on a street off Portobello Road. 'A shot of malt whisky for you?'

'No thanks.'

'Blimey! Still not drinking alcohol? I wonder how long you can go without it,' he said laughing.

After one shot of whisky, Frank B started. 'I just wanted to say a few things. As you probably know, your late uncle was my very good friend, my drinking buddy I should say. He was a very nice man indeed. We had some wonderful times together. Ever since we first met over thirty years ago, we always talked about going to Nigeria together. He wanted me to see his family house. He wanted me to meet his parents and to experience life in northern Nigeria. My ancestors were slaves taken from somewhere in Africa and I always wanted to visit any part of the continent. We made more than five arrangements. One thing or the other disrupted our plans. On one occasion we were about to buy the tickets when I fell ill. And he said he would only go to Nigeria with me. Then on another occasion, we actually bought the tickets but I lost my father and had to go to Guyana.

'Your uncle was an intensely private man. To be honest with you, there are so many things I don't know about him. He kept so many things to himself and took so many things to his grave. For example, he never told any of us, I mean his friends, what Matilda was to him. Who is Zoya and what was she to him? What was his relationship with these women? No one knew. Since he died, the two women have just vanished. They travelled abroad and never kept in touch. They have put the flat up for sale and have not discussed anything with me. It hurts because he must have helped them a lot and they knew how close I was to him. At least they should have kept in touch with some-one like you or me. But such is life. When we were younger, we talked about our liaisons and criticised each other. We were very direct like all young people were supposed to be. But as we got older we only drank and cracked jokes. I just mind my own business. Why didn't he go home, for example? No one knew. I asked him several times why he wouldn't visit his parents, but he just laughed. He told me he had plans for you to go to the US but I don't know much about it and I don't know the contact in the US. I know his death would in one way or the other affect your education but there is very little I can do. Such is life.'

There was a long period of silence.

Frank B went into his bedroom and came out with clothes, cufflinks and ties. 'I don't need them anymore,' he said. 'I've passed my 'display by date.' You need these fashionable clothes to charm and chase young women around. By the way, have you worn the T-shirt I gave you? You never know, it might work for you too.'

Frank drank more whisky and continued. 'There's someone you should meet. I don't know where she is at the moment but I can find out. Her name is Maureen. I've forgotten her surname. It'll come. She was your uncle's first girlfriend in the UK. It was love at first sight and I can tell that she was madly in love with him. She was his first and last love. Everyone after her was complete waste of space and time. She was lovely, lively, witty, intelligent and beautiful. She was somewhere in South Africa but I understand she's back or planning to return to the country. When I remember her surname I will check the phone directory and look for her. You must meet her. She was madly in love with your uncle. This was many years ago, probably before you were born. She even went to Nigeria to see where he came from before they marry. She came back and found him with another girl. She was devastated. She almost lost her mind. In short, she had a mental breakdown. Unfortunately so many men do things like this, but such is life. These things happen. And you know what Mo never had a good and trustworthy woman like her again. His life would have been completely different if he had remained with Maureen.' There was a long silence again. 'That's life,' he said as if resigned.

'By the way our team Arsenal lost today. Mo would have been upset.' When I stood up to the leave, Frank B gave one hundred pounds. 'Go to the pub here on Portobello Road or near your place, buy yourself a drink and pick up a woman and have a nice time,' he said laughing. 'Have fun when you're young and strong and then you'll have enough memories and things to remember or probably regret when you get to my age.'

I thanked him and walked out of the flat.

'I'm delighted to inform you that Bruno is feeling a lot better. The vet said it was a mild infection due to the changing weather,' Pat said with a broad smile as soon as I entered the flat. 'Dogs are affected by the change in weather too you know.'

'What's your immigration status?' Dr Asibong asked me one afternoon. The question caught me by surprise. I did not know what to say. 'I just have this strange feeling that I should ask you.'

'I'm still on the student visa,' I replied and told him about my problems with the scholarship board and with my solicitor.

'Try and sort this out as soon as possible. That's something you cannot afford to joke with in the UK. If I were you I would seek a second opinion. Unfortunately I cannot help you. However, I do know of an organisation that could be of help. They are called the West African Refugee Resource Centre. Call BT maybe they are listed in the directory.'

I brought out my address book. 'I met someone from the organisation called Taj. I've his contact details here.'

'Good. I know Taj but don't have his contact details. Call and tell him about your problems. I think you are leaving things too late. Feel free to use my phone.'

I dialled the number. Taj was in the office. He remembered me. I told him about my problems.

'I'm flying out tomorrow. Let's meet later today at Bozo's Joint. We've a Politburo meeting.'

At Bozo's Joint in Camberwell, South London, Taj was waiting in front of the shop. He was wearing a short African *kaftan* with embroidery in the front and around the neck. His pipe was still in his mouth when he introduced me to Bozo, the owner of the supermarket. He led me down to the basement puffing his pipe and introduced me to other members of the Politburo. 'You may not know this,' he said laughing and looking at me. 'But there's a Politburo in London, not just in Moscow, Beijing, Pyongyang, Hanoi and Havana.'

'And we meet in the basement of a supermarket. It doesn't matter where we meet. It's what we discuss that matters,' someone said laughing.

'Meet Mustapha, the young man I told you I met at Heathrow. He's trying to follow the footsteps of Ousmane Sembéne, the great African film-maker. I'm in a rush. Jarvo will handle your case,' he said pointing at one of the members of the Politburo. He gave me fifty pounds and left.

Jarvo and I found a quiet corner in the basement of Bozo's Joint. I told him everything about my immigration status. He listened attentively jotting down notes.

'On the one hand your case is very straightforward. And on the other, it's a bit complicated. We could have been able to do something when your uncle died but it is too late now. You can only ask for an extension, which the Home Office would not grant you because your tuition fee has not been paid in full. Had your fees been paid in full, you would have had at least a leg to stand on. Your solicitor can appeal against this decision but that's just buying time.'

Jarvo lit a cigarette and thought for a while. 'Your solicitor has messed you up big time. He should have been honest with you. He was interested only in money and probably hoped that you would be caught and deported or you would return to Nigeria out of fear. We all fall prey to people like these. By the way, he also overcharged you and did nothing. We'll give you money to pay him and we'll do our best.'

'I don't understand why he should be paid after all you said he did nothing.'

'Mustapha,' Jarvo interrupted me. 'It's in your interest to pay him. Now that he knows you are in trouble he can mess you up further by informing the Home Office about who you are and where you are and get you back to Nigeria tomorrow.'

'But he's a Muslim,' I said not fully convinced.

'So what?' Jarvo said and laughed. 'If he's a real Muslim, he would have been honest with you from day one, simple. Or he would have done all these things for you for free or charged you the minimum rates. After all, he knows you don't have much money. Forget about people's religion in London. It's their self-interest that matters here. London is full of all kinds of sharks. From now on make sure you swim with your eyes wide open.' Jarvo calmly explained the problem I was drifting into and concluded; 'you've two clear options. Either you become an illegal immigrant or you return to Nigeria.'

'Please don't sleepwalk into an illegal immigration status,' Jarvo said, the next day when we met at the offices of the resource centre near Elephant and Castle Shopping Centre. 'I've had time to think over your case since we met yesterday. Its better you walk straight into it with your eyes wide open, at least you know what awaits you. I'm not being funny but you have a big problem,' he concluded shaking his head to emphasise the point.

I sat there worried and confused.

'Mustapha,' he started after a long silence. 'You can make a world wherever you are. That's the joy of being adventurous. You're young and healthy so you can take risks. The bigger your dreams the greater the risks you have to take. I'm not saying you should return immediately or remain here. All I'm saying is that should you decide to stay here you can make it but it's going to be very difficult. In the final analysis, if your appeal is rejected, it's not the end of the world. It's the beginning of another world, a new chapter, a new dawn and a new dream. There are thousands, maybe millions of illegal immigrants living and thriving here even if that life is best described as a strange existence.'

With those words we parted company and agreed to meet again.

The realisation that I was going to put my dream on hold hurt me. The truth had hit me hard. I tried to pretend that things would be fine in the end. The reality was that things were getting worse.

I knew I had reached a crossroad and sooner or later I had to make the decision about which path to take. That night, the words of my father somehow found their way into my ears. 'Mustapha, whenever you think you have reached a crossroad and have difficulty making the right decision, there is one place for you to go to, the mosque. It's a place of worship so go there and seek guidance from the Almighty in prayers and seek refuge from *shaitan*. Whenever you don't have words and you need solace, go to the mosque. A mosque is a place where Almighty Allah will make you find the words that elude you because your heart is too full and your mind is probably weary. Also, please take time to contemplate before taking any action. It's when you contemplate that you understand the essence of life and understand the world around you. Remember that Prophet Muhammad (SAW) enjoined believers to contemplate. According to a Hadith, he was reported to have said, "One hour of contemplation is better than one year of worship."'

I felt numb. The realisation that I could not continue with my studies and that the dream of making a film had evaporated really hit me again. I felt dizzy. What am I going to do? I don't have money. That was the first and main problem. What's keeping me in the UK? If I decided to return to Nigeria, I would get a job. I could go back to the television station. I could join the radio station. There were other factors pulling me home too. I wanted to be with friends and my family. I wanted to be in the familiar environment. I missed the familiar noises, smells and people. I missed the rituals of everyday life in the northern part of Nigeria. I missed the seasons. But I asked myself several times, why should I return when I set out in the first instance to fulfil a dream? Why return and give up on my dream? The next morning, after my paper round, I asked Mr Patel if he knew where the nearest mosque was. 'There's one in Cricklewood.'

On Cricklewood Broadway, I asked a Pakistani butcher. 'You see that building there?' he said pointing to an old church. 'It's a *masjid*. It's an old church that has been converted to a *masjid*. Yes there's a cross at the top but inside is a mosque. Just go in and pray.'

I believed him. It was true. It was a mosque. I remembered my mother's advice. 'Never take a decision when you are hungry, angry and tired.' I was not hungry, angry or tired. I was in a normal frame of mind to take the most difficult decision yet. I performed my ablution and prayed as my father would have recommended: a two *rakat* prayer with the sole intention of asking the Almighty for guidance. I remembered my father's words. 'We need prayers to give us clarity of the mind. Once your mind is clear, you would be able to take a good decision.' After the prayer, I sat down in a corner of the mosque. I experienced a moment of stillness. A strong clear thought came to my mind, almost as if it had been spoken. The thought was compelling and I was happy when I stood up to leave that I had that wonderful experience. I smiled at myself. I knew the most difficult decision had been made.

Later that day I did an exercise. I wrote down why I should return to Nigeria: I had no money to live in the UK. I had no legal stay. I am not studying. I have no family. There is no sun. I have no close friends.

I do not offer prayers as I would love to and I'm in debt. I'm lonely and live in fear.

Then I wrote why I should remain in the UK. There was only one: to fulfil my dream of becoming a filmmaker. It was nine to one. Somehow I felt that my head said go and my heart said stay.

I woke up in the morning and decided I would stay. It was one of the very few times when my instincts told me to do something that defied logic. It was a crazy decision. I was ready to bear the consequences.

I called Jarvo at the resource centre and told him of my decision to remain illegally. I made it clear that I understood the risks.

We met again. That was the day the USSR collapsed; the day that I adopted the name Michael Danquah.

I resigned to living in the UK for an unforeseeable future. I reluctantly decided to close the chapters of my past life. I'm here in the UK and I might as well make the most of what was available. I was outwardly confident that I would succeed but I was also full of fear and apprehension. I felt I was entering the realm of despair; I was sliding into an abyss.

That was how I joined the TEMPSTAFF Recruitment Agency and how I got the job as a kitchen porter in the London International Institute of Business and Finance where I met the Hausa woman.

Chapter Five

Down and Out

The wait for the Hausa woman continued. I went to work at the institute hoping to see her, with practised sentences on my lips. From time to time I would look around the public transport and would check the library after work. I wondered if she was so upset that she avoided the institute. I had hoped I would see her one day and be able to apologize.

I was getting used to my double identity. I still reminded myself from time to time that Michael was now my name. 'You're not Mustapha, you're Michael.' I tried to avoid talking to people. I kept away from any crowd. I was trying to manage the transition from being legal to becoming illegal. When I arrived in this country I could walk around without fear of being apprehended. Now I knew that, technically, I should not be in this country. I was committing an offence by breathing the air and walking on UK soil. I had noticed that during the day I was fine. For some strange reason, walking around did not make me feel anxious. It was mainly at night that I felt as if someone was about to grab me. This state of mind affected my sleep.

Jarvo had assured me that this state of fear was temporary. 'It'll pass. You'll get used to it and with time you'll get used to being an illegal immigrant. Just make sure you have a good lie on your lips ready at all times. Try to be as invisible as possible. Illegal immigrants live but they don't exist.'

I did not tell Pat about my immigration status. I was happy she never asked. I had enough money to pay my rent and I tried to avoid her and her dogs as much as possible. I told Dr Asibong that I was technically illegal but that friends at the resource centre were trying to sort me out. Every morning I would say to myself before I opened the front door: 'you are no longer Mustapha' and as I close the door behind me I would repeat: 'you are now Michael.' When I returned from work, I said to myself before I opened the door: 'you are no longer Michael.'

As soon as I entered the flat, I said to myself: 'you are now Mustapha.' As time went by I settled into this life and I was happy with it.

'I'm going to Scotland for three weeks,' Dr Asibong told me one afternoon. 'Take as many books to read as you want.' I took three books and went back to the flat.

'I'll bring two things for you from Guyana,' Frank B said laughing, 'A bottle of real Guyanese rum and a beautiful girl to marry and take to Africa.' He told me that my uncle's flat had been sold but he had not heard anything from either Matilda or Zoya.

I went to Bozo's Joint. 'The entire Politburo is in Manchester. There's a Pan African Congress meeting taking place there,' Bozo told me as I walked into the supermarket.

Back in Kilburn, as soon as I inserted the key into the lock the dogs started barking as expected.

'Hi,' I said and went straight into my room. Pat said something I did not hear after I had closed the door. I thought she was talking to the dogs, as she always did. She opened the door to my room slightly.

'Are you listening? I'm talking to you, Mustapha. It's rude to ignore me and my dogs.'

I apologised. I could see she was upset. What have I done again? I asked myself as I walked towards the door. I've paid my rent. I didn't use the phone. I hardly entered the kitchen. I didn't perform ablution in the toilet and did not pray in the flat. I always made sure not a single drop of water was on the toilet floor. So what's wrong?

'We've got to talk,' she said holding Lilly. I began to panic. I thought my solicitor had informed the Home Office and they had informed her that I was living in the country illegally. Maybe Home Office officials went to my late uncle's flat and the new owners gave them Matilda's details and she gave them Pat's address.

Pat chased the two other dogs into the kitchen and closed the door, 'Don't be a nuisance,' she shouted at them. She returned to me. I was waiting in the hallway. At last she started. 'My mother will be coming here tomorrow evening.'

I thought about it for a second.

'I don't know what to do. She's very old. You see, I see her once or twice a year. The problem is my mother has a very close friend in North London whose husband died last year. She couldn't make it to the funeral then. Now she's decided to visit her friend. She has insisted on coming to London and staying with me. I couldn't say no.' She paused, stroking her dog Lilly. I still did not understand what her mother's visit had to do with me. 'Do you have somewhere to stay for three days?' she asked.

'No. As you probably know Matilda has sold the flat.'

'Yes I do. You have no friends?'

'I do but they're away, but why? Do you want her to stay in my room?'

'No, not at all, she'll sleep in mine and I'll sleep on the sofa in the sitting room.' She smiled. 'How do I put it? I hope you understand. My mother is not comfortable with black people, especially black men. Don't get me wrong; she's not a racist. No. I'm being honest here. She's not a racist. She just doesn't feel at ease when there's a black man around. She has nothing against black people. Trust me. Her carer is a black woman. The thing is, she cannot sleep in the same flat as a black person.'

'So you want me to stay away for three days.'

'Yes,' Pat responded emphatically with a smile looking straight at me.

There was a moment of silence.

'Can I come after she's gone to bed and leave as early as possible?'

'No,' Pat was categorically clear against the idea.

'I promise you she wouldn't see me during her stay here.'

'You don't understand. She is a light sleeper. She might see you on her way to the toilet. She just wouldn't be herself if she knew that there was a black man in the flat. She's very nosy and doesn't mind her own business. She'll open the door in the middle of the night to check if you are there. I told her that you have left the flat but, knowing my mother very well, she would want to be sure. She'd be very upset to see a black man in the flat.'

'But I have nowhere to go.'

'You must know someone who would let you stay for three days.'

'But I'm paying rent to stay here,' I reminded her.

'Okay I'll not charge you for three nights.'

I stood in the hallway speechless.

'Thank you for your understanding,' Pat said walking away. 'Just make sure the room is tidy before you leave.' She got ready to take the dogs out for a walk. They were barking. I could not think properly. I could hear her screaming at them. 'You must behave and be at your best because my mother is coming tomorrow. Don't worry she likes dogs. I'm sure she will bring you some presents. You have met her already and she adores all of you.'

I sat down in my room in total shock. What am I going to do? I thought about where I could go for two nights. The next morning I did my paper round.

I told Mr Patel. 'I'll find someone to do your round for three days,' he said. 'Unfortunately I cannot let you sleep in the shop for health and safety reasons. If something happened to you I'd be in big trouble with the authorities. What about your father's flat?'

'I don't have the keys.'

'Honestly that woman is horrible. She's stubborn, bitchy, always angry and bitter. She must have had a terrible childhood. She used to get her papers from me but she complained incessantly about trivial things so I told her to stuff it.'

I went back to the flat. I took my passport and my script. As the hours passed I began to feel unease. I needed a place to sit and think – an open space, a public space. I was looking for somewhere I could think for hours without being interrupted. If I went to the mosque, I'd be told to leave after the last prayers, then where to? I decided to go to Hyde Park. It was the only public space I knew. I took my rucksack and boarded the bus.

I found a bench and sat down. The first question that came to my mind was: how did I get to this? I began to notice that it was getting darker and darker.

Loud voices nearby disturbed my thoughts. There was a fight and those involved were coming closer to where I was sitting. I could hear sirens in the distance. I stood up and walked away.

From where I was, I saw policemen chase and arrest some men. I walked away quickly from the area. I noticed an ambulance arrived. I found another bench and sat there. There were too many things racing in my mind. Where am I going to sleep? What am I going to eat? I found it difficult to think straight. What I needed at this point was someone to talk to. There was no one. I was alone in the middle of a park in central London.

I was startled by the appearance of a middle-aged man. It appeared to me if he had come from nowhere. The man was not scruffy. He was modestly dressed and there were no signs of him being drunk. He sat down and threw his bag on the bench. There was a sleeping bag rolled on top of the big rucksack.

'What a life we're all living,' he said to himself loudly.

I did not answer.

'Nice weather isn't it?' he turned to me.

I nodded. I was not in the mood for any conversation. I wanted to be left alone. 'Where are you from?' he asked wanting to strike a conversation.

'Somewhere,' I said, not interested in talking to him.

'I see,' he said. 'What a strange life we're all living.'

A drunkard walking past stopped and looked at me. 'Have you got a cigarette or a beer? That's my bench you are sitting on,' he said and staggered towards me.

My companion on the bench stood up and shouted at him. 'Get out of here. Stop there or I'll call the coppers. Leave him alone. He has the right to sit here. This is public property.' The drunken man walked away cursing. 'He's all right, just drunk. He's got his own problems. By the way, my name is Mark.'

'Mine is Michael.'

'Pleased to meet you.'

We sat there for a few minutes in our own thoughts.

Moments later, he asked. 'Have your eaten?'

'No. I'm not hungry.'

'I see. When you're hungry let me know.'

I did not reply. We sat in silence. It was getting darker and darker. I looked at my wristwatch and it was 8:30 pm.

'Michael, let's go,' Mark said.

'Where?'

'To get some free food.'

'Where? Who gives free food?'

He laughed. 'There's a young man from Africa that does God's work. He works in a supermarket and gives homeless people stuff that is supposed to be thrown away. Let's go.'

I took my rucksack and followed him. We walked slowly through the traffic lights, side streets and then through some alleyways and to the back entrance of the supermarket. There was a small crowd of about ten people waiting patiently in front of the black back door. 'You know Michael life in the park has taught me a lot. I've also met some interesting people. It was a young man who looked Oriental to me that first brought me here. I was very hungry and as I yawned he told me there was a reason I yawned when he was passing right in front of me. He said God made me yawn so that he could show me where there was food. We spent time together and we ended up discussing almost everything but especially the existence of God. He believed we are constantly battling to control this world and that God is there watching but when I asked him why can't God do something to the suffering of so many people including us, he laughed and argued that God wants us to suffer so that we can learn but quickly added that sometimes he thinks that God is too busy with so many things including overseeing other planets in the universe to care about an individual in this world. But my Oriental friend strongly believed that we are not abandoned but what we experience is good for the soul. By the way he was a good friend of the security man that gives food.' Soon the door opened and a black man in a security uniform rolled out a bin full of foodstuff. Mark whispered into my ears. 'They've passed their display by date or sell by date. Instead of throwing them away, this young man allows us to pick what we want. Don't tell anyone okay! What he's doing is against the law. So don't get him into trouble. He's supposed to make sure we don't take anything from the bin.'

'Why throw them away when people can eat them?'

'It's for health and safety reasons. If you eat something from the bin and suffer from food poisoning you could sue the supermarket because they gave it to you.'

'I see.'

We waited for those who were there first to take what they wanted. When it was my turn I took a sandwich and a soft drink.

The security man walked closer and greeted me. I thought it was because I was the only black person there. He smiled and asked. 'How are you?'

'I'm fine thank you and you?'

'Glory be to the Lord, I am fine. Are you from Nigeria?'

'No. I'm from Ghana.'

'What's your name?'

'Michael.'

'Your face is familiar. I'm sure I've seen it somewhere in Nigeria. I cannot remember exactly where, but it's either in the newspaper or on television.'

'You know what? You're not the first person to say that. People look alike. So many people have told me that I look like someone from Nigeria.'

'Jesus loves you,' he said. 'Pray and the Lord will have mercy on you. Pray and the Lord will deliver you.'

I thanked him.

Mark and I returned to the park. On our way I suggested we sit on a particular bench. 'You're asking for trouble, big trouble. That bench is for Bill and Suzy. They sleep there. Bill is the head of the mafia in the park.'

'How do you know?'

'I've been in the park for three months now on and off.'

We found another bench and ate in silence.

Around about 11 o'clock, I told Mark. 'I'd like to lie down and sleep. I'm tired.'

Mark was shocked. 'What?' he screamed. 'Today is your first day in the park?'

'Yes.'

He laughed. 'There's a saying among the homeless, *never sleep before dawn*. Yes! From now till dawn is the most dangerous time for homeless people in public places. As they say, after dark all cats become leopards. There are so many crazy and angry people around and they take advantage of darkness to attack homeless people. Over the past three months, I've been verbally abused many times. Some people have been physically abused. You see, pubs have just closed and people are drunk and some are high on other substances. They do stupid things because they think they can get away with it. The other day a group of young men, about six of them started urinating on me. I was awake and they didn't even care. There are so many sadists around who enjoy seeing people suffer and when they see you on the ground instead of helping you they kick you. You must stay awake and be vigilant. If you must sleep, then sleep like a dolphin with one eye open!'

A particular type of fear gripped me. I looked around. The number of people in the park had reduced. There were a couple of people here and the odd person there. We heard noises and arguments from a distance. 'Ha, that's the mafia boss coming. That's Bill and Suzy. They are known as the first couple of the park. You always know them by their arguments. They are always arguing. She's a real tart,' he said laughing.

Around about 4.30 am I dosed off. I woke up around 8.00 am. Mark continued to sleep in his sleeping bag on the ground. I went to the public toilets to wash my face.

I returned and sat on another bench. I could not think of the future and did not want to think about the present. I decided to think about the past.

When I graduated from Ahmadu Bello University in Zaria with a

BA degree in History, I did my National Youth Service Corps in Lagos. I returned to my hometown of Bauchi where I was to teach History at the Government Girls Secondary School. A week before I was to start my teaching career, I visited an old friend at the state television station. He was one of the leading journalists. I was waiting for him in the newsroom when the then Head of News, Aminu Wunti, and the Head of Programmes, Yaro Ali, stood in front of me and where having a conversation.

'He's got the right looks,' Yaro Ali said.

'I think he's got the right smile too,' Aminu Wunti said.

'I understand he's a graduate,'

'But has he got the head for the job?'

'I'm sure he can do it. What's your gut feeling?'

'My gut feeling is, let's give him a try.'

'But we must ask him first.'

I remember Aminu Wunti walking closer to me. 'Mustapha, have you got a minute?'

'Yes I have.'

'Have you got the head for television?' he asked laughing.

'What do you mean?' I asked.

'Would you be interested in working for us? We need somebody urgently and your friend Ibrahim suggested we talk to you.'

I told them about the job waiting for me at the Government Girls Secondary School.

'Forget about them,' Aminu Wunti said. 'We'll give you a better package. And what more, you'll be on television and you'll be popular especially with the girls. We need handsome young men like you to attract female viewers.'

I still couldn't believe what they were saying. I thought they were just winding me up. I knew my friend Ibrahim liked playing pranks on me.

Aminu Wunti invited me into his office and told me what I was supposed to do. He sent me on two assignments with Ibrahim that day. 'I want you to keep a close eye on how your friend reports on events.

Look closely at how he holds the microphone and how he asks questions. Just watch him. I'm sure you will be able to do this on your own within a day or two. You don't look daft to me,' he said laughing.

The next day, the Head of News sent me to my first appointment. Tanimu, the cameraman, taught me the tricks of the trade. He was a very patient man and with his help, I recorded my first news item. I remember that day so clearly. I was standing on the stairs of the state assembly. We made sure it was after the session of the state assembly and there were state legislators walking past behind me when the cameraman signalled. I summarised the proceedings in the state assembly and finished with the line: *from the State House of Assembly, this is Mustapha Abdullahi reporting.* I was very happy. It was a life changing experience.

'Very good, you'll be fine,' Ibrahim said later after looking at the report. 'There were only two minor mistakes but that's excellent for your first report. I'll be your line manager. Go to the admin office and fill the necessary forms.'

From that day on I became a journalist.

With time I began to cover more and more events. And with time I became a household name. During the National Day celebrations, the main presenter was sick and I was told to present the live coverage. After that I was told to read the news as well. To perfect my news reading skills, I was sent to Lagos for a three-month course at the headquarters of the National Television Authority. When I returned to Bauchi, a former classmate at the university told me that a major general in the army would like to see me. We met at his residence and he told me that the army was not happy with the state of affairs in the country. I asked if he would say that on camera. We agreed that the general would draft the questions that would be comfortable for him and I would ask him and he would give his answers. On the appointed day I went with the cameraman and had a three-hour interview with the general in full uniform.

'Would the military just stand and watch the country degenerate? At what point would the military leadership decide that enough was enough? Does the military have what it takes to rule? The questions

I asked were direct. The answers were also direct. There were veiled threats in the answers the general gave. When I showed it to the Head of Programmes, he decided it should be on national television. 'The general talked about national issues and I feel the whole nation should listen to him.' Eventually I did a six-part series based on the interview on the state of the nation. The title was NIGERIA: *A Nation Adrift.* The six-part series was shown all over the country. It gripped viewers because the problems facing Nigeria were laid bare. In the programme, I spoke openly about the indiscipline in all spheres, wastage, corruption, nepotism and maladministration. How could a country like Nigeria be where it is today? We needed answers from our leaders and the earlier the better. Nigeria must not be allowed to drift further into chaos and obscurity, something must be done, somebody must rescue our beloved country from total ruin, I concluded.

Three months after the series was broadcast nationally, the military seized power in a bloodless coup. The timing of my film was great. The series was repeated after the military took over. The new military leadership used my film to justify their campaigns against indiscipline, waste, corruption and nepotism. Nigeria needed good leadership with vision and commitment.

It was when I was making the series that I had an idea. I wanted to make a series of films not for television but for the big screen on the state of affairs in the country. I wanted to be free to decide the content. I felt that I had a message and I wanted to convey *my message.* I did not want to do what my bosses wanted me to do. I noticed that so many ideas were added to my script for the six part series. Some of my ideas were removed. I wanted to be creative, independent and free. I thought that was the next logical step. I remembered vividly my then girlfriend, Hauwa said. 'Mustapha, I honestly think you'll be a very good filmmaker. You need good education at a good film school in the US.'

I applied to study filmmaking in the US. I dreamt of returning home with a degree from a recognised US institution. I dreamt of setting up my own studios on one of the many hills around Bauchi town.

I wanted to see how films were made in Hollywood. My application was rejected on the grounds that there was no audience for films in Bauchi State.

There was a commotion on Park Lane and a lot of drivers were blasting their horns. I was temporarily brought back to real life in central London.

Soon after the traffic had cleared, my thoughts went back to my past life.

In particular, I remembered my last day at work. It was at the height of my career. I handed in my notice after I had secured a place at the Film College in London. On the very last evening I read the final news item. My colleague Fati Adamu Wunti read the summary of the news and instead of the usual signing off, she said, 'My colleague Mustapha Abdullahi has some news for you.' There was silence. I knew the camera was now focusing on me and for the last time. I looked straight into it. 'After all these years working first as a reporter and then as a newscaster, it is with a heavy heart that I inform you that today is my last day. I have thoroughly enjoyed every minute of my stay here. I feel it's time to move on to something else. I would like to use this opportunity to thank those who gave me the opportunity to work here. I thank you all for everything and I wish you all the best. Good night and for the very last time, goodbye.'

As I sat there on the bench in Hyde Park, I remembered the lights going off in the studio, the tears that rolled down my cheeks when Fati whispered, 'I'll miss your company. I'll always remember your laughter and your jokes. I wish you good luck. I hope you succeed in making the film.'

I remembered the last time I walked out of the studios and then out of the television station. Mallam Yau, the security man at the gates greeted me cordially as he always did. 'May your stay in the UK be successful,' he prayed. I wondered if that was the highest I could reach in my life. Is it downhill from now on? Can I ever reach that height again in my life? Can I ever come close to replicating such success in future? How did I come to where I am now, sleeping on a bench in Hyde Park? I tried to avoid answering these questions. Luckily I heard a familiar voice.

'Michael, so this is where you are.' It was Mark. He looked fresh and happy. 'I was looking for you. I thought you'd gone.'

'Gone where?'

'I don't know, anywhere. The world is big.'

'I've nowhere to go at least for the next couple of days.'

'You're not alone. If we had a place to go we wouldn't be here. Hahaha! There are many lost souls like you around.'

'Did you have a good sleep?' I asked.

'Of course I did and you?'

'No I couldn't. The noise was constant.'

'What do you expect from central London? This part of the town never sleeps. Make sure you find a quiet place next time but then there is no fun. Anyway I'm used to it now. I can sleep right next to the traffic. It doesn't bother me anymore.'

Mark walked away saying he wanted to stretch his legs.

Alone on the bench I counted my money. Five pounds and forty-seven pence was all I had. How can I live on this? I asked myself.

Mark came back. 'I've decided to continue my journey into the unknown.' I did not reply. 'You may not see me again. You never know. I might change my mind and return. At the moment I want to continue my search for that thing. The thing we all look for in life. If I see you again fine, if not then good luck to you. May you find that which you're looking for in life.' He picked up his bag and walked away.

I had lunch. It was bread and sardines in tomato sauce. Both items had passed their sell by date.

Later, I called members of the Politburo. No one was back yet from Manchester. Just as I was wondering how long I would be in the park, Mark reappeared. 'A voice inside me said I should return. I thought I'd forgotten something,' he looked around the bench. I let him talk. I was tired and getting weak. My head was aching from lack of sleep. Mark brought out a small radio and started listening to music. I dozed off. I did not know for how long for but when I woke up, it was a little bit dark.

'Had a good kip?' Mark asked.

I did not answer.

'I hope it doesn't rain,' Mark said.

I looked up. 'See,' Mark pointed to the sky. 'There are dark clouds there and if you see clouds coming in from that direction, it means rain.'

I looked at the clouds but made no comment.

'You see those men coming,' Mark whispered. 'They are coppers.'

'Who are coppers?'

'Policemen. Don't worry they're not going to give us trouble.'

The two men had baseball caps on. One had a blue raincoat and the other was wearing a grey raincoat. They both wore jeans and sneakers.

The two men slowed down as they approached us. They greeted us cordially. One fixed his eyes on me. I looked away.

'Seen anything unusual?' the man in blue raincoat asked.

'No, nothing, all quiet,' Mark answered.

'Calm before the storm?' the other man commented.

'Oh yeah! It's definitely going to rain,' Mark replied.

'Got a new mate?' he asked looking at me.

'Yeah! He's all right, just hanging around. He's not into making trouble. He's clean.'

'All right then. Be careful and stay safe.'

They walked away.

There was a rumble of thunder in the distance. I hoped it was something else. I looked up and the sky was dark with clouds. I prayed it would rain elsewhere and not Hyde Park.

The wind started picking up.

'I had better go,' Mark said and left hurriedly.

Once again I was alone and confused. There was lightning in the distance followed by thunder. I lost my bearing. It started to rain. It was raining heavily within minutes. The nearest place I could think of was the public toilet. I ran into it.

Bill and Suzy were there already. There were others, too, drinking cider and beer.

'I remember your face. I saw you a few days ago – no it was yesterday.

Yes! You and that fella called Mark or whatever his name is,' Suzy said pointing her fingers at me. She was holding a cigarette. 'Yes I remember you,' she said staggering forward. 'You were there drinking lager with that dodgy fella and took the piss out of me.'

'Leave him alone,' Bill said pulling her back. 'He's decent.'

'He's a spy. I'm positive. He's following us. He wants to *grass* us to the coppers.'

'No way, he's not a spy. He doesn't look like a spy. He's just lost like his drinking mate Mark.'

'No. He's a black copper. A black undercover,' Suzy insisted.

Bill laughed. 'He can't be a copper. I can smell a copper from one hundred yards. This is not one of them. I bet he has no clue what you're talking about.'

'Okay,' Suzy said smiling. 'How come he's not drinking? Coppers don't drink. They just watch and collect information.' She paused and continued, 'Alright then, you like our weather don't you?'

I did not answer.

'He came all the way from Africa to enjoy this weather,' Bill said laughing.

The rain continued to fall. An old man with two bags stood next to me. He was drenched. 'How long have you been here?' he asked.

I was not sure what he meant, in the park, toilet or in the UK?

'Not that long,' I replied.

'Lucky you,' he said laughing. 'For some of us we've been here too long.' He paused for some time. He looked at me and started laughing. 'It all her fault isn't it?' he asked loudly.

'Who,' I asked.

'You know who I'm talking about.'

Another man joined our conversation. First he nodded in agreement. 'Yes you're right, it's all her fault.'

'It's because of that woman that we are all here today. I would have been somewhere else if we had another person in charge. She changed our lives completely.'

'Oh yes. She's very mean. That woman called Maggie.'

It was then I made the connection. They were referring to the then Prime Minister, Margaret Thatcher.

The rain eventually stopped.

'Next time it rains, we should go to the underpass over there,' the old man said on the steps as we walked out. 'The underpass is better than the toilet. It stinks there.'

Later in the evening I found my way to the back door of the super-market. I noticed that there were about half a dozen other people waiting. When the security man opened the door and brought out the bin containing foodstuff, he looked around. 'I still think I know you,' he said to me. 'It's not that often I make mistakes about faces I've seen before. Your face is definitely familiar. I've seen it before. I'm one hundred per cent sure. You're not just an ordinary person. You're somebody.'

I didn't answer.

He gave me a leaflet titled *Signs of Our Times*. 'It's about hope in troubled times. I can see you are going through a difficult time right now otherwise you wouldn't be here. Trouble times come to us all. We do have money, health, personal and family problems and there are days that are bleak and we feel that tomorrow will not be better. There are times we find ourselves helpless, homeless and poor. What we need is hope – hope that someone somewhere is looking, is listening to our prayers and that He cares about our situation. Hope that tomorrow will definitely be better than today! Take it from me my brother from Nigeria, someone does care. God cares. According to the Bible, Lamentations: 3.25.26' (he showed me the verse in the leaflet): *The LORD is good to those who wait for Him, to the soul who seeks Him. It is good that one should hope and wait quietly for the salvation of the LORD.*

He gave me a bag full of food. I thanked him.

'Praise the Lord,' he said.

I returned to the park. I found a place and sat and ate. I heeded Mark's advice that night. I stayed awake till about 4.00 am before I closed my eyes. It was cold but there was nothing I could do.

Around about 10.00 am the next day, I went to the telephone booth.

I decided to call Taj. I was very happy when someone picked the phone. 'Hello!' I shouted.

'Yes I can hear you.' I told him about my predicament. I was very brief.

'I've just returned from Manchester,' he said. 'Let's meet at Bozo's Joint around 6.00 pm. I promise to get you somewhere to sleep tonight.'

From the moment I replaced the receiver in the telephone booth in Hyde Park, I was very happy. I knew Taj wouldn't fail me. Hope suddenly overtook despair. I asked loudly outside the booth: A roof over my head? I pinched myself several times. It was like a dream. But I was not dreaming. Indeed, I've just spoken to Taj and he promised to get me a room. Wow! I stood in front of the booth with a big smile on my face.

When I was ready I decided to go to the Kilburn flat to pack my things. On my way I decided that whatever Pat said I had made up my mind to go. I had had enough.

I had no idea whether Pat's mother was still in the flat so I timed my arrival in the area to coincide with the dog's time. I waited by the corner of the road.

'You see, he recognised you,' Pat said holding tight to Bruno who was barking and jumping excitedly. 'Bruno really missed you. How did I know that?' she asked. 'He kept on scratching the door of your room.'

'Can I go into the flat now?'

'Of course you can.'

'What about your mother?'

'Oh! She changed her mind and did not come.'

'I see.'

'Did you have a nice time?' she asked smiling.

'Oh yes I did.'

'Where did you stay?'

'At a friend's place,' I replied and walked away.

I went into the flat and packed my few belongings. I locked the door from the outside and dropped the keys through the letterbox.

Six

Moving to South London

On the upper deck of the bus, I continued to review my life. 'What you have gone through and what you are going through is a test,' I thought I heard a voice say as the bus moved slowly. I could not say why, but as the bus moved south I began to feel a lot better. I was beginning to feel that somehow I would be happier in south London. There was something in Taj's voice that gave me hope. It was not only the promise of a roof over my head. I was beginning to hope and to dream of a better future.

'I'm sorry to hear what happened to you,' Taj said as he embraced me at Bozo's Joint. I told him it was confidential. 'Of course, this is not what you'd want everybody to know. Trust me,' he laughed and looked at me as if he did not believe my story. 'Why should I tell people a made up story?'

'Honestly Taj, I slept in the park for two nights,' I said laughing.

'I'm knackered,' he said as we walked towards his car. 'I'm off to Kampala, Addis Ababa and Tripoli. Later I'll go to Cairo, Dakar and then São Paulo.'

'Why are you going on these trips?' I asked entering the car.

'I'm trying to organise the next Pan African Congress,' he disclosed.

It did not take long to reach the house in Herne Hill. He opened the door and led me straight to a room upstairs. 'Here it is. A roof over your head as promised. I'm sorry there's nothing in it except this thin mattress but it's better than a bench in the park.' He laughed.

'Perfect,' I said and thanked him.

He gave me the key to the house. 'Jarvo has moved in to one of the rooms. He's also in a mini crisis. Let's meet tomorrow in the office,' a tired looking Taj said. 'I need some time to rest and I'm sure you need time to rest too.'

I rested for a while.

'Welcome to South London,' Jarvo shouted laughing as he closed the door. 'Taj told me you are in some kind of mini crisis too. That's what life is made of, mini crises all the time. That's how our characters are tested. The most important thing is to avoid a major crisis.'

He opened a can of beer and gave it to me. 'This is for you. It helps a lot you know. I don't know what you've been through but what you need is a bit of something like this from time to time.' Later he gave me a duvet and pillow. 'We'll sort you out soon,' he promised as he settled down to read through some notes. 'I'm preparing for a seminar at the centre tomorrow and as usual I have left things a bit late. The conference in Manchester took a lot of my energy.'

I had a good shower and sat on the floor in my room.

Later there was a knock on the door and Jarvo came in with another can of beer. 'Have one before you sleep,' he said and sat on the floor too. He wanted to know the nature of my mini crisis. I told him an edited version. I did not tell him about sheltering from the rain in the public toilet.

'Mike, what you went through is not unique. We all go through such humiliating experiences from time to time here in the UK. Actually, come to think of it, it's always a positive thing to have reality checks in life, especially early in life. Carl Jung once said: *We don't get into consciousness without pain.* We definitely don't get wiser by having everything going for us. We need a little bit of suffering from time to time to have a better understanding of life and to shed some misconceptions of life. Your experience in the park would do you good in the end. You need such rough patches in life to appreciate the smooth ones. I envy you. From now on, the only way is up. One way or the other you have to make sure that you never sleep in a park again, that is a lesson learnt. As Friedrich Nietzsche once said, that which does not kill us, only makes us stronger. Sleeping in the park did not kill you so it will only make you stronger. Congratulations! Let's celebrate.'

We drank beer.

'When you look back later in life, you'll laugh. You must have learnt something and that knowledge will never be a waste. In life we all go down but not everyone gets up and moves forward. So Michael, it's a new beginning. Just like a snake changes its skin, your move to south London should be that change. Good night'

I thanked him.

The realities of London had forced me to change but I thought I must change my attitude to life too. I blamed myself for what had happened. I thought about Imran and Pat. The two did not make my life easy. I decided I would never blame them. Instead, I would forgive them. After all, my mother always told me not to be angry. "If you're angry and bitter when you are hurt, you can never achieve anything," she always advised. I tried to think about how to take things forward. To make life easier, I thought it would be better to be known as Michael from now on. In North London, I had two identities, which complicated my life. I thought that being Michael would make things a lot easier. I was conscious that this resolution meant I would not be performing my religious duties but I said to myself: *once I sort myself out, I will return to practising my faith properly.* There is time for everything. This was the time to do everything to survive as a human being. I had no idea where to face in prayers and it did not bother me.

The mattress was very thin. I could feel my bones touching the concrete floor. But I was happy. I looked at the ceiling in disbelief. A roof over my head! I began to relax before going to sleep. I looked at the ceiling from time to time to be sure I was not on the bench in the park. Before I eventually fell asleep, I did not know why but I began to think about the Hausa woman. I remembered the voice on the bus: 'what happened to you was not an accident. There's a reason why it happened.' I tried to decode the message. Maybe I'm now in south London to meet her. After all, I saw her in my dream at the end of that period of darkness. I began to ask myself why whenever I thought about her I felt different. Maybe she was the only person that could solve my problems.

I had a dream. One evening I was walking by the side of the river. It was during the rainy season. The river was full and flowing fast and there were people on both sides of the river washing clothes. When I got to a certain point, a young boy told me to follow a particular path. I could not understand why he told me to get off the main path and continue my walk. But I obeyed and followed the path. At the end of the path, to my great surprise, I saw the Hausa girl sitting alone on a bench. She smiled and invited me to sit next to her. We sat facing each other. She looked straight into my eyes and said. 'I'm going to give you the best gift in life which is a part of myself. It's not just any part of my body, it's my heart. Mustapha, I want you to have something special from me that'll be inside you forever. I also want part of you in myself; something I will forever cherish, something that will always remind me of you.' As soon as she touched me I woke up.

I looked around nervously. It was dark. I had a mini panic attack. I thought I was in the park. I thought I heard distant noises and thought I heard Bill and Suzy arguing. I looked around and realised I was in a room. I was scared. It took me a few minutes to recall how I ended up in a room with a roof over my head.

I went back to sleep.

At dawn, I felt different. I no longer heard the prayer calls floating into my ears. I could hear Bruno's howling but faintly.

Later that day, Jarvo and I went to the offices of the resource centre. 'Taj is preparing for a speech in parliament on immigration and we want to brainstorm on the issue before he speaks,' Jarvo said before we all settle down in the conference room. He was excited and without any formal introduction started to speak. 'You must look at the issue of immigration as a whole from a Marxist perspective otherwise you will not fully understand it. The main aim of allowing immigrants to settle in capitalist societies is to greatly increase competition among workers and put downward pressure on wages. Immigrants, who are part of the *lumpen-proletariat* are exploited mercilessly by the capitalists to increase surplus in the value of capital. To be very honest with you all, immigrants put more money into the new country than they take out. We immigrants spend the money in the new country on rent, bills, taxes and so on.

'Illegal immigrants are the worst group of workers in western societies because they have no job security, not entitled to social welfare benefits, no health-insurance and they live in constant fear and are often coerced, deceived, bullied to work in dreadful conditions. They are the cheapest source of labour available. Illegal immigrants are worse than slaves. Slaves don't have to pay for the chains. Illegal immigrants pay for the invisible chain around their necks. Criminals serving in prisons have shelter, food and when they are sick, they receive free medical treatment. Yet illegal immigrants who have not committed any offence apart from breathing the air without permission are not entitled to free health and have to pay for every other thing ... Surpluses extracted from these illegal immigrants are higher than those from normal workers ... You may not know this, but a lot of illegal immigrants pay taxes and national insurance contributions, which are not properly accounted for and so it does not benefit them. They cannot claim social security benefits when unemployed and have no state pension when they are old. All these taxes and national insurance contributions that illegal immigrants pay are bonuses to the Treasury.'

When Jarvo stopped and there was a general discussion.

I did not take part.

'That mad woman said you moved out of the flat,' Mr Frank B said with anger as soon as I entered his flat. 'She's a crazy woman. I honestly don't know how you were able to put up with her for such a long time.' I did not answer. 'What happened?' he asked still angry.

I told him.

'I know how it feels when you are at the end of such horrible things. You just have to bear these things before you finish and return. It's a mad world. You could have complained to the authorities you know. She should have provided alternative accommodation for you because you were a rent-paying tenant. It's not fair. She just took advantage of you. Some people are like that. Do you want me to take it further? I could get that horrible woman to pay you compensation. I can make life difficult for her too you know. I'm not going to let her get away with it. She'd try it on someone else.'

'Let's forget about it.'

Frank B was very upset. 'I'm really sorry. Anyway, here,' he said giving me a bottle of rum from Guyana. 'This is the type Mo liked. For years, whenever I went to Guyana I always brought back a bottle or two for him. This is locally distilled not far from our house. Definitely one of the best you can get but the rum from Barbados is the best, I must admit. You can be sure of one thing after drinking this rum you will not have any hangover.' He opened a bottle of whisky. 'A shot of whisky for you?'

'No thanks.'

'Nothing better than a shot of whisky you know.'

Frank B told me that Matilda had moved to an island in the Caribbean. 'Such is life, young fella. Life is strange. The older I get the less I understand people, human beings.'

Later I visited Dr Asibong. 'I'm really happy to see you,' he said. 'Mr Patel told me what happened and I was worried. I'm so pleased you found a place and more importantly you are with the guys at the research centre. It's important to stay close to people that would make you develop mentally. You need a lift right now and they are the best people around to help you. I did a bit of research and found this institution where you can do some courses by correspondence. Study anything. I guess you got a lot of time now but don't waste it. One thing you can never get back is wasted time and one thing nobody can take away from you is the knowledge you have acquired. I suggest you study philosophy. It'll give you some valuable insights that should help you articulate your ideas when it comes to making your film. When you study philosophy your core beliefs would be challenged which will be a good thing.'

'What happened to you?' Sandy asked when I called the agency.

'I had problems with the landlady and I'm now in south London.'

'I had a very good job for you last week.'

'At the institute?'

'No.'

'Okay, I'm available for work.'

'I'll try to get something for you next week okay?'

'That's fine.'

The prospectus of the college Dr Asibong suggested arrived. I could not decide what to study, philosophy or filmmaking? Dr Asibong and Jarvo wanted me to study philosophy. I wanted to study filmmaking. I was still holding onto the dream that one day I would direct my own film. I tossed a coin three times. Philosophy came up twice. I decided not to go against the toss. I filled in the form as Michael Danquah.

'Comrades,' I could hear Taj saying from the corridors of the resource centre, 'it's time to take the battle to the chambers of the mother of all parliaments. It's time to take the message to Westminster.' The offices of the resource centre were teeming with people. The campaign for amnesty for illegal immigrants was at its climax. Taj was to speak in one of the halls in the Houses of Parliament in Westminster. His enthusiasm was infectious and his sense of humour lit up the offices. 'Great to see you,' he said as I entered the conference room. 'I'm glad you're coming. I'm so happy because I've got an exhibit to show them. I look forward to saying something like this: Honourable parliamentarians, ladies and gentlemen, illegal immigrants are not monsters. Look, we have one in the hall. I would point at you and tell them to see how an illegal immigrant looks like.' Taj laughed and everyone around him laughed too. He was wearing a white African top with embroidery around the neck. He was excited and it showed.

I whispered into his ears. 'Taj, honestly, I'm scared of going to the houses of parliament in case they check our documents.'

'It's all right,' he said loudly. 'They will not check. One of the benefits of living in a democratic country like the UK is that you have rights, even as an illegal immigrant. Do you know that you have the right not to cooperate with the police? Yes it's your right. Don't worry, they'll not check our documents,' he assured me laughing. 'If they ask just tell them I'm your uncle. They know me very well.'

I laughed and left him alone.

'Forward Ever,' Taj shouted when we were ready.

'Backward Never,' a group shouted.

'Comrades, off we go,' he said and led us out of the offices. We made our way to Westminster. As we approached the Houses of Parliament my heart beat rate increased. What if they decided to check our documents? I could be walking straight into the hands of the authorities. We went through the security barriers without any problems. I was surprised that the policemen were cracking jokes with us. In the hall, a black MP stood up and spoke about immigration in the UK. He then introduced Taj who stood up. He was very calm and smiling.

'No western country could function without immigrants. Western countries need us more than we need them ... Population is destiny. The population in the West is declining so they need young men and women from other parts of the world to come and work for them.

'Historically, people always moved from one place to another for different reasons. We immigrants came from far-flung places to toil away in your farms, shops and offices ... We put more into the system than we take out ... In any case, we ensure that wages and taxes are lower and annual deficits smaller.

'Do you know that I like it when I hear the British people talk about how they had dinners or spent their weekends in exotic restaurants. Hear them say something like, 'I went to the Turkish, Persian, Korean, Mexican, Vietnamese, Thai, Chinese and Indian restaurants.' My question is this: Who owns and runs these restaurants? Immigrants!

'Just look at the hospitals, yes go to the hospitals and do a headcount of immigrants working as doctors, nurses, porters, midwives and pharmacists. You'll see that from birth to death, you Brits are in the hands of foreigners, immigrants.'

'That's correct,' the black MP interjected shaking his head in agreement.

Taj then threw a challenge to the authorities and right-wing politicians. 'If you all think that we are not useful, that we are a drain on your society, if you think you can live alone on your island, do one honourable thing: send all of us back to our countries. When you get rid of all foreigners from the UK then we'll see what happens to your economy in particular and the whole society in general. Who has the money to buy the goods in the shops? Who will pay to sustain your transport system? Once you get rid of all of us, we'll see who will drive your trains, who will sweep the streets for you, who will teach your children in schools and who will represent you in athletics? Just imagine the filth all over the country because most cleaners are immigrants.'

Taj paused, drank water, looked at me and continued with his steady smile and fluid eloquence. 'The reality is that illegal immigrants are here with us. They are here to stay. They all came into this blessed and glorious country with hopes and dreams. They might be illegal but their dreams are not illegal. Make their dreams come true.' He looked at me again. 'They came here chasing dreams. They want to do something positive in this country. Most of them can't because they live in constant fear.

'As politicians it would be a political masterstroke if any of the two parties were to grant amnesty. There are over half a million voters who would be forever grateful and vote for whoever granted them amnesty. An amnesty would bring immediate and measurable relief to millions of immigrants and their children. I hereby plead on behalf of all illegal immigrants. Please grant them a one-off amnesty.

'Honourable members of the parliament, ladies and gentlemen, go to the city of London every evening or during the weekends, when the men in suits from outside the city have made their money; when they have traded and have had meetings and left. Now let us ask ourselves who on earth ensured that the toilets were clean, who ensured that the streets were clean, who ensured that the traffic was orderly, who ensured that the meals were cooked? When you are sleeping, resting and having all the pleasures of life at the small hours of the day, it's the immigrants who keep the towns functioning; from bakers to mini-cab drivers, from cooks to cleaners.

'Immigrants are here to stay. We're not parasites; we're an asset.

We're not a burden we are a blessing. We need you to survive, you need us to prosper.

'DON'T AGONISE!' Taj concluded with his trademark clarion call and a clenched fist.

'ORGANISE!' His supporters responded rapturously.

Outside the hall, in the corridor, someone tapped me gently. 'Taj said you are an illegal immigrant.'

The woman was wearing a red coat and had red hair. She said with a raised voice. 'Taj said you are living in the UK illegally.'

'No. I'm not. He probably meant someone else.'

'I'm on the side of illegals,' she said smiling. 'I'm writing a paper on them and would like to interview you.'

'I'm not an illegal immigrant,' I insisted.

'By the way, my name is Elizabeth. I'm Scottish as you might have guessed from my accent. I'm a PhD student.'

'So what can I do for you?'

'I want to interview you, as an illegal immigrant.'

'I don't think I'm the best person to talk to.' I turned and walked away. I left the Houses of Parliament immediately. I kept looking over my shoulder until I took a bus to Elephant and Castle.

Two weeks after the visit to the Houses of Parliament, Jarvo came in while I was studying in the kitchen. 'What are you doing?'

'Reading. You know I'm doing this course in philosophy.'

'But today is Friday. Friday evening – time to have fun.'

'There are so many parties and discos around.'

'I don't want to get into trouble.'

'But you cannot live like this. You have to have fun from time to time.'

'All right then, let's go.'

'Let's hit the town. All work and no play will make Michael a crazy man,' he said as he entered his car. 'Do you remember the Scottish girl with the red hair?'

'You mean the one that was in parliament?'

'Yes, she is still around.'

'So?'

'I saw her talking to you in the corridor.'

'Yes she asked me some funny questions.'

'She was in the office today and asked about you.'

'What does she you want?'

'She wanted to know where she could meet you.'

'Why?'

'I don't know. She probably fancies you,' he said laughing. 'No actually she's doing research on immigrants. You never know, maybe she wants something more.'

'I'm not sure. As an illegal immigrant you have to be very cautious. Also I don't have the money for entertainment and all this going out and having fun.'

'No harm talking to her. I don't think she's the type that will report you.'

I did not answer.

'You've to be adventurous. As they say, fortune favours the brave.'

'But curiosity killed the cat.'

'That's true. You can't just sit indoors and expect your luck to come in. If you don't seek you don't get. She might just be the one for you.'

'Where's she now?'

'She's at a party in Napo's flat in Islington. Get ready to chat her up.'

The party was in full swing when we arrived. There was music and the sitting room was full of people dancing. 'This will give you the courage to talk to Elizabeth,' Napo said handing over a can of beer. 'She's expecting you.'

'Ah, here you are,' I heard the Scottish accent of Elizabeth. 'Nice to see you again.' She was holding a can of beer. 'So what have you been doing with yourself?'

'Nothing really,' I said looking at her.

'Jarvo said you are studying.'

'Yes.'

'What are you studying?'

'Philosophy.'

'Let's go out it's a bit crowded in here,' Elizabeth held my hand and led me out of the kitchen to the hallway. 'After so many years of studying, now I've time to let my hair down,' she said excitedly. Elizabeth and I did not dance. We sat in a corner of the sitting room talking. I told her about myself. My real name and what I did before I came to the UK.

The party ended.

'So Mike I noticed you got along very well with Elizabeth. You talked for hours,' Jarvo said on our way home in his car. 'Don't let her off the hook. Keep chasing. Try and keep the relationship going. She might be the one to get you out of this jail called illegal immigration.'

'I'm meeting her on Thursday.'

'Go for it,' Jarvo teased me.

On the appointed day I went to the cafe an hour before the meeting. Elizabeth walked in smiling. She was well dressed in a two-piece suit.

'You look very smart,' I commented as I kissed her on both cheeks.

'Thank you,' she said. 'I've just had a good meeting with my supervisor.'

We ordered hot drinks. Again I allowed her to do the talking. Elizabeth wanted to know everything about me. I was honest and told her the truth.

'You should always have another plan. Plan B, just in case this one doesn't work.'

'What you mean?'

'If your plan of becoming a film director doesn't work, what would you do? Would you consider moving to Scotland for example? It's an option. I'll finish my PhD soon.'

I was shocked by her approach.

'Are you with me?' she asked.

'I'm listening,' I stammered.

'I don't suppose you were married in Nigeria.'

'No. I wasn't.'

'Fine, it's important to know that.'

Elizabeth concluded. 'I'm going back to Scotland next week. 'This is my telephone number,' she said handing over a piece of paper. Call me only on Sundays at 11.00 am when my parents would be in the church. If you call and anyone else picks the phone, just put the receiver down. If I pick up the call, I will start by saying 'Lizzy here'. Sorry about that but when you live with your parents you have to learn to tolerate some things. I don't intend to live with them forever.'

I could not entirely understand what Elizabeth wanted, even though it was straightforward. One minute I thought I understood her and the next minute I felt I did not. What does she really want? Imran the solicitor told me that the only way to get to stay legally was to marry someone from the UK or EU. Elizabeth would be ideal but I felt something was missing. I did not feel anything towards her.

Later, I told Jarvo everything.

'You have to consider all the options. You cannot continue to suffer like this. You have to conquer the fear in you. I know being an illegal immigrant makes life difficult but you have to rise over the ordinary and live a full life. If you allow fear to defeat you, there's nothing you will succeed in doing. Don't destroy your future because of your past. I know it's tough for you but you have to grab your opportunities as they present themselves. Don't be the architect of your own sadness and misery. You have a choice to make your life happier. She's there for the taking, what are you waiting for? She ticks all the boxes, what else do you want? You don't have to marry her tomorrow. Meet her as often as possible and see how it goes. If she wants you to relocate to Scotland, go for it. Where is it written that your life must follow a particular trajectory? Going to Scotland would be fun, part of the adventure. You want to remain in this jail forever? When opportunity knocks open the bloody door.'

Elizabeth returned to London. She wanted me to meet her brother-in-law and her sister Leona.

'We need to talk,' Elizabeth said at the bus stop. I noticed she was distant and not happy.

'What's wrong?'

'My brother-in-law thinks it's not a good idea.'

'But what has it got to do with him?'

'You don't understand. He's like that. It's important for you to be calm, okay.'

I followed Elizabeth who was still being distant, but tried to put on a brave face.

'You're Mustapha?' I heard someone ask as soon as I entered the flat.

'Yes I am and you are Don.'

'Please sit down,' Leona said introducing herself. 'I'm Elizabeth's sister.'

'I guessed so, nice to meet you.'

'Thank you, tea or coffee?'

'Tea, no milk and two sugars please.'

'What's going on?' I asked Elizabeth. 'What's wrong?'

'It's a bit complicated,' she whispered.

'I understand you are seeing Lizzy,' Don said, looking very upset.

'Yes, and as far as I know she's not married to you. What's the problem?'

'There's a big problem here. I want to be a Councillor and after that I want to be an MP ...'

'What has that got to do with me and Lizzy?'

'Shut up!' he shouted. 'I don't want my reputation tarnished and my political career ruined by an illegal immigrant. You want to marry Lizzy so that you can get a residence permit. You don't love her. You are a cheat. You see her as an easy target just because she's naive and young. I can see the tabloids full of stories about how my sister-in-law was hoodwinked by an illegal immigrant into a bogus marriage. My political career will then be over for good.'

I was numb. I looked at Lizzy who said nothing.

Don continued. 'I don't trust you Nigerians. Unfortunately I was born in that country but I'm British now. You Nigerians are crooks. You want to use my sister-in-law to legalise your stay in the UK and then abandon her.'

Don looked very upset and bitter. 'I know who you are. I have all your details. If you talk to Lizzy again I'll report you to the Home Office and get you deported immediately.'

I thought I've had enough. I stood up and thanked Lizzy and Leona and walked out.

I was preparing an omelette when Jarvo came into the house. 'So how was it?' he asked excited.

I told him. Jarvo was quiet for a while. 'Mike, this man called Don has a problem. He has a huge ego. I know him but not very well. He's not a pleasant man. I didn't expect him to interfere in the affairs of his sister-in-law. For God's sake Lizzy is not a teenager. This woman is about to finish her PhD. For goodness sake he's not even a Councillor yet. He's not even sure the party would endorse him as a candidate. This is ridiculous. I think its pure envy and stupidity.'

Jarvo drank beer and continued. 'Do you know that Don recently called on Britain to recolonize the part of Nigeria he came from? He wants to be a local chief in the new British Empire just as his ancestors were local chiefs under British rule. Luckily no one paid attention to him. I think he's deluded.' He paused and concluded. 'Come to think of it, you should consider yourself lucky. Imagine if this bastard waited until you were about to marry her and if he has such control over her, he would make life difficult for you later. Count your blessings. Be grateful he showed his true colours right at the start of the relationship. Disappointments could be blessings in disguise. What is destined to be yours will be yours. No one can take it away from you. She's not for you, simple.'

Seven

First Narrow Escape

On Monday Sandra asked over the phone. 'Do you want to work?'

'Yes.'

'The job is in a bank, as a kitchen porter.'

'Thank you very much.'

Sandra gave me the details and how to get there.

About an hour later, I told the security man. 'I'm from the agency to see the Head Chef,' at the door.

'What's your name?'

'Michael Danquah.'

He printed a badge and told me to wait. Moments later, a door opened and a tall, black man in chef's clothes came up to me smiling.

'Michael?'

'Yes.'

'Please follow me,' he said. 'How are you?' he asked as we went downstairs to the basement. He stopped looked at me and started laughing. 'Where are you from?'

'From Ghana and you?'

'Sweet Jamaica maan,' he laughed again. 'Just the right guy I'm looking for.'

'What do you mean?'

'I'll explain to you later,' he continued to laugh and sing. When we reached the kitchen, he turned and, still smiling at me, asked, 'You know how to dance?'

'No. Why?'

'I know a woman who's looking for a dancing partner. Well, if you don't get what you are looking for you might as well make use of what you have. I hope this woman comes for her lunch later.'

I was busy washing pots and putting plates into the machine when Leonard shouted. 'Michael the lady is here. Come with me.' He gave me a tray full of food. 'See that beautiful lady?' I nodded. 'That's the woman I want you to befriend. I promised her a boyfriend,' he said loudly. The woman in her forties wore a two-piece suit. 'As you can see she's on a special diet and this is her food.'

We walked close to her. 'Marina this is what you ordered, a fresh man from the savannah, fed from birth only on organic food. He's healthy and unadulterated with no additives and no preservatives. No added sugar and one hundred per cent natural. I can assure you he will perform all year round and no need to recharge his batteries. Just be careful, he can go wild if you touch the wrong buttons. Michael comes with no emotional baggage, very low mileage and maintenance costs. I promised you a bull and here he is.'

The lady was smiling at Leonard when I gave her the tray. He told her that I would be joining her for lunch. She pointed at a particular part of the restaurant. Leonard was getting excited. 'Take your break and go and sit with her. She's a lovely woman.'

I joined Marina moments later.

'I was born in Moscow. My father emigrated when I was two years old,' she started telling me about herself. 'I hate Communism but I would like to visit Moscow soon. My heart is still there. I could have been brought up here but I'm still a Russian. I was married in the US but it did not work out. I married here but it's a bit complicated. I've never been to Ghana. I'd love to go there. I've been to Kenya, Madagascar, Mauritius and South Africa.'

Marina did not eat. She took her meal with her. 'I'm not really hungry. I'll see you tomorrow.'

She left. I finished eating.

'So Michael what's next?' The chef asked. 'Are you taking her out tonight?'

'No boss. I've no money.'

'And have you got her contact details?'

'No.'

'I've done all this introductions for nothing?' He looked surprised. 'You want a woman and you don't want to spend? You have to take her out even if you have to borrow money. Think of the return on investment.'

'She's too expensive for me.'

'So, she's not a mannequin. You've to do something with her.'

'Why should I?'

'Because I promised her,' he said looking very serious. 'You've got to.'

I was not bothered by his comments. I knew that chefs had a way of winding up kitchen porters. The next day at lunchtime, Leonard shouted, 'Michael your sweetheart is here. She's waiting for you.'

He gave me her food. 'Hello gorgeous,' he said to her. 'You look great today.'

'Thank you,' she said and blew a kiss at him.

Leonard was excited. 'It's all happening. I want to be the best man when you're getting married and I hope be invited to wherever you're going on honeymoon.'

'Maybe I should clarify one thing about my husband,' Marina started. 'He's at home depressed. I'm not really married to him anymore but I haven't really divorced him yet. We've technically separated. It's a bit complicated. We always had an open marriage anyway. He lives in a separate bedroom and minds his own business.' Marina then told me she would be travelling to Egypt for ten days over the Christmas period. 'I'm tired and stressed out. I need some sunshine. Look at the horrible weather out there. It has been snowing all morning and the forecast is for more snow till March next year. You want to go to Egypt with me?'

'No thanks. I've made other plans.'

'Okay! Next time but if you change your mind and you really want to go and get some sunshine, let me know. Don't worry I'll pay for everything.'

On Friday, my last day, I went to see Leonard in his office after changing into my overalls. 'What am I going to do with Marina?'

'I don't know. It's up to you. No harm in having fun with her. She likes you and she wants to have fun so go for it. She's a nice woman but terribly lonely. Remember this Michael money is not the tonic of life.

It's love. Whispering something like, *I love you* is worth a million pounds to her. She'd appreciate it.'

'I'm not interested.'

Later Leonard said. 'Your sugar mummy called to say she'll only pop in to say hello to you. She's not having lunch today.'

At lunchtime Marina, who was casually dressed came and was waiting for me in the canteen. 'Nice to see you Michael,' Marina started with a sweet smile. 'I'm on my way to my cottage for the weekend. I forgot to tell you yesterday. You and I could go to the cottage next weekend. I have a few things to do there and I would need an extra pair of hands.' She walked closer. 'Here,' she said. 'This is for you. I'm back in the city on Tuesday. Have a nice weekend.'

I thanked her. Marina walked away. As I was about to look into the bag, she turned around and came back to me. 'By the way, there were some Home Office officials at the reception when I was coming down. I overheard one of them saying they were looking for some Nigerian cleaners and porters. I know you're from Ghana. Just thought I should let you know.'

I froze – torn between the desire to run and to be courteous and not to let her suspect I was affected by the sentence. 'Thank you very much,' I said.

Marina continued talking. 'The weather is awful out there.' I began to panic. I stopped her. 'I'm sorry I really have to go. I've got tummy ache.'

'Poor you,' she said.

I left the bag on the table and ran into the toilets. I locked myself in one of the cubicles. I thought that the Home Office officials might check the toilets. I remembered the cleaner's cupboard nearby where buckets, polish, detergents and mops are kept. I ran out and into the small room. I closed it and urinated in the bucket. I was trembling with fear. My heart was pounding in my chest. All the stories of illegal immigrants being arrested and deported came to my mind. From the day I became an illegal immigrant, this was the moment I feared most. Would Home Office officials catch me, detain me and then deport me? I thought of running out of the building through the back exit. I did not do that. I thought they would be downstairs already. I don't want to go straight into the arms. I decided to remain in the small, dark room hoping that I would not be found out.

Later I heard Leonard singing near the door of the cleaners store and into the toilet. 'Please don't go, don't go ... I want you to stay right now.' I thought it was a coded message for me. I remained there shaking with fear. There was a long period of silence. I could hear footsteps going in and out of the toilets. Just when I thought it was safe to come out, I heard a conversation very close to my hideout. 'Michael must be somewhere, we've checked everywhere.'

'The fucking bastard has done a runner,' someone said.

'The fucker is hiding somewhere,' another voice added.

'We'll get him next time.'

'It's amazing because he didn't go through the back door. That was secured.'

My body was shaking. There was a moment of silence. I expected the door to open. There was a long period of silence. I could tell that lunch was over and the canteen was empty.

Moments later I heard the chef's voice. 'Now you're free to go. All clear.'

I let out a deep sigh of relief. I was sure Leonard meant it. I took my time. I opened the door and peeped out nervously. There was no one in the toilet or in the canteen. The lights had been switched off. I tiptoed into the changing room, grabbed my winter coat and rucksack and ran out through the back door. I hid behind the huge black rubbish bins. I scanned the area nervously. There was no one around. I wore my winter coat over my overall and walked calmly from behind the bins to the side road. From time to time I glanced over my shoulders nervously. I saw a bus approaching a bus stop on the other side of the road. I did not care where it was heading. I waved it down and ran across the road. I showed my weekly travel card and entered. I noticed that people were looking at me. I couldn't understand why. It was only later that I realised I was still wearing my overalls under my winter coat.

I spent the weekend alone in the house.

'You lucky bastard,' Sandra said on Monday afternoon as soon as I entered the Willesden Green branch of the agency. 'The chef called and told us what had happened. They cleared three buildings and arrested all illegal immigrants except for you. They came here looking for you this morning. I gave them the wrong address. Michael,' Sandra whispered leaning forward. 'You need a new name and a new national insurance number immediately if you want to continue working for us. I really want to help you, you're a nice guy but I don't want us to get into trouble.'

'Thank you very much Sandra.'

Sandra whispered. 'Get a new identity. Don't come in. From now on everything would be on the phone. Either fax your timesheet or drop it through the letterbox very late when the office is closed. Off you go.'

I took hurried steps out of the office. Sandra followed me. 'Michael,' she started with a smile, 'I saved you from the Home Office, now I want something in return.'

'What's it?'

'A Masai man! We don't have them in Australia. I've wild fantasies about Masai men.'

'Okay! I'll get you one.'

'One more thing, go and get a white shirt, black trousers, black shoes and a bow tie. I'll train you to do silver service. You'll earn more money and less hassle but in return what are you going to give me?'

'A strong Masai man.'

'I've a job for you.' Sandra pulled me into the office. Giving me the details she added. 'The manager is called Julia. Don't fool around with her. I hear you like older women. The chef told us about your love affair with a banker.'

I whispered into her ears. 'So the Home Office are looking for me.'

She did not look concerned. 'Don't be neurotic. They are looking for thousands of others too.'

'I'll get you a Masai man. I promise.'

'I like the way they drink the blood of cows.'

'Is that the only reason why you want a Masai man?'

'Off you go.'

I cashed my cheque and decided to walk to West Hampstead to see Dr Asibong. As I walked I looked around more than I usually did. I would glance over my shoulder to be sure no one was following me. Whenever I was suspicious of someone I saw more than once, I would enter a shop hoping that the person would walk past.

As I walked on Chichelle Road towards Cricklewood Broadway, I noticed two uniformed policemen walking purposefully behind me. I panicked, as I had not seen them earlier. I thought: that's it! They are following me. When I reached the junction on Cricklewood Broadway, I noticed they were talking to two other men and I thought I saw one of them pointing at me. My heart began to race. I wasn't sure what to do. I crossed the road at the traffic lights. They crossed the road too. I decided to take a bus on Cricklewood Lane. I was hoping to take any bus going in any direction. I was now fully convinced they were following me. I cast anxious glances around and, to my horror, I noticed two uniformed policemen walking towards me. I felt like running across the street but there was traffic. Within a split second I pushed opened a door and entered a smoke-filled place where some middle-aged men were looking at some TV screens. I joined them. One screen showed many dogs running. I kept an eye on the screens and an eye at the door. On another screen, I saw some men wearing colourful jerseys riding horses. I continued to look at the door nervously. The horses were now jumping some hurdles. Some of the men in the shop were shouting, 'Co'mon Magic Carpet. 'Co'mon Invisible Star.'

The door did not open. I was not sure if the policemen had past or were simply waiting for me to come out. I went to the door. I saw four policemen talking and laughing right in front of the door. I remembered the voice in front of the toilets at the bank: *We'll get him next time.* I thought they were laughing because they knew they had got me. I felt like handing myself over to them. By the time I went back to the door, they had walked away.

I continued my walk on Cricklewood Lane. I walked past the two policemen talking to a traffic warden. They did not pay any attention to me.

I asked Dr Asibong why some men would stand and watch television during the daytime, urging horses and dogs on. He laughed. 'It's a betting shop,' he explained. 'I suppose you don't have that back home.'

I told Jarvo about my experiences. 'Let's celebrate at Bozo's Joint.'

'There's another reason to celebrate,' I said opening an envelope from the college where I did my correspondence course.

'What's that?'

'It's my certificate. I've got a diploma in philosophy.'

'Congratulations, as Michael or Mustapha?'

'Michael Danquah.'

'At the end of the day, it's the knowledge that matters not the name. I'm really happy you're conquering the fear. A lot of illegal immigrants are paralysed by fear. Someone called Edwin Cole once said: *You don't drown by falling into water, but by staying there.*'

'I need a new national insurance number,' I reminded Jarvo.

'No problem. I'll get someone to sort you out. We might just be lucky and we'll meet him at Bozo's Joint otherwise we have to ask Bozo for his number.'

'Who's he?'

'Femi, the fixer.'

The bar at Bozo's Joint was very crowded. 'Let's have one for the road,' Jarvo said ordering two bottles of Guinness.

Son-of-Adam staggered to me. 'Why call it sink when it never really sinks no matter how much water it takes? Have you ever seen a sink that sank in the kitchen or bathroom? Why call it toothbrush and not teethbrush after all it cleans not one but many teeth?'

He walked away singing loudly.

I wanted to know more about *The Silent Man*.

Jarvo thought for a while. 'It's a really sad case. Michael, you should count your blessings you don't have some of the problems these people have,' he said and lit a cigarette. 'This man called Adu graduated from one of the best universities in West Africa and came here to continue his studies. I don't know exactly what happened but I understand that he sent his passport to the Home Office for renewal or extension of his visa. Those days, it took the Home Office weeks, months and in some cases years to process applications. Unfortunately for him, his father died and he had to decide whether to retrieve his passport and return to Ghana for the funeral or wait to hear from the Home Office. He decided to wait. His father was the traditional ruler and he was the first son. According to their tradition he was supposed to be the first person to put a spade full of gravel on the father's coffin in the grave. There were lots of traditional rites and rituals that he must partake in. In the meantime, the Home Office took their time. It was very complicated because if he retrieved his passport and returned to Ghana, the chances of returning to the UK to continue his studies would have been lost. Back in Ghana, the whole community waited for him. When it was clear he could not return for the funeral and assume the traditional leadership of the village, the council of elders allowed his younger brother to perform the rites and rituals and become the chief of the village. As a form of punishment, the council of elders told him never to set foot on the village soil again. He had disrespected the traditions and had to be disowned. He was so shell-shocked by the news that he had not had any meaningful conversation with anyone since he was told that he had been banished from the village. This happened over ten years ago. He lost everything. He could not study. His wife left him and returned to Ghana. He was excommunicated by his community in the UK. So Mike yours is more of an adventure. Enjoy it.' He lit another cigarette and continued in a reflective mood. 'If everyone in this bar was to wrap their problems and put them in the middle of the bar, when you see the problems of others, you would happily take yours back. Your main problem now is finding a woman, not just any woman but the right woman.'

He ordered two bottles of Guinness. 'We might as well have one more.'

'Look who's here,' Jarvo said smiling at a young man walking down the stairs. 'How is Niran? Did you see him in Nigeria?'

'Yes. I did. *The Peacock* is doing well. He was in the detention centre for several months before they deported him. He's planning to come back soon. Don't ask me how.'

We laughed.

'Femi, just the man I'm looking for. Do you know where we can get NI number,' Jarvo whispered into his ears looking at me.

'For him?' he asked.

'Yes.'

'I do but ...' He looked at me again. 'Is he a Nigerian or a Ghanaian?'

'Nigerian.'

'Hmm, he must be careful not to be *shopped*,' Femi added looking straight at me.

I did not understand what he meant.

'It means when someone is reported to the authorities,' Jarvo whispered into my ears.

Femi continued. 'Nigerians are reporting fellow Nigerians to the Home Office for a fee. I don't know if it's true. Don't ask me how much they're paid because I don't know.' Femi paused for a while. 'I know some Nigerians in the Peckham area that have so many NI numbers but they're not trustworthy at all. They ask for ridiculous amounts of money and if you can't pay them they *shop* you,' he complained. 'One minute,' he opened his address book. 'I know some guys from North Africa who are into such things. They're okay but you must be very careful. Unless you double-cross them, they'll not *shop* you.'

'Thank you very much,' I said after receiving the telephone number.

Femi joined another table.

'Should we have one more for the road?' Jarvo asked.

'Why not, would one more make a difference?' I replied laughing. Jarvo went to the bar and bought two more bottles.

'Are you going to work or are you going to lie low for a while?'

'I'm going to work tomorrow. I cannot afford to lie low.'

'Generally, I think you're on the right track. Just keep a low profile and just keep working. In Ghana we have a proverb that says: *It's by going and coming that the bird builds its nest.* Just keep doing the ordinary things and somehow, somewhere the extraordinary will happen.'

On Saturday I went to work around Bond Street. 'Julia comes in late on Saturdays. The head chef will look after you.' I was directed to the kitchen.

'Where are you from?' was the first question the head chef asked.

'Ghana.'

'So sad, I thought you were from Nigeria.'

'Why?'

He laughed. 'My country Algeria defeated Nigeria twice during the 1990 African Cup of Nations Football championship. We defeated them in the opening game, 5-1. Can you imagine five good goals went into the net of the Super Eagles. Then we met in the final where we defeated them again. This time around we did not want to humiliate them so we scored only one goal. It was the happiest day of my life. To beat the Super Eagles twice was a great achievement and it made every Algerian proud. To beat them once could be luck but to beat them twice means we are superior. Normally when Nigerians come here to work, I give them something to compensate for the loss and humiliation.'

'I don't like football and I am from Ghana.'

'Anyway nice to meet you.'

I changed into the overalls.

'By the way, what's your name?'

'Michael.'

'And you?'

'Alan. That's my English name. My Muslim name is Abdul. And your African name?'

'Danquah.'

'That's too difficult for me. I'll call you Abdul Agency. It's easier for me. Look,' he pointed at another chef. 'He's also from Algeria. And he's also an Abdul. So we have three Abduls in the kitchen today. I'm Abdul Malik and he's Abdul Justine.'

'Abdul Justine?' I asked.

'Yes! If you've never heard that before, you're hearing it for the first time. Abdul in Arabic means a servant or a slave. Did you know that?'

'No I didn't,' I lied.

'Abdul Malik means the servant of the King or Ruler. In this country I am the servant of Her Majesty. Abdul Aziz means servant of the powerful; Abdul Karim means servant of the noble one. Abdul Justine means he's the servant of Justine. His wife's name is Justine and he's her slave. I'm not kidding you. He's been doing two jobs for over a decade just to keep her happy. Is that not slavery? He sleeps on the floor while she sleeps with her dogs. He pays for everything including holidays for the dogs. She's French you see and she spends a lot of time in France with her dogs while he works day and night here and sends her money. He washes her clothes, cooks for her. He does everything. That's why I call him Abdul Justine. He's simply her slave.'

'Don't listen to him, he's making things up.'

'His real name is Assad. In Arabic it means a lion. Does he look like a lion? Justine has tamed him to the point that he roars like a mouse. He's become a toothless gutless lion.' He asked me. 'You are Abdul what?'

'Abdul Nothing.'

'No way! You must be Abdul something. You must be a slave of something or somebody. We're all slaves. In our world today, we are all slaves of money. Doris there,' he said pointing at a woman at the till, 'is Abdul gambling. She spends all her money and her husband's money on scratch cards, pools and bingo. Some people are Abdul banks, slaves of banks. They work all their lives to pay off different kinds of loans and others debts. Some people are Abdul Cars because they spend all their money on cars they hardly drive.'

'He's talking about himself,' the other chef shouted. 'At least I'm a servant of what Almighty Allah created; a human being and animals. He is a servant of objects which is like idol worshipping. He has two cars parked in front of his house and he comes to work by public transport. He spends a fortune on these cars. He's also Abdul Football. Abdul Cigarettes. He's Abdul so many things.'

'He's right. I'm Abdul many things because I'm weak. Don't we human beings like it when we are chained by our own desires? So young man from Ghana, now you know the meaning of Abdul.'

'Thank you for educating me.'

I could not tell him that my surname was Abdullahi, the servant of Allah.

'So Michael, we're all programmed to be servants of something or someone. That's why I called you Abdul Agency. You work hard and the agency makes money out of you. When you marry then you become an Abdul of your wife. It's in our genes. Actually, we're all born free but because of our desires we voluntarily become slaves. Only those free of desires are totally free.'

I stood there looking at him.

'Sooner or later, all of us will be called to account for what or who we served in this world. A voice will ask you one day: were you Abdul-Shaitan or Abdul-Allah?'

Eight

Identity Crisis

As I was about to leave the house in Herne Hill on Monday morning, the phone rang. 'Don't come into the office today,' Sandra said. 'Home Office officials are conducting an operation in the Willesden Green area. We saw them picking up illegal immigrants and loading them into a van. I've a bag for you. Leonard dropped it this morning.'

'I'll come and collect it once you give me the all clear.'

'Let's meet at The Met around 7.00 pm. Remember the pub?'

'Yes'

'Andy, my new boyfriend will be performing there later. I don't need a Masai man.'

I remained indoors till about 6.00 pm.

Just after 7.00pm, I entered the pub in Willesden Green. Sandra was sitting on a man's lap. 'Meet my boyfriend Andy. He's from New Zealand and, as you can see, he's into music.' Andy had a guitar next to him and he looked a bit tipsy already. He had a long ponytail and prominent tattoos on his arms. He wore earrings and had three chains around his neck. Sandra gave me the bag I had left in the canteen after Marina told me about the presence of Home Office officials in the building. 'That's from your sugar mummy. Leonard said it was love at first sight. I like hearing such romantic stories.'

I did not answer. There was a moment of silence.

'What's it like to be a toy boy?' Andy asked after sipping from his pint of beer. 'It's weird when a young man dates an older woman. I think he's very insecure or emotionally immature. He's looking for a mother not a lover. I'm right, yes?'

I did not answer. I thanked Sandra and left.

On my way back to South London I looked at the bag again. There were two notes. One was from Marina with all her contact details and the other one from Leonard. I could not make up my mind if I should call and thank Marina for the presents. After all, if she had not brought them she would not have told me about the raid by Home Office officials. I was not sure what to say. I was not sure what the chef had told her. Maybe she guessed right that I was an illegal immigrant.

What bothered me most that evening was my new identity. I was wondering what name I should adopt. It suddenly occurred to me that I had attended a Christian missionary school in Bauchi town. And in those days, European missionaries made sure that all the pupils in missionary schools had baptismal names. Mine was Emmanuel. That's it. I smiled to myself on the bus. My new name will be Emmanuel. Then I thought about my new surname. I wanted something from Nigeria; something closer to home. I thought about districts of Bauchi town. Babayo! My new name will be Emmanuel Babayo. Now I was ready to meet the Arab guys in North London for my new national insurance number. I called from the public telephone booth. We agreed to meet the next day.

At the agreed time I waited outside exit 6 at Manor House underground station at 6.00 pm. Also, as agreed, I was wearing an Arsenal scarf for easy identification.

A red Ford Escort pulled up. 'Emmanuel?'

'Yes, that's me.'

'Come in. My name is Bobby,' he said as we drove off. 'So how are you my friend, bloody Arsenal supporter?'

'I'm fine thank you and you?'

'Why didn't you come in your car?'

'I don't have one.'

'I thought all Nigerians had cars.' He laughed. 'Your country is so rich. You have good footballers.' He named his favourites: Jay Jay, Finidi George, Kanu. 'I like Nigerian footballers. When they play it's as if they are dancing.'

'Where are you from?' I asked.

His expression changed. 'I'm a citizen of the world. I have British, Algerian, Moroccan and French passports. Are you happy now?'

I did not probe further.

'We all come from somewhere and it does not matter where we come from. You and I now want to do business. I give you what you want and you give me money for it. That's what is important. Everybody is happy.'

Bobby drove through the back streets of North London. I was worried when for no reason he would do a U turn. When we reached a junction, he asked himself, left or right? He waited for a while and said. 'First we go left and then later we go right.' I was getting worried but I did not want to say anything. I wasn't sure what he was doing but I kept quiet.

'No don't get out,' he said after parking on a narrow road. 'Do you want a passport? We can make you a genuine EU or UK passport, easy. You just choose the country you want.'

'I don't have the money for a passport.'

'Look my friend, if you have UK passport or EU passport you can claim benefits and get a council flat.'

'I've no money.'

'Your country is rich, how come you have no money?'

'Okay. Let's do the NI first and once I make enough money I'll get a UK passport. Trust me. I'll call you as soon as I have enough money.'

'Okay,' he agreed.

I gave him my name on a piece of paper and fifty pounds deposit. 'Don't forget to bring the balance this time next week. Don't call me. People might be listening to my telephone. And don't forget to wear the Arsenal scarf, you bloody Arsenal supporter. You poor Nigerian!'

That evening I called Leonard.

'I'm really happy to hear your voice Michael. You're damn lucky. They checked everywhere. They even checked the freezers. They checked everywhere except where you were hiding. They were convinced you were in the building and waited in the main reception for hours. How did you get out?'

'I escaped through the emergency exit at the back.'

'That's interesting because I disabled the alarm before I left hoping and praying you'd use it. I knew you were somewhere because your coat and bag were in the changing room. Also they came in as soon as Marina left, which wouldn't have given you enough time to go to the changing room. Thank your mother for her prayers. Bless her. In Jamaica we say a mother's prayer is like a shield.'

'You know what, Marina told me they were in the reception.'

'Oh my God. So she saved you. She wasn't meant to be in that day you know. How do you explain such strange coincidences?'

'Should I call and thank her?'

'No. I told her you had left for Ghana. But it's up to you. If I were you I wouldn't. She was sent by the Almighty to save you and she did just that. Leave it at that. The way I see it is that if you call her she would expect a full-blown relationship. She would ask you some questions and would want to travel abroad with you. How long can you keep lying to her?'

We agreed to keep in touch.

'So Mr Emanuel,' Bobby started as soon as I entered his car at exit 6 Manor House underground station. 'The last time we met I made a mistake,' he continued as I fixed the seat belt. 'Kanu is not the best player from Africa. George Weah is the best. He's a magician.'

I did not argue. 'Did you see the goal he scored last weekend?'

'No I didn't.'

'You sure you don't want passport? Very cheap and all your problems will be solved. We'll give you all the documents you need. Trust me.'

'Would you give me these documents for free?'

'No, of course not, you have to pay.'

'So, I've to work first and earn the money.'

'Can't you play football and earn money? After all, Nigerians have some of the best players in the world.'

'I'm too old.'

He parked the car near a school. 'I trust you that is why I'm giving you this NI number. Don't tell people about us unless they are genuine. If you get into some problems just tell them you've forgotten where you got the number. If you send people, I mean the police or government officials to us we will send our people to you. Understood?'

'Yes.'

'We know who you are and where you live,' he said laughing. 'Remember this. We don't forgive. Only Allah forgives.' Bobby brought out an envelope and handed it over to me. I looked at the card inside. Emmanuel Babayo. I gave him an envelope.

'That's the balance.'

He counted the money and thanked me.

'I'll contact you for the passport soon,' I promised and shook his hand.

'I'm waiting for your telephone call.'

The next day I registered as Emmanuel Babayo at the agency. Back in Herne Hill, I could hear Russian music even before I reached the front of the house. Jarvo was full of smiles when I entered. 'Meet *tovarish* (Comrade in Russian) Thomas,' he said. 'We were mates in Moscow.'

'Michael,' Thomas said shaking my hand. 'I tell you! Our Moscow days were certainly the most interesting days of our lives.'

Jarvo opened a bottle of vodka. 'This is fresh from Moscow,' he said bringing out three small glasses from the cupboard. 'There's nothing better than Russian vodka.'

Thomas nodded in agreement. '*Pravilno*', he said in Russian.

'Too strong for me,' I said.

'Listen, *tovarish*,' Thomas started. 'This is one of the best vodkas you can get. Just a little bit. *Chut-Chut,*' he said explaining using two fingers, just a few drops. It's an offence you know to sit and watch others drink vodka. It's a grave insult indeed. In Russia we say tea is not vodka, you would not drink much. Come on just a drop or two, *Chut-Chut.*'

'We have to celebrate your transition from Michael to Emmanuel,' Jarvo said giving me a glass of vodka with a few drops in it. 'In Russia there's always a reason to celebrate, always a reason to drink vodka,' Jarvo insisted.

'Agreed, *Chut-Chut*,' I said.

I reminded them that Jarvo gave me the name Michael Danquah the day the Russian parliament voted to get the Russian Federation out of the USSR.

'I remember that very sad day in late September 1991.'

'One of the saddest days of my life,' Thomas confessed looking very glum.

'Suddenly the Union of Soviet Socialist Republic we knew was no more.'

'Soyuz Sovetskhih Sotsialisticheskhih Respublik.'

Jarvo gave us slices of Russian rye bread. *Nu davaite! Na zdarovie tovarishi.'*

'May we always have a reason for a party,' Thomas recited Russia's oldest toast. They both sniffed the rye bread before drinking their glasses dry. 'That's how we drink vodka. *Harasho pashla!'* He nodded several times eating bread and sardines. 'I know someone in a security firm,' Thomas said. 'I'll tell him to get you a job. He's one of us.'

'That would be very helpful,' Jarvo said. 'This agency work is too risky.'

Thomas stood up to go. 'Michael, you'll hear from me soon. I'm going to see Gideon now. I've some bottles of vodka for him. I'll tell him to give you a job.'

'Have one for the road,' Jarvo implored. '*Na pososhok* as we say in Russian.'

'*Nu davai,*' Thomas said and knocked back one last round. 'Michael, you never say no to a drop or two of vodka.'

One morning the phone rang. 'Michael oh sorry Emmanuel,' Sandra said. 'One of our clients wants a very good kitchen porter. Do you want to work today?'

'Yes.'

Sandra gave me all the details. I dropped everything and rushed out.

I reminded myself several times that I was no longer Michael but Emmanuel. The security man in the building off Marylebone Road printed my name badge EMMANUEL BABAYO.

'Mr Babayo, take the lift to the third floor. The manager is waiting for you.'

'My name is Jenny,' said a short slim woman as soon as the lift opened.

'Nice to meet you.'

'I hope you're not going to run away when you see what's waiting for you.'

'I fear no jobs.'

'Good to hear that. My worst nightmare is for you to walk away from this job,' she said leading me to the washing-up area. It was full of pots, pans, cutlery, trays and cups. Jenny looked at me.

'No problem,' I said smiling. I looked at the machine. 'I've used this type of machine before and I'll do my best,' I promised.

It took me a couple of hours to clear the whole lot. 'Wonderful Emmanuel, thank you very much. I'm really impressed. I'll give you five more hours. Take your break now and mop the whole kitchen when the chef has finished. I'm off now. I will sign your timesheet tomorrow morning and fax it to the agency. Once again thank you very much.'

I was mopping other parts of the kitchen when I heard a huge noise. It sounded like a huge blast. It shook the building and I was scared. The alarm went off. I knew there had been an explosion somewhere and could hear people screaming in the distance. I dropped the mob and began to run around. I knew I must not use the lift. I had no idea where the emergency exit was. I could see through broken windows that the blast had partially destroyed the adjacent building. I surveyed the kitchen area. I heard someone scream where I thought the chef was. I looked around and saw him writhing in pain. He had been caught by broken glass and was bleeding. I tore his apron and used it to stem the flow of blood from his leg and arm. I heard sirens and later saw the fire brigade crew at the adjacent building using cranes to rescue people.

The chef was dizzy and lay on the floor for a while. 'I banged my head when I fell and I need time to recover. I'm still dazed.' When he felt better we started walking down the stairs slowly. It took us a long to emerge from the front door. An ambulance crew ran towards us. I was covered in blood but not injured. They took the chef away into an ambulance. I told them I was fine just shocked. Later a policeman came.

'Were you caught in the blast?'

'No Sir,'

'Sir, what did you see?'

'I saw nothing.'

'Then what did you hear?'

'I heard a huge blast and the building shook.'

'And were you injured?'

'No I'm fine.'

'How did you get that blood on you?'

'I helped the chef who was injured.'

'Where were you when the incident occurred?'

'I was in the kitchen on the third floor.'

'Is there someone in the kitchen right now?'

'As far as I know, there's no one.'

'Are you sure you're okay?' the policeman asked looking at the blood on my overall.

'I'm fine.'

'What's your name Sir?' another policeman asked moments later.

'Emmanuel Babayo.'

'Could you spell your names for us please?'

I spelt out my name.

'Thank you.'

I was later allowed to return and retrieved my belongings.

I arrived at Bozo's Joint just before the 7.00 pm news. The Politburo had just finished their meeting. The main news showed a clip of fire fighters on cranes and a clip of the chef and I coming out of the building. I was covered in his blood. Everybody in the bar came round the TV set. 'Mustapha is in the news. Mike is in the news.'

The main report was about the gas explosion in central London. After the initial shot of fire fighters rescuing people down the crane, I was shown at close range, in my white overall, partly covered in blood.

I looked genuinely dazed and shocked as I described what happened. EMMANUEL BABAYO flashed up on the screen during the brief interview.

There was laughter in the bar.

'Comrade, so you've changed from Michael to Emmanuel?' Ama asked.

'See what London can do to someone, from Mustapha to Michael and now Emmanuel,' Wassa added shaking his head.

Taj gestured for silence and walked closer to me. Holding his pipe, he started. 'Mustapha, God forbid, something serious had happened in the accident and you went to meet your maker? Imagine the amazement and confusion up there. God would be puzzled wouldn't He? He would look at this register and say something like, "But I don't have any Emmanuel Babayo on my register. I sent you out into the world as Mustapha and you come back to me as Emmanuel?"'

There was laughter in the bar.

'Let's celebrate that you are alive,' Jarvo said going to the bar to buy more drinks.

'Na zdarovie,' I managed to say.

That evening I was touched by what Taj had said earlier. I wondered, just before I went to bed, that's if in reality I had died in the explosion, I would have been identified as Emanuel Babayo. If no one claimed my body, I would be buried as Mr Babayo. I began to wonder if this wasn't the time for me to return to my real identity.

On a Saturday, Sandra took me to a private Club in Pall Mall in central London to see how waiters worked. I was wearing black trousers, white shirt, black shoes and a bow tie. Sandra and I went early. I did not serve anyone. She taught me how plates and cutlery were arranged, how white wine was served in small glasses and red wine in large glasses. How cutleries were polished and she taught me how to set the table for breakfast, lunch and dinner. When the regular waiters came, she suggested I watched how they worked.

The next day, I joined five other waiters at the club; four women and one man. I was nervous. I watched and copied them. When we were on a short break, the young man who supported Juventus Football Club wanted to know my favourite football club. I told him I was not interested in football. When he insisted, I told him I supported AC Milan. He left me alone. I did not like the way the women were looking at me while giggling and laughing. I decided to sit on the staircase and read a novel.

'What are you reading?' A female waiter asked me in a strange accent.

'A novel,' I answered without looking at her.

'What is it about?'

I gave the novel to her to read the blurb. 'That reminds me of the book I'm reading right now. It's about a life's ambition. What do you want to be in life?' she asked me. I couldn't understand her accent. I knew it was not English or Scottish. I thought she was from Australia.

'A film director,' I said without paying attention to her. I thought she would make fun of me. The young woman was excited.

'Are you serious?'

'Of course I'm serious,' I answered without looking at her.

'Exciting stuff, look at his face,' she said. 'Now he's grumpy again.'

I found her irritating and wanted her to leave me alone.

'Would I ever see your film?'

'I hope so.'

'Good luck.'

The work at the club ended. Sandra went to Australia on holiday. Several weeks passed without work.

One evening, Leonard called while I was reading.

'I've got a weekend job for you. Are you free?'

'Yes I am.'

'It's cash in hand not through the agency.'

'That's even better.'

He explained. 'My wife and I will be opening a restaurant soon in the city. We need someone to help us with the cleaning.'

'Fine.'

He gave me the details.

'Long time no see,' Leonard said the next morning. 'How's life treating you?'

'Fine, thank you.'

I noticed immediately he was a different person. He had grown a beard and looked calmer. He was not the all-singing, all-dancing chef I had known months before. He told me what he wanted me to do and I started working immediately. I was surprised he never mentioned Marina.

'Take your break Michael,' he said later and gave me sandwiches and drinks. 'I'll be praying soon, so pick up the phone please.' He went into the office and brought out a prayer mat and laid it on the floor. He wore a small cap and started to pray. I couldn't believe my eyes. I sat there staring as he stood still, bent down and later sat down on the prayer mat. So Leonard is a Muslim. I had so many questions I wanted to ask him but I couldn't. I was living a lie and was not prepared to get out of it.

'I didn't know you are a Muslim,' I started after he finished praying.

'Oh yes, I converted months ago.'

'So what's your Muslim name?'

'Bilal Abdullahi Muhammad.'

'I see. Can I ask a question?'

'You ask me any questions you like.'

'Why did you convert?'

'It's a long story. It can also be short. I was born into a Christian family in Jamaica. I came here as a Christian and was raised and educated as a Christian. But I began to question a few things. I wasn't satisfied with so many answers provided by the Church and by the educational system. Aisha, my wife was interested in Islam and did some research into the religion. She converted a long time ago. Initially I found it hard to understand her and why she converted. But as time went on she explained the religion to me and I watched how she practised it. It was only a matter of time that I converted too.'

'I see. Thank you.'

'The main thing Michael is that I am at peace with myself. I pray five times a day and I don't drink alcohol. I don't eat pork. I try to be as simple and modest as possible. I look forward to observing Ramadan soon. And *Insha'Allah* my wife and I would be going to Saudi Arabia to perform the holy pilgrimage. You know what Mike, and I am being honest with you, the moment I recited the *shahada*, something clicked inside me. It was magical.'

'What's *shahada*?' I pretended not to know.

'*Shahada* is the Muslim declaration of belief in the oneness of Allah and in Muhammad as His final prophet. There is no god but Allah, and Muhammad is the Messenger of Allah.'

At that moment I wanted to tell him that I was also a Muslim and that we actually shared the same name in Abdullahi but something closed my mouth.

I continued to work.

'Are you sure you want to work tomorrow?' he asked when I was ready to go.

'Why did you ask?'

'It's Sunday. It's important to remember and serve God.'

'Yes I know that I have to keep the Sabbath day holy. But I also have to survive. I pray at home and as you probably know God is everywhere and religion is inside us.'

'Since you're a Christian I've to respect your belief.'

'I'm alright I will see you tomorrow.'

'*Insha'Allah*.'

The next day, Sunday, a female voice welcomed me as I entered the restaurant. 'Good morning Michael, Nice to meet you. My name is Aisha. Since you know my husband as Leonard you might as well call me by my former name, which is Beverley. I'll call him Bilal and he'll call me Aisha so don't be confused.'

'Nice to meet you Aisha. It's alright I'll call you by your Muslim names.'

'That's very considerate of you Michael.'

Without wasting any time she told me what to do. 'Bilal is running late. He'll be here any moment.' I looked at her closely. She did not wear anything to suggest she was a Muslim. She had a T-shirt over jeans. Her head was not covered. Aisha started talking to me about Islam. She thought I knew nothing about the religion and I pretended to know nothing. 'Before you start anything, say *Bismillah Rahman Rahim.*' (In the name of Allah, the Most Gracious, the Most Merciful)

I repeated it deliberately making some mistakes.

'When you finish you say *Alhamdullilah.*'

As we continued to work, Aisha would from time to time say one or two things like, 'Don't say anything with certainty about the future for you don't know what it holds, so always say *Insha'Allah.*' She explained what *halal* and *haram* meant and why the new restaurant was a *halal* restaurant. Later in the day, she whispered, 'I'll remember you in my prayers so that one day you will revert to Islam and enjoy peace of mind.'

I thanked her and continue to clean the kitchen.

'Take a break Michael,' Aisha said. 'Time for prayers' she said looking at her husband who had joined us in the restaurant. They both went away for some time. When they emerged Aisha was wearing a *hijab.* I sat there and watched them as they prayed.

We continued to work. While we were cleaning the tables and chairs, she asked. 'Have you ever heard of *Qiyamah?*'

I lied. 'No, never heard the word. What's that?'

'The end of time! When everything comes to an end. There are signs that indicate that we are in that period or approaching it.' She told me ten major signs. I knew them already but I pretended I was hearing them for the first time.

Later Aisha asked me to help her put up a poster on the wall which read;

There is no word as beautiful as Allah
No example as beautiful as Rassulallah (SAW)
No lesson as beautiful as Islam
No song as melodious as Azan

No charity as meaningful as Zakat
No encyclopaedia as perfect as Quran
No diet as perfect as fasting
No journey as purposeful as Hajj

'Beautiful isn't it,' she asked with a smile.

When I was about to finish, Bilal gave me an envelope full of money. 'Please count it before you go.' I did. It was three times what I would have earned had I got the job through the employment agency.

'*Insha'Allah,* we'll call you soon.'

Thomas was very happy to see me as soon as I entered the house.

'We've just opened a bottle of vodka.'

'I'm really tired and I need some rest.'

'But we have to celebrate.'

'Celebrate what?'

'Gideon has agreed to give you a job. I'll take you to his office tomorrow. But first let's drink,' Thomas repeated, '*Chut-Chut.* Drink just a few drops. I like the way you say *Chut-Chut.*'

'Alright then, *Chut-Chut,*' I said smiling and reluctantly lifted a glass.

'*Nu davaite tovarishi do kontsa,*' Jarvo said.

Nine

Seeking Refuge in Brixton

The next morning Thomas and I went to Canary Wharf. 'Gideon was my roommate in Moscow many years ago. He's a very nice man,' Thomas said as we approached the offices of SAFEFORCE Security. As we were about to enter, I noticed that Thomas removed his hat. I wanted to remove my cap. 'You don't have to,' he told me. 'It's a Russian tradition to remove your hat or cap before entering a friend's place. It's a sign that you're a friend not a foe.'

'*Nu shto, starik! Privet,*' Gideon greeted and hugged Thomas in the office. '*Kak dela, maladoi chelovek?*' he added looking at me.

'Meet Michael, the *tovarish* I told you about. He's one of us.'

'I understand you drink vodka,' Gideon said with a smile shaking my hand firmly.

'He's Jarvo's drinking buddy,' Thomas added sitting down.

'*Chut-Chut,*' I said laughing.

'That's good. Now I've a drinking buddy here,' he went and brought a bottle of vodka. '*Nu shto ribyata, soabrazim na triakh?* Should the three of us do justice to this bottle?'

'*Nyet. Spasiba,*' Thomas responded shaking his head. 'We want you to get a job for him, *po tovaricheski,* (in the spirit of comradeship) as we say in Russian.'

'*Ladna,*' Gideon sighed returning the bottle. He then gave me a form to fill out.

There was no interview. Gideon gave me uniforms and said he would call me later.

The next day, Gideon called and told me to report to a supermarket in Ilford in East London. I did. It was a twelve-hour shift. I lied to the supervisor in the supermarket that I had worked as a security man before. I familiarised myself with the aisles and I asked where the cameras were. I watched as the shoppers walked through the aisles. No one told me exactly what to do. I kept a close eye on people I instinctively thought might be shoplifters. Nothing happened. At the end of the day I was very relieved.

I worked in the supermarket for two weeks.

Gideon told me that my next job would be in an industrial estate outside London. 'I'll drop you there before 6.00 pm. You have to ensure all the doors are locked when everyone is out of the building. The guard dogs will be released on the premises around 7.00 pm. Your job is to keep an eye on the CCTV monitors for signs of any breach of security. There are alarms fitted all over. By 6.00 am the dog handlers will come and take the dogs away and then you are free to go.'

I was thrilled. For the next three weeks I did exactly as Gideon said. When the job was over I was sent to work as a security officer at a fashion shop in Bayswater. It was upmarket and posh. I was beginning to gain confidence in the uniform. My job was to stand at the exit all day and keep an eye on customers. I knew that another colleague was downstairs watching customers on remote circuit cameras.

On the third day, while standing at the exit, the alarm went off as a Japanese woman walked past the doors.

'Excuse me, Madam. Could I have a look in your bag please?'

'No not you, somebody else,' she protested.

'It's my job to check,' I insisted. 'I am the security officer on duty.' I collected the bag and checked the contents. 'Can I see the receipt please?'

She reluctantly showed me.

'Sorry about that,' I said when I was happy that she had paid for it. 'The cashier must have forgotten to remove the security tag.' I took the item to the till. The security tag was duly removed. The Japanese woman was very upset. She was murmuring and pointing a finger at me. 'Why touch it? I said don't touch it. I want another one,' she demanded. The cashier went and picked another one for her. The cashier asked: 'why don't you want this one?'

'Because that black man has touched it,' she said within earshot, visibly upset.

Later the manager told me to always be polite to customers. 'As we say in this country, customers are always right. The Japanese have lots of money. I wouldn't want such a rich woman to say anything negative about our shop. Next time don't argue. Don't touch it. Just tell her to go and see the cashier. If the cashier is black send her to a white person.'

The manager signed my timesheet and told me not to come in the next day.

'I'll send you to work with people from your country,' Gideon said the next day.

I reported very early on Monday for my next job. 'My name is Emanuel Babayo.'

'Nice to meet you. Mine is Oluwasegun. You're welcomed. We've been expecting you. I'm the supervisor here and you'll be working with Tola,' he said with an air of authority.

'Nice to meet you, Tola.'

We shook hands.

'Your main job will be to stand here and ensure that all visitors coming into the building sign in and have a badge to display. Although you have the right to search their bags, we usually don't do it. Unless of course you strongly suspect they are carrying explosives or dangerous weapons,' he smiled. 'Please be alert at all times. Sometimes the authorities check our state of alertness by trying deliberately to breach security. Keep your eyes open. You understand?'

'Yes I do sir,' I said and saluted.

He liked it and smiled.

I noticed over the next few days that Oluwasegun was reading a lot of books, especially in the evenings. I asked him what he was studying.

'Forensic psychology,' he explained in an empty office surrounded by books. 'Since I came to this country I've been studying by correspondence,' he said. 'I have five degrees; three Bachelor degrees and two Master's degrees. I've been in this country for twenty years. I've been working here doing this job for twenty years.'

In the evenings, Tola and I went around the building to ensure that the windows were closed, all the doors locked and the alarms systems were switched on.

One particular evening, a lady cleaner asked me where Pastor Segun was. 'I didn't know he was a pastor,' I said. When he came back, he confirmed to me that he was really a pastor at a church in Peckham. He invited me to a naming ceremony.

'I'm not going to take part in any of the rituals.'

'You're invited for the food and drinks. You can also dance if you want. It's Sunday at 6.00 pm. Just come and enjoy yourself.'

On Sunday I decided to go to the naming ceremony. By the time I arrived, the party was in full swing. From afar, I could hear music blaring from the community hall. Women dressed in elegant and colourful attires and men in big gowns and three piece suits. Children were running around. It was a typical Yoruba party. The music was loud. The food was tasty. The atmosphere was noisy.

Tola, who was wearing a hand-woven gown, welcomed me with a big smile. 'As you can see, we Yorubas know how to enjoy ourselves. We call it *Gbaladun* (enjoyment). We have the best music, best dresses, dancers and best food,' he said proudly. He gave me cow leg pepper soup to start with. Then I had pounded yam with *egusi* soup. Later I had *moi moi*. When I finished eating, I settled in a corner of the hall with a bottle of Guinness. Tola asked me if I had any particular song I'd like played. 'Anything by Fela Anikulapo Kuti but I'd really like *Suffering and Smiling*. Within a few minutes the disc jockey played the song. I was on the floor dancing. I enjoyed the music. It reminded me of my university days and my year-long national service in Lagos. I noticed that two elegantly dressed young women were dancing very close to me. When the song ended, one of the girls invited me to dance another song by Fela called *Zombie*. We danced and sang together. When the music was over I decided to rest. 'I like the way you dance,' one of the girls said. She sat next to me. 'I want to dance the next song with you.'

'I don't know how to dance to the tune of traditional Yoruba music.'

'It's simple I will teach you,' she grabbed my hand and pulled me to the dancing floor. She showed me how they danced. The other girls joined her. I was really impressed.

'My name is Iyabo.'

'Mine is Emmanuel.'

'Are you a member of this Church?'

'No. I'm an invited guest.'

'Nice to meet you, my friend Bisi wants to ask you a few questions. I think we should talk outside. The music is too loud.' I stood up and followed Iyabo. Outside, she whispered smiling at me, 'my friend who was dancing next to you,' she pointed at her, 'likes you.' There was a particular type of smile on her face. 'But she's shy, very shy that's why I'm talking to you.' I looked at Bisi closely. She avoided eye contact. Iyabo continued, 'you see she's been very lonely and is looking for friends. I think the two of you would get along very well. I can see you are made for each other – a perfect match.' She gestured that Bisi should join us.

Bisi was shy. She told me she would like to know more about me. 'When can we meet? I'm going back home soon because I do early morning cleaning somewhere in the city.' Stepping closer to me, she held my hand. 'Can we meet tomorrow evening after work?'

'Of course.'

'Where do you live?'

'Herne Hill.'

'I live in Camberwell. Not far. Give me your telephone number and address and I'll call you around 7.00 pm. That's when I'll be free,' she said and stepped even closer, her body touching mine. 'We need to talk. I can see many things in your eyes,' she rubbed her body against mine. 'You and I need to sit down and talk.' Without any hesitation I give her my contact details with a big smile. 'I will call you tomorrow evening, I promise.' She waved goodbye with a big smile and walked slowly away shaking her buttocks.

I went back into the hall and sat down looking forward to the meeting with Bisi tomorrow evening. I thanked Iyabo for introducing me to a soul mate when she brought me more drinks and food. 'That's love at first sight. She's a nice girl but she is very shy. She needs someone who has experience in life to teach her a few things and be her friend. She needs a good man like you. Just be patient with her. Take it easy. When you meet her again you will love her more I promise you. Don't worry everything will be fine.'

The evening dragged on.

'The music is too loud, can we talk outside?' Iyabo complained again.

'Will you marry Bisi?' She teased me.

'We'll see,' I said.

'Are you married?' another girl called Bimbola asked.

'No.'

'It doesn't really matter does it?' Iyabo argued.

'What you mean?'

'You can marry more than one wife. Bisi can be your girlfriend.'

'But I have to know her first. I have to talk to her and see if we are compatible – you know get along.'

'She's free, and we don't want you to waste her time.'

I noticed Iyabo's expression changed. 'When are you going to marry Bisi?'

'I don't know. I have to take things slowly and talk to her first.'

'But I've just told you that she hasn't got the time,' looking very serious.

'We've agreed to meet tomorrow. We shall take things from there. I don't have the money to marry straight away.'

'You want her to visit you. You gave her your address. And now you say you don't have money to marry her. What do you think she is – a prostitute?'

'Listen, she suggested we meet tomorrow evening. I didn't invite her.'

'You didn't invite her but you are ready to welcome her,' Bimbola added her voice. 'Emmanuel, we need to talk,' she said in a commanding tone.

I began to sense that something was wrong. I could see in the body language and the way they looked at me that this was more than just an ordinary meeting. It occurred to me that I had been very careless by giving them my contact details. The girls now surrounded me. I felt outmanoeuvred. Bimbola grabbed my shirt. 'Emmanuel,' she started looking very stern. 'We know that you are an illegal immigrant. In your own interest just do what we tell you to do okay?'

'See,' Bisi said showing me a British passport. 'If you want to have a stay permit, if you want to be a legal citizen you can marry me.'

'But it's not cheap. It cost a lot of money. We need money,' Bimbola insisted.

'But I don't have money,' I insisted.

'You want to be legal or not?' Bim asked looking straight into my eyes and tightening the grip around my neck. She repeated the question slowly.

'I do.'

'So, Mr illegal immigrant, go and get the money wherever you can.'

'But I didn't ask for this. I only came here for a party. Now if it is a joke I think it's enough.'

'We are not joking.'

'By the way who told you that I'm illegal?'

'We can smell an illegal. We know who you are. We have all the information about you.' She released the grip. 'Well if you think you are legal then why do you have to worry? I'll call the Home Office and give them all your details. They will check and then we'll see what happens to Mr legal immigrant.'

'*Abio*,' hissed Iyabo.

'What do you want?' I asked again.

'*Owo*! Give us three thousand pounds immediately.'

'For what?'

'For a stay. Once we have the money, you can marry Bisi.'

'I don't have the money and I think that's enough now.'

I tried to walk away. Bimbola pulled me back. 'You like her but you don't have money. What's free in this country?' she asked.

'*Abio*!' Iyabo exclaimed loudly.

They laughed at me and clapped their hands. They started singing and dancing. I could see that they sensed I had fallen into their trap.

Iyabo laughed scornfully at me. 'Listen to an illegal immigrant talking about love at first sight. He wants to have a girlfriend and cheaply too. This is one thing illegal immigrants are not allowed to do.'

'Okay,' Bimbola said. 'I've an idea. Let us reach a compromise here. Give us a deposit and we'll let you go. Give us something now and the rest later. Remember that the moment you stop paying I'll call the Home Office and you'll be on your way home – home sweet home. You want to go back to *Nija*? Then you know what to do.'

'Okay I agree the game is over. I've lost. Can I go now?' I asked laughing.

'Go where? Who's playing a game with you? The game is over for you?'

'Listen to this illegal immigrant talking to us like this.'

The three young women blocked me. 'You're going nowhere Emmanuel; it's in your interest to cooperate with us,' Bim said forcefully.

'What's this?' Iyabo asked showing me something.

'Razor blade,' I answered.

'You know what I am going to use it for?'

'No I don't.'

'I'm going to cut myself, remove my clothes and when the police arrive I'll tell them that you attempted to rape me. And Mr illegal immigrant, I have witnesses. Two women here witnessed you trying to rape me. Isn't it true girls?'

'Yes you are right. We tried to stop him but we couldn't.'

'So Emmanuel, Mr illegal immigrant, if you don't cooperate with us not only are you going to be in jail for attempting to rape my friend but you'll also be deported after your term. Double whammy!' Bimbola said excitedly.

'What do you women want?' I asked a bit frustrated.

'*Owo*! We told you many times we want money.'

'I don't have it here. I did not come out with money. I didn't expect such a scene at the party.'

'You've to be prepared all the time. Is that not the first rule of being an illegal immigrant?'

'You have my contact details. Now could I have your contact details? I promise to give you something by the end of next week.'

They spoke in Yoruba. Bimbola wrote something on a piece of paper.

'Okay. I will pay the first instalment next week.'

Bimbola stepped closer to me. 'If you fail to honour your promise, you should be ready to return to your blessed country. Listen Mr illegal immigrant, it'll cost me only ten pence to get you back to our beloved country. Ten pence to make a phone call and your fate is sealed,' she emphasised without showing any emotions. 'One phone call and you're on your way. No appeal; no way back.'

'Where you would be going to enjoy a lot of sunshine and parties.'

I nodded in agreement.

They let me go.

I called Taj that night. 'I'm in trouble.'

'Are you in a police station?'

'No.'

I told him what had happened and gave him the address they had given me, as well as the contact details of Pastor Oluwasegun. 'You go underground somewhere. Look for temporary accommodation and lie low. You never know, they might just call the Home Office. This is just a precaution. I'll talk to the pastor and see if we can find them. I'll try and sort this out as soon as possible,' Taj promised.

The next day, Jarvo and I went to Bozo's Joint.

A Jamaican guy has just left an advert for a room in a house in the Brixton area, Bozo said giving me a card with the details. I called the number and we agreed to meet immediately.

'Yah man!' A tall man with dreadlocks greeted me as I approached the house on Cold Harbour Lane. He was holding a lighter but not smoking. 'What can I do for you?' he asked.

'I called earlier looking for a single room.'

'You're looking for a room right?' he asked in a lyrical Jamaican accent, revealing two gold-coated teeth.

'Yes.'

'Say no more. Follow me,' he opened the door and shouted. 'Melody, your man is here.' I followed him into the sitting room. 'My name is Leroy. What's yours?

'Michael.'

Leroy didn't respond immediately. He stared at me. 'Why have you a Christian name?'

'Because I'm a Christian.'

'You don't understand. Are you African?'

'Yes.'

'Why do you have a slave master's name? Do you know what Christians did to Africans?'

I did not answer.

'Don't you have another name?' he asked shaking his locks.

I still did not answer.

'I'm not gonna call you Michael here you know. You're African so I want an African name.'

While I was thinking of what name to give him, I told him there was no big deal in names. I thought if I gave him Mustapha he would question why the change from a Christian to a Muslim name.

A woman appeared and greeted me cordially.

'That's Melody,' he said pointing at her. 'That's her name. It's not European and not Christian.' He turned to Melody, 'Listen to this man, this African man, this black man,' Leroy said pointing at me. 'This young man calls himself Michael.' Turning to me Leroy continued. 'Don't get me wrong. I'm not saying this to antagonise you. No. I want to call you a proper name – a name with meaning. I want to be your brother. I want to be your friend. But I don't want to call you, my blood brother from Africa, I don't want to call you Michael. Understand me?'

'Oh I see. I didn't understand.'

'So what's your name? What's the name your parents call you in Africa? They definitely didn't call you Michael. I'm dead sure of that.'

'You're right brother. You're dead right. They call me Kimani.'

'Yah man. Now you're talking,' Leroy was happy. 'That's exactly what I want to hear, proper African name. What does it mean?'

'Love. Peace. Respect.' I lied.

Melody shook her head in disagreement. 'I know that it means someone who is spiritual.'

'That's what it means in my place.'

'It doesn't matter. Say no more. It's African and I like it. Look at it this way. If you love other people, you're at peace with yourself and with others. If you respect others and others respect you then you're spiritual.'

'My cousin in America is called Kimani,' Melody said.

There was a moment of silence. Leroy lit a cigarette and started singing Peter Tosh's song, *Everybody Wants To Go Up To Heaven, But Nobody Wants to Die*. As we sat there getting ready to talk, it suddenly dawned on me that I had given myself yet another name in London.

'You smoke?' Leroy asked.

'No.'

Leroy showed me the room. I agreed to take it for a couple of weeks. I went back to Herne Hill and took some belongings.

Later, Leroy said. 'I give you jerk chicken and rice as a friend. You don't have to pay. Melody is cooking right now.'

'Thank you.'

Leroy brought out a bottle of Jamaican rum. He started to roll something with his long fingers. 'Brother Kimani, you don't smoke cigarettes but do you smoke this herb?'

'No I don't.'

'It's good for you. It's medicinal you know.'

'I'm not sick.'

He laughed. 'Hear him, me no sick. All of us have something wrong inside us. You take *ganja* and it makes it right. It's preventative medicine,' he said laughing. 'Just in case you have something in there that is wrong – something lurking under your skin.'

'I think I'm fine thank you.'

'You trust Western medicine just as you trust Western religion. You even have a Western name. *Ganja* is the best medicine you know. I'm not joking. People have been using it as medicine for a long time before the white man came with all these tablets and tonics that harm our bodies. Listen to this. Bob Marley once said that: *Herb is healing of a nation, alcohol is the destruction.* In Montego Bay when I was young, my mother used to make us *ganja* tea. I'm strong and healthy because of the *ganja* tea you know. So Kimani, everybody has their medicine and this herb is mine.'

Melody brought the food. We ate in silence.

'Tell me Kimani, you porky?'

'What's that?'

They both laughed.

'Blackman messing around with white woman,' Leroy winked.

'Your girlfriend is white?' Melody asked.

'No.'

'You have a girlfriend?'

'Now? No I don't.'

They both looked at each other.

'What do you do when it's cold?' Leroy asked.

'I've a big problem with my girlfriend now,' I lied.

'I see,' Leroy said shaking his locks.

'Will she visit you here?' Melody asked.

'No.'

'Any man visit you here?' Melody asked.

'You batty man?' Leroy said.

'What's batty man?'

They both laughed. Leroy coughed for a long time.

'African man doesn't know who's a batty man.'

Melody explained. 'Man who sleeps with another man.'

'No. No. No.'

'Why take room for two weeks then?' Leroy asked looking at me.

'Problem with my girlfriend,' I lied.

'How many do you have?'

'One.'

'And she cause you trouble?'

'Yes.'

'I see that's why she sent you to the doghouse. It's your fault. Get more girlfriends. The more the merrier. She cause you trouble because she's the only one. When you've several girlfriends they don't cause you trouble, they fight each other.'

Leroy gave me a bottle of Guinness. 'You know what, Brother Kimani. I like talking to you. I somehow feel as if we are related.' Melody nodded in agreement. 'I want to test your knowledge about Jamaica.' Leroy stood up and played Eric Donaldson's song, *Sweet Jamaica*. He danced and told me, 'You know, that's our national anthem. You believe me?'

'Yes,' I said.

'In other countries, when the national anthem is played, people stand at attention but in Jamaica, when this song is played, people dance.'

Melody laughed.

'Do you know that Jamaica had electricity, water, phone cards before the USA?'

'No I don't.'

'Yes we did and Jamaica was the first country in the Caribbean to gain independence? We love football too you know; not only you Africans like football. We play good football too. As you know we like athletics. Yes, we're blessed with sprinters. Look how small the country is and see how many Olympians Jamaica has produced and how many medals we have.' He smiled. 'You know Melody can run? She was one of the fastest in her school. You want to compete with her? Thief something from her and run and see whether you can get away. Snatch her purse and run and see how many steps you take before she runs past you. You like Jamaican rum?'

'Yes,' I said nodding.

'It's the best in the world,' he said and sipped a bit. 'Now to the interesting thing about Jamaica you didn't know. We've the most beautiful women on earth. Honestly, see, we come third in Miss World titles.

Look how small the island is and how many times our women win Miss World. And all our girls are natural, not artificial. Not plastic. I'm telling you the truth brother Kimani, the first time I saw Melody she was walking on the other side of the road. I looked at her till I hit a lamppost.'

I laughed loudly.

'It's no laughing matter. You can laugh but I wasn't that day. I almost fainted. I said to myself, I must know this woman who almost made me faint.'

Leroy paused for a while. He started rolling a joint with his long fingers. 'You sure you don't want to try some?'

'I'm sure brother Leroy.'

'Alright then, remember Bob Marley said when you smoke herb, it reveals you to yourself.'

'Thanks. I don't need the herb to see myself.'

When he had finished rolling and started smoking, Leroy asked. 'Why do you think, I should believe that your name is Michael or Kimani? Why? Tell me?'

'Why not?'

'Don't get me wrong. I'm not trying to antagonise you. The thing is, we live in a lie lie society. Everybody lies to everybody else. Husband lies to wife, wife lies to husband. Father lies to the children, children lie to father. How do you know my name is Leroy? You trust everything everybody say? Even if I show you my birth certificate you believe everything written there? What if my name is not Leroy? Maybe I'm lying. You believe her name is Melody? Ever heard of such a name? Tomorrow you go away and you tell people I know Leroy and Melody. You go away thinking you know something. You know fuck all. I give myself the name Leroy. You believe me?'

Leroy laughed. He drank more rum. 'Kimani, here, government lies to people every day. People lie to government every day – the bigger the lie the better. Politicians lie, sports men cheat, shops lie, everybody lies. Why you see I don't watch TV, because it's all lies. Even the pictures they show us can be fake ones. Same with radio. I don't read newspapers because they all full of lies. You think those girls in page three in the tabloids are real? They are all fake tits – all plastic. When you hear spin doctors, what do you think these people do? They spin lies and doctor the truth. You come here and tell me your name is Michael and you're from Ghana. Bullshit. Rubbish. Big lie. You think Melody is my wife?'

'Yes.'

'No. She's not. Listen to this my brother. Three women say I father their kids. Lie. They want me to pay something. I've no money. Pay for what? Pay fuck all. They agreed to sleep with me. I didn't force them. Crazy world we're living in. What father? After sleeping with me that day do I know who else she sleep with? Or who else she sleep with before she sleep with me? Too many lies in our world today. Do you trust the blood test they do in the hospitals to check who the father is? I believe nothing that comes from people's mouths.'

'No one tells the truth any more,' said Melody.

'That's true. Brother Kimani. I know a woman on this street. She has a daughter and lied to her daughter that her father is dead. Imagine. The man is alive and kicking. The man doesn't know he has a daughter. They probably meet in the bus or in the market or somewhere and don't know each other. Listen to this. Last year, a well-known musician died here in Brixton. He was respected. Everybody talked about how good a father he was to his six children. One day the wife let slip that only three of the kids were his. This well-known and well-respected man went to his grave thinking he had six children.'

I did not go to work. I remained indoors during the day and went out only at night.

The phone rang one evening during the second week. Melody said it was for me.

'Michael you can come out of hiding now. We're at Bozo's Joint if you want to join us.' Jarvo said.

I told Leroy. 'My missus says that I can return home.'

'Treat her well,' Melody advised.

'Thank you very much for everything,' I said smiling at them.

'I'll miss you,' Leroy said hugging me. 'Feel free to come and visit us. Just knock the door and we shall open it for you. Melody will cook your favourite jerk chicken with rice and peas. I'll get you some Jamaican rum or Guinness.'

Taj and Jarvo were outside Bozo's Joint when I arrived. Taj was smoking his pipe. Jarvo was smoking a cigarette. The two laughed at me for a long time.

'Michael, what *really* happened?' Jarvo asked laughing.

I told them.

'You got a bit excited. The Yoruba girls got you.'

'Don't be so philosophical,' Taj said laughing. 'You succumbed to temptation. It's normal. I can understand and sympathise. These Yoruba girls must have enchanted and mesmerised you with their bodies! Some of the clothes they wear and their looks had a magical effect on your imagination. You lost your guard and gave them your details.'

'You're lucky. No harm done in the end. It could have been worse. You should learn from this experience and remain vigilant all the times,' Jarvo advised.

'What sort of clothes were they wearing?' Taj asked laughing. 'Were they wearing clothes made of see-through fabric? You know the Yorubas call it lace material. Did you dance with them?'

I did not answer. They continued to laugh.

'I've a feeling one of them shook her buttocks in front of you and the other asked for your contact details.'

I refused to talk. I stood there watching them laugh at me. I also decided not to tell them that I had adopted another name in Leroy's flat.

'Since you're so nostalgic about Nigeria,' Taj said walking to his car. 'I've some clothes for you.' He came back with the bag and handed it over to me. 'One of my brothers gave them to me but I think you need them more than me. I have enough. By the way, I met the pastor and with his help we tracked down the girls. The address they gave you does not exist. The church leadership was really angry with them. It turned out that the passport they were using for this scam was a fake one. In fact, one of the Church leaders called me today to say they had tried it on someone a few days before but the young man was actually born in the UK – a British citizen. He was so angry that he informed the police. The girls are now in hiding. I told them that we don't want to press charges and they must not tell the police about your incident. Otherwise, the police might ask you some questions you don't want to be asked. I also told the pastor and the church leaders that we do not want to be called as witnesses. From our side, case closed.'

I thanked him.

'Next time, don't go near any Yoruba woman,' Taj said, laughing as he bade farewell.

'Now we've a good reason to celebrate,' Jarvo said leading me into the bar. 'What do you want – vodka, beer or Guinness?'

'After what I've been through, give me anything.'

Ten

Love is in the Air

The sun was warm when I stepped onto the streets of south London.

'You look like a Sheikh,' Dr Asibong commented on the clothing I was wearing as soon as I entered his flat. I was wearing the long, white kaftan Taj gave me.

'It's been a while since I wore a traditional dress.'

'I know. The weather here is awful.'

'Your visit is well timed. I've an appointment at the GP's surgery and I'd like you to come with me. I find it hard to walk straight. I need someone to support me.'

'That's fine.'

Dr Asibong and I walked slowly into the surgery.

'Hi Doc,' the receptionist said as soon as we entered. 'I didn't know you had a grown-up son.' She looked genuinely surprised.

'You never asked,' he replied smiling. 'Ask and ye shall be told.'

'How many children have you got?'

'Mind your own business.'

'That's not an answer. I want numbers, five, seven, ten.'

Dr Asibong laughed and said. 'I don't know how to count.'

'What's his name?'

'Sheikh! Can't you see he's a Sheikh?'

'Is he a Muslim?'

'Of course, he's a Sheikh. See what he's wearing.'

'How come he's a Muslim and you're a Christian?'

'His mother is a Muslim.'

'Doc, you went out with a Muslim woman?' she asked with her mouth opened.

'What's wrong with going out with a Muslim woman? Is it forbidden by law?'

'No.'

'She was old enough to see a man and chose to see me.'

'Okay, I know where this is going to end up. That's enough,' she said shaking her head.

'You don't ask a woman her religion before …' Dr Asibong said looking at her.

'I can only date a Christian from my Church and he must come from Barbados.'

'Rubbish! You have to look beyond your limited horizon. God created all these wonderful things around the world for us to explore and enjoy. The Bible didn't say you should taste only one fruit in the garden.'

'It's enough. I told you I know where this is going to end,' she laughed and looked at me.

'You can date Sheikh. He's available,' Dr Asibong suggested.

'What if he's married? Someone once told me that Nigerian men, especially the Muslims, marry many wives.'

'Not only Muslims; even Christians marry several wives. What's wrong with that? Four wives give a man the physical and mental exercise needed for survival. You could be one of his wives. Look at him; he's young, strong, healthy and religious. What else do you want?'

'I've a boyfriend.'

'So what! A bit on the side is not a mortal sin. One is never enough in many things. You need a spare man, just like a car needs a spare tyre.'

'You cannot convince me on that, Doc. We're dealing with emotional issues here. I cannot serve two men, just like I cannot serve two Gods.'

'I can serve at least three women.'

A woman walked closer smiling. 'My name is Jamila. I'm a nurse here and I'm a Nigerian.'

I stood up and bowed.

'Thank you,' she said and turned to Dr Asibong. 'Your past is catching up with you. You cannot hide your kids from us forever,' she said smiling.

Dr Asibong laughed but did not reply.

'I have your notes, let's go,' she told him and helped him stand on his feet.

'Where's your mother?' the receptionist asked me.

'She's in Nigeria.'

'Why didn't she come with you?'

'She doesn't want to.'

'Has she got another family?'

'Yes.'

'Have you been to England before?'

'No.'

'Do you like it here?'

'Yes.'

'Are you registered with a General Practitioner?'

'No.'

'As the son of Dr Asibong you can register with us you know.'

'I didn't know that.'

'Just in case something happens to you while you are here; you don't have to see a private doctor. I'll give you the necessary forms.' She stood up and gave me a form to fill out. 'Just write your full names and your date of birth. We have your father's address on our records.'

I wrote SHEIKH ABDULLAHI. I did not want to write another name.

'Is it true that practising Muslims fast for a whole month?'

'Yes, from sunrise to sunset.'

'The maximum I can go without food is four hours. And you pray five times a day?'

'Yes we do.'

'My God! I don't even pray once a week. I really admire your discipline and commitment.'

'If you admire his discipline,' Dr Asibong said walking slowly into the reception, 'why not marry him and you would be able to have the same discipline and commitment.'

'I'm just curious. I just want to know more about Islam.'

'In that case why not invite him to your flat and he will introduce you to a new world, something you've never experienced before.'

'No thanks. I'm not going down that road,' she replied laughing. 'It's your turn to see the GP,' the receptionist said. 'Dr Helen Louise Armstrong is waiting for you in her consulting room.' I walked with him to the GP's room.

'You can sit there and wait for your father. There is nothing confidential, unless your father objects to you sitting with him.'

'I've no objection at all.'

'I'll tell you to leave if necessary,' the doctor said.

I sat there and watched as she did the usual checks and filled out some forms for blood tests. When she finished with Dr Asibong, the GP said. 'Can I quickly check your son? I've noticed something unusual.'

'You can have him if you want. He's available.'

'Shut up, Doc. He's got bulgy eyes.'

The doctor walked closer and looked at my eyes. 'I think you've got a hyperactive thyroid,' she opined and asked me questions about my sleep, appetite and whether I tired easily or not. She checked my blood pressure and gave me three different forms for blood tests at the Royal Free Hospital. 'Don't eat or drink anything before the blood tests, which should be done first thing in the morning. Once the results are in, the receptionist will call your father and make an appointment.'

I thanked her.

'Please don't listen to your father when it comes to women's issues. He's certainly not the best person to seek advice from. He's got some weird ideas about polygamy. Have you read the article he published recently on polygamy? If you haven't, don't bother … outrageous views.'

'I cannot stand this one man–one wife nonsense. Men are not monogamous by nature …'

The doctor interrupted him smiling. 'The door is open. I've other patients to see.'

At the reception, Jamila the nurse explained what a hyperactive thyroid was and how it was not dangerous or life threatening. 'You will be alright,' she assured me. When we were ready to go, Jamila gave me her telephone number. 'Call me if you have any problems or any questions. I'll be your mother in the UK. I'll introduce you to my children. I live just around the corner.'

In his flat, I asked Dr Asibong about his article on polygamy. 'Sheikh, my main argument was that monogamy is not natural. Marrying for love and desire is a new concept. Broadly speaking, marriage as an institution was created to con human beings. Human beings are still animals at heart and especially men, are not meant to be in a monogamous relationship. The whole idea of one man–one wife is a con primarily to get children to follow the religion of their parents. Also, one man–one wife ideology was meant to control the society and ensure that property passed from one generation to another in a particular order. The whole concept of monogamy to me is unrealistic because we have the capacity to mate with people outside our partnership. You go and tell most animals in their natural habitat to sign an agreement limiting them to one partner. I can see human beings reverting to one form of polygamy or the other in future, monogamy is just too restrictive.'

Several months later, Sandra called one Monday morning. She started with an apology. 'Michael, I'm sorry I let you down. I left TEMPSTAFF without telling you. We had lots of problems there. Anyway, I've set up my own agency. We're based in Queens Park. I'd offer you better rates than TEMPSTAFF and I promise to give you lots of work. Do you want to work for me?'

'Yes.'

'Great. I've a job for you right now. Do you remember where I sent you to a couple of years ago when you first joined TEMPSTAFF? The International Institute of Business and Finance in central London?'

'Yes I do.'

'They need someone in the kitchen as soon as possible.'

There was a moment of silence. My mind went back to the Hausa woman – her smiling face, her mild fragrance, her gaze. I could see her eyes looking at me. I thought I heard her voice asking? *Yaya kake?*

'Are you there? Hello? Michael, are you still there?' Sandra asked.

'I'm still here. What about Miss Robertson?'

'She's left. They've reorganised the whole structure and the new boss is a Nigerian woman called Joy. I'm sure she won't be jealous if you talk to a fellow African woman,' Sandra said laughing.

'Okay. I'm on my way.'

'You are a star Michael.'

'Sandra, one last thing.'

'What's it?'

'Who am I there: Michael or Emmanuel?'

'Michael. By the way, Joy is off sick today so report to Suzanne.'

The only shirt that was clean enough to be worn was the one Frank B gave me with the inscription: *I'll Make Your Dreams Come True*. I wore it and dashed out of the house.

In the canteen, I recognised the chef. He was from Sierra Leone and was called Joe. He recognised me and smiled. 'Nice to see you again.' We shook hands. The radio was playing Lionel Richie's hit *Hello, Is It Me You're Looking For?*

'I'm looking for Suzanne,' I told Joe.

A young woman came out of the office singing the song.

'Hello, is it me you're looking for?'

'Yes,' I answered. 'I'm from the agency.'

She stopped singing. 'What can I do for you?'

'Whao!' Joe said grinning, 'I'm jealous.'

'I can see it in your eyes that you're looking for me,' she said with a meaningful smile. 'What can you do for me?'

'Can't you see his T-shirt? He'll do exactly what is says on it.'

I did not know what to say. 'I'm only here to work as a kitchen porter.'

'I know. I'm just winding him up,' Suzanne said looking closely at me. I tried to avoid eye contact but could not move my eyes away from hers. We stood there looking at each other. For a few seconds, I felt different. She ran her left fingers through her thick, luscious, dark brown, wavy hair. 'I think we've met before,' she said nodding and smiling. 'I cannot remember exactly where.'

I remembered the face vaguely and her accent too.

Joe washed his hands and tapping my shoulder said. 'This is the man we've been waiting for. You came just in time; not too early and not too late.'

'The agency called me this morning. I'm sorry if I'm late.'

'Just ignore him,' Suzanne said with a genuine smile. 'I'm sure we've met before.'

'Is that the best chat up line you can think of?'

'I'm not making it up.'

We stood there looking at each other. She was biting her pen. 'Your name is Michael.'

'That's correct.'

'But the agency told you that this morning,' Joe said.

'You are from Ghana,' Suzanne said.

'That's correct.'

'You want to be a film director.'

'That's correct.'

'So Joe, I wasn't making things up.'

Joe smiled. 'Yes, he is the one,' he uttered. 'The man we've been waiting for.'

'Follow me Mike,' she said looking very relaxed and happy. 'Now I remember. Yes! We did silver service years ago in Pall Mall. You were with Sandra the first day. You came and worked with us the following day. You had an argument with an Italian guy and you went and sat on the stairs reading a novel.'

'Spot on,' I said nodding and smiling. 'Now I remember.'

Joe was excited. 'We don't just meet again by chance especially in a big city like London.'

'Follow me. I'll show you the changing room,' she said.

'He knows where it is,' Joe shouted. 'He's been here before. Mike, be careful you don't let one thing lead to another in the changing room.'

'Shut up,' she said smiling. 'You're simply jealous.'

'Of course I am. You've never shown me the changing room.'

'Just ignore him,' Suzanne said. In front of the changing room,

Suzanne stopped and stood there for a moment looking straight into my eyes. It was an expectant look. It was as if she expected me to say something. I avoided eye contact. She was still smiling but breathing heavily. 'You haven't changed a bit. You've lost weight and your eyes are bulging. When you've finished changing, come to the kitchen and I'll show you what to do.' She walked away slowly. I stole glances at her rounded bosom, long legs and waspish waist.

'Before you start work in the washing-up area,' Suzanne said after I had changed, 'I want you to write the menu on the board over there.' She held my hand. 'I want to see your handwriting.'

'Don't mind her,' Joe said. 'She still doesn't know how to write omelette, that's why she wants you to write it for her. She still can't figure out whether it's double m or double l.'

'It's true,' Suzanne admitted casting a meaningful look at me. 'I still get it wrong.'

I wrote omelette correctly and she was pleased.

'Good start,' Joe said. 'He passed the first test.'

Suzanne I noticed timed her movements to coincide with mine in the kitchen. She would either deliberately touch me or rub her body against mine. To give me any simple instruction, Suzanne would hold my hands or put her hands on my shoulder. I knew these signals but did not know how to respond. I was afraid. What if it was in her nature? What if that was how she related to people? I did not want to risk touching her. She might report me to the authorities.

'What do you want for lunch?' Suzanne asked later.

'Anything you give me.'

'What would you like, beef or chicken?'

'Chicken please.'

'Then here comes the most interesting question,' Joe shouted. 'Leg or breast?'

'Breast,' I said laughing.

'You see he likes tits and I like legs. Michael, the model on Page 3 today has some nice tits.'

'Why would someone in their normal senses look at those filthy girls on page 3?'

'You call them filthy I call them pretty girls. You're simply jealous,' Joe said.

'Why should I be jealous?'

'Because I like appreciating their assets. Show me yours and I'll appreciate them.'

'Shut up, Joe.' Suzanne said frowning at him. 'I hope you're not like him,' she added while serving me. 'The last time we met you were reading serious stuff.'

'Pictures of topless models are a celebration of women's body,' Joe argued.

'Absolute nonsense,' Suzanne replied and led me to the staffroom where we settled down for lunch. She told me to sit next to her. She read *The Guardian* and talked about Glastonbury: the mud, the rain, the music, the leaking tent and the general madness of the music festival.

'Why would someone in their normal senses go through this hell?' Joe asked.

'Just for the fun of it! There's magic in Glastonbury and you're guaranteed a good time and an incredible experience. One thing is for sure, there's method in the Glastonbury madness where we girls just want to have fun.'

'Did you enjoy the breast?' Joe asked turning to me.

'Don't talk like that here?' Suzanne protested. 'So naughty you are.'

'But he's just finished eating the chicken breast I cooked.'

'Just ignore him.' Suzanne said looking at me. 'He thinks about only one thing all day.'

Suzanne turned to Joe and said, 'African gypsy read his palm.'

Joe laughed. 'Not today, maybe another day. Where's MKJ?'

'The silly cow is off sick today,' Suzanne answered. She whispered into my ear. 'We call the catering manager, Joy MKJ. It means, Miss Kill Joy. She's a nightmare. She hates seeing people having fun. Everybody has to be sad and miserable like her. Are Nigerian women like that?'

'I don't know. I'm not from Nigeria,' I answered.

'No,' the chef said laughing. 'The other Nigerian woman that used to study here was very nice. She was always smiling and greeted me cordially. Very modest and she's the only woman who asked me if I had a good sleep whenever we met in the morning. She was the only woman who asked if I was well and wished me all the best every time she walked away from me. She was the only woman who prayed for my success and good health every time she saw me. She was simply the best – the most beautiful and well-mannered girl I've ever met.'

'Here we go again,' Suzanne said shaking her head. 'He's gone mad. He should be in a mental home. He's going to talk about this African woman all day.'

'I still believe she'll come back.'

'Opportunity knocks only once,' Suzanne said.

'Lightning can strike twice in the same place.'

'Here's a chance to win two cinema tickets,' Suzanne read an item in *The Guardian*. 'The answers are very simple: Table Mountain, Springbok and Robben Island.'

'What about the last competition?' Joe asked.

'I've the two tickets at home.'

'When do the tickets expire?'

'Next week, I think. I'll have to check.'

'Why not take Michael with you?'

'No I want to go with you.'

'Nah! Go with Michael.'

'Want to go?' Suzanne asked me smiling.

'Say yes. The tickets are free anyway,' Joe implored.

'It's up to you Michael. Have you ever watched a film on South Africa?'

'No.'

'Here's a chance then. Let's go if Joe doesn't want to go.'

'Now I'm jealous. The two of you will sit up there and eat popcorn. You'll probably be in the back row. What are you going to do when the lights are switched off?'

'Watch the film,' Suzanne answered. 'You can join us.'

'Threesomes are no fun for me,' Joe replied casually. 'Three is a crowd.'

'Shut up Joe,' Suzanne said smiling.

The next day at lunchtime, I heard a woman's voice say 'Mr Kitchen Porter.' I looked up. 'This pot is not supposed to be on the floor,' she said pointing at a particular pot. 'For health and safety reasons they should be somewhere else. You have to be very efficient when you work here, okay? No pots on the floor.'

I apologised.

'Are you from Nigeria?'

'No, Ghana.'

'Oh I see. You look like a Nigerian.'

'There's no difference between us anyway. Maybe the accent but people from different African countries can have a similar accent sometimes, while people from the same country can have different accents. The borders in Africa are artificial.'

'That's enough,' she said. 'You are not here to educate me. My name is Joy and I'm your boss. I'm the catering manager here.'

'Nice to meet you.'

'Stop what you're doing and put the deliveries in the cold room,' Joy ordered.

'Yes Ma.'

I was in the cold room arranging the deliveries when Suzanne came in. We were both in there for some time. She took out a box of chicken cutlets and we both went out together.

'Jesus Christ!' Ms Joy shouted. 'What are you two doing in the cold room?'

'You said I should put the deliveries there,' I said in my defence.

'I went for this,' Suzanne showed her a box of chicken cutlets.

'But that shouldn't take a long time. And you Mr Kitchen Porter, how long does it take to put things on the shelves?'

'I'm new here and I have to learn where things are stored and in a proper way,' I explained.

'I'm serving a customer; what do you want me to do?' Suzanne asked.

'What's the problem?' Joe asked.

Ms Joy was visibly upset. 'Didn't you see them? They were in the cold room together. You know what they've been doing?'

'What do you think they're doing?'

'But they were there for over a minute.'

'But there's no health and safety regulation that states only one adult at the time or only same-sex adults at a time can be in a cold room. Whatever two consenting adults are doing behind closed doors is not my problem as long as they close the door to keep the temperature at an acceptable level. Some like it hot. Some like it cold,' Joe said smiling.

'You follow me,' she ordered. I followed her to her office. 'You came here from Nigeria to work and not to play.'

'From Ghana,' I corrected her.

'You're not supposed to interrupt when I am talking. It's un-African. I'm older than you and I'm your boss. That's very rude. You have no manners. I've noticed within the few hours I've been here today that Suzanne has changed. It's because of you. Leave this white girl alone.'

'I was only doing what you told me to do,' I protested my innocence. 'If you hadn't told me to put away the deliveries in the cold room, I wouldn't be there in the first place.'

'You did more than what I told you to do. I'm a woman. I can tell from her body language that something is going on between the two of you. As from now on, you and Suzanne must not be in the same place, either by accident or by design. You must not be in the same store, cold room, washing-up area or dining room together. During break time you must eat somewhere else, not in the staff room.'

'Yes Ma,' I said obediently and went back to the washing-up area.

'I've been moved to the sandwich bar upstairs,' Suzanne whispered when she passed through the washing-up area. 'That silly miserable cow is so jealous and vile.'

'I'll see you later.'

'Yes, come to the bar when you've finished.'

Later I went to the senior staff bar.

'Just what I'm looking for, a man with muscles to help me with the barrels of beer,' Suzanne said as I walked into the bar.

'I see, so this is your partner in crime. Now I know why Joy sent you here to serve your time,' Leslie the Head of Catering said smiling. 'I was wondering why she wanted you to work here. So it's because of this young man.'

Suzanne did not answer. 'Is it going to be busy?' she asked Leslie.

'Yes. The conference ends around six or so. They'll all be here around seven. You've time to get prepared.'

'Can my partner in crime help me then?'

'Do you really need him?' Leslie asked looking at me.

'Yes, I do.'

'All right then, you can have him. He might as well serve his time with you since you both committed the crime together,' Leslie said looking at me. 'You can have him here every evening for a couple of hours. Do whatever you want with him. You can even sign his time sheet.'

'What about Joy?'

'Tell her I said he should help you. I know she can be a nuisance but ignore her. I'll move her to another campus soon and then you can go back to the kitchen,' Leslie said with an air of authority and walked away.

'So,' Suzanne said looking very happy, 'my partner in crime, are you thirsty?'

'No.'

'From now on, you'll be my partner in crime, my PIC. It takes two to carry out the perfect crime.'

I nodded. I noticed she had used the future tense, not the past. I could see from the corner of my eye that she was smiling when she added. 'You need a good partner to carry out the perfect crime.'

Suzanne and I sat behind the bar. 'It's a bit quiet. Why not tell me something about yourself?' she asked.

I hesitated for a while.

'All right then, if you're not going to talk, I'll tell you about myself. I was born in the northern part of South Africa, in a small town that is predominantly white, a Boere enclave. It's not very far from Johannesburg. The name will be difficult for you. I went to a boarding school and later studied Literature and Sociology at university. I'm into French literature. I speak French and Balzac and Voltaire are my favourite French writers.'

She then told me about her family. 'Strange enough, my grandfather is somewhere in Holland. I hope to visit him one day. We were never told many things about him. We knew he was in Holland but no attempt was ever made for us to know him or to contact him. But I hope to do that soon. I'm old enough now to ask and find answers to some of this troubling part of my life. I have two brothers. One is here in the UK. I live in one of his flats. He's a businessman. Another one is in South Africa. Don't ask me about my age because I'm not going to tell you. Like most women, I fancy my hairdresser.'

'Why did you come to London?' I asked.

There was a long silence.

'Like everyone else I came to London chasing a dream. I believe London is where dreams come true, where you know who you are. London is where you meet your match. I always wanted to live in a multicultural environment. I was tired of the politics at home. I was looking for new challenges outside South Africa. I wanted a bit of adventure. There were so many changes taking place in South Africa that I found hard to take. I was old enough to leave the country and I wanted to see the world,' she paused and sipped her drink. 'Living in London is challenging. I like the fact that things are a bit chaotic. But I hate London in a way because it can be very harsh if you're lonely. I'm lonely,' she confessed looking at me.

I noticed she was sitting closer and closer to me as the day wore on. Our bodies started to rub against each other. From time to time Suzanne would put her hand on my lap. I started to do the same. 'Here, try a bit of this,' Suzanne would say, offering her drinks. I drank from her glass.

'I look forward to going to the cinema with you on Friday. I'm sure you'll enjoy the film. I'll bring the tickets,' Suzanne said before leaving. 'I'll see you there, darling.'

It was the first time she had used the word *darling*.

Suzanne waved and called my name as soon as I entered the cinema hall. '*Howzit?*' she asked and held my hand. Suzanne was excited. 'I hope you enjoy the film,' she whispered as she led me into the hall. We were both relaxed in our seats. Our legs were touching each other, elbows too. Soon her hands were resting on my shoulders. I looked at her. She smiled – a seductive smile. I gently touched her hands. I put my hands on her open palm. She kissed it and said, 'Beautiful hands.' A strange pleasantness flowed through my body. I was happy but I reminded myself as the lights were switched off that I had to be careful. 'The *kraal* is very dear to my heart,' I heard her say at the end of the film. Outside the hall, near the bus stop, Suzanne embraced me longer than expected. It was a tight hug. I felt her large warm breasts against my body. I looked into her eyes. Her smile and strong eye contact were indications of romantic interest. The eye contact made me more attracted to her. I knew she wanted to hold my hand. I decided to put my hands in my pocket. 'I'll see you on Monday. Have a nice weekend,' she said and hugged me tightly again.

On Monday I was late for work. In the kitchen, I thought I saw someone that looked like Suzanne in the office. But the woman had short red hair. I stood next to Joe and looked at her strangely. I had not expected such a transformation.

'Come on say something Michael,' urged Joe. 'It's Suzanne, looking sexier. Tell her she's beautiful. Tell her she looks great!'

'You look great,' I struggled to say.

The phone rang. She picked it up.

'Shit Michael,' Joe whispered. 'It's my fault. I should have warned you. I told her last week that you fancied red heads with short hair so that's why she cut her hair and had it dyed. I completely forgot to tell you.'

'That's all right.'

'You men can't stop gossiping,' Suzanne commented after the telephone conversation.

I was washing the pots when Joe shouted across the kitchen. 'Michael, come and listen to Suzanne.' She was singing Dolly Parton's *The Bargain Store*.

My life is like unto a bargain store
And I may have just what you're lookin' for
If you don't mind the fact that the merchandise is used
But with a little mending it could be as good as new …
Why you take for instance this old broken heart
If you will just replace the missing parts
You would be surprised to find how good it really is
Take it and you never be sorry that you did …
The bargain store is open come inside
You can easily afford the price
Love is all you need to purchase all the merchandise
And I will guarantee you'll be completely satisfied.

The bargain store is open, come inside
The bargain store is open, come inside

Joe winked at me.

'What's your problem?' Suzanne asked. 'Common, Joe. It's a classic and I really love it.'

'There's a hidden message in the way you sing it.'

'I'm off to see Leslie for the weekly meeting.'

During lunch break Joe asked me. 'How're things with Suzanne? Have you gone out yet?'

'Yes to watch the film but that was it.'

'Are you very close? You know what I mean.'

'No, we're just friends, nothing more than that.'

'I'm not trying to interfere but I think she's expecting you to make a real move. It's time to take things forward. Suzanne likes you and everybody can see it. Don't let her wait for too long. She has changed so many things in her life to accommodate you and has created the space for you to come into her life. Go out and have fun with her. If she tempts you, don't resist. Fall for the temptation. You're young and strong and by the time you grow old, such temptations will not come your way. So you might as well enjoy her. She's a genuine match for you.'

He was quiet for a moment.

'Michael, timing is everything. I think her birthday is coming up soon. Let me check,' he said and entered her office. 'Yes, I'm right. I've just checked her passport. This coming Saturday is her birthday. When you get an opportunity, ask her out for dinner or a drink. Don't be shy. She can only say no. But I'm sure, ninety-nine per cent sure that Suzanne will say yes.'

'Okay why ninety-nine per cent?'

'In life only two things are one hundred per cent certain: death and taxes.'

Before I left that afternoon, I mustered the courage and invited Suzanne out. I could tell immediately that she was pleased with the invitation. 'I'm not sure at the moment,' she said smiling and holding my hand. 'I'll tell you tomorrow if I can make it. If I can't, we could do it another evening.'

That night I could hardly sleep. I had the fear of being rejected by a potential partner. I was also afraid that Suzanne might find out my secret. I felt that whatever decision Suzanne took would have some impact on me. If she said no, I would have to crawl back into my shell and ask Sandra for another job. If she said yes, I'll have to explain who I am to her at some point. And that was one of the things I feared most. I felt I could handle the rejection of a potential lover but was unsure whether I could handle Suzanne knowing my secret. Before closing my eyes, I hoped she would say no.

'Mike, I'm free on Saturday,' Suzanne whispered standing very close to me in the washing-up area early the next morning. She touched me. 'Here's my home number. Give me yours, just in case something happens.'

I told Joe. 'You're on Mike,' he said excitedly. 'If a woman gives you her home number, you are ninety-nine per cent there; it's yours to lose now. If a woman listens to you, you're twenty five per cent there; if she talks to you, you're another twenty five per cent closer and if she goes out with you, you're another forty nine per cent there!' he said. 'I'll give you the details of an Iranian restaurant called Persia restaurant. It's one of the best in town. They have very good food. The people there are very nice. The atmosphere is wonderful and the music is great. They have a lover's corner; just for two with a very romantic setting called Rumi's Corner. I'll book it for you straightaway. It never worked for me. I tried three times and all the women I took there didn't eventually fancy me. So I gave up. I know the head chef and manager called Dara.'

Joe called and booked Rumi's Corner. 'Now we're in business. Suzanne is madly in love with you. Don't hesitate. He who hesitates loses badly – especially in love. I hesitated before speaking to the African woman and see what happened. She's gone. Make Suzanne's dream come true, who knows she might make your dream come true too. The first minutes in the restaurant are the most critical. Seize the initiative. Look straight into her eyes. If she blinks you've won the battle. Tell her anything. Don't be shy. This is London. Lie to her. Women like bullshitters. Tell her anything that will excite her; something that will be music to her ears. Tell her you'll love her. Create an illusion around yourself and let her chase that illusion.'

I stood there looking at him. I could not tell him the truth. I could not tell him what was bothering me; what was holding me back. I could not tell him that Michael was not even my real name; that I was not from Ghana and that I was an illegal immigrant.

'Listen Michael, this woman is no ordinary woman. She's got very good manners and she's well educated. She can take care of herself and would not be a liability to you at all. She's just working here because she wants to keep herself busy. Listen to this. She was supposed to fly out of London for good last week. She cancelled it because of you. She didn't tell me but I knew. This is a once-in-a-lifetime opportunity.'

'How much does it cost? I mean the dinner?'

Joe looked at me, brought out his wallet and gave me one hundred pounds. 'Do you have any other excuse? You've no clothes to wear? You want to borrow mine? They'll be too big for you anyway. You don't know where Piccadilly Circus is?'

I thanked him.

'Make sure you dress well. Remember it's her birthday so you have to get her some flowers, at least one rose. If you want to get to her heart you have to say it with flowers. That's the only way.' He repeated. 'You've to say it with flowers. I'll call my friend Dara to make sure you're taken care of,' Joe paused and thought for a while. 'I'll order the cake. I know what she really likes.'

On Friday, Joe was visibly excited. He winked at me several times and whispered when Suzanne went to the toilet. 'I've ordered the cake and it'll be delivered to the restaurant later today. It's very posh and is baked in only three places in London. I remember the last time she had it, she was so excited. That's the key to her heart. It should do the trick. She'll be wowed. Getting a woman to love you is like a war; you have to attack from all sides and use every means necessary.'

'Why are you so quiet?' Joe asked her. 'I can take you out for dinner you know?'

'No thanks. I'm already going out with someone.'

'Aha! I see. So there's someone in your life that we don't know.'

'Mind your own business.'

'Who could that be? Who's the lucky man?'

'Mind your own business.'

Later Suzanne came to me in the washing up area. 'Where do we meet?'

'Piccadilly Circus 7.00 pm by the statue.'

'Perfect.'

'See you tomorrow.'

The next day, Saturday, I wore a two-piece suit Frank B had given me and arrived half an hour before the appointed time. Holding a bunch of flowers, I walked briskly to the restaurant to be sure I knew where it was. I went back to the statue at Piccadilly Circus. I stood there and practised my initial lines.

'Michael,' I heard Suzanne voice. I turned. She was standing in front of me. Suzanne was wearing a red figure-hugging dress that revealed the curves of her body. She looked radiant and happy and was holding her black coat.

'Wow!' I said looking at her. I thought she looked more beautiful, especially on her high heel shoes. She looked taller, confident and sure of herself. 'You look fabulous.'

She smiled and said; 'Thank you.'

I gave her the flowers and kissed her on her cheek. 'Happy birthday gorgeous.'

'How did you know?' she asked, radiant with joy.

I did not answer. 'You're the most beautiful woman I have ever seen,' I said mesmerised. She remained standing as I continued to admire her.

'Sorry I'm late. I was doing my hair. As they say, better to arrive late than to arrive ugly.'

'You look beautiful with or without doing your hair.'

I looked at her again and shook my head. She knew that I admired her. She smiled and looked down. 'This way,' I said pointing toward the street leading to the restaurant. As we walked our hands touched and our fingers slipped around one another. Walking hand-in-hand we crossed the street slowly, eyes down. I could sense that she was nervous too. We did not talk for a while. I noticed passers-by looking at us. When we reached the restaurant, I opened the door.

'Ladies first,' I said.

'Thank you *Messieur*.'

'Suzanne and Michael?' a waitress asked as we entered.

'Yes,' I answered.

'I guessed right. Please follow me.' She led us to a corner, near the stage of the restaurant. 'You reserved Rumi's corner. This is it! Could I have your coats please?'

'Ladies first,' I said looking into the excited eyes of Suzanne.

'*Merci beaucoup*,' she replied with a smile.

Sara, the waitress lit the candle in the middle of the table that was secluded from the main restaurant. There were some carvings on the wall. From time to time the sayings of Rumi were illuminated on the centre of the table. She took the flowers from Suzanne and put them in a vase.

I looked at Suzanne as we settled down. I did not talk. I decided to let her do the talking. I looked straight into her eyes. I showed her that I meant business. I noticed she was not comfortable. She blinked twice, took a deep breath and placed her right hand on my left hand on the table.

'Michael,' she started. 'Thank you very much for the invitation.'

'It's your special day. You're a special person.'

'That's very kind of you.'

Sara poured rosé into two glasses and put the rest of the bottle in a bucket. 'I'll come back to take your order in a minute,' she said smiling at us.

'Happy birthday,' I started raising my glass. 'Suzanne, I wish you long life, success, good health, peace of mind but, above all, I wish you love.'

'Thank you my dear Michael and may your dreams come true.'

'And yours too and here is to your health and happiness.'

Suzanne agonised over the menu stealing glances at me. She flipped her hair many times and fidgeted with the cutlery. 'I like the colour of your shirt,' Suzanne said at one point. 'It's my favourite colour.'

I did not know what to say. I smiled.

Sara came to take our order. 'Vegetarian for me please,' Suzanne said.

'Whatever the head chef thinks is good for me.'

'That was very easy,' Sara commented smiling as she dimmed the lights around Rumi's corner.

'M&S, nice to meet you,' Dara the head chef said. He was short and had receding hair and reading glasses hanging from a long chain around his neck.

When the food came, we ate in silence.

When Suzanne went to the toilet, Sara told me. 'Mike, the cake will be here soon. There'll be champagne later but it's on us; don't worry. We're not going to charge you for it. You're doing well,' she said winking at me.

When Suzanne returned, Sara dimmed the lights further. The cake with lit candles was rolled through the restaurant slowly on a trolley. When the cake was placed on the table, the musician on the stage played *Happy Birthday to You*. One! Two! Three! Suzanne blew the candles. There was a great applause.

'What a surprise?' Suzanne remarked excitedly. 'How did you know my favourite cake?'

I smiled.

When the bill came, Suzanne brought out her credit card.

'It's your birthday. It's just customary that I should pay.'

I brought out my wallet and paid the bill.

We thanked Dara and Sara.

'You did well Michael,' Dara whispered as he walked us to the door. Opening the door, he said. 'See you soon and have a lovely evening.'

'Taxi!' Suzanne flagged down a black cab as soon as we stepped out of the restaurant. 'Earls Court,' she told the driver opening the door. Still holding hands, we entered and sat down.

Eleven

The Pain of Love

Suzanne woke me up in the morning with a kiss. 'Mike, good morning and thank you very much for yesterday, you've rekindled my fire.'

In the early afternoon, Suzanne played a message on the answering machine. It was in Afrikaans. Her mood suddenly changed. 'Damn,' she said in a panicky voice. 'It's my flatmate. She's been suffering from depression.' Suzanne hurriedly walked out of the room and came back agitated. 'Oh my God, she's not in her room. I'll have to go and look for her before she harms herself. I think I know where she'll be.'

About an hour later, Suzanne returned looking relieved. 'She was exactly where I thought she'd be. I was afraid she'd do something stupid.'

In a cafe where we were eating Suzanne explained. 'Elmarie my flat-mate is also from South Africa but she's having great difficulties adjust-ing to life in London. In South Africa she lived in the countryside, on a big farm. They had a big house, with a swimming pool, beautiful gardens and servants. She was not used to doing things for herself. We used to play in a waterfall on their farm. Moving to London was dif-ficult and stressful for her. She lost it. She found it hard to sleep at night and found it difficult to keep any job. She doesn't know what to do with herself. She's like a fish out of water, in short, she lost her perspective.'

'Let her go back to South Africa.'

'It's not easy to just pack up and return. We're all trying to escape from something, aren't we?'

'Okay! Get her a boyfriend then.'

'You men always think our problems can be solved by having a man around.'

'At least she'll have someone to relate to.'

'You don't understand. She's got lots of problems.'

On Monday Suzanne and I went out together. 'I'll see you in the

kitchen,' she said as we approached the newspaper kiosk near the institute. 'I buy my paper here. Give me a kiss, my magnificent lion.'

I kissed her.

'I love you Michael.'

'I love too but why lion?'

'You're as magnificent as a lion. We have them in South Africa and
I've seen them in the wild. They're gorgeous like you.'

'Thank you.'

Joe was full of smiles. 'Dara said you did well. How was it?'

'Great.'

'You see, he who dares wins. Courage is everything.'

Suzanne walked in later singing.

There is nothing like the real thing baby
There's nothing like the real thing
Thank God we've got the real thing.

'You would say that wouldn't you?' Joe commented.

'Shut up.'

'So how was your weekend anything good?'

'Can't complain, had a good time.'

'So that's why you're singing the song?'

'Mind your own business. You're simply jealous.'

'Of course I am because I don't have the real thing.'

'He who seeks' finds, so go and look for the African woman and
you'll have the real thing.'

'Now you're talking. One day she will come back to the institute.'

'I'm off to see Leslie for the weekly meeting. Back after lunch,'
Suzanne said and pinched me.

Joe stepped forward. 'Michael, keep the momentum going. Don't
feel any guilt. Are you Catholic?'

'No. I'm a Protestant.'

'A word of caution,' Joe said looking serious now. 'Don't have high
hopes. Women in this part of the world are really unpredictable.

Women's liberation means they can choose and dump at will. She probably just wanted to try someone like you. Now that she's satisfied her curiosity, she might just dump you. A lot of women like the comfort and freedom of a secret relationship. Some enjoy the thrills of one night stand.'

'What's that?'

'It's when a woman has a relationship with a man for just one night. A lot of them like a short secret relationship, something to be proud of secretly. I'm not saying Suzanne is doing it. No. I can see she's dead serious. But you don't know what's going on in people's minds. When I first came to this country many years ago, I couldn't understand it but now I specifically go out for a NSA.'

'What's a NSA?'

Joe laughed. 'No strings attached. It may sound weird to you but that's what people do here. And I do it too. Listen Michael, London is full of surprises: negative and positive. So always be prepared. Just enjoy what comes your way. London is where you lose your innocence, where people come to discover and know themselves. Suzanne is a very nice girl. Be nice to her and treat her well. I can see the two of you getting far together. Try and do some crazy things with her. Explore your wild side but not too much. You know what I mean. Do things that when you look back later you'll say, yes, I had fun. When you're old and reflecting on your life, what are you going to say? I came, I saw and I suffered? No way. I came, I saw and I enjoyed life.'

I thought it was time I told Joe some home truths.

'Joe,' I started, 'the truth is my name is not Michael. I'm not from Ghana.'

I looked at Joe's expression. He didn't look surprised. He shrugged and smiled.

'But that should not stop you from having fun.'

'You men are always conspiring ...' Suzanne's voice could be heard as soon as she entered the kitchen area. 'When two men are talking you can be sure they're talking about only one thing.'

'We certainly are not talking about the food and the weather.'

'Oh yeah, still dreaming of the African girl?' Suzanne asked putting her hand around my waist. 'Dream on, young man. The bird has flown away never to return,' Suzanne teased him and turned to me. 'He's in love with the African woman that studied here some time ago. He's hoping she will come back and they'll fall in love and marry and live happily ever after. Good love story isn't it? Pure fiction.' Suzanne laughed, shoving me. 'He's got two dreams. To win the pools and use the money to look for her wherever she is, win her love and then marry her. He's even willing to convert to Islam. She's a Muslim you see. Some men can be crazy.'

'I'm not crazy. I'm in love. The African woman is the best woman I've ever seen. She's as pretty as a picture. I don't need the sun when I see her. Her beauty radiates and brightens my day. She's unbelievably beautiful – stunning. She dresses in simple but fitting clothes –not too bright and not too dark. She's modest in almost everything. She's got a soft, healing voice. She's humble and polite. She knows how to relate to human beings. Everything about her is just perfect. Did you see the way she walks? Like a gazelle – with style and magnificence. I can still smell her fragrance even though she stopped coming here years ago. I can still see her beautiful mesmerising eyes; eyes that confess the secret of her heart. The light that shone from her eyes was definitely light from a pure heart. A heart made of gold.'

'Michael, did you ever meet the girl?' Suzanne asked me.

'I don't think so.'

'I saw you talking to her when you first came here to clean the tables.' I pretended not to remember the incident. 'I saw the two of you talking.'

'You see, he stalks her. He's crazy for the woman.'

'Oh!' I said. 'You mean that African woman? But that was a long time ago.'

'Yes, that Muslim woman wearing multicoloured clothes. It may be long for you but not for me. The one Ms Robertson saw you talking to and was very upset. Remember? She almost sacked you because of that African woman. She reported you to the agency. She said she didn't want you back. I remember very well because Ms Robertson came here fuming. "Look at this kitchen porter talking to that African woman," she said so many times in her angry Scottish accent.'

'And what did you do?' Suzanne asked. 'You must have been very happy.'

'Of course I was,' Joe said smiling, 'One rival down! I was happier when the African woman came back the following day and didn't talk to Michael. She just walked past him. I said great. Now she's all mine.'

'Oh yes, now I remember her,' I said smiling.

'Ms Robertson was a pain in the neck,' he said.

'Joe is crazy about this African girl,' Suzanne said holding my hands.

'Michael, did you see her feet?' Joe asked.

'You mean you saw those too?'

'Because she's a Muslim, she covered almost all of her body so I'm left with a few things to look at and a lot of imagination in my head.'

'He wants to go all the way to Nigeria to look for her. Love can make someone mad.'

Joe went into the manager's office and came back with an envelope. Showing it to me, he said. 'Here's her name, address and telephone number in London. She forgot it here. When I called they said she'd moved to another address. Do you know where this name originated from in Nigeria? Do you know where I can find her? I asked the Nigerian High Commission but they said they could not help me.'

I looked at the envelope and managed to suppress my delight.

'Tell me the truth Michael. I've a feeling you're hiding something.'

'I'm not from Nigeria. All I can say is that she's from the northern part of the country.'

'That's not helpful at all,' Joe said looking disappointed.

I was very happy. At last, I knew the name of the Hausa woman. Zainab Zubairu Bakaro. She was indeed from Bauchi, my hometown. Bakaro was a district in the town, not far from where I was born and brought up in the Kobi district. Now I know how to track her down, I thought smiling to myself.

'Go and have your lunch,' Suzanne said walking away into her office to answer a phone call. Joe looked at me closely. 'Give me some time to think about your next move,' he whispered to me in the staff canteen. 'Don't tell Suzanne anything about your real identity. It might not be necessary.'

'What you mean?'

'As it's often said, there are three things you cannot trust in this country. Work because no job is safe; weather because you can have four seasons in one day here; women because they're so unpredictable here. If she wakes up one day and says "Michael you are history," at least you haven't told her your most important secret. Also, should something happen between the two of you, she cannot use it against you. She looks nice but we don't know her character.' Joe thought for a while. 'You know women don't like too much truth. It's always important to give them a lie. Believe it or not, too much sincerity makes women suspicious.'

I nodded.

'In exchange, Michael, you will help me to find that African woman.'

'Agreed, deal done,' I said laughing.

As the days passed, Suzanne and I became closer and bolder. We went to work together hand-in-hand and returned to her flat later.

'I always wondered how these machines work,' Suzanne said one day pointing at the photo booth near Holborn underground station. I need two passport photos.'

Suzanne looked at herself in the small mirror.

'How do I look?' she asked.

'As always, you look great.'

'If I don't look great in the photograph you'll refund me my money,' she joked as she entered the booth and adjusted the seat. She inserted coins into the machine and sat still for a while. It flashed twice. She pulled me into the both and it flashed twice again.

Later Suzanne gave me one of the photos in which we were both smiling.

'Look,' Suzanne said on the bus one day. 'A short, intensive, three-month course on filmmaking and it's not far from here. Better still, its evening classes. Meet famous film directors and experience the magic of filmmaking.'

'I know about them,' I said showing no interest.

'Look it says here. Learn about shooting, screen writing, editing, producing and so on...What's wrong with you?'

'Nothing.'

'I thought you wanted to be a film director?'

'The course is too expensive.'

'Okay I'll pay.'

'Why?'

'First of all, I can afford to pay the fees. Secondly, I want you to fulfil your dreams, darling. Who knows, one day we might see your film on a big screen. Look it says, the sky is the limit, unleash your potential ... we nourish and nurture young talents...'

'What's your dream?' I tried to divert her attention.

'I'll tell you one day. Now we are talking about your dream.'

That evening Suzanne gave me a cheque for the course.

The next day, I went to the college to register. 'We want to see the first six pages of your passport and proof from the Home Office that you are allowed to study in the UK,' a woman told me in the administration office.

'Fine, I didn't realise you wanted all these documents. I'll bring them tomorrow,' I said and walked out of the office.

'The course is full,' I lied to Suzanne before she asked me any questions. 'It's oversubscribed and I was a bit late.'

'That's a shame because it's ideal for you.'

'Next time,' I said giving her the cheque.

'But you should have insisted.' Her mood suddenly changed. '*You* should be on the lookout for such courses, not me. It's your future we're talking about here.' I looked at her. I couldn't understand why her mood had suddenly changed.

'Please calm down Suzanne,' I said holding her hands. 'What's wrong? Not getting a place on the course is not the end of the world is it?'

The flash of anger worried me. It was frustrating for me because I could not explain to her why I could not study. She continued to show signs of being irritated and unnecessarily angry. I sensed that something else was disturbing her. A couple of hours later, she came to me and apologised. 'I'm sorry my love. I don't know what came into my head.'

'It's all right. We all have such moments in life. Maybe I should stay away for a while.'

'It's not you. What's bothering me has nothing to do with you. There are a lot of other things happening in my life. My father is ill in South Africa and wants me to return for good and I've been postponing it. I don't want to return now, maybe later. My mother seems to have lost the plot. My flatmate has been sectioned under the Mental Health Act. One of my brothers is giving me a lot of problems. He's a real bastard. Come to think of it Michael, you're the only one not giving me any problem at all. You're my oasis. You're lucky Michael, you haven't got problems.'

'I've got problems too.'

'But you've managed to deal with them and be able to smile and be happy.'

I held her closely. 'I love you.'

'I know that.'

It was true – I loved Suzanne. I was having difficulties trying to understand her. Loving Suzanne was a big challenge. She was white and Christian. I am black and Muslim. What bothered me was where the relationship was heading. Ideally I would have liked to marry her despite her race and religion. But because Suzanne was South African, she did not have the necessary documents that would make my stay in the UK legal. It was a strange relationship. We never spoke about our immigration status. I thought she was a legal immigrant. I thought that all white South Africans because of the historical connections with the UK had some kind of legal residence in the UK. I was beginning to think that it would be better at this point to split up and find someone who could help me to stay in the UK legally because this seemed to be my only option. But the thought of walking out on Suzanne filled me with dread. She had shown the world that she loved me. She had told me on many occasions that I was the love of her life. I enjoyed this particular type of love with no conditions attached. What both of us needed was an honest discussion about the state of our relationship and where it was heading. But I did not want to talk about it. I was afraid that during the course of the discussion, I would have to tell her about my real identity and my immigration status. The truth was I was enjoying the ecstasy of loving someone and being loved back.

Weeks later, Suzanne told me that she would like to take some time off work to sort out a few things. 'The pressure is getting to me. Michael, it has nothing to do with you. Some parts of my life are in a mess.'

I left her alone and returned to the house in Herne Hill.

Suzanne did not report for work after the agreed one week off.

'You know where she is?' Joe asked.

'No.'

He called her home number. No one picked up the telephone.

I called Sandra. 'I've no clue where she could be. I heard through the grapevine that you are going out together. I'll do some detective work for you.'

Later that day Sandra called. 'It's not looking good Michael. I tracked down her landlord and someone in his office said that she had left the flat and given them the keys. They have no idea where she is and they were not bothered at all.'

'Do you have the details of her brother?'

'I didn't know she had a brother. Hang on, the man I spoke to was South African. Maybe that was her brother. Anyway, I'll do some more detective work for you.'

I took a deep breath. What was I going to do? Had I said something to annoy her? But that shouldn't make her leave her flat. I reminded myself that she did say what was bothering her had nothing to do with me. Was she pregnant and had she decided to leave the country without telling anyone? Was she ashamed of being pregnant? But she could have told me. She always wondered: *what happens when your dream comes true?* Has her dream come true? Maybe she was pregnant and decided to have an abortion. She was probably ashamed of carrying a mixed-race child. Maybe the abortion went wrong. Oh my God!

Where is she? Is she alive? Is she sick? Or is she dead? Maybe the love she had for me had worn off and she decided to leave the area and move somewhere else. Maybe she met another man and decided to move into his flat. That's possible. She probably met a white South African and decided to settle down with him somewhere. No, maybe it is an English man. But she could have moved in with another man and still continued her work. Why did she stop coming to work? Maybe she and this man are on a romantic dream holiday to some exotic places.

I noticed that Joe was not bothered at all. 'Women are like that,' he said smiling. 'The good thing is that you've had your fun. You've something to look back on and smile to yourself. Don't worry,' he said, putting his hand on my shoulder. 'One day she'll turn up and behave as if nothing has happened. Listen, when you have a bird and it flies out of its cage, let it go. If it comes back, it was meant for you. If not, it was never meant for you.'

'But Joe, we're talking about Suzanne here.'

'Michael, she'll come back; don't worry. She wants to mess you up a bit,' he said laughing. 'Now you know why God created Eve – to mess up Adam.'

I could not smile and be as calm as he was. I was restless and anxious.

'Do you think I should contact the Missing Person's helpline?' I said out of desperation.

'Are you mad? No way! If you contacted the helpline they would definitely contact the police. And who is the first person the police would want to talk to?'

'Me.'

'Are you comfortable talking to the police?'

'If I could find out and know where Suzanne is.'

'But can you answer all the questions they'll ask you?'

'No. But I want to find her.'

'Do you have to? There's a reason she disappeared. Don't worry; she's somewhere chilling out. If I were you just I'd pretend it doesn't bother me at all and continue to live my life. What can you do? If you go to the coppers they will ask you some hard questions and the next thing you know, you're in a detention centre waiting to be deported and then she'll turn up.'

That night, I dreamt I was in a public place where there were lots of people watching television. Then it was time for the programme *Crimewatch* on BBC. The presenter turned to the camera and announced in a very clear voice: 'This is our special appeal for the month. Do you know where Suzanne van Anhalt Zerbst is? Suzanne is from South Africa and has been in London for over two years. She speaks with a distinct South African accent. She is 5 feet 8 inches tall and has short, dark wavy hair. Her brother, who lives in Earls Court, is worried about her safety. Suzanne was last seen in the Earls Court area with this man. An enlarged photo of the picture we took in the photo booth was shown on TV. We understand that this man was originally from Nigeria and his name is Mustapha but he has many aliases, including Michael and Emmanuel. He is known to frequent various addresses around the Brixton and Kilburn area where, we believe, he has friends. If you see him,' the photograph was shown again close up, 'please, please, please don't approach him. We believe that he might be carrying dangerous weapons. Just call the police immediately.' The photograph was shown again at close range. I turned around. And all eyes were on me. I started running but so many people chased me. I was eventually caught. I woke up in the middle of the night panting with sweat. 'Thank God it was a dream,' I said myself.

Twelve

A Second Narrow Escape

As soon as I entered the house in Herne Hill, Jarvo announced in a desperate voice, 'Michael, we have two days to leave this house. I'm not joking.' I stood by the door looking at him. I could see in his eyes and his body language that he was serious. He was touching things but not really lifting them. He was swearing in English, Russian and his native language. Jarvo, the usually calm and smiling philosopher, was now very agitated and angry.

'The person who was responsible for renewing the agreement to remain in this house deliberately did not do it. This idiot was sent reminders by the authorities but he hid them away from other members of the Politburo. He could have just given me the file or at least show me one of the letters and I'd have renewed it. It does not cost a penny to do it just to sign and say yes we are going to remain in this house for another year. Now the authorities are sending in bailiffs after tomorrow. Someone by accident saw the letter from the bailiffs. We could have gone out in the morning and come back and found that the house had been boarded up with all our belongings inside.'

'What happened?'

He thought for a while. 'The infighting within the Politburo has reached a dangerous level. It's moving from trench warfare to hand-to-hand combat now. There are two factions and this idiot is in the other faction.'

I did not know what to do.

'I don't even know where to start from,' he confessed loudly looking at me. 'Look Michael, honestly if I had a gun I'd go and finish this idiot,' he started. 'Look at all the inconvenience he has caused.'

'Finishing him off will not stop the bailiffs coming,' I said.

'At least he'd be gone for good.'

I went to the nearest newsagent where I saw an advert: ROOM

TO LET. I took down the details. From the nearby telephone booth, I called the number. We agreed the terms immediately. I returned and packed my belongings.

Tunji, a Nigerian welcomed me at a council flat in a tower block on Boyson Road in Camberwell. He showed me the room on the second floor. There was a bed and a table.

'Perfect, I'll have it. That's all I need,' I said and paid the deposit. I opened the window and had a good view to the train tracks.

I returned to Herne Hill to collect my belongings.

That night, lying in bed in Camberwell, I began to ask myself if going back to Nigeria would indeed be better than what I was going through in London. I was fed up with life here, I concluded. How can I continue to live like this? What was I achieving? What are my goals in life? It was time I returned to Nigeria. I was beginning to feel that life in London for me would only get worse, not better.

When I settled into the new flat, I called my friends and acquaintances and gave them my new telephone number. 'Michael, I was just looking for your number when you called,' Bilal said. 'What a coincidence! We need someone to help us work in the mosque.'

'I'm free.'

On Saturday I went to the city. Aisha was very pleased to see me again. 'Could I have a word if you please?' she whispered. I followed her to a corner. 'We're expecting some other people to come. There'll be builders, painters and others putting finishing touches. All of us are Muslims,' she stopped and looked at me closely. 'Please don't be offended. If you don't mind, we would like you to have a Muslim name, just for today. We respect your religion but it would be a bit awkward if everybody was calling you Michael in a mosque. Do you understand what I mean?'

'Yes, I do.'

'Do you want me to give you a name or would you choose a Muslim name?'

I thought for a while. 'Call me Mustapha.'

'Great. Thank you very much, Mustapha,' Aisha said with a big smile on her face. 'This is just for today and probably tomorrow. We just don't want to complicate things if it can be simple. Hope you'll remember the name.'

'Mustapha,' I repeated.

'Thank God you didn't choose Mohammad.'

'Why?'

'There are three Mohammads already.'

The work began. Aisha would explain to me from time to time what was happening. 'The Mufti wants to be one hundred per cent sure that those praying in the mosque face the right direction. It's important,' she explained what a man in coloured robes was doing with a compass.

On Monday Sandra called the institute around lunchtime. 'What's wrong with your number?'

'I'm really sorry. I've been kicked out of the house.'

'Poor you, the good news is your Suzanne is in South Africa.'

'You must be joking.'

'I'm not. She's okay. At least that's what someone told me in the pub on Saturday. Give me your new number and I'll give it to somebody who would see her sometime next week.'

'I told you she's okay,' Joe said. 'Women are like that. You completely freaked out for nothing. She's there enjoying her life in the sun.'

'What am I going to do?'

'Nothing, if she comes back fine, if she doesn't, that's life.'

A week later, Joe looked at me with a worried expression on his face as I entered the kitchen.

'Are you all right?' I asked.

He walked closer to me and whispered. 'MKJ has been looking for you.'

'What's wrong?'

'She said she wants to see your passport. She confided in me that she thinks you're an illegal immigrant and if that were the case, she'd call the Home Office and report you. She thinks that you are a Nigerian and not a Ghanaian.'

'Shit! I have to get out of this place.'

'I'm not being funny but this woman is out to get you. The sooner you disappear the better,' Joe said looking at the door. 'I'll call the agency to send someone. I'll tell her that you called in sick.'

'Thank you very much.'

'Good luck and keep in touch.'

'Lie low for a while. I'll get you something,' Sandra promised.

I could not help but think about Suzanne every day. Maybe she was depressed like her friend and needed a little bit of sunshine and a change of environment. But why would she just pack and leave the country? If she were pregnant she wouldn't be seen in the shopping centre in Johannesburg with friends, laughing. Why return to South Africa? What could have happened to her? Maybe she never loved me. I also remembered moments we shared together. I liked her frankness. I don't think she was lying to me that she loved me.

I wondered if Suzanne had returned to Africa because of the weather. 'I love the sun,' she once said. 'I'm meant to walk around in the sun not wearing jumpers all year round. I love the African skies that can be overwhelmingly huge. And it gives you a sense of security somehow. I like the nights – they're very dark and there is nothing better than looking up and seeing the stars.'

There was a knock on the door. 'Someone from the agency for you,' the landlord said and gave me the cordless phone.

'The love of your life is doing fine in South Africa,' Sandra said with excitement. 'As they say in South Africa, she's *jolling*, which means she's having fun.'

'How did you know?'

'I've just spoken to her. She needed some documents from the agency for some paperwork in South Africa. So she called and I've faxed all the relevant documents.'

I wanted to ask if she was pregnant but kept quiet.

'Did she tell you what happened? Why she just disappeared?'

'She said she needed a bit of rest, that she would explain when she talks to you. She still loves you she says. I've given her your new number and told her that you are as sick as a parrot. Take it easy Michael. What on earth did you do to her that she had to run all the away to South Africa. My God! Get me a Masai man who can make me run to Australia for a break,' Sandra teased me.

Two days later, I was lying in bed watching television in the evening when the landlord knocked on the door and gave me the cordless phone. 'It's the agency for you, Michael,' he said smiling. 'Why are they calling you in the evening?'

'Maybe they've got an early morning job for me.'

I was expecting to hear Sandra's voice. There was silence. 'Hello Michael here.'

I could hear a faint voice saying something. 'Hi, my partner in crime.'

I asked loudly. 'Hello, can I help you?'

'*I just called to say I love you,*' a female voice was singing on the other side. I recognise her voice immediately and I sang the Stevie Wonder song with her.

I shouted, 'Suzanne, where are you?'

'I'm terribly sorry. I hope you'll forgive me. I'm still in South Africa. I didn't realise you'd miss me. I've so many issues that would take a lifetime to explain. Anyway, I'm fine, enjoying the sun, the food, the wine. Just tell me what you want and I'll bring it.'

'A lion …'

Suzanne laughed.

'When are you coming back?'

'Mike, my real lion, I've no idea, *just now.*'

'Now?' I interrupted.

Suzanne laughed. 'In South Africa, when we say *just now* we mean something else. It could mean tomorrow, it could mean never. I've so many things to sort out here. To be honest, I've no idea – one month or maybe more. I know I should have told you or written to you but I was overwhelmed.'

I wanted to ask if it included pregnancy. I didn't.

'Mike, you're the love of my life. The best time I've spent has been with you. I shall always love you. Good night my sweetheart. I've your new number and I promise I'll call you soon.' To sign off she sang Whitney Houston's *And I will always love you.*

And she hung up.

Two weeks later, Suzanne called. We had a long chat. When we finished I returned the telephone, went to the toilet and decided it was time for me to sleep. For some reason, I did not close the door to my room. It was quite unusual. It took a while for me to sleep. I was lying in bed thinking about Suzanne. Half asleep, I smiled, warmed by the duvet and the voice of Suzanne. I was woken by voices and hard steps on the stairs. I recognised the voice of Kunle, a co-tenant who worked as a minicab driver. I opened my eyes when I heard what sounded like the voice of an Englishman. 'We want to see all your documents,' the voice said. My eyes were wide open as soon as heard that. I became anxious and my heart was bounding in my chest. I sat on the bed and looked through the gap of the unclosed door. I didn't know what to do immediately. I felt like hiding under the bed. I heard what sounded like a conversation over a police radio. I knew there were policemen in the flat. I looked at the door again. I wanted to go and close it properly but felt it was too late. The trained eyes of the police would have seen that the door was partly opened and would notice if it were now closed. My eyes were fixed on the door. I saw a policeman walked past the door.

'This is my room,' I heard Kunle's voice. There was a moment of silence. 'Here are my documents,' he said later. Through the gap I could see a policeman talking over his personal radio.

'Accident at the junction … suspect….' Then silence. 'Cheers, confirmed.'

The policeman asked. 'Who lives in this room?'

'That's Dele's room,' Kunle answered. 'He's a security man and works nights only.' The policeman opened the door, switched the light on and off then closed the door.

'And here?' he asked.

'He's sleeping. He's inside.'

The policeman knocked on the door and opened it a bit. 'Can I see your passport please?' Tunji came out and showed them his British passport.

'And here?' the policeman was now in front of my room.

'That's Michael's room. He's working as a night porter at a hotel in the West End. He'll be back around 6.00 am,' Kunle told them.

'Has he got his documents?'

'Of course,' the landlord said. 'You can come back in the morning.'

'We surely will come back,' the policeman said moving closer to the door. He lifted his hand as if he wanted to push it wider but stopped. 'Alright chaps, thank you for your cooperation and sorry to disturb you. It was a routine check. We'll come back in the morning to see the papers of Michael,' he said but did not walk away. I could see him raise his hand and tried to push the door again but again did not push it. He stopped. 'I believe you. See you later,' he said and raced down the stairs.

I ran out of my room to the toilet.

'You're the luckiest illegal immigrant in the UK,' Tunji said in low voice.

'Today would have been my last day as a free man in the UK,' I whispered still shaking.

Kunle was genuinely surprised to see me. 'Honestly I didn't know you were there. I just lied.'

'Thank you very much.'

Kunle explained what had happened. 'I had a minor accident on Walworth Road. The other driver and I came to an agreement amicably. There was nothing serious, just a minor scratch on my car. Just as I was about to drive off, the police arrived at the scene. We both said we had resolved the matter but they wanted to see my documents. I showed them everything relating to the car. Then they wanted to see my residence permit. That's how they came here.'

'I'd have been on my way to a detention centre by now,' I said. 'I've got to get out of here before they return.'

'Wait for about an hour or so. Give them time to leave the area. They could be in their car watching. Don't switch on the light in your room.' Kunle advised. 'Go to the sitting room downstairs but don't switch the lights on. At least if they change their mind and decide to surprise us you're not in your room.'

'Thanks,' I said. My body still shaking. I packed a few things and waited for about an hour. When I was ready to go, Kunle went out to his car and did a quick check around the area.

'They're not around. They're too busy to sit and wait unless, of course, it's a serious offence. No one has reported you so there's no need for them to hang around waiting.'

'They have probably forgotten by now,' the landlord opined yawning. 'I don't think they'd come back.'

I could not afford to take the risk and remain in the flat. I dashed out into the darkness. Later in the morning I called Leroy. 'Yah man! Brother Kimani, feel free to come any time. Consider this your second home. If someone is in your room, you can stay in mine but don't touch my missus,' he said laughing.

In the evening, Leroy brought out the bottle of rum singing a Peter Tosh song: *It doesn't matter where you come from/as long as a black man/you are an African.* 'It's the best rum in the world you know.'

'No thanks.'

'Alright, I respect you.' He brought out a bottle of Guinness. 'Kimani, my brother, there's a reason we meet again. So tell me why your missus send you to the doghouse again.'

'You know what women are like.'

'Yeah I know but Melody doesn't send me to the doghouse. As I said you should have more.'

Melody joined the conversation. 'If he has more women then he's not going to come here.'

'No my brother will always come and visit me.'

The next day I called my landlord. 'I told you they'd not come. They've forgotten the case by now. By the way, Suzanne called saying there is a change of plan. She's not returning to the UK as planned. I told her you were at the agency.'

I was shocked by the news. One minute she loved me and was coming back, the next minute she was not. After a while I decided the best thing to do was to forget about Suzanne and start thinking about returning to Nigeria. I started to cough slightly. 'Do you have cough syrup?' I asked Leroy.

'You don't need syrup. You need a night nurse,' Leroy said laughing.

'What's that?'

'I knew he wouldn't know the meaning,' Leroy said, still laughing.

'You mean you don't know night nurse?' Melody asked laughing.

'You need a woman for the night,' Leroy said laughing. 'Let's go to the nightclub down the road.'

'No thanks.'

'You don't want to get into more trouble do you?' Melody said.

'No, I told you the more the merrier,' Leroy paused for a while. 'You're not a porky, you no battyman, you've one missus and she send you out to the doghouse and then you rent a room to chill out before you return, very strange man.'

'He's not strange.' Melody argued.

'What!' Leroy shouted. 'You begin to like him too?' he winked.

'Look at your brother. He's a Church man. He has only one wife and he doesn't drink alcohol. He doesn't smoke. Never entered a nightclub …'

'Say no more. I don't want to talk about Ian. Kimani here is my brother.'

'But Kimani talked about his wife from Africa.'

'She's the one you're running away from?'

'Yes.'

'What? Your woman is African and she give you trouble?'

'Yes.'

'Something is wrong with you.'

'What do you mean?'

'Leroy thinks African women are the best and believes they make no trouble for their men at all, not like we Caribbean women who always fight for our rights. Sometimes we rough the men up too.'

'Okay Kimani I'm serious, I'll get you a girl.'

'Why?'

'I like to see my brother happy and enjoy life. You know what? I chat with Bozo. Remember him? I checked with him and he said to me you're very genuine. I like people who are honest.'

Later Leroy brought out a rasta wig. 'Let's have fun.' He threw it at me. 'Wear it. I want to see you like a real rasta man.' *One good thing about music, when it hits you, you feel no pain,* Leroy started singing Bob Marley's song. Later he played *No Woman No Cry* which we sang together.

'So, your missus send you to the doghouse just because she has bad mood. As Bob Marley said: *Truth is everybody is going to hurt you: you just gotta find the ones worth suffering for.* He shook his head. 'I can understand. I say have more. Put it this way, the more women you have the less you care. It's all in the mind as they say. See, Kimani, whether you have one, two, three or four you'll have problems so why not have four?'

'I don't have the energy.'

'What you mean you don't have the energy? Okay me know the answer. If women here send you to the doghouse, I'll take you to Montego Bay in Jamaica and get you a nice girl. So many girls looking for young honest and genuine men like you.'

After five days I decided to return to the flat in Camberwell.

'My African friend and brother,' Leroy said as I was about to leave. 'I'm really sad you're going but am happy to see you again. I hope you resolve the issues with your missus. Going to the doghouse is not good for a man. Give her a child. If she has a child then she will not send you to the doghouse. I get inspiration when I see your face. Truth has only one face. Lie has many. I look at you and I see only one face, I see only truth. I have your number. I'll call you from time to time to touch base. Feel free to come and visit. We'll drink, talk and dance reggae.'

'And we'll go to Montego Bay to get a woman.'

'That's for sure. Say no more.'

Thirteen

Desperate to Return Home

From the sitting room of the flat in Camberwell, I saw some boys playing football. I remembered I was once a goalkeeper. Goalkeeping taught me many things. First of all, to be vigilant all the time, whether the ball was in your half or in the opponent's half. Goalkeepers must be able to read the game very well. *Anticipation. Preparation. Concentration. Flexibility. Focus. Timing.* Goalkeepers must expect shots from any player on the pitch at any time, including their own team-mates. 'The opponents don't have the entire team to beat. They have only the goalkeeper to beat to win the match. You're the last person on the line and cannot afford to make a mistake.' These were some of the words of my coach, which I had not forgotten. 'Whatever happens, don't find yourself in no-man's land. Once you come out for a ball, you must either catch it or punch it out of the danger zone,' the voice of my coach echoed in my ears. 'How did I get myself into a no-man's land?' I asked myself. It was the place where the goalkeeper was neither on the goal line to make a save or near the ball. It was one of the worse decisions a goalkeeper could make. I was not in Nigeria doing something positive with my life nor was I doing anything positive with my life in the UK.

As I stood there watching the boys playing football, I asked myself. Where did I take the wrong step and made the wrong judgement? Where did I fail to anticipate something? Where did I lose concentration and focus? At what point in my life wasn't I flexible? Did I make the wrong move by leaving the television station to pursue my dream as a filmmaker? Was it when my visa expired and I did not return? Was I wrong to follow my instincts and remain in the UK? I asked myself many more questions. As I stood there, I said I could face my father and say at least something: I have avoided the *four gates of hell* as he always used to put it. Anger. Greed. Lust. Envy. And yet I had not achieved anything. I knew I had to 'raise my game' somehow and somewhere. It was impossible to remain in the UK and raise my game. The earlier I returned to Nigeria the better. Another voice, faint though, reminded me of what our coaches told us before any match and during half-time breaks. 'Stick to the game plan. Don't let the opponent change your game plan. Whatever happens, don't panic and don't take stupid decisions and play out of position because you've conceded a goal. Stick to the game plan right to last minute. Keep playing until the final whistle.'

As the minutes ticked by, my resolution to return to Nigeria became harder. I've had enough. I took the chance to try my luck. I ended up in this tunnel and I cannot see myself coming out of it soon. The longer I stay in this tunnel the darker it became. I feared that the longer I stayed in the UK, the more I would lose my dignity and self-respect. I didn't want to be arrested and deported. That was my greatest fear. I would rather go voluntarily. I've had two narrow escapes. It might be third time lucky for the authorities. I have to decide, as soon as possible, the timeframe to get out of the United Kingdom.

'Michael or whatever your name is,' Kunle said laughing at me as he entered the sitting room. 'There's a weekend job in the Accident & Emergency unit in a hospital as a porter. My friend David just rang me. I'm too tired. Do you want to do it?'

'Of course, I need the money.'

'Good,' he said and gave me the details.

David welcomed me at the A & E reception. 'Follow me please,' he implored leading me to the changing room. He was in a hurry. 'How body?'

'Fine, thank you.'

'Have you worked in an A & E before?'

'No.'

'Some things will shock you but I think you're old enough to handle them,' he said giving me an overall to wear. 'It can be like a war zone sometimes, especially Saturday nights but just remain calm. Let the best in you come out. Patients need help and as a Christian you'll find that helping sick people is a very rewarding and spiritual experience.

There will be blood, tears and pain around you but you have to be strong. You'll be doing the cleaning. You'll not be moving patients to and from theatres and ambulances. You'll be called upon to mop the floor and clean the trolleys and so on and so forth,' David said giving me gloves and showing me the necessary detergents.

I started immediately. I went round with a bucket and mop cleaning the area. 'Michael we need your help,' a nurse shouted waving at me. I dropped the mop and ran to her. 'Come with me please. I want you to restrain a son from attacking his mother.' A middle-aged woman was on the floor. A young man was swearing and kicking her. I could see they both had some injuries. Two other people tried to restrain the young man. The nurse went to protect the mother while I pulled the young man away. He was agitated and determined to hit his mother. I could see and smell he was drunk. 'You bitch,' he would swear at his mother. The young boy in his early twenties freed himself from my grip and attacked his mother again. I ran after him and pulled him back. He turned to me. 'I'll beat the shit out of you, fucking black bastard.' He hit me. I did not hit him back. He tried several times to hit me again but I managed to stop him. 'If you hit me,' he threatened, 'I'll do you GBH' (grievous bodily harm).

Two male nurses came and took him away. I cleaned the vomit off the floor and the blood on the seats. 'If you see the full effects of alcohol as I have seen over the years you'd not put a drop of it in your mouth,' David said.

'Can you believe it, a son swearing and beating his mother?'

'Alcohol destroys families and lives. So many come here with wounds you cannot imagine. Saturday nights are the worst. We spend so much time and energy attending to people who are drunk. It hurts me to see law-abiding, tax-paying citizens, especially pensioners, sitting and waiting while alcoholics are attended to first. These are people who deliberately intoxicated themselves.'

The next day David wanted to know more about me. I told him a lie and concluded that I was looking forward to returning to Nigeria in a matter of months 'with my head intact.'

David was sympathetic. 'I know a lot of us come here and we don't get what we really want or what really brought us here. Sometimes maybe what's good for us is back home not here. Sometimes it's good to return before one gets stuck here. You see, not all dreams are meant to come true.' He paused. 'But I know a place where if you work hard, you can make a lot of money within a very short time, real money. Cash in hand. No taxes.'

My eyes were wide open, 'Where?'

He did not tell me immediately. 'From the money I made there within the last six months, I bought a big piece of land and built a four-bedroom house in my village in Nigeria.' He counted his fingers smiling... 'Six months. I swear by the name of Jesus Christ.'

'Where is it? I'd like to work there too.'

'It's very hard work.' He hesitated for a while. 'It's outside London but there are places you can do the same job inside London.' He stepped closer and whispered. 'Washing dead bodies gives you good money.' He could see that I was not excited any more. 'Well some-body has to do it. Money is money. If you want I'll introduce you to a Nigerian who recruits people for the job.' David guessed from my silence and body language that I was not interested. 'It's up to you. Who would know what you did to earn the money in your village? At least you're a good Christian – you didn't steal the money. You're per-forming something important and you're being paid for it. Michael, at the end of the day money is money and it is good money.'

I nodded.

I was called to the reception to take away and clean a blood-soaked gurney from a stabbing victim.

I finished the work and was paid. 'If I had got to the point of wash-ing dead bodies to earn a living, then it was *really* time to return to Nigeria,' I concluded on the bus on my way home.

I was in the kitchen talking to my landlord on Monday when the telephone rang. 'I'm sorry who, Kimani? There's no Kimani here. I think you've got the wrong number.' I waved at him frantically point-ing to myself saying 'It's me. It's me.'

'Okay, hold on for Mr Michael Kimani.' He gave me the receiver laughing. It was Melody on the phone.

'Leroy is not feeling well but that's not what I'm calling to talk about. There's a job in the care home at Sloane Square where I work. Leroy says I should ask you first before we get somebody from the agency. Do you want to work?'

'Yes.'

Melody gave me the details.

'I'd rather care for old people than washed dead bodies,' I said to myself as I turned onto the street where the old people's home was located.

'Ah Michael!' Melody said as I knocked and entered the staff room. 'Everyone please meet Michael Kimani. He'll be working as the temporary general assistant.'

'Hi everyone,' I said to the dozen people in the staff room.

I followed Melody to her office. 'You wouldn't believe it Michael, the girl doing the job ran away with her brother-in-law. Someone married to her sister. Crazy world we live in.'

'How's Leroy?'

'He's all right. I notice he's always happy when you are there. There's a kind of chemistry.' Melody said and brought out a file. 'It's a four-day-a-week job. 6.00 am to 5.00 pm. I'll need your NI number. Your job is to help with everything here, understood?'

'Yes.'

'You can be called upon to work in the kitchen, work as a security man, help old people walk around and so on and so forth.' Melody showed me around the building. 'Hello young lady,' Melody said to a very frail woman who was struggling to walk. 'Where are you sneaking out to?'

'I'm going out to do some naughty things,' the old woman replied smiling.

'Michael, be a gentleman. Take her for a walk in the garden.'

'Thank you,' the old woman she said.

'You see, young lady, you're never too old to be taken out for a walk.'

I helped the old woman walk to a bench outside in the well-groomed garden with tastefully arranged flowers. 'That's very kind of you,' she said sitting down on the bench. 'My name is Rosemary. Please do me a favour. Could you get me any newspaper from the reception?'

I went and took a copy of *The Telegraph.*

'Read any news for me please, anything including obituaries. It doesn't matter which one. Just read it into my ears. I'm a bit deaf.'

I started reading the main story. 'Thank you,' she said. 'Your voice is really African. It reminds me of my days in Salisbury, Rhodesia. Where are you from?'

'Nigeria.'

'Why do the military in Nigeria like taking over power?'

'I don't know. I'm not in the military.'

'But it's your country.'

'Yes it is.'

'What are you doing in this country?'

'I'm studying.'

'Do you intend to return home?'

'Yes I do.'

'When?'

'I don't know, when I finish my studies.'

'Are you married?'

'No I'm not.'

'Why are you not married?'

'Because I don't have the money.'

'I suppose you need money to maintain a family.' She smiled. 'I was born and brought up in Salisbury, Rhodesia. I suppose you're too young to know the history of that country.' I did not answer. 'My husband and I came to the UK after the world claimed that Ian Smith had lost the elections. Henry, my dear husband, died a few years after we came to the UK. He was heartbroken that we had lost Rhodesia.' She paused. 'Such is life isn't it? Never thought I would be in an old people's home in London. Always thought I would die and be buried in Salisbury. Mind you I'm here for a short period of time, I mean in the old people's home. My sons are too busy to look after me so they put me here so that I can talk to other people and be taken care of. What is your African name?'

'Danquah.'

'That reminds me of one of our servants called Mahangwa. He was a very nice boy. Mind you he had five children but we still called them boys. We treated the natives very well. They never complained. Are you coming to work tomorrow?'

'Yes.'

'Remind me to read you some poems I wrote about Rhodesia. As I said my son brought me here for some days. I'm going back to Teddington tomorrow.'

There was a long silence. She started something I thought was one of her poems.

Land of Cecil, land of plenty
Land of joy, land of glory
Land of hope, land of peace
I can hear the thunder
I can hear the sound of the falling water
I can see the magnificent Falls of Victoria
I can feel the sun right in my bone
I can see the thick darkness of the night
Bury me anywhere in Rhodesia
Somewhere near Salisbury
My hero forever remains Cecil.

Rosemary remained silent for a while. She looked sad. 'That's life.' She stood up and admired the flowers in the garden. 'We used to have a beautiful garden in Salisbury but we had to leave everything behind.'

The next day, Rosemary told me that she was going back that day. 'Will you come and say goodbye? I'll miss your voice and your kindness when I return to Teddington.'

At 4.00 pm I waited at the reception. Melody came out with Rosemary and her belongings. 'Michael,' Melody started looking a bit stressed, 'A minicab will come and take you and her to her son's office. He'll drop her there and bring you back.' When the minicab arrived I helped her into the car and sat in front. In front of her son's office in Mayfair, I helped her out of the car.

'That's very kind of you Mr Mahangwa,' she said smiling.

A young woman came out of the building. She was wearing high-heeled shoes and walked carefully towards me. She had a very posh accent and wore very bright lipstick. 'Hi, I'm Danny's secretary. Danny is her son. He's very busy right now would greatly appreciate it if you could wait with her for a while. I'll release the minicab driver. Danny will sort you out.'

I helped Rosemary into the lift and then into the spacious and well-decorated office which had a huge chandelier hanging from a high ceiling. We sat on a thick leather chair.

'Hi mum,' said a man wearing a blue shirt over jeans. He waved at her and asked, 'Are you okay?'

He was holding a mobile phone. Rosemary did not respond. He continued to speak on the phone. 'Yes, I'll be there. No. Not with her. I've got another one. Don't mess this up for me. Please be sure you get her name right. Yes the event is going ahead. No idea. Bye.'

He looked at me and smiled. 'Busy busy busy! It's non-stop. That's my life. Louise,' he called his secretary. 'Please arrange for another minicab to take my mum and Mike to Teddington?'

'Done Danny,'

The two went into his office. The moment the door was closed, Rosemary whispered with a hint of sadness. 'Since we sent him to boarding school in the UK he's never really sat down and talked to me. It's business, money, girlfriends, hobbies, horses and cars. You name it but no time for me his mother. Such is life isn't it? Sometimes I wish I'd remained in Salisbury, at least I'd have many natives around me. I would never be lonely. But I would never go back. Not with that man in power there.'

I was watching the huge television in the office. There were small cars racing on a circuit.

'Formula One,' Rosemary said shaking her head. 'That's what he's into.'

Louise came out of Danny's office. 'The minicab is here. The cab will take you to Teddington first and drop you at the care home.'

As I was about to enter the lift with Rosemary, Danny ran out and stopped the doors from closing. Still talking on his mobile phone, he opened his wallet and gave me £200. 'I'm sorry for all the inconvenience I've caused. I'm so confused today. Thank you very much Michael.'

'Thank you Danny.'

The next morning Melody whispered on the corridor. 'That's Mr Why.' An old man was standing holding the handrail on the corridor with his mouth partly opened, looking at us. His expression was like someone in a state of shock. He stared at us.

'Why?' he asked in a faint voice as we were about to walk past him.

'Mister, I don't know why,' Melody replied politely. When we passed him Melody explained. 'Mr Why, as we call him, is from either Greece or Cyprus. We were told that he made a lot of money in mining somewhere in Africa. Then he went into shipping, real estate and retail. He had businesses everywhere in the world. He has three children, two boys and one girl. Some years ago they started fighting over this money. Not just with lawyers. We heard that one brother almost killed another. There was another fight between the son-in-law and another brother. There is one big divorce case going on. The old man tried and failed to reconcile his children. In the end one of them dumped him here. But even here he's not at peace with himself, that's why he asked all the time '*Why?*' From time to time I sit and talk with him. I listen to him. It's sad, very sad. He asked all the time why they fight over his money. He thinks there is enough for all of them till they die. Why are they treating him like this? Why are they not listening to him? Why do none of them even visit him? All of them live within 10 miles of here but no one visits him. Christmas comes and goes, Easter comes and goes and no one visits or even sends a card to their father. Not even a phone call. They are busy fighting each other day and night and he wants to know what he has done wrong. He wants to know why?'

'How's life treating you comrade?' Ama asked as I entered Taj's car one Sunday morning.

'I'm fine but I'm returning to Nigeria soon.'

Taj looked at me seriously. I could tell he was very concerned. Jarvo let out a deep sigh. I sensed they were not happy with what I said. I regretted blurting it out.

'Why?' Ama asked.

'I'm fed up.'

'That's not an excuse,' Jarvo stammered. 'You have to keep fighting. We're all fed up here but we just don't pack our bags and leave.'

Taj started driving.

Ama sitting in the front of the car turned and looked at me. 'You can't just give up the struggle like that Comrade. The struggle continues until total victory is achieved.'

I did not answer. I regretted telling them that I wanted to return to Nigeria. 'How's the infighting in the Politburo?' I asked, trying to divert their attention.

Jarvo laughed. 'We're still at it and I can see it going on for a long time – to the very bitter end. I'm enjoying it.'

Taj cleared his throat as we approached a traffic light. 'Our future Sembène, I can still remember the face you came into this country with that day at Heathrow Airport. I would like you to return to Nigeria with pride and confidence that you have achieved something here. There's time for everything and this is not the right time for you to return. It is true Africa needs us, people like you and me but we must return with the right attitude and qualifications not as a defeated person. You can make your contribution to the Pan African liberation struggle in many forms and in many places. In life we always reach crossroads – all of us but we also need to sit down and reflect before taking any path because we may not get the opportunity to come back and take another path. There is a reason why you are where you are now.' He paused. 'See, we're waiting at the traffic light. It's red. Now look, it's yellow and then green.' He engaged the gear and continued to drive. 'Life is not that automated to switch within given time. God does not put specific time limit for all of us as to when we experience the red light, the yellow and the green. Look, the signal up ahead says what?'

'Diversion.'

'Minutes ago we were driving on a dual carriageway hoping it would take us to a particular place within a particular time. Now, we're being diverted. We have no idea how far this diversion will take us. It's possible for us to be diverted elsewhere. That's life. Things happen and we change direction. If you're travelling on a road and everything is coming your way, are you in the right lane?'

I thought for a while and then answered. 'No.'

'What's likely to happen if you suddenly change lanes?'

'Accident.'

'As a Muslim you should always remember the concept of *Sabr*, (Patience). As you know in Hausa we say: *Hakuri maganin zaman duniya* (patience is the panacea for living). We also say something like: *Mai hakuri yakan dafa dutse* (patience often wins in the end). You've got all the tools to make you succeed in the UK and I'm sure you will succeed one day. What if Allah is testing your patience? What if what He's got in store for you is scheduled for next year and you decide to leave this year? If Almighty Allah says this is where you will get what He has planned for you, why go? Do you remember what's written on buses in Nigeria? 'GOD'S TIME IS THE BEST.'

Jarvo quoted Confucius: *It does not matter how slow you go as long as you don't stop.*

'I can see Babu is here already,' Taj said parking his car in front of a pub. 'That's his car there.' Turning to me, he said. 'You'll enjoy the gospel according to Babu. The best analysis you can get on Africa. Feel free to ask him any question.'

We entered the pub called The King's Head. Taj introduced me to Babu. He was an old man with grey hair and moustache. He was a soft-spoken, measured man who had a sharp look in his eyes.

'This is what we call Babu's corner,' Taj said laughing.

'I'm pleased to meet you Mustapha. We need filmmakers like Sembène. Where are we with the film?'

I did not know what to say. I did not want to lie to a respectable elder like Babu. I moved closer and whispered, 'I'm thinking of leaving the country soon. My immigration status is making it difficult for me to survive, let alone pursue my dream. I'm in a dark tunnel and I've no idea when I'm going to get out and see the light.'

Babu listened attentively. Just as he was about to talk, a group of Sudanese arrived in Babu's corner. He stood up and welcomed them.

About three hours later we left the pub. 'So Sembène,' Taj started while driving. 'Life is full of challenges. I hope, pray and believe that one day you'll look back and laugh at the decision to return home at this point in time. If every time you have a scratch on your body you scream, you'll lose your voice. We need these wounds in life from time to time to make us stronger and wiser. It's through these wounds that we get enlightenment, that our lives are enriched.'

'Don't be a quitter Comrade,' Ama added. 'Keep fighting. Challenges make life more interesting and your life becomes more meaningful when you overcome them.'

'Nothing is straightforward in this country. London is testing you; don't fail the test,' Jarvo joined the conversation. 'I think you need a little bit of vodka to help you see through the fog. It was George Bernard Shaw who rightly said that alcohol is the anaesthesia by which we endure the operation of life.'

I allowed them to talk. They don't know how I felt and what it was like to be an illegal immigrant, I thought. I resolved not to discuss this matter with anyone. I'll just leave the country. I've made up my mind and there was no going back.

I arrived at the old people's home around noon several days later. I was on a different shift. I went through the side entrance and changed into my overall. It had become a habit to go into some of the rooms and greet the old people. On this particular day I thought I would greet Mr Why. I knocked and opened the door. As I tried to enter, I felt as if someone or something was blocking me or holding me back. I could not take the next step. I noticed there was someone lying, fully covered with a white sheet on the bed. It was unusual for him to be in bed at that time of the day. Usually he would be staring vacantly at the gardens from his window with a cup of tea. I felt that something was not right. I closed the door and went to the staff room. Melody, who was the closest to the door, said in a whisper. 'Mr Why died less than an hour ago. He complained of a headache. We called the hospital but before they could get here he was gone. You'll see his body later. You know what, Michael, he died still asking why. He never had peace or answers right up to his last breath. Why?'

The daytime security man called John suggested that we meet and pray for the departed soul of Mr Why. John, a Nigerian, said in a loud voice, 'We are his last family. We cared for him and we have a duty to pray for his soul.'

No one objected.

We gathered in his room, eight of us, around his bed. From where I was standing, I could see his face. The same expression that greeted me the first time I had met him in the corridors – a tired face, full of bitterness and anger written over it. His eyes were wide open and his mouth too. It was as if he were asking, 'why?'

John spoke first. 'We all knew and called him Mr Why. We found his surname too difficult to pronounce. I remember very well the first time he was brought to this care home. The first question he asked when he alighted from the car was, 'Why did they bring me here? Why are they doing this to me? Why? They could have left me at home. I didn't want to come here. Mr Why made us laugh when he was not asking the same question. This man thought that his problems would be solved by money but they were not. I now call on Michael Kimani to lead us in saying the Lord's Prayer.'

I was taken by surprise. I looked sharply at him. He smiled. Luckily I went to a missionary school and memorised the Lord's Prayer. I cleared my throat and started slowly:

Our Father who art in heaven
Hallowed be thy Name
Thy kingdom come
Thy will be done on earth
As it is in heaven …'

The pace at which I was reciting the Lord's Prayer was probably too slow for John. He joined the prayer with his loud voice and hastened it to the end. John said a prayer. 'Our Father, please forgive Mr Why for all his sins. May his soul rest in peace. May he at last sleep without asking why.'

A couple of hours later the daughter of the deceased arrived with friends and relatives in two Mercedes-Benz cars. She was dressed in black. She wore huge dark glasses with golden frames over her eyes. Two female relatives held her as she appeared to be sobbing. A photographer accompanied them and took pictures at every turn. Another man had a video camera, which he used to record every movement of the daughter. The woman spent a few minutes in her late father's room with his remains. When she emerged, she went straight into her car and they drove off.

'You see the type of person she is?' Sangita the woman at the reception asked. 'Not a single word to us. Not even greetings. Not even how are you? She could as well have said *thank you*, at least we cared for her late father.'

'We'll miss him,' John said thoughtfully. 'I really liked watching him when he asked why. It made me think. His life is a big lesson for all of us.'

'We don't know how he made his money,' Melody said. 'What goes round comes around.'

'You're right,' Sangita joined the conversation nodding. 'He must have done horrible things in his past life.' She said something like *bad karma*.

'Whatever our opinions are, it's still a tragedy that shouldn't have happened. He was denied love because of the love of money, which as we all know is the root of all evil,' John said.

I cleared my throat. 'As a Christian, I would say that we shouldn't judge him because the Holy Bible says *Judge not so that ye shall not be judged.*

Later Melody called me to her office, closed the door and whispered. 'Remember Rosemary, the old woman you took to her son's house in Teddington?'

'Yes.'

'She called to ask if you could call her.' She gave me a piece of paper with a telephone number on it. 'Go outside the building and call from the public telephone booth. We don't want anybody else to hear your conversation. Walls have ears. Listen Michael, if she wants you to help her, and I think that's why she called, then it should be cash in hand to you. Don't let them pay you through the care home, okay?'

I nodded.

'They have money. You need money.'

'Thank you very much.'

'Listen Michael, I didn't tell you anything.'

'Of course, you didn't.'

I went outside the old people's home and called the Teddington number. 'Ah Mr Mahangwa, so sorry I mean the Nigerian man,' Rosemary said as soon as she was given the telephone. 'Nice to hear your voice again! I would like you to come here and read the papers to me or just talk. It doesn't really matter whether it's morning or evening. So either before you go to the care home or after – if you have the time of course. You can spend longer hours here over the weekends. Don't worry, my son Danny has a lot of money and he'll pay you cash and not the care home.'

I was delighted. I went to Teddington the next day. 'I knew I would meet you again. I know something no one knows and I've told my two sons some things about you. That's why when I said I wanted you to come, Danny did not object.'

I pretended not to listen.

The next Sunday I went to The King's Head. I joined Taj and Jarvo who were already seated in Babu's corner.

'I hope you have discarded that nonsensical idea of yours,' Taj said offering me peanuts.

I did not reply.

Jarvo drank from his pint of Guinness and said, 'It happens to all of us. We all reach the point where we feel it cannot go on like this. Every one of us wants to leave this place at some point. You are not unique. There are millions of people like you.'

'I'll hold fort before Babu comes,' Taj said and joined a group of Africans that have arrived to meet Babu. I did not join him immediately. I sat there thinking of what next to do with my life.

'Let's hear what Taj has to say,' Jarvo suggested when he returned from the toilet.

Taj smiled and concluded. 'Instead of constantly enumerating what this leader or that leader is doing wrong, why don't you ask yourself what, no matter how small, you are doing as an individual, a member of an organisation, part of a community, your profession and in whatever station you are, to advance the cause of Africa and the dignity of the African. We can either do something or do nothing.'

When the discussion was over, Taj sat next to me. 'I know that you've suffered some hard knocks, but don't fall into despair. I know how you feel – as if all the doors are closed. They're not. There's always a secret path for you but you don't know it. Only Allah knows. You cannot see it yet but the future is bright for you. You know the Hausa proverb that says: *Kowa da abin da aka rubuta masa* (Each has his own destiny).' I nodded. 'What you should do is to be grateful to the Almighty all the time because only Allah can guide you out of this tunnel. Remember that every bad situation will have something positive: *Allah Shi Ya san gobe* (Only Allah knows what will happen tomorrow).'

Babu came in. 'Mustapha, let's talk for a minute or two outside before I sit down,' he said and led me to the car park. 'I've been very worried about you, our future Sembène. I wish I could help you but I can't.' He paused and thought for a while. 'Nigeria is not what you think it is. It has changed. You have changed too. The last time we met you said you were in a tunnel. I like the way you put it but what I don't like is the context. We all go through tunnels in our lives. It's part and parcel of life. It's how you endure the walk that determines the way in which you see and receive the light at the end of the tunnel. What you need now is a bit more composure and guile. Look at life in a positive way. Refocus. Change your attitude. We did not arrive at where we are on a straight and well-lit path. We don't attain enlightenment by walking on well light paths with full stomachs. Remember that the darkest hour comes just before dawn. In Swahili we say: *Giza likizidi, kucha kunakaribia*, which means when darkness becomes more intense, dawn is near. *Haiko kule afua* (Relief is not far away) our Sembène. Life has taught me that you cannot rush into light. You have to go through the entire course of the darkness without any rush to appreciate the light you'll receive. I don't want you to be blinded by the light. I hope you get out of the tunnel at the right time. The Masai say daylight follows a dark night. The Gikuyus say water does not stay in the sky forever. Some Africans say you have to be lost to find your way. Keep walking. You never know, one more turn and suddenly light.'

'Michael Mahangwa,' Rosemary said welcoming me one day. 'Very nice of you to be taking care of an old woman like me. I really like the natives because they are very caring…they have strong family values and look after and respect the elderly. I have to admit that I learnt a lot from the natives including the fact that they see aging and dying as a normal natural process and not as a failure; not like here where people see aging as a disease. I hope my son is paying you well. He has the money.'

Danny arrived in a chauffeur-driven car. He walked into the sitting room still talking on his mobile phone. 'Hi Mum,' he managed to say as he went straight into a private room.

'He has been like this since we sent him to boarding school outside London,' Rosemary repeated the story over and over again with a tinge of regret. 'He has no time for me at all. Just to sit down and talk. I really want to talk to him but he simply hasn't got the time. A little bit strange isn't it? If there was a time when he should actually sit down and talk to me it is now. But that's life. What can I do? He's always busy. He has married three times and has divorced three times. He's got five kids. You know what Mr Mahangwa, Danny tells me that he's not happy with his life.'

I could not understand how such a rich man would not be happy.

She continued. 'Why did all these women leave him? He could not relate to them. He still cannot relate to his children. He just throws money at them instead of his time and attention. I still cannot understand why he constantly runs away from things that are supposed to make him happy. Maybe I'm getting too old to understand anything. But, you know what Mr Mahangwa his father was different, completely different. His father was very modest and displayed no extravagance at all. I loved Henry for all his good qualities. Henry was a good Christian. We belonged to a different breed. We were good to the natives. We treated them well and I still can't understand why they stood up against us. I loved Ian Smith. He tried to protect us from that horrible dictator – please don't mention his name in this house. I cannot bear to hear his name.' She paused for a while. 'Why did they want to take our land when everything was fine? We treated them well, I mean the Rhodesians. And this man, this horrible man came and ruined our beautiful Rhodesia. Please don't mention his name. I want to see my beloved town Salisbury again.'

I sat there listening.

Rosemary had a nap. 'Michael,' she said when she woke up. 'You know what?'

'No.'

'I always wanted to tell you something. That's the reason I told my son to employ you.'

'What's it?'

'It's something about you that I know.'

'What do you know about me?'

'Michael is not your real name. You're a Mohammedan.'

I turned instinctively, as if something had pricked me. Then I pretended I did not hear what she had said. 'Yes! I know you heard me. I can see it in your forehead that you're a Mohammedan.'

'I don't understand what you're talking about.'

Rosemary smiled. 'You understand everything. Stop pretending. I always wanted to tell you. From the first day I saw you I knew you are a Mohammedan.'

'Who are Mohammedans?' I asked.

'You know them very well – those people who wear funny caps and kneel down and pray. You're one of them. I can see your forehead has touched the ground many times in prayers.'

I looked at the huge mirror nearby.

'There's no sign on your forehead but I know.'

A couple of weeks later Rosemary fell ill and was admitted to hospital.

I was determined to return to Nigeria. I told my flatmate Kunle I needed an extra job. He made calls and got me a job that suited me. It was a job as a night kitchen porter at a hotel in Chelsea.

I decided not to inform anyone about my plans. Once I was in Nigeria, I would call some people and tell them. That was it. I planned a clean break. Kunle gave me the details of a travel agent at Elephant and Castle Shopping Centre. I did not tell him it was for me.

'Rosemary wants to see you,' Victor said in his heavy accent one evening over the phone. He gave me the details of the hospital.

'Ah Mr Mahangwa, nice to see you,' Rosemary said in a faint voice as soon as I entered her room. She looked very frail and had difficulty talking. I notice that her hands were shaking and her eyes were watery. 'I still remember you. You're a Mohammedan. You've been very nice to me. I've got something for you.' She gave me the envelope. 'I want to thank you and say goodbye while I still have the energy to say that today but you never know, I may not have the energy or be around to say it tomorrow. Pray for me so that my final journey will be smooth and swift. I don't want to experience unnecessary delays. Pray for me so that I can go while I'm still alive. Thank you very much and good-bye my Mohammedan friend.'

I almost cried. I thanked her. I knew that it would be the last time I would see her.

There was a moment of silence.

I looked at her for the last time and bade her farewell.

I stood up and left.

I stopped and counted the money in the envelope in the toilet. I walked out of the hospital with a big smile. There was enough money there to buy my ticket to Nigeria. My dream of returning to Nigeria was coming true. I was so happy. The next thing I thought was to book my flight. I decided not to inform my friends and relatives in Nigeria that I was coming back. I wanted it to be a surprise. I repeated my plan. Buy the ticket, clean my room, give all the books and most of the clothes to charity. Don't tell anyone. Take only one or two bags to the airport. Fly out. Arrive in Nigeria and take a good rest. Tell everyone that everything was fine. I could even lie that I had finished my course. After all, no one would want to see the certificate. I would then go to Abuja and look for work. With a bit of luck I might meet the Hausa woman, Zainab Zubairu Bakaro, and we might click again and this time, no more lies and probably never part again.

I was beginning to hope for better things in Nigeria. That evening I went to a telephone booth and called the number for Suzanne in South Africa. A female voice asked. 'Is that Michael?' I said 'yes'. 'She's away in Europe at the moment. She said we should tell you she's busy with her research for her MA in sociology.'

'Thank you very much.' Perfect, I thought. Now I can fly out of this country and return to Nigeria with a clean conscience. I owed no one anything. I met people in peace and was happy I was going to leave them in peace. I was very happy that Suzanne would not be hurt or feel abandoned. She was busy doing her research, which was more important than our relationship.

The next morning, although I woke up happier than when I went to bed, I was disorientated. Working night shift had thrown my body into chaos. But I was very excited. I had finally fixed the date for my departure. At last I was beginning to see the light at the end of the tunnel. I would call Olu at the travel agency to book my ticket. The feeling that finally I was going to leave this country was very liberating. Even the air felt different. In just a matter of days I'd be out of this place for good, I thought. At last, the sun is about to shine on me. I could see myself entering the aeroplane, sitting down. I could see the plane taxiing and taking off. I could see myself on the plane as it flew over the Sahara. I could even hear the pilot announcing that we were about to descend and land at Kano Airport. I could see myself walking out of the plane, a free person. I was thrilled. I had taken the final and most decisive step; I'd decided to call the travel agent.

Mr Sam Olu, the travel agent and I agreed to meet on Saturday, midday by the statue at Elephant and Castle. I worked overnight at the hotel in Chelsea. It was very busy. I was really tired. I had only a few hours of sleep in the changing room in the morning. I was exhausted when I eventually opened my eyes, my whole body ached. I managed to count the money in the envelope again, four hundred and thirty-five pounds. I put the envelope in the inner pocket of my jacket. The substandard sleep was affecting me as I sluggishly walked out of the hotel. Before I changed buses and took the number 38 bus, I checked the inner pocket of my jacket and felt for the envelope. It was there. I went to the upper deck where there were empty seats and sat by the window. I showed the bus conductor my weekly ticket. The night shift had altered my alertness. Within a few minutes I dozed off. I felt someone sit next to me but I didn't open my eyes. When I did open my eyes, we were very close to Elephant and Castle. I began to rehearse what I would say to my parents. I would start by admitting that the trip to the UK was a failure but that I had learned a lot about life. The death of my uncle and the fact that my scholarship was stopped created unforeseen problems. I tried to do the impossible by staying to fulfil my dreams but the problems were just too daunting. I would have to explain to them what illegal immigration was all about. I would not tell them about my stay in Pat's flat and her dogs. I would confess that life became so difficult that I was unable to practise my religion and this was one of the main reasons I decided to return. I would tell them that I wanted to return while I was still healthy and fit and able to pursue other goals in Nigeria. I would tell my father that I was not tempted by any of the deadly sins he had warned me about. I was not greedy. I did not commit adultery. I was not unnecessarily angry with anyone. I did not envy anyone. I would add that I was always grateful for what I had no matter how little. I failed in the UK due to circumstances that were beyond my control. I was sure they would understand and accept my explanations. I knew them very well. They would appreciate the fact that I had come back in one piece and was healthy. I would argue that it was difficult to find a wife and have a family and that was the main reason why I was returning to Nigeria. I would tell my mother that I could not find a Muslim woman in the UK and did not want to marry a white woman.

I alighted from the bus at Elephant and Castle and went straight to the statue. I looked at my wristwatch. I was ten minutes ahead of our scheduled meeting time. Then I decided to check the inner pocket of my jacket. To my surprise the envelope was not there. My first thought was that I had forgotten it in the changing room. No, I said to myself, I definitely touched it when I entered the first bus. I also felt it while I was waiting for the second bus. I touched other pockets but there was nothing. I stood there in disbelief. I checked my bag in case I had somehow thought it safer to put the envelope there. It was not there. Gradually it began to dawn on me that someone had picked my pocket while I was asleep on the bus. I was very confused when Mr Sam Olu from the travel agency greeted me. He was a big tall man. 'Mustapha,' he asked with a broad smile. I nodded and we shook hands. I did not know what to say immediately. I looked straight into his eyes and said, 'I'm really sorry to have wasted your time. I changed my mind. I know I should have informed you earlier but something happened and I had no time to call you.'

Mr Sam Olu smiled. 'That's okay, no worries. Just let me know when you want the ticket. You have my number. Here's my card. Next time, just come straight into the office. God bless you and have a nice day.'

I stood there in a state of shock. I looked up to the sky. 'Haven't I suffered enough?' I asked loudly looking around without directing the sentence to anyone. 'I just want to return to Nigeria with my dignity intact. I want to return to some kind of normal life. I want to be Mustapha again. I want to do something positive with my life, to make a contribution. I just want to end this long walk in this dark tunnel…'

Someone was rushing to enter the bus and pushed me aside. I stopped talking to myself. I went to the nearest telephone booth and called Jarvo.

'Nice to hear your voice,' Jarvo said. 'Thomas and Gideon are here. We'll wait for you.'

I went to a nearby supermarket and bought two bottles of vodka, a loaf of bread and sardines. I took the bus to Greenwich.

'You look knackered,' Jarvo said as soon as he opened the door.

'I'm fine,' I said entering the flat.

'We were about to eat something.'

'Thanks. I'm not hungry.'

I brought out the bottles of vodka, bread and sardines.

'What?' Jarvo shouted. 'What's wrong with you?'

I did not answer.

'*Nalevai*,' Gideon said excitedly bringing out four small drinking glasses. He looked at Jarvo and asked. '*Slava Bogu!* What's wrong with you? *Gospodin*, a *tovarish* has brought bottles of vodka and *zakuski* (little bites) and you're asking what's wrong with him?'

'I tell you! Just what I need,' Thomas said opening a tin of sardines.

'But that's a lot of vodka,' Jarvo added looking at me, still perplexed.

Gideon filled the four small glasses. 'What do you mean a lot? Have you forgotten the Russian proverb that says: *There cannot be too much vodka, there can only be not enough vodka.*'

'*Pravilno*,' Thomas said giving me a glass filled with vodka.

'*Nu tovarishi, Na zdarovie* …' I struggled to say the few Russian words I had learnt.

'*Davaite ribyata, do dna*,' Gideon added excitedly.

We poured the drink down our throats and ate bread and fish to push it down.

'*Eta da!*' Thomas said. 'I did not know you could speak Russian.'

'After what happened to me …' I stopped talking.

'What happened?' Jarvo asked.

'Nothing, I'm talking about life generally – nothing specific.'

'I was really worried you'd pack and returned to Nigeria,' Jarvo said.

'No I wouldn't do that.'

'You seem to have given up any hope in this country.'

Gideon had filled the glasses again.

'Let's celebrate the fact that I'm still here,' I said.

'*Pravilno!*' Thomas said. 'Now you drink a glass or two not *Chut-Chut!*'

'I'm really happy you decided to stay,' Jarvo said raising his glass. 'To live here you must have the spirit and stamina of a marathon runner. Not that of a sprinter. It's going to be long and hard but there is a finishing line. I'm happy you've discovered the secret of living in London; that is to be able to confront one fear a day. You've confronted the main fear and defeated it. I'm beginning to admire your gut and courage ...'

'*Khvatit baltat* Toast,' Gideon shouted. He was impatient. 'We can have a long lecture later. Now let's drink to the success of our *tovarish* Mikhail. You see in Russia your name would have been Misha.'

'To *tovarish* Misha,' Thomas said raising his glass.

'Yes,' Jarvo added. 'Let's celebrate the fact that Michael has decided to remain in the UK.'

'*Davaiti ribyata, na zdarovie,*' I said and emptied my glass.

Fourteen

Hitting Rock Bottom

'A woman called Aisha wanted to talk to you,' my landlord said two weeks later. 'She said you should call her husband Bilal.'

I went out to the nearest telephone booth and dialled his number.

'What are you doing this weekend?' Bilal asked.

'I'm very busy,' I lied.

'Shame! I've got a job for you. My wife sends her *salaams*.'

'How's business?'

'*Alhamdullilah*. Business is fine. Whenever you need any job just call me.'

'I will,' I promised.

'What's wrong with you Michael?'

'Nothing.'

'I can detect from your voice that you're not well.'

'I'm fine. I'll keep in touch,' I promised and hung up.

I was confused. I could not understand why I had said what I had just said. I desperately needed any job. It had been a very bad fortnight for me. First someone picked my pocket. I was still in shock when I was told the following night that the restaurant at the Chelsea hotel would close for a couple of months for refurbishment. I was not needed any more. Then Melody told me that the care home had been sold to developers. All the residents would be moved to new premises outside London. I was not needed. It was as if one after the other, the lights inside me were being switched off by a hidden hand.

Whoever picked my pocket took more than the airfare. The person took away my hope. It was as if I was getting out of a well full of water and then suddenly someone came from nowhere and pushed me back into the bottom of the deep well. The tunnel I was in ever since I decided to become an illegal immigrant was getting darker and darker by the day. I could not see how there would be light at the end of this tunnel. I stared and all I saw was darkness – total darkness. No sign of that promised light at all.

I could go back to the telephone booth and call Bilal. I knew he would give me something to do and pay me very well too. I could call Gideon. The security agency would have something somewhere for me too. I just did not feel like making any of the calls. What for? What's the point in working? What's the point doing anything at all? I was fed up with washing plates and pots in so many kitchens. I was fed up with cleaning tables and mopping floors. I was fed up of taking care of older people. I was fed up of living a lonely life. I was fed up of living under the umbrella of fear with multiple identities. I wanted to have a family. I wanted to be surrounded by friends. I wanted to have laughter and joy in my life. I wanted to have a structured life. To wake up with purpose and to do things I wanted to do and at my own pace. I wanted to do things that would make me happy that I had done them. I longed for this structured and predictable life of my childhood and adulthood when I knew what to expect every time of the day. I was tired of struggling for years to make ends meet. I knew I had to work but I needed to sit down and think too. I was having difficulty thinking. I had worked for years but what had I achieved? Nothing!

No one, I thought seemed to understand me. The only person I thought loved me had left me. I wondered if Suzanne had ever loved me. What sort of life is this? I asked myself several times. I have no *real* friends, no family, no education, no good work, no money, nothing. What was I doing here?

It was quiet in the flat. Nothing, except the trains disturbed my thoughts.

No one understood what I was going through. No one understood what it was like to live as an illegal immigrant. One is not a human being. It was fun initially, changing names and walking around with a new identity. I enjoyed that bit. With time, it had become a burden. I was not enjoying it any more. No one seemed to understand my pain and despair. I could share my joys with people but I have to suffer alone. How could people understand that you go to bed as Michael and wake up as Mustapha or vice versa? How can you fall in love with someone and share intimate moments together and she doesn't even know my real name, she doesn't even know what I believe in? She doesn't know the country I came from. Should something really bad happen to me, God forbid, for example, accidentally dying, I could be buried as Michael, Emmanuel or Kimani. Who understands the permanent state of fear of illegal immigrants? Every day could be the last day before being arrested and deported. How can I live such a life? To make a mistake is human unless you are an illegal immigrant. All it would take is one mistake and that would be it. All I had to do was be in the wrong place at the wrong time and talk to the wrong person. Within a minute or two all my hopes, dreams and aspirations would be dashed. We have blood in our veins too. Our heart beats just like others too. Wars begin and end. Prisoners are exchanged. Forgiveness follows. The state of fear of an illegal immigrant lasts a lifetime. Prisoners know exactly why they are behind bars and except for those serving life, they have a release date. I don't know what I have done but I can feel the punishment twenty four hours a day with no release date.

I sat in bed doing nothing. I had stopped reading. I no longer watched television. Nothing interested me any longer. I could tell that I was lethargic and inept. I used to be very active so I knew the difference. I was not happy with myself. I forced myself into idleness. Would I get out of this situation a sane person? Tears began to roll down my cheeks like hot water from a burst pipe, tears of sorrow, self-pity, despair and disbelief.

The phone rang. It was Leroy. 'What's happening? Just wanted to touch base with my African brother,' he said and invited me over.

Leroy was in the front garden drinking ginger beer when I arrived. He was wearing a tracksuit in the national colours of Jamaica. 'I was away in Montego Bay, Yah man.' I liked his lyrical accent and his plain talk. It brought a smile to my face. I also liked his carefree attitude to life. 'Nice weather there you know and really really nice women. I can't understand what we're still doing in this country. Having said that, home is where the pension is,' he said and laughed. 'Babylon system is a real vampire, where they beat you and they don't want you to cry.'

Later Melody served jerk chicken with rice and peas. 'We have received news that Rosemary is about to die. She has been unconscious for days now,' Melody said before leaving for work. 'It's very hard, working now with very few people.'

'Don't complain,' Leroy said. 'Our African friend here has no job. He's still smiling.'

Leroy told me about the song he has been thinking about. 'It's in my head but I can't get it out. You look intellectual. Maybe two heads are better than one.'

'Tell me what it's all about.'

He told me and I wrote it down.

'Let's sleep on it and see what we come up with tomorrow,' I suggested.

The next day I came up with something like this:

Where there is money, there is war
Where there is war, there is money.
When you hear the guns of war
Follow the colour of the money

War in the East, they make money
War in the West, they make profit
War up north, they make money
War down south, they make profit

Where there is money, there is war
Where there is war, there is money
Humans are killed to make money
Souls disappear in search of profit

Real money, blood money, big money
Real money, blood money, big money

War is peace, peace is war
War is business, business is war
Love is war, war is love

When you hear the guns of war
Follow the colour of the money
Where there is war, there is money

We don't lie, we tell the truth
We don't lie, we tell the truth.

Leroy was very excited. 'You've put down my thoughts correctly.' We started practising the song in his front garden. Within a few days, whenever we were practising, people would gather and enjoy the free music.

A month later, Leroy welcomed me with a big smile. 'Kimani, you wouldn't believe this. We've been invited to do a show on Saturday.' I didn't believe him of course. It was only when we were in the nightclub that I believed the story.

Wearing my fake rasta wig, I imitated the way Leroy spoke in a Jamaican accent. We had shots of Jamaican rum backstage before the show began. 'Don't be nervous. You will be alright,' Leroy assured me. 'Just close your eyes and sing from your heart.'

Just before the interval, we were told it was our turn. From the backstage I could hear, 'Ladies and gentlemen, please welcome the Brixton Brothers, Leroy and Kimani.' Leroy entered the stage first. I followed him. He sat down on a chair and retuned his guitar. Three. Two. One. He said and started playing.

I sang the song to a great applause.

When we finished, I collected the guitar and with a perfect Jamaican accent enjoined the crowd to sing along with me while I played Bob Marley's *Redemption Song*. Everything went as planned. 'That's a bonus,' Leroy said. 'Well done Kimani. You did well.'

We were paid and I returned to Camberwell to pay my outstanding rent.

'What a failure you have been Mustapha,' I thought I heard a voice tell me several days after our show. 'You couldn't even successfully get yourself out of the country. If you were in Nigeria by now you could be doing something with yourself, something useful, something meaningful. What are you doing now? Wearing a rasta wig and singing in a nightclub in Brixton in a fake Jamaican accent. Your late uncle made money from songs. He was famous, well-loved and even bought a flat. You cannot even afford to pay your rent. He helped you to come over and study.'

Life was now full of 'if onlys'. If only I had not left my job in Nigeria. If only I had not left my country. If only I had told Zainab the truth I could have been her friend and maybe her husband by now. I could be somewhere sitting next to her enjoying the radiance of her smile, the fragrance she wore. If only my uncle hadn't died. If only Alhaji Tanko hadn't stopped my scholarship. If only I had taken the right decision and returned to Nigeria as soon as my student visa expired. If only I had not abandoned my dream of being a film director. If only I hadn't lost my airfare to a pickpocket. If only I hadn't slept on the bus that morning. If only ... if only ... if only.

I reached out for a can of beer from my rucksack. Alcohol now soothed the transition from day to night. A can of strong beer was now what I used to help me switch from one emotional state to another. It made my life easier. I did not have to think hard. All I needed was a can of strong beer to forget my problems. It was painful to accept that I was destroying myself.

Leroy called. He was very excited. I could tell from his voice over the phone. 'I've good news for you brother Kimani. We've been invited to perform at two places. We're going to perform in Streatham on Friday night and somewhere in Crystal Palace on Saturday night. You see, we're being noticed. We will soon need an agent to manage our business. Our song *War is Business* could be a big hit. We could sell millions and make money. Then we can retire in two places – in Africa and the Caribbean.' He laughed. 'You look depressed sometimes. You must change your attitude.'

We performed and made money.

After those engagements nothing else came.

'Let's go and play outside Brixton tube station. A producer or an agent might just be passing by and could like our song and that would be it. These things do happen you know. We have to put ourselves out there to be seen and noticed. I dream of making an album. Listen brother Kimani, in life you make your own luck. Our luck could be outside Brixton tube station.'

I reluctantly agreed. We played for a week but nothing happened. Some people dropped coins into a hat we placed in front of us. 'Don't give up the fight,' Leroy implored from time to time. He brought out a small loud speaker and microphone. 'I think we'll make more money if we mime popular songs. They would give you more money when the tune is familiar.'

I nodded.

'So you look a bit like Bob Marley. You don't have to be a copy. Wear dark glasses. The most important thing is the music.' We tried the trick. It worked. We made money. 'Easy money and it's tax-free,' Leroy put it that way.

Leroy suggested we moved to central London. 'You know what I mean. Places like Piccadilly Circus, Leicester Square, where there are lots of tourists. We're going to make lots of money there. We'll sing only Bob Marley songs. That's all these tourists know about reggae anyway.'

We had a good couple of weeks at Piccadilly Circus. Leroy fell ill. I was on the pavement at Piccadilly Circus one evening when two female Japanese tourists sat next to me.

'My name is Yoko. Meet my friend Taka. What's your name?'

'Michael,' I answered with a fake accent. 'Happy to meet you beautiful ladies.'

'Where are you from?' Yoko asked.

'Jamaica! The most beautiful island in the world.'

'No, Japan is the most beautiful island in the world.'

'I like your dreadlocks,' Taka said. 'Can I touch them?'

'Of course, I don't charge for it but if you give me money I'll take it.'

'Can we take photograph with you?'

'Sure. Say no more. I don't charge for that either.'

I stood up and we posed. First I took a photograph with Yoko, then with Taka. A passer-by then took the three of us.

'We want to hear your music,' Yoko said smiling.

When I was ready I performed an impromptu set for them.

I want to be free
I want to be myself
I came with a dream
Now my dream is gone
I came a free man
Now I'm a slave
I came here clean
Now I know I'm not
I came here healthy
Now I know I'm sick
Somebody help me
I want to be myself again.

I came with a clear vision
Now I'm lost in the mist
I came with an identity
Now I don't know who I am
I was dreaming of a highway
I ended up in a cul-de-sac
Somebody help me
I want to be myself again
Somebody help me please
I want to fulfil my dream.

I came with a dream
A dream of light and shine

All I see now is darkness
As I walk in a tunnel
On my broken hopes and dreams
Somebody help me if you can
Somebody help me please!

The two Japanese tourists clapped when I finished singing and gave me money.

'You need love,' Taka said.

'What do you mean?' I asked.

'It's only when you're truly in love that your dream will come true.'

'That's right. Only love has the power to release your luck. Love is like a fountain from which fortune flows. Fall in love with someone and fortune will knock on your door.'

'But nobody loves me.'

'That's not true. Every human being has a soul mate.'

'Except me. You want to be my Yoko?'

'No I've a husband already.'

'What about you? You want to take me to Japan with you?'

'My boyfriend is in the hotel waiting,' Taka said laughing.

'See what I mean? No one loves me. I'm alone in the midst of people and in the middle of London. Say no more.'

'As soon as you fall in love you'll be fine,' Yoko said smiling.

They walked away giggling.

I felt a bit dizzy. Two local council officials; a male and a female walked up to me. The female official showed me her card and said. 'Hi there, just to remind you that serial begging, busking and street-drinking is an offence punishable under various sections of the law.'

I looked at them. I could not see them clearly. My eyelids were heavy.

'This is the final warning,' I vaguely heard the man saying.

When they left I decided to rest along the nearest alleyway. I sat down under a sign that said FIRE EXIT for a while, not knowing what to do. As time went on I decided to lie down. I was very weak and tired. I do not know what happened next. When I woke up, I realised

I had vomited and was lying near my vomit. Someone had stolen my guitar. It was the early hours of the morning. I managed to stand up. 'Mustapha,' I said to myself, grateful I was alive. 'It's enough. You cannot go on like this.' I returned to Camberwell feeling sick. I went to the toilet and looked at myself in the mirror. I could see that I was a different person. I could hardly recognise what I saw in the mirror. Something was missing from my face. I did not like the face I saw. The eyes of the person in the mirror were dull. I had not expected to see that face. 'This is not me,' I said. 'Something has happened to me. This is not the Mustapha that came into the UK. This is not the Mustapha that was once a TV journalist. This is somebody else. Something had definitely entered and changed me.' I looked at the mirror again. 'You are the problem,' I told the face in the mirror. 'You are the solution,' I thought I heard the face replied.

The person who picked my pocket kicked me back into the deep well just when I was climbing out. It was my responsibility to climb out again. He or she must have spent the money they took from me. But here I was still suffering from it. It was time to let go and change course and, if possible, start all over again. It was time to prove that I could do something positive with myself. It was time to come out fighting. The thief had cleaved my hopes but they must not extinguish my dreams. I needed a roadmap out of this hell.

That evening I resolved to stop drinking with immediate effect. I also resolved to call all my friends and greet them. I would just greet them, nothing more. I resolved that I would not see Leroy again. I promised I would resume practising my faith. It had given me peace of mind, a sense of direction, an inner strength, a structure and purpose to my life, and stability. I had had a first-hand experience of what it was like not to practice the faith. I had no peace of mind, no direction, no purpose in life, no real friends and no … Now at least I knew what I had been missing. I would call Bilal and tell him I needed a job. I would tell him that I wanted to convert to Islam and lead a strict life. In a way, I envied Bilal and Aisha for practising Islam the way I should be practising it. Once I had talked to them and converted to Islam, I would try and get a good job and get my life back. Then I would be myself again.

I went to the telephone booth. I opened my address book and brought out some coins. I lifted the receiver and held it for some time and put it back. I could not dial Bilal's number. I had lied to him. I was afraid of telling him the truth. I stood in the booth for a while. A black woman with a baby on her back wanted to use the phone. She noticed I was not making any calls. She opened the door. 'What are you doing? What's wrong with you? I hope you're not peeing in the telephone booth? Why are you standing there doing nothing?'

I apologised and got out of the booth. Once I solve my immigration problems, I would change and practise my faith. I know what to do. I said to myself.

As soon as I returned to the flat, Bilal called. 'Michael, are you okay to work now? Are you feeling a lot better now?'

'Yes.'

'Great. I'm so happy. We need someone for at least a month. Aisha and I will be going to Makkah and Medina for the holy pilgrimage, *Insha'Allah*.'

I went to the restaurant in the city the next morning.

'*Assalaam Alaikum* brother, I'm very happy to see you again,' Aisha said as soon as I entered. 'This is Jawi. She will run the restaurant in our absence. Sister Jawi is from Somalia.'

I knew I must not shake her hand. I looked at her and said, '*Assalaam Alaikum*.'

'*Masha'Allah!*' Aisha was ecstatic. 'You see Michael has picked up a few Islamic sentences already.'

During break time, Bilal called me aside and said, 'If you don't mind, I want to teach you how to wash before prayers. It's called *wudu* in Arabic. It's important for someone like you to know these simple things. Ignorance is the source of our problems. Once you know something then you don't fear it. A lot of people don't know anything about Islam so they fear Muslims. It hurts me to see a young man like you not bowing down in prayers.' We performed *wudu* together.

'You don't have to pray,' Bilal said. 'I wanted you to learn something today.'

'It's alright,' I said standing slightly behind him. 'I want to learn how to pray.'

He led the prayers in silence.

Fifteen

Third Narrow Escape

The moment I opened my eyes at dawn, several days later I felt a very strange sensation. I was beginning to feel happier. I smiled at myself and I knew I was happy. I was beginning to have a structured life. I had somewhere to go to and something to do. I went to the toilet and returned to bed. I closed my eyes and slept as I usually did for a few more minutes. I usually enjoyed this short sleep, which produced vivid dreams. I had a short dream.

'Be positive. Joy will come when you least expect it,' a voice said. 'You have unwittingly allowed the person inside you to go to sleep. It's time to wake him up. Mustapha, please stop looking around and dreaming. Look inside yourself and wake up.'

When Bilal and Aisha returned from holy pilgrimage, I took some days off work.

I knew the route back to my usual self. It was through fasting, prayers and meditation. I was beginning to think that as time went on maybe I would one day perform the holy pilgrimage. I was far away from satisfying the minimum requirements before embarking on such a spiritual journey. I felt, that morning that telling them would be the first step. If I told them that I was a Muslim I also felt I would untangle the whole web of inconvenient truths about me. I knew that they would ask me some awkward questions. I was not prepared to answer those questions. I decided not to tell them that I would like to be a Muslim. Something inside me said when it was time I would find the right words to say it.

Several days later, and alone in the flat, I was reading when the telephone rang. I picked it up. 'Hello,' I said. There was silence. 'How can I help you?' I asked. There was silence. 'How can I help you?' There was a little bit of noise. I thought it was one of those nuisance calls. As I was about to replace the receiver when I heard something like:

'Hi my P.I.C, my lost lion, of all the big cats in the wild, lion is my favourite.' I thought for a while. The female voice sounded familiar. PIC, meant partner in crime. Lion was the pet name Suzanne once called me.

There was silence. I screamed, 'Suzanne, where the hell are you?'

'I thought you'd forgotten about me,' she said laughing. 'I'm sorry I wasn't sure what to say. I thought, out of sight was out of mind.'

'How can I forget about you my sweetheart,' I started singing. *'I've got just enough love for one woman, and that woman is you.'*

'Thank you, darling. I thought you're angry with me. I wasn't sure whether to call or not. You might be with someone else.'

'No way, Suzanne, you're my first, my last, my everything.'

'Thank you my lion. You know what, sometime ago, I called and your landlord said something like you went to see Sandra. I wasn't sure if she was your girlfriend now. I wasn't sure if she was with you right now.'

'No. I'm alone. I think my landlord meant I went to the agency for work. For him Sandra was my employer.'

'I see! And there I was thinking you were *seeing a woman called* Sandra.'

'Where are you?'

'Earls Court. I came back from South Africa yesterday very tired of course. I needed a bit of rest. I thought I would take some time off before I called you. Michael, I've also been very busy with my sociology project. You know what it's like, you think something is going to take three months and it ends up taking six months.'

'Welcome back.'

'Thank you my love. Are you okay? Did you miss me?'

'Of course I did.'

'I missed you too, lots to catch up, lots of stories. Are you free tonight?'

'Yes I am.'

'Great! Can you come over?'

'Of course Suzanne,' I sang the first line of a song: *Just call my name and I'll be there.*

'MICHAEL! I'm all yours,' she shouted over the phone.

I heard her footsteps running towards the door moments after I pressed the buzzer. Suzanne opened the door and hugged me. 'Come inside darling.'

'I miss you sweetheart,' I said in the flat, holding her tight.

'This is incredible. You've changed. Something has happened to you. I can see it in your eyes,' Suzanne said looking into my eyes.

'You haven't really changed, except for the haircut and the tan.'

'Yes, I had enough sunshine to last another year.'

Suzanne brought out a bottle of white wine. 'This is one of the best wines you can get – very expensive. My uncle gave it to me months ago and I promised to share it with only you even if you're with someone else.' She poured two glasses. 'I missed you Michael,' she raising her glass and started to cry. I held her, stroking her hair. 'I thought I would never see you again.'

We sat down on the sofa. Suzanne started. 'So many things happened at once in my life and I couldn't handle them. I was on an emotional rollercoaster. Where do I start? First of all, I'll start with an unreserved apology. I'm sorry I didn't tell you I was going to South Africa. It was the wrong thing to do and I apologise. I should at least have told you and made it clear that it had nothing to do with you. I didn't realise it would affect you until Sandra told me. Have you forgiven me?'

'Of course I have. If I want God to forgive me, I must first forgive those who consciously or unconsciously hurt me. I was shocked by your sudden departure. I was surprised because it happened just when we were getting to know each other. I thought something had happened to you. I'm very happy to be with you again. Suzanne I love you and that's the most important thing.'

'Thank you honey,' she said. 'I just thought that after a very painful event I should leave you alone and concentrate on the issues I was struggling with. I didn't think through it properly. I just bought a ticket and flew out. Honestly I just wanted to get out of this place.'

I didn't answer.

'Let's get this issue sorted. I called once and your landlord said you're going to see Sandra or something like that. I said uuh, so they're together. So Sandra is his new *cherry*.'

I laughed. 'He meant I had gone to work for Sandra. He's a foreigner like me. When he mentioned Sandra he meant that I was going to work for the agency. It has nothing to do with *seeing* Sandra. I was not dating her. That's his way of saying I was either going to look for work or at work. By the way, he also said that you had shelved your plans and was not returning to the UK. That's why I gave up on you completely.'

'Oh my God! No. I didn't mean I wasn't coming back. What I said was that I had changed my plans. I said I would be in Europe but I was not coming to the UK. Instead of coming to the UK, I would be returning to South Africa. I meant I wasn't coming immediately as I had promised, but later.'

'I was here thinking that you were not coming back to the UK forever.'

'And I was there thinking you were seeing Sandra.'

'Anyway these things happen.'

'Michael, I completely lost it when my best friend and flatmate, Elmarie, died. I just couldn't handle it. I lost something inside me too. Imagine Michael, we grew up together. Their farm was next to ours. She and I went to the same schools. We went to the same university. We stayed in the same room. She and I left South Africa together. She sat next to me on the plane. We both came to London searching for something, dreaming of being everything. Within months it was clear she couldn't cope. The problem was I didn't know what to do. Along the way she started to lose her mind and bearings in this big city. The truth was she refused to change. She wanted to live a particular life, a life that London cannot tolerate. I told her many times, you have to change to fit into life in London; London will not change to accommodate you. Anyway, her death affected me seriously. When I received the news of her death, I experienced a complete shutdown. Nothing prepared me for something like this. I was hysterical. I honestly didn't want you to see me in that state. I couldn't reconcile many things in my head. Luckily, I had money and could travel to South Africa immediately. Maybe the sunshine, air, mountains, the birds would help me to think and grieve properly. It was not easy there too. I was alone. And I thought if only I had told Mike, I could fly him to be with me. But then I said, no let me deal with this alone. I wouldn't bring you in as my therapist. As soon as I am feeling better, I became embroiled in a big family dispute. It's a long saga and you definitely don't want to hear the story. My brother Albert, the one in London, is a real bastard. He's unbelievably selfish. I thought I had run away from these problems but I wasn't at peace, even at home. I had serious issues with my mother. She's something else. It's either her way or no way. My father is sick and remains detached as ever – a very bitter and angry old man. My brothers are at each other's throats. The atmosphere was toxic. I tried to remain calm. As if that was not enough, the atmosphere in the country was not so peaceful either. You know all about these things anyway – the crime, the carjacking, the murders. You name them... But I tried to keep sane. In the midst of all these troubles, I made a startling discovery about my past. That was why I decided to fly out to Holland.'

Suzanne stood up and brought a bag full of presents from Holland and South Africa. There were T-shirts, key rings and chocolates. 'I thought all the while, this guy made my birthday so memorable. He even knew my favourite cake. I must buy him something, even if he's with Sandra. I have to get some presents for this man, my lion, who, for the first time, made me feel that I'm loved.'

I thanked her.

As I looked at Suzanne, hope seemed to return to me. 'To be honest with you Mike, at one point I didn't want to return to the UK but whenever I remembered you and Joe, I laughed. How is he?'

'He's alright. I haven't seen him for ages.'

'Is the African woman back?' she asked laughing.

'I don't think so. I haven't been sent there to work for a while.'

'Why?'

'I don't know. I didn't ask Sandra why,' I lied. I did not want to tell her that MKJ wanted to report me to the Home Office.

'So how have you been coping?'

'A bit of work here and there.'

'I had some job offers in South Africa you know but I said no. Meeting you has changed me and the way I see so many things in the world,' she confessed earnestly. 'Even my father, the man who is always detached, looked at me and said, "you've met someone and that person has changed you." I asked him for better or for worse. He laughed and said for better. If I had told him about the person I had met, he would have gone berserk.'

Someone knocked on the door of the sitting room and opened it.

Suzanne introduced me to her new flatmate, Joanna from Yorkshire.

'Let's go out for a walk and then find something to eat,' Suzanne said holding me. 'I want to rediscover you, my wild lion.'

In her favourite Indian restaurant, Suzanne said. 'If you're not working, how do you pay your rent?'

'It's been tough. I do work but normally I spent almost everything I get on rent.'

She thought for a while. 'Okay Michael, here's a proposal. I'm supposed to start work in a month's time with a new South African telecom company here in Vauxhall. I met one of the directors on the plane. He wanted me to start immediately but I said I needed time to sort out a few things. When I'm ready I'll call them and give them a week's notice. I have some money right now. The only good thing that comes from my brother, Albert, is that he's not charging me for rent. I'll pay your rent for one month and you can stay with me. I'm not suggesting you move in. Not yet anyway. My brother is a real bastard and he owns the flat. I don't know how he'll react. That's not true, I do. But I don't want that problem now. So I'll pay your rent for a month while we get to know each other again. Is that alright with you?'

'Yes.'

The more we sat and talked, the more I was feeling closer and closer to Suzanne. The longer we stay together, the more worried I became.

I was struggling with one big issue – the best time to tell her my real identity. I wanted her to know the real person she had falling in love with. The person she had been sharing her secrets with. If she found out, I thought, the trust would be broken. I had so far succeeded in showing her only the face of Michael. I wondered how she would react if I told her the truth. I knew that the earlier I told her the better. If she said it was all over, that she would not want to be seen dating a Muslim, fair enough. It wouldn't be the worst thing to go through.

'I'm going to Holland soon and I want you to come with me,' Suzanne said one morning.

'I'm not sure darling.'

'I'm going to see someone. You don't have to see them. You can spend a night in Amsterdam. I want to walk with you along the canals, visit the coffee houses that don't serve coffee, eat cheese and try the real pancakes.'

'Next time,' I assured her. 'Yes, I want to visit the coffee houses that don't serve coffee.'

Suzanne laughed. 'Take that place off the list. I didn't expect it to excite you. Don't worry I'll pay. We'll take the ferry after all we have the time.'

'Now I'm excited. But I'm really sorry Suzanne, I can't.'

'Alright then,' she gave up. 'Let's go and have dinner at the Italian restaurant.'

I did not object.

'I like London,' she said as she walked slowly on the street holding hands.

'Why?'

'One can be anonymous here. London has some kind of intoxicating effect on me. I don't know why,' she stopped and looked me in the eyes. 'Michael, you are an angel, I'm so glad I met you. I love you.'

'I love you too.'

We sat down and held hands across the small table in the Italian restaurant. Looking at each other, I felt it was time I told her the truth.

'Suzanne, there's something serious I want to tell you before it's too late; before you find out.'

'Oh my God,' she exclaimed and started blushing, her faced reddened as she looked at me strangely. 'I just told you that you are an angel and you want to dump me? You mean there's another woman in your life?' Suzanne was flushed by my statement.

'No. It's a confession I want to make. I'm not leaving you. I love you and will always love you. You're the only woman in my life.' I tried to calm her down.

'So what's it then?' She said, sipped her wine and smiled, looking relaxed. 'What a good story that would have been. I came back from South Africa, mainly because of you, and then, thank you, off you go, goodbye, I love another woman.'

'How should I put it?'

'It doesn't matter anyhow.'

'It's nothing to do with you and with our relationship.'

'So go on.'

'I just wanted you to know more about me before it's too late. Just as I've not asked you a lot of questions about yourself. I mean intimate questions. You also have not asked me some serious questions about myself.'

'That's true.'

'Michael is not my real name. It's an alias.'

'What's your real name then?' she asked chuckling.

'Mustapha.'

'I've heard the name before. At least I can pronounce it. Go on then.'

'I'm not from Ghana.'

'Good heavens! Where are you from planet Mars?'

'Nigeria.'

'I know where it is on the map, not that far from Ghana, next confession.'

'I'm a Muslim.'

'Of course, if your name is Mustapha then you are a Muslim. I was in Morocco and someone called Mustapha was in charge of the hotel. I also read about Mustapha Ataturk. What else? You're not from planet Earth, a UFO. What else? Is that all? I'm enjoying it.'

'I just wanted you to know that I'm not a cheat.'

'So what's the story behind the name Michael?'

'It's a long story.'

'Shorten it to three sentences. Food will be served soon.'

'Circumstances forced me to change my identity. I came here as Mustapha but circumstances conspired against me and the only way I could survive was to adopt a new identity. Are you happy with that?'

'Yes I am. Do you want to be a film director or did you make that up too?'

'I always wanted to be a film director. I came to London with a script. I was almost there before things happened. I've been meaning to tell you but just before I picked up the courage ...'

'I disappeared. You've a very good excuse,' she said laughing.

'Yes. I could not tell you the whole truth the moment we met. I had to wait for the right time. I don't want to go into this relationship lying about myself. I want to know if it's going to be a problem.'

'What do you mean?'

'I just want to know if being in a relationship with a Muslim would be a problem?'

Suzanne sipped more wine and thought for a while. She looked at me close smiling. 'My partner in crime, my wild lion, thank you for being honest. I appreciate it. Actually Michael, I suspected that you had a different identity the first time we met. Something about you struck me. I looked at you and I said no, there is something in this guy that is more than what the ordinary eye can see. You sort of looked too intelligent to work as a waiter. I can fully understand someone having an alias in London. I think very few foreigners don't have a second or third identity. That's the reality of life in London. For so many people, unfortunately, that's what they have to do to survive. Someone once told me that London is best lived in disguise. So to answer your question, I've no problem with your religion.'

'Thank you very much. I will always love you.'

Suzanne started laughing so loudly that other diners in the restaurant looked at us.

'Actually, I worked for months using somebody else's identity. That was before I got my papers sorted,' she whispered. 'My name was Mary O'Connors. I went around London working and pretending to be an Irish woman. It was fun but I couldn't cope with the dual identity. So I knew Mike wasn't your real name and I was waiting for you to tell me your real name.'

'My landlord told you?'

'No. I knew before I left.'

'Joe?'

'No.'

'How?'

'I called you Mike a few times and you didn't respond immediately. There wasn't that split second response to one's name. You thought for a while before you turned. I was in a similar situation before. It's said that a thief knows how to catch another thief,' she laughed loudly again.

'Thank you very much for your understanding,' I said, letting out a deep sigh.

'So you're relieved now that you've got it off your chest.'

I nodded.

'Don't worry Michael, a rose will smell the same if it had another name. Michael, Mustapha or whatever, it doesn't really matter to me. I'm in love with the person not the name.'

'Thank you Suzanne. You'll remain my sweetest and dearest forever!'

I wanted to tell her that I was an illegal immigrant. The waiter brought our dinner.

'*Bon appetite*,' I said.

'*Merci bien* and you too,' Suzanne said looking at me and chuckling.

'Sheikh I'll be 60 years-old next week and I'd like you to help me prepare something for some invited guests,' Dr Asibong said over the phone.

'No problem at all. I'm free.'

'I want to meet the lucky woman too.'

'She's in Holland right now.'

'What a shame! I'm expecting about 10 people and would like you to cook some African dishes.'

'That's fine. I'll be there first thing in the morning on Saturday.'

I always wanted to show him my identity cards. When I was ready to go, I made sure I concealed the other identity cards, except for that of Michael Danquah. I had been warned by several people never to carry more than one identity card on me at any given moment and that I had to know the names on the identity card. Jarvo had warned me several times that it was a very serious offence to have more than one form of identification on oneself in the UK. On that day I ignored all the warnings.

Later in the evening, on Sumatra Road, when all his guests had eaten, I decided to show them all my cards. Michael Danquah (catering agency); Emmanuel Babayo (security agency), Michael Kimani (care home), Sheikh Abdullahi (NHS card) and Mustapha Abdullahi (Nigerian passport)

Dr Asibong and his guests were amazed. Some were flabbergasted.

'I've never seen anything like this before.'

'Always heard about something like this but never seen it.'

'You often hear on the news about people with so many identities.'

'Aren't you confused?'

'How do you remember all these names?'

'My God, you must be confused all the time.'

'Do you always remember who you are?'

When I was ready to go, Dr Asibong warned me. 'Sheikh, don't let the police see them.' I nodded and laughed. I put all the identity cards and other documents in my breast pocket.

I came out of the flat on Sumatra Road in West Hampstead and turned right. After taking five steps, I saw the flashing blue lights of a police car and heard the siren. I remembered that all the identity cards were in my breast pocket and prayed that the car would speed past. The police car came to halt with screeching brakes. The doors opened. Two officers jumped out. The female officer shouted in a clear commanding voice. 'Stand where you are. Drop your bag. Put your hands up. Don't move.' The blue lights were flashing.

I stood there frightened. I could not get rid of the documents. The female police officer stepped closer. She had pulled the handcuffs out. I noticed that the male officer had rushed back into the car and was communicating over his radio. 'Come again Serge, alright Serge.' He looked at me and continued loudly. 'No does not fit the description.' I thought I heard him say. The female officer also listened to her personal radio. She stood right in front of me with the handcuffs. Something came through the radio, I did not hear what it was and she turned and ran towards the car. 'Wrong suspect, sorry about that,' I thought I heard her say. The sirens were on again and they drove off at full speed.

I stood there in shock and disbelief. I looked up and could see Dr Asibong and his guests looking at me from the first floor flat. I went back into the flat and ran into the toilet to ease myself.

'You know what? I had all the identity cards in one pocket,' I disclosed when I came out.

'What a narrow escape Sheikh,' Dr Asibong said, looking at me. 'In Swahili, there is a saying: *The day you go out naked is the day you meet your in-laws.* You're damn lucky. If they had searched you and found the IDs they would have arrested you straight away. Sheikh, you were born under a lucky star. You're the luckiest illegal immigrant in the UK.'

Suzanne was shocked when I told her about my narrow escape. With her mouth slightly opened, she asked. 'Why are you so *dof*? How could you do such a stupid thing?'

'Every human being is allowed to be stupid for five minutes every day. I was stupid for more than five minutes at the wrong place with the wrong things at the wrong time.'

'You are damn lucky. Now tell me about the other aliases I didn't know you had. I only know Michael Danquah.'

'When I had my first narrow escape, Sandra advised me to change my identity.'

'What happened?'

I told her about my first narrow escape at the bank. 'So I changed to Emmanuel Babayo and worked mainly as a security man in many places. I also worked for Sandra's new agency as Emmanuel.'

'After we met?'

'No, before we met. I can't even remember now.'

'God,' she exclaimed. 'You cannot even remember when you had an alias. Okay, you'll tell me more about all these escapes later. Next alias please!' she said smiling.

'After the first narrow escape ...'

Suzanne started laughing.

'I'm serious, policemen visited the flat I was living in but didn't push open the door. I could see the policeman through the small gap standing in the hallway. He was under the light and I was in darkness. I could see him and he could not see me in the room. For some reason he just didn't open the door. Had he pushed the door a little bit wider, he'd have seen me sitting on the bed. I was like a sitting duck ready to be taken away. They promised to come back so I had to look for another place. I sought refuge somewhere in Brixton, where I was known as Kimani.'

'Next alias please?'

'Sheikh.'

'That makes sense – at least it's a Muslim name. How did you get that? You had another escape?'

'No. Dr Asibong and I went to the GP's surgery and he introduced me as Sheikh. It was summer and I was wearing a long white dress. The receptionist wanted to know if I was registered. I said no. And she gave me the form. I wrote Sheikh because I didn't want to complicate things.'

'So when you go to see the GP, you have to be called Sheikh from now on.'

'Yes.'

Suzanne took a deep breath. 'So anymore names?'

'Let me think. Ah! Rosemary called me Mr Mahangwa.'

'Jesus Christ! Who's Rosemary?'

I told her about the work in the old people's home.

'Life is really hard for you. I'll tell the DJ to play two special songs at the discotheque later today.'

We remained silent for a while.

'What else happened when I left for South Africa?'

'I decided I'd had enough and planned to return to Nigeria. I worked in the care home and at a hotel as the night-shift kitchen porter. I saved a lot of money and luckily for me, Rosemary gave me some money too but on my way to the travel agents to pay for my return ticket to Nigeria someone pinched the envelope from my pocket.'

Suzanne laughed. She almost choked. Minutes later, still coughing, she said. 'You're making this up! That's extraordinary.'

'Honestly I'm not making it up. Why should I lie to you? What else was left for me in London? I thought I'd failed in everything and wanted to return while I had a bit of dignity and self-respect left. I had nothing left to do here and the only woman I loved said she was not coming back. At least in Nigeria, I could do something with myself. But someone had better ideas and nicked the envelope. I was really fed up with life here.'

Still laughing, Suzanne said, 'Your experience reminds me of a quote I once read about London. A writer called Samuel Johnson once said that: *When a man is tired of London, he is tired of life; for there is in London all that life can afford.*' She paused and continued. 'You're meant for me, simple. We're destined to be together. Michael, honestly, I was not supposed to return to the UK. I had an amazing job offer in the foreign ministry, my dream job. I always wanted to be a diplomat and one of my brother's friends is an ambassador somewhere. He told me to join him in a faraway country but I said no. Very good pay and very good country but I flatly rejected the offer. Another job offer was in a mining company. My brother has connection with a lot of people in the mining industry and one of them offered me a very good job. I don't know why I turned it down. I went through a period when I did not want to do anything. I was fed up too and a voice kept telling me to say no to the offers and return to London. My father wanted me to take over a few of his business concerns but I refused. He was angry and I left the house and went to stay with my mother. When I was flying back to South Africa from The Netherlands, the guy sitting next to me was an employee of South African Airways. We got talking and he told me to apply for a good job at South African Airways. I actually applied for the job when we arrived in South Africa because I thought yes this is an opportunity to see Michael or to fly Michael to South Africa three or four times a year.'

'Why did you change your mind?'

She took a deep breath. 'For me, love is all or nothing. I cannot love you on a part-time basis. I want to love you in whole not in part. I have experienced the love that you've given me and I want to give it back to you in whole.'

I looked at her. 'Honestly Suzanne, I'm not lying. It was a terrible experience that affected me badly. I was depressed and upset. It was great that you didn't come back around that time. I wouldn't have wanted to talk to you then. I was not interested in anything. I just wanted to be left alone or go home.'

'And I was in South Africa, also not interested in anything but just wanted to come back to you,' Suzanne looked at me and started to smile. 'If I knew who stole your money, I'd give them more.'

'What do you mean?' I asked with a frown.

'If I knew who picked your pocket, I'd say thank you very much for keeping Michael in the UK for me. Here's your reward.'

'Listen Suzanne, I really suffered after the incident. The person who picked my pocket really punished me.'

'I can imagine! It must have been very hard. One minute you're dreaming of going home. And you were even on your way to buy the ticket and then ...' Suzanne stopped and started laughing. 'Don't worry, there's a reason why that person succeeded.'

Later that evening, a Friday night, Suzanne and I went to her favourite discotheque in Shepherds Bush. It was called Somersault. Inside the crowded discotheque, as we stood chatting, Suzanne pulled a man walking past. 'Dave, meet my boyfriend Michael. I want you to dedicate two songs.' She whispered the songs into his ears. Dave nodded.

About half an hour later, the DJ announced that the next two songs would be dedicated to Michael from South Africa, the Rainbow Nation.

Suzanne laughed. 'Michael from the Rainbow Nation. This is hilarious!'

'They are requests from Suzanne also from South Africa. She wants me to tell the whole world that Michael is the sunshine of her life.' The first song was: *The Only Way is Up!* The next one was Barry White's: *I Love You Just the Way You Are!*

The next Saturday I went to Brixton market. As I walked around I heard a familiar voice shout 'Michael'. I turned. It was Sandra. She was with another man. 'Meet Fred, my boyfriend. Fred lives in Streatham and we're here to do some shopping. Any news about your Suzanne?'

'Oh yes she's back in London.'

'Are you still together or …'

'We're together.'

'I'm back at the agency now. Have you got any jobs?'

'No.'

'Call me on Monday. I'll try and sort you out.'

'Thank you.'

'Speak to you soon. Bye.'

As I was about to walk away, Bilal called me from a nearby shop. 'I'll call you by your adopted Muslim name. Brother Mustapha, how are you?' I noticed he was holding prayer beads.

'I'm fine thank you and you?'

'*Alhamdullilah*, we're fine,' Aisha answered. She was wearing a red *hijab*. She stepped closer smiling. 'Listen Brother Mustapha remember the Somali sister called Jawi who works for us?'

'Oh yes, of course I do.'

'She has established a dating agency for Muslims.'

'That's interesting,' I said laughing.

Bilal laughed. 'Now there's a good reason for a young man like you to convert.'

'But you have to be a Muslim to join,' Aisha insisted laughing too. 'Who knows, maybe you'll meet your soul mate there. But you've to go and recite the *shahada* in front of an Imam. Then we'll get you a good practising Muslim sister, a good companion, a good wife.'

'Thank you very much. I'll think about it,' I said smiling.

'Brother Mustapha,' Bilal said. 'We're trying to open a branch of our *halal* restaurant in Brixton. Since you live in the area, I'd like you to do some work for me.'

'I'll call you, *Insha'Allah.*'

'*Insha'Allah,*' they said in unison.

I walked further. There was a group of Christian evangelicals giving out religious tracts. Someone was preaching on top of his voice. 'The Lord Jesus will save you,' I could hear from afar. The voice was familiar. I walked toward the gaily-dressed men and women. Some of them were singing hymns.

'How're you Mr Emmanuel?' Pastor Oluwasegun asked smiling. 'Remember me?'

'Of course I do. I'm fine thank you, long time. How're you?'

'We thank God,' he replied and gave me a tract about Jesus the Saviour. I thanked him.

Later when I was walking towards the Brixton underground station, someone tapped me on my shoulder. 'Yes I was right,' I heard a familiar voice. I turned. It was Leroy. He was laughing. 'You know what brother, I saw you earlier, talking to those Jesus people,' he started in his lyrical Jamaican accent. 'But before I could cross the road you were gone. Like always, the moment I see you something inside me clicks. Something inside me said that this is your African brother. How are you?'

'I'm fine. How's Melody?'

'She's alright.' He was quiet for a while looking at me shaking his head. 'You remember the days we used to play around here?'

'Of course I do.' I pointed to the spot where we usually played.

'I still go out to perform here and there. A girl from Barbados called Latisha sings and I do the guitar. We've new songs now. She's a very nice woman. You want me to introduce you to her?'

'No thanks. I'm very busy with my missus.'

'I know but I'm happy to see you. Now that your African woman does not send you to the doghouse, we don't see you anymore. No bitterness, only brotherly love. I like it. Good African woman taking care of you. You're a nice man and you deserve a good woman.' He paused. 'I better tell you something now because I don't know when I will see you again. You know what Brother Kimani, as I say long time ago, a lie has one thousand faces, but truth has only one. Whenever I see you, I see only one face, the truth.'

Sixteen

Gamble Everything for Love

On Monday morning, Sandra called. 'Do you want to work or are you still on your honeymoon? Who knows with Suzanne back, you're probably trying to make up for lost time?'

'I want to work.'

'Do you want to work at the institute?'

'No.'

'Why?'

'Remember Ms Joy.'

'Of course yes. I do. She's no longer there.'

'Alright then.'

'The job is for four days starting tomorrow but you never know they'll probably keep you there for a while, on and off. You don't need anything from the office. They have blank timesheets and a reminder that you're Michael there not Emmanuel.'

'Thank you very much.'

Over the past several weeks, I had been thinking of what next to do with my life. I wanted to study. I enjoyed studying philosophy and would like to obtain a Master's degree. I saw a course advertised in the papers. That afternoon I called the university. I was put through to the course tutor, Dr Phillips.

'I'm in a hurry. Where are you from?' he asked.

'Nigeria.'

'I see, from Africa. Did you study in the UK?'

'Yes, I have a certificate ....'

'I mean your secondary education and first degree.'

'No. My first degree was obtained in Nigeria.'

'I'm not really sure the course is tailored for people like you. I don't think you have the necessary background knowledge to understand what is being taught. Don't get me wrong, from my experience people from Africa and the Arab world do struggle with understanding Western philosophy. I honestly don't want to spend so much time explaining these concepts that are totally strange to you. It wouldn't be fair on other students who would be frustrated.'

'Thank you.'

'Bye.'

It was only moments later I realised a mistake. Had Dr Phillips asked to see my diploma certificate, I could not show him because it was issued to Michael Danquah. I called the admissions office again. I wanted to know if there were places left on other courses.

'There are two places left in the political economy of course.'

'Okay put me through to the course tutor please.'

The course tutor, Dr Beatrice Flowers, had time for me. She was very cordial and polite on the phone. We spoke at length. When we finished she said, 'I'd like to see you in person. A face-to-face interview is part of the procedure.'

'That's fine.'

'Five o'clock tomorrow?'

'Perfect. I'll be there tomorrow.'

The next day I went to work at the institute.

'I've heard a lot about you,' said Adrian the chef. 'Joe is on holiday so I'm here to cover from the agency.'

I was then introduced to the new supervisor called Collette.

I told her I'd like to leave early. 'I've a dentist appointment.'

'No problem. That's fine,' she said. 'I understand you know what to do in the kitchen.'

I nodded. 'I'm off to see Leslie for a meeting.'

Just before lunch break, the chef shouted, 'Michael where has the packet of sausages gone? The packet was here one minute and now it's gone.'

'I don't know what you're talking about.'

'A packet of sausages is missing, that's what I'm talking about.'

'Why are you asking me? I've been in the washing-up area all morning.'

'But you went into the cold room. I saw you,' he insisted in a raised voice.

'Yes I did. You told me to put the deliveries in the cold room.'

'The point is, a packet of sausages is missing. These things don't have legs.'

'You probably looked in the wrong place,' I argued.

'You and I should have a look together,' he suggested.

We checked. The packet was there.

'I still believe it's short. I can count okay. I'm not an illiterate. Listen Michael,' he was visibly upset. 'You're here to work as a kitchen porter and I'm here to work as a chef. I'm a trained chef. I know when things go missing so don't argue with me. Now I want you to apologise for shouting at me.'

I did not want to. I did not shout at him. Still, I apologised.

'Can I have a look in your bag in the changing room?'

'Why?'

'The packet of sausages must be somewhere; it could be in your bag.' He was adamant. 'Listen Michael, admit it before we check. If the packet is in your bag its theft and I'll call the police,' he threatened on our way to the changing room.

I opened my locker, brought out my rucksack and opened it. There were only books inside. Adrian removed all the books and checked the rucksack. He checked the locker and my jacket. He was not happy. He found nothing. He walked away without an apology.

When it was time for me to leave I changed and went for my interview with Dr Flowers. I tried to suppress my anger throughout the journey to the university. Dr Flowers was busy with other students. I waited in front of her office. I could not get the earlier incident out of my head. 'How could someone show such disrespect? How could he accuse me of stealing sausages? How could I, Michael, steal sausages?'

'Mustapha, Mustapha,' I heard a female voice but did not respond. I was still asking myself: 'how could I, Michael, steal sausages?'

'Are you Mustapha?' a woman asked me. I looked up.

'Yes, I am.'

'My name is Dr Flowers. I spoke to you over the phone yesterday.'

'It was a pleasure talking to you and thank you very much for inviting me for an interview.'

'Follow me please,' she said. As I followed her into her office, I reminded myself several times. 'You are Mustapha not Michael. Your name is Mustapha not Michael.'

We sat down. Dr Flowers was a middle-aged woman with shoulder-length blonde hair. 'I think I asked you most of the questions yesterday. I wanted to be sure that the person I was talking to was real. Sometimes people just call and waste our time.' We went through the procedure of admissions, the whole course, the duration, the fees and the timetable. She brought out the pack that contained everything I should know about the university and the course. She gave me a form to fill in and asked for two passport photos. 'Finally Mustapha,' she said before signing the form. 'What's your immigration status?'

'I've got an indefinite leave to remain in the UK,' I lied looking straight into her eyes. 'If I knew I'd have brought my passport with me.'

'It's my fault. I completely forgot to ask you to bring it. But I trust you,' she said and signed the form. 'Here you are. Pay the fees and complete the registration at the admissions office. I've done my bit. I look forward to seeing you in my classes.'

I thanked her and walked out. I couldn't help but smile because I had just lied my way into a Master of Arts course in a well-known university.

I told Suzanne what had happened. She laughed and wrote out a cheque for me.

'That's good news Michael,' Jarvo said when I told him over the phone. 'You're getting better and better at lying. The ultimate challenge is to lie your way to the truth. But listen Michael, there's nothing you'll do in the future without a computer. You must have basic computer skills. We run computer courses for immigrants in our office and you can come once or twice a week. These courses are mainly in the evenings. It's important to have the skills and it's free and everyone here would be very happy to see you on the course. Since your woman came back you've completely forgotten about us,' he concluded laughing.

That evening Suzanne came in excited. 'I'll be going to South Africa for about three weeks over the Christmas period. The company will be having a big meeting somewhere outside Johannesburg and we all have to attend. It's called *Bosberaad*, a meeting held usually outdoors in a game reserve. So Michael, put it in your diary. Suzanne is going to South Africa in December for Christmas and she'll definitely be coming back.'

'I'll not forget.'

'And this time, no plans to go back to Nigeria.'

'I'll make sure I succeed this time around,' I joked.

Weeks later, Jarvo started. 'Michael, Taj and I are worried about your immigration status and it's an item on the agenda of the next Politburo meeting. We think you ought to do something. You cannot continue like this. It's too risky. All it takes is one mistake and you're gone.'

Taj joined in. 'Sembène, remember the Hausa saying: *Ka tsalake rijiya da baya*. You have successfully jumped over deep wells running backward. You've been running on luck – a commodity that tends not to last. Remember that where there's good luck there's also bad luck. No one is suggesting you get rid of the Boer woman. What you should have is a plan B. You know very well that as a South African, marrying her will not give you a legal stay.'

I nodded.

'So we have to find someone who could give you a stay. We want you to live freely and succeed here but your immigration status has to be addressed and the sooner the better. Unless you and Suzanne relocate to South Africa or Nigeria for good, one form of solution must be found.'

'I'm more worried than you. I'm not very comfortable in going into pubs or nightclubs and chatting up women. I also don't think I can use a dating agency.'

Jarvo laughed. 'It's okay Michael, the Politburo has mandated me to put a plan B in place as soon as possible. It's on our priority list.

I've called it Operation SVABODA, which in Russian means freedom. I've made a few calls and a Senegalese poet said he would introduce a woman to us. Her name is Stacy. She's from East London. She's a single parent and I'm not sure if she was ever married. Her former partner is from Nigeria and they have an eight-year-old son. I understand she's not interested in money. What she's more interested in is having a father figure for her son. But it'll cost something to arrange the wedding. The Politburo will pay for everything. Don't worry about that. All you have to do is turn up for the wedding. Of course, you'll meet her before the wedding. I suggest, if you have the time, that you visit her as many times as possible before the wedding. You never know, along the line she might be interested in the real thing so in that case you can kill two birds with one stone.'

'What does she do?'

'She sells flowers outside an underground station in East London during the day and at night she works in a pub. So Michael, get ready to move to East London and sell flowers and work in a pub. Well that's what it will take you to get a residence permit. Consider yourself very lucky it's not expensive. People pay thousands of pounds for a sham marriage.'

'You and Stacy might click and you might have a real cockney wife and child,' Taj opined.

'No way.'

'Have you ever heard a beggar that has a choice?' Taj asked laughing.

'I'm in love with Suzanne and cannot have two women in my life at the same time. What if the Home Office checked and found out that I don't live in East London and Suzanne hears about it? I could lose both. You understand?'

'Our assumption is that they would not check because she's British. There are thousands of marriages and they don't have the resources to check them all. They just pick one or two. You might just get away with it. Once you are married, we'll get a very good solicitor to handle your application and you might receive your stay within a few months. You're right. It's complicated but you cannot continue like this. *Tak zhit nelzia*'

'Want to go to the Thai restaurant?' I asked Suzanne.

'No I'll stick to my Indian restaurant.'

'Okay, get ready and let's go.'

'*Bitter koud*,' (very cold in Afrikaans) Suzanne said complaining about the weather. 'It's terribly cold out there and raining,' she said wearing her winter coat. 'I'm happy I'm going to South Africa tomorrow where it is summer. There's one thing I cannot share with you or bring some back for you and that's the sun.'

When the food was served, Suzanne said, 'I'll try some of yours.' I filled a spoon and fed her. 'Now try some of mine.' In the end she ate half of mine and I ate half of hers.

'Have you got anything to tell me?' she asked on our way back to the flat. 'I can tell something has been bothering you over the past couple of days. Just tell me – I'm not going to eat you. We women have six senses you know. We've evolved over time to sense if something is wrong with our partners.'

We continued to walk in silence.

'Say something. You're too quiet. Something is wrong.'

'Suzanne, nothing is wrong.'

'I know something is bothering you. I know you well enough to know your moods. Money worries? I can help you. Just ask.'

'I always have money worries. So that's not a problem.'

'I like it when you talk.' She put her hand in my back pocket as we continued to walk. 'Look at that,' she showed me a mixed race couple with a pram approaching. Suzanne stopped and looked at the baby boy in the pram. 'He's cute.'

'Thanks,' the black man said with a huge smile.

'My dream is to walk around with a baby boy in a pram.'

I stopped. 'What did you say?'

She repeated the sentence and added. 'We all have dreams, don't we?'

The next day I went to Heathrow with Suzanne. After checking in Suzanne said. 'Michael, don't worry I'm coming back this time around. If that's what is worrying you, I can assure you that I will not disappear again. I love you and I will definitely come back to you, and only you.'

I nodded, smiled and kissed her.

'So that's not what's bothering you then. One day you will tell me.'

'You're right. It has nothing to do with you.'

'Write it down and posted it to me. Writing is a form of therapy. You have my address.'

We kissed and she left.

Later I called Jarvo. 'I'm in trouble.'

'Where are you?' he asked in a panicked voice. 'What happened?'

I laughed. 'Relax Jarvo, I'm at home.'

'You almost gave me a heart attack you know. What's wrong?'

'Suzanne is talking about babies.'

He laughed. 'I was afraid you were arrested and in a detention centre. I see. If the Boer woman is talking about babies then you're in real trouble. I don't envy you at all. This woman means business. Let's meet and talk. Where's she?'

'She's on her way to South Africa.'

'Hold on Taj has something to tell you.'

'Sembène, I can see things are getting serious with the Boer woman. What an irony. When a bird flies for a long time in the air, it is allowed to perch on any branch strong enough to carry it. I can only wish you the best of luck.'

I visited Dr Asibong. 'Sheikh, you have a good woman. It's very rare to meet such a delightful young woman who's intelligent and witty but, above all, she has a sense of understanding. No trace of arrogance at all which is rare considering her background and that she's a descendant of the Boers. To be honest with you, I was shocked by her humility, but Sheikh, what about your residence permit?'

I told him about Plan B.

He thought for a while. 'I'm not sure it would work. You might get yourself into a real mess dealing with two women at the same time. The one in East London might not see things the way you and your friends see things. Her expectations might be different. What she's got in mind will probably come out later. Talk this through with her first because I don't want you to lose Suzanne. She's a good companion of yours. The only thing I can say is Allah knows how to test you.'

Jamila was very forthright. 'As long as you get along very well, that's the most important thing. There's a reason the two of you met and are still together. No one knows what tomorrow will bring. As a Muslim, put your faith in Almighty Allah. He has a way in making things work out in the end. Listen to your heart. So long as you do your best whatever happens will be for the best!'

I called Frank B. 'You should have married her yesterday. Blimey, what are you waiting for? This is the best time of your life – enjoy it. Jump on each other every day like mad rabbits. You will not be young forever. Man o man, you have a woman like Suzanne and you're dragging your feet? What is life if not a great adventure? When you embark on an adventure any point of departure will do. Just get on with it.'

I went to the resource centre for my weekly computer course. 'Today,' Jarvo started, 'we'll be talking about word-processing.' He said switching on a computer and tried to explain some terminologies like DOS, floppy disk, Wordstar, WordPerfect. Wassa interrupted as soon as he entered.

'Look who is here, the African man who wants to marry *oyinbo* (white) woman, the black man who allows a white woman to dominate and control him.'

'What's your problem?' Jarvo asked.

'I think this *oyinbo* woman is the one running the show and it is unAfrican for a woman to run the show. Men must be in charge.'

I ignored him.

'As we say in my part of West Africa,' Wassa continued. 'It's the he-goat that sniffs, chases and then mounts the she-goat, not the other way round. Have you ever seen the hen chase the cock? This white woman is the one chasing Mustapha at will and that's not natural.' He looked at me and laughed scornfully. He was categorical. 'The he-goat chooses his own mate. You don't let females sniff out the he-goat.'

Jarvo hissed and disagreed. 'You're not serious, you've got to be broadminded. This is not your village in West Africa. He's got a woman that likes him, what's your problem? Leave them alone.' He continued and turned to me. 'Michael, we have a problem that sooner or later we have to resolve.' Jarvo paused and thought for a while. 'The best way out of this is to propose to her. If she says no, then you're free to marry Stacy and have your documents sorted. One way of getting around this is for you to see if she will marry you first. Would you go down that road?'

'Of course, I would. I have no hesitation at all.'

'If you propose what do you think she would say yes or no?'

'Suzanne would say yes.'

'And you?'

'I'll marry her and damn the consequences.'

There was a moment of silence.

'Michael, this is about your future,' Jarvo stammered.

'I don't think what I'd go through with her would be worse than what I've been through already. I've nothing to lose any more.'

Jarvo nodded.

'This white woman has completely turned his head upside down,' Wassa said sitting down next to me laughing. 'Our brother here cannot think straight any more. This is what people call love in Europe. I bet she'll say no. I don't see that white woman from South Africa agreeing to marry our confused and deluded black friend. No way! I cannot see her saying yes. She's just using you as her winter blanket; something to keep her warm. You are her medicinal choice; someone to lift her mood.' He paused, looked at me and added. 'This Boer woman is simply enjoying what she cannot enjoy in South Africa. I cannot see how this relationship could work.'

I was angry but decided not to show it.

'Wassa, you have a problem,' Jarvo said in my defence. 'Because ninety-nine white girls from South Africa wouldn't marry a black man does not mean that the hundredth girl will not. She might say yes. One thing life has taught me is that we must never generalise. There's always an exception. She is white and has just got out of an apartheid environment but she might just be different. We don't know what's going through her mind. She could be rebelling against the system – we do not know. Remember that the moon changes every blessed day. We human beings change every blessed day.'

Wassa insisted. 'I'm one hundred per cent sure she will say no. She's white, Boer, Christian and South African. Come on guys, there's no way she would say yes.' Wassa brought out his wallet and counted one hundred pounds and put the money on the table. 'Mr Philosopher put your money where your philosophy is.'

Jarvo accepted the challenge. He opened his wallet and counted a hundred pounds and put it on the table too. 'Personally I don't want her to say yes. But for the purpose of this argument I'll put my money down. I would prefer if she said no so that plan B can kick in immediately and there wouldn't be any complications. Plan B is straightforward.'

'You hold the money,' Wassa said handing over the total amount to me. 'There's a reason why philosophers are never rich,' he muttered to himself after a short sarcastic laugh.

'Just a reminder that Stacy will be coming in later,' Jarvo said before the computer course resumed. A couple of hours later, two women walked into the offices.

'Hi Stacy,' Jarvo waved at her. 'How're you?'

'Hi love,' she replied. 'Meet my friend Alison.'

'Haya,' Alison said and waved at us.

'You support Charlton Athletics,' Jarvo said to Alison who had a scarf around her neck.

'Of course,' she said proudly.

'And you?' he asked Stacy.

'West Ham of course! The Hammers are the best team in London.'

'Tea or coffee?'

'Doesn't really matter,' Stacy said.

'As long as there's lots of milk and sugar,' Alison added.

I sat and looked at them speaking in plain cockney. I could only pick up a few words clearly. 'Tell you what,' Alison would say before almost every sentence and giggle from time to time.

Jarvo called Stacy and I into a room. 'This is Michael,' he said, introducing me to her.

'I thought it was you I was to marry,' she said giggling.

'I'm not that lucky,' Jarvo answered smiling.

'Not bad looking.'

'Thanks for the compliments.'

'What does it mean?' Stacy asked pointing at Jarvo's t-shirt.

'*Ignorance is Bliss* means it's good not to know many things.'

'I agree,' she said nodding her head. 'What you don't know doesn't hurt you, *innit*?'

'Exactly. Correct.'

'I'd definitely be happier if I didn't know so many things,' she added sitting down.

Jarvo looked at me and smiled. 'The purpose of this meeting is for the two of you to get to know each other,' he started. 'This is not a sham marriage as the poet mentioned to you.'

'Of course not,' she said. 'I thought he was joking when he said sham.'

'You Stacy will get a man. An African man, just as you wanted and you Michael will get a woman, an Englishwoman, a cockney, a West Ham supporter who would give you TLC. (Tender, Loving Care)'

We looked at each other and nodded and smiled.

'The way I see it is this,' he continued; 'This is a win-win relationship. I'm just trying to arrange a marriage that would be beneficial to the two involved. We're not a dating agency but circumstances have forced us to introduce the two of you so that you can meet your individual needs. You're both consenting adults. I must reiterate that it's not a sham marriage. If everything goes according to plan, we'll meet in the New Year and take things forward. Michael will visit you, know the area, meet your son Jason and you get to know him too. Once we've done that then we'll move to the next stage, which is the registration of the marriage and then the ceremony will come later. This is just to get the ball rolling as they say.'

'Yes get the show on the road,' Stacy said smiling at me.

'Correct,' Jarvo said smiling at me.

'What are you doing for Christmas?' Stacy asked Jarvo.

'Nothing really.'

'What a shame.'

'And you?'

'I'll visit my parents in Canning Town.'

'Looking forward to that?'

'Of course, I am.'

'Alison and I will be attending a hen night on Christmas Eve. It's going to be fun.'

'Why?' Jarvo asked.

'We're going to see members of the Chippendales,' she said giggling.

'That's really worth going to.'

'I've a few questions for Michael'

'Go ahead.'

'What's your star sign?'

'Cancer.'

'Where would you like to go on holidays?'

'Greece.'

'If you won the pools, what are you going to spend it on?'

'Pass. Next question.'

'What football team do you support?'

'Arsenal.'

Stacy didn't look excited. 'I can tolerate them,' she said smiling. 'At least you don't support Liverpool. I cannot imagine myself living in the same flat with a *bladdy* Liverpool supporter. They are a real rubbish team. I can't stand their attitude. Tell you what! I was really worried you'd support Man U you know. My ex was a Man U supporter and he used to get on my nerves. I thought, not another *bladdy* Man U supporter. The Gunners are boring but I don't mind.'

'Do you want to know how old I am?'

'No. It doesn't matter does it? You look old enough for me.'

'Merry Christmas and have a wonderful time,' I said as she stood up to go.

After he had seen them off at the bus stop Jarvo returned to the office, cleared his throat and announced. 'Plan B of OPERATION SVABODA has commenced. To remind you, Plan A is this: Michael will propose to Suzanne as soon as she returns from South Africa. We hope she says no so that we can move to plan B. By the way, you can get a second-hand ring in good condition from a jeweller on Walworth Road in Camberwell.'

I went to the jeweller with an old ring of Suzanne in my wallet. I bought a refurbished engagement ring. 'It looks as good as new,' the jeweller said. 'She wouldn't know anyway. She will be too excited. By the way, where's she from?'

'South Africa.'

'Perfect. This ring is called *Some Like it Hot* and it's pure diamond on it.'

I thanked him and paid.

On Christmas day the telephone rang.

'My lion of the Timbervati, *howzit*?'

'Fine and how are you?'

'I'm *cool*. I want to wish you a Merry Christmas and just to make you a little bit jealous. I'm wearing a T-shirt over a short skirt. It's 28 degrees here. I'm sitting on a *stoep*, what you'd call veranda singing to the birds. I've just had a *braaivleis* and I'm relaxing in the shade with a glass of fresh mango juice – and you?'

'I will definitely not swap the beautiful weather we have in London for that of South Africa. I'm wearing two woollen jumpers. It's raining, windy, gloomy and very cold. This is the perfect weather for me. So you cannot make me jealous.'

'I've some *biltong* for you.'

'What's that?'

'It's dried seasoned meat.'

'How's your father?'

'He's still the same. What can you do?'

'And how's your mum?'

'She still lives in her own world.'

'How was the company meeting?'

'It went well. Hey Michael, I had a fright of my life some days ago in Jo'burg.'

'What happened?'

'Someone who looks almost exactly like you waved at me near a robot.'

'You have robots in South Africa?'

Suzanne laughed. 'That's what we call traffic lights.'

'I see.'

'I was waiting to cross the road and he waved and drove on.'

'I was not in Jo'burg.'

'Now I know it's not you. I thought why would Michael come to South Africa without telling me? Anyway, I had a dream about your film.'

'I always dream about you.'

'Ah thank you.'

'I'll be here waiting for you.'

'I'm also counting the days.'

'Ten more days.'

'Merry Christmas and a Happy New Year to you. May the New Year bring you love, success and good health.'

'I will always love you.'

Ten days later, Suzanne walked into the arrival hall at Heathrow Airport. 'Michael, I told you I'd be coming back.'

'I wasn't worried you wouldn't return to London.'

'I was worried you'd go to Nigeria for good. You tried it once and might succeed second time around.'

'You look relaxed.'

'It's the sun.'

'And look at what you came back to. Lovely weather isn't it?'

'*Bitter koud,*' she said in Afrikaans. 'Horrible weather! I hate the cold weather.'

Later that day I suggested that we go to the Iranian restaurant again.

'You mean Persia restaurant?'

'Yes. Saturday evening?'

'Perfect. There's something on the menu I'd like to try.'

Great! I thought she had fallen for it.

I called the restaurant and booked Rumi's corner. Dara said. 'Ah, I remember the two of you very well. The last time you came here you were both nervous, especially you Michael, you were shaking like a leaf. I said to myself poor Michael, why is he so nervous. It's just a date. But you were all right. I'm glad to hear that you're still together.'

'I intend to propose to her on Saturday.'

'Now you are talking. We'll buy the flowers and hide them. Don't worry about that. When the time comes, Sara will give them to you. This is really exciting. We'll get her to sing. She told me she likes singing.'

'Jarvo, Plan A in motion,' I said over the phone.

'We'll be there for you. I hope she says no. I cannot imagine the complications if she said yes. Losing a hundred pounds is nothing. If your woman says yes, we're completely screwed big time!'

I called Joe. 'Great Michael, I'm very happy for the two of you. I think she would suspect something if I came along. I'll stay away for a while to make it more real. I know she will say yes. Don't worry. I'll be at the wedding.'

'Table for M&S?' Sara asked smiling at us as we entered the restaurant.

'Yes please,' I said.

'Rumi's corner is reserved for you.'

'Thank you,' I said.

'Nice to see you again,' Suzanne said.

'You look well-tanned,' Sara said after collecting Suzanne's coat.

'I've just returned from South Africa.'

We settled down.

'Very nice atmosphere,' Suzanne commented. 'Lots of people today.'

'We'll start with the usual rosé,' I told Sara.

From the corner of my eye I saw Jarvo, Wassa and Taj enter the restaurant. I waved at them.

'Michael, what are you doing here?' Jarvo asked laughing.

'Sembène, so this is your hideout,' Taj said.

'Mustapha, I didn't know you liked Persian cuisine,' Wassa said.

I stood up, greeted them and introduced them to Suzanne.

'So what are you doing here?' I asked, pretending not to know.

'We just wanted to try something exotic,' Jarvo answered first.

'Actually, we had a meeting nearby and thought we might as well eat in the area to support the local economy,' Taj added laughing.

'Nice to meet you,' Jarvo said looking at Suzanne. 'We've heard a lot about you.'

'I've heard a lot about all of you too,' Suzanne said smiling.

'Enjoy your meal.'

They left us alone.

Suzanne did not suspect anything.

'I am back to this man with many names. The first one called you Mike. The second one called you Sembène. And the last one called you Mustapha. Amazing how you can cope with it. Head spinning for me. By the way, why Sembène? Did you experience another narrow escape in my absence?'

'No, after the famous film director called Ousmane Sembène.'

'I see. I thought you had added another name in my absence.'

Suzanne talked about their farm and the film she saw in Johannesburg. We finished eating. Suzanne went to the toilet. Dara stepped closer. 'We're ready. I've announced in Farsi that you'll be proposing to your one and only love. Everybody is excited and is looking forward to the magic moment. You know we Iranians like romance a lot. Rumi once said: *Gamble everything for love if you are a human being. Half-heartedness does not reach into majesty.*'

'But it's tough.'

'Who says love is easy?' he asked with a shrug.

Dara stepped away when Suzanne returned. He called for silence in Farsi and continued speaking in English. 'It's time for music. I'd like to invite Suzanne to sing for us but before that, her boyfriend wants to say a few words. Keep it short and simple please Michael.' He passed the microphone to me.

I checked for the twentieth time that evening, the ring was in my pocket. I stood up. I was very nervous. There was absolute silence in the restaurant. I thanked Dara and Sara for their delicious meal and the wonderful atmosphere. Dara illuminated Rumi's line. 'As you all know, Jalaluddin Rumi once said: *The minute I heard my first love story I started looking for you, not knowing how blind that was. Lovers don't finally meet somewhere. They're in each other all along.*' I went down on my right knee holding Suzanne's hand. 'Suzanne I love you – will you marry me?'

Suzanne looked at me and her face lit up. She looked round in amazement. There was silence. After about five seconds, Suzanne took the microphone from me. First she wiped the tears from her eyes, and said, 'Michael, you're the love of my life. Yes I will marry you.'

There were cheers, whistles and claps. I stood up and inserted the ring onto her finger. We grabbed each other and kissed passionately. We sat down both shaken by the experience. Suzanne was blushing. 'Oh my God! That was a surprise. You got me there. I could guess so many things but I couldn't guess this one. Well done! Well-planned! I wasn't expecting it, at least not now. That was a shocker. I love you Mike.'

Sara brought the bunch of flowers and Dara brought two glasses of pink champagne.

I looked around to see where my friends were. I saw Wassa walking out of the restaurant. When we had calmed down, Dara invited Suzanne to sing. She sang Whitney Houston's *I Will Always Love You*. When she finished she was crying. 'Mike I'm overwhelmed,' she whispered and ran to the toilet.

Taj and Jarvo came and congratulated me. 'This Boer woman has really complicated our lives,' Jarvo said, smiling. 'That was great. Wassa lost the bet.' They laughed and left. Dara stepped forward to clear the table.

'Dara, do you know that I literally gambled everything for love.'

'Rumi would be proud of you. It's great to see a man gamble everything for love. It means you have guts.'

'Listen Dara, you don't understand. I gambled everything.'

'Then majesty awaits you.'

Suzanne came back and we got ready to leave.

We thanked everybody and left.

Outside the restaurant, holding the bunch of flowers with one hand, Suzanne stopped on the snowy street and held my hands very tight. 'That was one of the biggest surprises of my life. Do you really mean it?'

'Of course I do. Do you really want to marry me?'

'Of course I want to.' She looked at me. 'You know my greatest fear?'

'You're going to slip and fall on the snow.'

'I'm not afraid of that. If I fall, I'll get up. If I'm injured it'll heal.'

'Then what are you afraid of?'

'That one day I will stop loving you.'

'Taxi!' I flagged a cab.

The next morning Suzanne said, 'Let's go to Amsterdam to celebrate our engagement. It's just forty minutes by air and just for two nights. We fly out Friday evening and return Sunday afternoon. It wouldn't affect your work.'

'I'm sorry darling I have to say no again. I still have a few things to sort out.'

She did not argue. 'I thought it would be a bit romantic to go somewhere. I think we need a change of environment – a place like Amsterdam where you and I can walk along the canals.'

'And go to the coffee shops that don't sell coffee?'

'I told you to take it off the list of places to visit but if that's where you really want to go to, get your passport ready and off we go.'

'Unfortunately I have to say no again. I think I'll have some problems with visa.'

'I actually wanted to surprise you and buy the tickets. You might be right. I just remembered the hassle I went through to get a visa. It was a nightmare. The queue at the high commission was horrendously long and the staff asked all kinds of stupid questions and they wanted to see so many documents. The experience almost drove me mad. It took me three days to get a visa for a two-day visit. Forget it. You wonder how such people were let out of the country in the first place let alone selected to work in foreign missions. They were so arrogant and stupid.'

'You see what I mean?'

'Okay! Let's go to Cornwall. I always wanted to go there and you don't need a visa.'

'You're right. I don't need a visa.'

'Typical English weather; damp and miserable,' Suzanne said as we checked into the hotel drenched in rain. 'We should be somewhere nicer like Barbados or Mauritius, Botswana or Kenya.'

After dinner, Suzanne started. 'Now that you want to be my husband, tell me more about yourself.'

'What do you want to know?'

'What I've not been told before.'

Lying in bed, I told her an edited version of my life until the day we met at the college.

'How many children do you want?' she asked.

'As many as God gives us. Remember I'm a Muslim and for me only Allah gives.'

'What would you prefer? Boy or girl?'

'It doesn't really matter. I pray they are healthy.'

'What's your secret wish? I notice you look at baby girls more than boys.'

'A girl. I even have a name for her, Amira.'

'What does it mean?'

'Princess! Daddy's Princess.'

'Have you got a name for a boy?'

'No. When he arrives I'll find one.'

'You want to make me jealous. Then I want a boy.'

'I know. You're always looking at baby boys.'

'I always wanted to have a boy. And wait and see what I'm going to do with my little Prince.'

'Remember only one cock can crow in the courtyard.'

'Hahaha! You feel threatened already. By the way, you will not be able to visit my family in the immediate future. When things settle down a bit, I hope they do, we'll go to South Africa together and I'll show you our farm. Some things have to fall into place and the time must be right.'

'As an ancient philosopher called Heraclitus once said: *Nothing endures but change*. Hopefully things will change for the better and I will be able to visit.'

'Can I visit your family in Nigeria?'

'Of course you can. Why did you ask?'

'Because I'm white and Christian.'

'We've seen white people before and we've Christians. You were in Morocco and no one harassed you because of your religion.'

'I was there as a tourist, not as someone married to a Moroccan. The relationship would be different if I was staying with my in-laws.'

'Don't worry about my family. You'll be alright.'

'Do I have to convert to Islam?'

'Who told you so?'

'I read somewhere in the papers that a woman who wants to marry a Muslim man must first convert to Islam.'

'No!' I was categorical. 'No! That's not part of the deal. You keep your faith I keep mine. You worship your God, I worship mine. Personally, the main task before me now is not to change you but to change myself. I want to be a better person tomorrow than I am today. To be a good husband and a good father, I must change myself for the better. The responsibilities ahead of me are huge. If, however, you want to convert to Islam we would welcome you. I cannot and will not make it a condition.'

'I really love you Michael.' She kissed me. 'Do you really want to make a film?'

'Of course, that was what brought me to the UK in the first place. I even have a script that was accepted. I'll show you one of these days. I kept forgetting. All I had to do was rewrite the script and there were even corporate sponsors for the film. I was almost there before everything unravelled.'

'And then you were so fed up and wanted to return home and someone stole your money on your way to buy a ticket,' she said laughing. 'I still can't get it out of my head.'

'It's not funny.' I said laughing too. 'Coming back to your earlier question, I hope to return to the college, finish the course, rewrite the script and with a bit of luck direct the film.'

'I had this strange dream while I was in South Africa. In it you and I were staying somewhere. I cannot remember exactly where but you had a dream and had this mysterious way of being able to hold the dream in your hand. You would say, "Suzanne, look this is my dream." You then put it in a wooden box and closed it. I remember the wooden box very well. From time to time you'd bring it out and show it to me and say my darling, this is my dream and one day I hope it will come true. Then one day, you brought your dream out and showed it to me, as you always did. Then I said Michael, there is no point showing me every time, turn it into reality. You can make your dream come true. You have the power to do it. You said you needed some magic. You and I went out into this thick forest where we thought we'd get the magic. We searched and searched for days. It was exhausting. Just when we were about to return empty-handed you tripped and fell. In the process of getting back on your feet, you took a seed from the ground. "I might as well take this with me" you said. We returned disappointed with only the seed. Then one day you said you had a dream that you should plant the seed. So you planted the seed and as soon as it started germinating your dream disappeared from the wooden box and came true. I will never forget that lovely smile on your face. I hope that when your dream comes true, I'll be there to see the smile in real life.

'I still remember your face the first time I saw you. You looked very tired. You came with Sandra to do silver service but you didn't do anything that day. You were just there watching us. I thought Sandra was your cherry, your girlfriend as we say in South Africa. You know there are some men who would not let their girlfriends out of their sights. I thought you were one of those insecure men. Then you returned the next day and we worked together and you annoyed the Italian guy.'

'Yes. Antonio.'

'Then you and I talked on the stairs. And I asked you what you want to be in life? And I still remember you said, "I want to be a film director."'

'I cannot remember that.'

'Selective memory, you said it with such confidence because I remember the face.'

'And then what happened?'

'Then we talked about South African writers.'

'You mean Peter Abrahams and Alan Paton. And then what happened?'

'Then you disappeared or rather, you never turned up at the club again. Then many months later, you walked into the canteen in the institute where I was working wearing this t-shirt. One thing led to another and here we are in a hotel in Cornwall celebrating our engagement.'

'What have we got out there? Typical English weather. Rain! Rain! Rain'

'We're going to be husband and wife soon.'

'And we are talking about babies and dreams.'

Back in Camberwell, south London, my landlord told me that an Englishman called about three times during my absence. The man promised to call that particular evening. He did not leave this contact details. I decided to wait for his call. Later the phone rang.

'Good evening, could I speak to Michael Kimani please?'

'Speaking,' I recognised the voice of Danny.

'At last, I got you at home. How are you Michael? This is Danny here. The son of Rosemary, remember me?'

'Of course I do.'

'I'm sorry to bother you.'

'It's alright. How's your mother?'

'Ah, so you haven't heard. She died months ago. I was told you left the care home. I was lucky to be at her bedside when she died. One of her last requests was that I call and thank you. She said, very faintly of course, thank my Mohammedan friend. We noticed that she got on very well with you and that she was very happy when you read her the newspapers. I'm sorry I left it so late. As you know, I am very busy. I've been all over the world. I'm calling you from Tokyo. That was one of her last wishes and I must respect it.'

'I'm sorry to hear about her death.'

'Oh well, that's life. How's life treating you?'

'I'm okay, sort of. I'm doing an MA course right now in political economy. I did a diploma course in Western philosophy and I'm about to start rewriting my script. I came into this country to be a film maker.'

'Wow! I'm amazed. Honestly I never thought you could read very well or write properly and I used to laugh when I saw you talking to my mother. I wondered how you were able to communicate with her. But I'm really impressed, Mr Kimani. I like to hear such stories. My mother said some interesting things about you.'

'She said that I'm a Mohammedan.'

'Yes among other things.' He paused. 'Michael, I'm not just into cars. I mean I'm not into F1 only. I also do charity work and I'm about to set up a Rosemary Foundation to support certain good causes. I'm mentioning this because if you need any support later please do contact me. If I cannot help you, I will send you to the right people. I know a lot of people in the film and entertainment industry. I know the chairman of a football club in London who supports creative writers for example. It is one thing to have ideas but it's another thing to have the money to put those ideas into the real world. I look forward to meeting you again and, who knows, maybe one evening we shall see your film on the big screen. My late mother certainly thought you would be someone. Good night Michael and good luck.'

Seventeen

The Power of Love

'Sheikh, make sure you buy Suzanne something special on Valentine's Day or take her somewhere special for the weekend. She deserves a good present or a treat or both from you. Remember she's no longer a girlfriend, she's a fiancée now,' Dr Asibong said as I was about to leave his flat. 'That woman of yours is very special.'

'Maybe flowers,' I said on the stairs.

'There's no *maybe* here. Definitely flowers! But there must be an element of surprise to it too. You could pay for the flowers and get them delivered to her first thing in the morning. Make sure she opens the door.'

'But flowers would be very expensive, especially on that day.'

'Love is not cheap! Suzanne is worth every petal! This woman hasn't given you any headache as far as I know. You're lucky to have such a wonderful woman so you have to learn to appreciate and pamper her.'

I did not answer.

'I know what you're thinking. Back home we don't give flowers but Sheikh, when you are in Rome?'

'Do as the Romans do.'

It was a cold day. I was shivering on the platform at West Hampstead underground station when a female voice interrupted my thoughts. 'Sheikh, how's your thyroid?' I did not respond immediately. I connected the name Sheikh and my thyroid. I turned and looked at a woman standing behind me. It was Dr Helen Louise Armstrong.

'Ah,' I lied. 'It's okay now.'

'Let's see your eyes,' she said and had a very close look at both eyes. 'Remove your scarf for me please and sit down on the bench,' she requested. I did. She stood behind me and using two fingers on each hand touched the lower part of my neck. 'Hmm, thank you. There's no improvement from the last time I saw you. It's still swollen. You need to be checked by a consultant. Are you still on medication?'

'Yes,' I lied.

'That's weird. Your eyes and the thyroid gland are bigger, definitely bigger than when I first saw you. Hmm, anyway when you have time, go to the surgery and get the nurse to send you to the hospital for blood tests. I'll send you to a consultant at the Royal Free Hospital after the tests. A specialist must see you immediately.'

'Thank you very much.'

The train arrived. We entered. 'I haven't seen your father for some time.'

'I think he's very busy.'

'It's good when I don't see him because it means he's healthy. So I suppose he's busy chasing all the women,' she whispered smiling. 'He's trying to prove to the world that monogamy is bad for the human race. I hope you don't subscribe to that idea.'

'I don't.'

'That's good! Anyway, I must leave you here. There's a train on the other platform,' she said and ran across onto another train at Finchley Road station.

The train driver announced that the train was being held at the red signal. I decided to go to the surgery.

'Funny enough I was just thinking about you the other day,' Jamila said after welcoming me cordially. 'I thought you must be getting ready for a romantic weekend somewhere with Suzanne. You know its Valentine's Day soon,' she said smiling. 'So have you proposed to her yet? If not, this is the right time for you to go down on a bended knee and do the necessary. Any knee will do – it doesn't matter left or right.'

'Actually I have proposed to her and she has agreed.'

'That's great news. I'm so happy for you. So when is the wedding then?'

'No date yet.'

'Don't forget to invite me. It may interest you to know that I can bake cakes,' she smiled and teased me. 'Soon we're going to have an *Amarya*' (new wife).

I nodded smiling.

'Don't forget I am your mother in the UK. So feel free to talk to me about anything.'

'Thank you very much. By the way,' I whispered. 'Dr Asibong is not my real father.'

'Of course I knew that. He likes winding people up. Anyway, how are your real parents at home? It's important to keep in touch with them you know. We parents get anxious too, especially when we don't hear from our children. So make it a point to call them at least once a month.'

I told Jamila about my conversation with the doctor. She gave me the necessary forms for the blood tests. 'Go and do the blood tests first and come back after one week. The result should be here. Then you will see the GP who would refer you to a consultant if necessary.'

In the flat in Earls Court, I asked. 'Suzanne, there's a place I'd love to take you to next weekend.'

'Where's that? Botswana or Zimbabwe? Seychelles or Maldives?'

'None of the above.'

'I want to go to where the sun is shining. I need sunshine.'

'In reality this should have been a surprise. I had Paris in mind.'

'Ah! For Valentine's weekend?'

'Yes.'

'I saw a lot of deals in the papers.'

'Where else could we go and have a quiet weekend all by ourselves?'

'Mauritius?'

'It's too far to go to Mauritius for just a weekend. Anyway, the point is I still have a few things to sort out before I can travel out of the country. As you probably know, I am not a British citizen and for some foreigners getting the necessary documents to live takes a while. It's too late for me to take you to Paris right now, because the process of getting the visa takes such a long time that by the time I get it, Valentine's Day would have come and gone. As soon as I am sorted, I promise you, we can go all the way to Mauritius.'

'I understand darling,' Suzanne said. 'I've been lucky with the Home Office, maybe because I'm a South African but I do understand what you're talking about. Even some South Africans do have some issues with the Home Office. As you said, even when you have the documents, getting the visa to France could be another nightmare. I saw the queue the other day at the embassy. It was horrendously long. And then once you enter the staff ask for all kinds of documents; where is this letter, whose signature is this? And all those stupid questions they ask. Why are you going there, do you have enough money to support yourself? How many days are you going to stay? By the time we go through all these problems of getting visas, we don't even have time for romance anymore.'

I was very pleased with myself.

'So, if we are not going to be kissing under the Eiffel Tower in Paris we might as well go to the Persian restaurant. I want to try their food again. I like Dara and Sara, they're a very nice couple.'

I was delighted. 'I'll book a table,' I said.

The phone rang. 'Okay thanks, Jos. I'm really grateful. No. Don't. I'll come immediately. Tomorrow evening. Yes, one night. Thank you. See you tomorrow evening.'

Suzanne replaced the phone.

'I'm going to Holland for a night. There's an emergency family meeting. That was Jos on the phone. I'll fly out tomorrow, back the day after. Honestly Mike, if you wrote a book about my family, it would be a bestseller. Michael, you're damn lucky you have no relatives to make your life a misery.'

'Other people have replaced my relatives.'

'Who are they?' Suzanne said looking at me.

'Definitely not you. I should say other things.'

'Alright I hope no one annoys me there.'

'Please do me a favour. Remain calm. Whoever succeeds in making you angry will succeed in destroying you in the end. Once one is angry, one does the most stupid things.'

The next day, as I was still holding the door handle at the resource centre, Wassa started to mock me. 'Look at the strange man who is being chased around by a white woman.'

I entered, closed the door and greeted everyone in the conference room. 'Okay,' he continued. 'I lost my bet but I still don't think she meant it. She's going to find an excuse soon to dump you. She didn't want to embarrass you in front of everyone in the restaurant that night.'

Jarvo cleared his throat. 'Wassa, you're taking things too far. It's enough. Let's accept what has happened and celebrate the love between them.'

'Bullshit! What sort of love? It's not natural for a woman to be chasing a man. Back home, the man does the chasing. That's what being a man is about. The he-goat chooses his own mate. You don't let the female sniff out the he-goat.'

'Please,' Jarvo pleaded. 'Let's get over this he-goat thing. We're human beings and have different ways of expressing our love. What made you think that she's doing the running? You and I don't know what transpires between the two of them. I think your assumptions are wrong.'

'What has Mustapha got to gain from marrying that Boer woman? What? Why should he be chasing her? It does not make sense at all. She has more to gain by having him around her. That's why I think she's doing the chasing. If he marries her, as he intends to, he cannot get his residence permit. He's an illegal immigrant and marrying someone like Suzanne will not help his cause at all. Also, Suzanne is white and Christian. If he marries her, Mustapha cannot marry another woman. Back home, he could marry more wives. I simply don't see the logic in him being in a relationship with that woman. What's wrong with you?' He turned round and looked at me. 'Mustapha, what did the Boer woman put in your food for you to be so madly in love with her? Back home when a man behaves like this we say that the woman must have used some love portions on him. You are marrying someone who will make your life even more difficult than it already is. You're not a teenager. You have two eyes and two ears and have been in this country long enough to know the difficulties you're going to face. Yet you still decide to marry this woman. I don't know what it is if this is not madness. Mustapha, honestly don't take this as an insult but you are the most stupid man walking on the surface of the earth.'

I was not angry. He continued. 'Back home I would have taken you to see the very popular medicine man who would be able to free you from the grip of this woman.'

'What's your problem?' Jarvo said getting irritated. 'Are you jealous?'

'I'm not. I'm just worried because my brother is getting himself into one of the biggest problems in this country, which is living illegally for the rest of his life. He has lost his senses completely.'

Jarvo said. 'We know we've a problem on our hands and that's the problem of his immigration status. We've got two plans. It's true that so many things are outside our control but we must bear in mind that we are dealing with the emotions of two people. The former Chinese leader Deng Xiaoping once said that: *It doesn't matter whether a cat is white or black, as long as it catches mice.* In other words, it doesn't matter where the bicycle is made as long as it can take one from point A to point B. I am not very happy that he has chosen this option because of his immigration status, but I would be the last person to condemn him. Michael, it's a big gamble.'

'I've reached the point where I'm ready to gamble everything for love.'

Wassa laughed loudly. 'Listen to him. Gamble everything for love. You think you are acting in a film or what? Be real man! I think our brother here has been watching too many Hollywood films that he's confusing fiction with reality. Mustapha something is wrong with you. My friend you should go and get your head sorted. Hear him, gamble everything for love. I cannot believe that all this madness is for a white woman.'

Later, after Suzanne had arrived, she asked. 'Michael, why haven't you asked me about these issues? I mean you have not shown any interest in knowing more about the problems.'

'Suzanne,' I whispered. 'We all have problems. In Hausa we have a saying: *Gidan kowa akwai.* Literally it means it's there in everyone's house. Each household has its own peculiar issues. As a matter of policy, I always tried to mind my own business. I have enough problems to deal with. Whenever you feel like it, you can tell me more. It all depends on you.'

On Valentine's Day I left the institute with a big smile. I arrived at Piccadilly Circus on time. Wearing my best suit and holding a bunch of flowers, I stood near the ticket machines where we agreed to meet. A group of girls came up to me.

'Are the flowers for me?' a girl asked.

'Wow! Yes,' another one screamed. 'I will marry you.'

'I'm the one you have been waiting for. You mean you don't recognise me?'

'Yes I'll be your Valentine – thank you.'

They walked away giggling.

As I stood by the tube map looking at the names of the stations, I felt two hands cover my eyes from behind. I could smell her perfume. 'Guess who's going out with you for dinner tonight,' a female voice whispered in a distinct South African accent.

'My one and only Suzanne,' I said.

'Sorry I'm late.'

'I've all the time in the world for you.'

'Wow! What a lovely bunch of flowers. For me?' she asked excitedly. She was wearing an orange silk top over a faux-suede pleated skirt.

'Of course, they're for you.'

'Oh! Thank you so much darling.'

We held each other and kissed passionately.

'Excuse me! I want to look at the map,' someone said angrily and pushed past me.

'Nice flowers,' she said looking at them.

'Nice perfume,' I said putting my hand around her waist.

We went out of the station and walked slowly towards the restaurant holding hands. From time to time, Suzanne would stop and kiss me. I noticed that she did it when she saw other couples. After all it was Valentine's Day. It was like a message: we do it better! In front of Persia restaurant, Suzanne whispered and pinched me. 'This is my first real Valentine.'

'Every day is Valentine's Day since I met you,' I whispered into her ears.

Sara was at the door. She welcomed us and led us to Rumi's corner.

'Every dress you wear fits you perfectly,' Sara commented looking at Suzanne.

'Is he taking good care of you?' Dara asked, opening a bottle of pink champagne.

'If he remembers Valentine's Day and he invited me out then I think he's taking care of me.'

'Just tell me when he doesn't and I'll put something in his kebab,' he said smiling. 'By the way, you look great.'

'Thank you Dara,' she said.

'To our everlasting love,' Suzanne said raising her glass of champagne.

'To the most beautiful woman my eyes have ever seen.'

I could see she was excited and a bit nervous. 'Now close your eyes and open your hand.'

I obeyed. She placed something in my hand. 'Open your eyes.'

'What's in it?' I asked looking at a small box.

'Open it.'

'Wow! Thank you very much,' I said and pulled out a silver chain from the box.

'Do you like it?'

'Of course, what does it say?'

'*Ek smaak jou stukkend* means I love you madly in Afrikaans. I had it made in Amsterdam.'

'You mean in one of those coffee shops that don't serve coffee?'

'No. They don't do chains in those shops.'

'They must sell something to make money! Thank you very much for the present.'

We ate.

I looked closely at Suzanne and not for the first time that evening I felt entranced. She looked more bewitching than ever.

'You've something to tell me?' she asked. 'I can tell.'

'Yes I do. Do you want to use the loo first?'

'I might as well. I don't want to pee in one of my best skirts. It's very expensive.' She stood up and showed me the faux-suede pleated skirt. 'I bought it in Amsterdam, from one of the most expensive fashion shops,' she whispered.

'You definitely have the figure for it and I like the top too.'

'Thank you,' she said and told me that the washed-silk, v-neck top was from the same shop. 'So I might as well go to the loo. You're full of surprises.' She walked away slowly jutting her buttocks.

When she returned she asked. 'So what have you got for me today? Mr surprises!'

I bought a piece of paper and read a short poem I had written entitled 'Crazy for You' It started with how I felt captivated whenever I was with her and that I had never before met anyone as sweet, kind and understanding as her. It ended with the line; 'There's no other woman like you; that's why I'm crazy for you.'

'Is that why you wanted me to go to the loo first?'

'No! It's about being crazy for you.'

'But that's not a surprise.'

'In our lives we do some crazy things and often we enjoy them. What we should not do are stupid things so as not to regret them. Loving you could be both. After I had proposed to you, a friend said that I was the most stupid person walking on the surface of the earth. He suggested I should go and have my head examined. It's true I'm crazy but I am crazy for you.' I paused. Looking straight into her eyes, I asked loudly, 'How do I put it?' I took a deep breath. 'Suzanne, you know that I haven't got my papers sorted at the Home Office. I've mentioned something to this effect several times.'

She nodded.

'That's not the whole truth. Suzanne, the truth is I'm actually an illegal immigrant.' I paused to see her reaction. She blinked and smiled.

I continued. 'Let me set the record straight. I came into this country legally, as a student to study filmmaking and prepare my script for the screen. What I've not told you was that circumstances conspired to make me an illegal immigrant. That's why I had to change my name to Michael in the first instance. It's a long story.'

'I see,' she nodded smiling.

'My uncle, who provided me with board and lodging died a few months after I arrived. Then my scholarship was stopped. So I had to choose whether to remain in the UK and try my luck or return to Nigeria. I chose to stay. It meant that I would be illegal but I desperately wanted to fulfil my dream. Given the circumstances, the only way I could get a residence permit was to marry either a UK citizen or an EU citizen.'

I noticed that Suzanne had a big smile and sipped her champagne.

'Not a South African.'

'That's correct, definitely not a South African.'

'Go ahead. I love the story, sounds interesting. Life knows how to give you tough choices.'

I nodded and continued. 'But I followed my heart and proposed to you because I love you. The thing is, my friends wanted to arrange a sham wedding to a UK citizen. The woman was willing to marry me for the money and I would get my documents sorted – a kind of marriage of convenience.'

'South Africans do it too. These were the friends that came here the day you proposed?'

'That's correct! I told them that I love you and will not leave you. I told them that it would be too complicated to have both of you in my life. I love you and that's it. But if you said no, I may consider marrying her just to get a residence permit. Life is not easy as an illegal immigrant.'

'I see. And when you proposed I said yes,' Suzanne said chuckling. 'I'm thoroughly enjoying this story.'

'It's not funny.'

'I bet it's not.' Suzanne sipped more champagne and smiled. 'The picture is getting clearer now. The plot thickens. I'm really enjoying this engaging story. Go ahead, so they did not come here to eat.'

'They came to hear what you would say. Anyway, I chose to marry you because I love you. One hundred per cent love. You remember what you once said when you returned from South Africa? You said something like, "for me love is all or nothing. I cannot love you on a part-time basis."'

She nodded.

'Same here, it's either Suzanne or nobody and it must be fulltime love. I've enjoyed every minute that I have spent with you. I strongly believe that love can conquer everything. Where there is unconditional love there is magic, there are miracles, there's peace and there's luck.

'Suzanne, at the end of the day, I do need a residence permit. I'm hoping and praying that there would be an amnesty in future. And I hope that between now and when there is an amnesty, I will not be arrested, detained and deported. If things work out according to plan, and we have children, I cannot maintain a family by washing plates or relying on you to be the main breadwinner. Maybe I could but it would be hard, a real struggle. Above all, I don't want to live in fear of arrest and deportation for the rest of my stay in the UK. How I am going to resolve this I don't know but I want to reassure you that I'll never leave you. I shall not marry that woman so as not to cause any misunder-standing between you and me. To love is to be crazy and I am crazy for you. Yes love makes people crazy but what are we without love? We're dead. I'm happy I'm crazy for someone like you. I feel I am a human being now that I'm in love with you. Love has no logic. Suzanne, I want you to love me but, above all, I want you to understand me.' I went down on my knee holding her hand, 'I love you and will love you until the day the sun refuses to shine. My sweetie, will you marry me?'

'Yes,' Suzanne said wiping away tears.

I stood up and kissed her.

'Has he proposed again?' Dara asked.

'Yes,' she said laughing.

'Michael, you propose only once and then you marry.' Looking at

Suzanne he asked, 'Suzanne, what have you been putting in his food?'

'I should ask you Dara,' Suzanne replied laughing. 'What have you added to his kebab?'

'It's Rumi's magic. Rumi would be proud of you, especially Michael, who has gone completely crazy. Any request for music?'

'Yes please.'

'In ten minutes.'

Suzanne held my hand across the table. 'I like that. Where there's love there's magic. Where there's love there are miracles. Beautiful quote,' she said smiling shaking her head. 'So you're an illegal immigrant?'

I nodded. 'Yes, I am.'

I looked at her and let out a sigh of relief. I felt as if the weight of the world had been lifted off my back.

Suzanne was invited to sing. She sang Whitney Houston's song *The Power of Love*.

After her song Dara invited us onto the dance floor.

Suzanne immediately placed her two hands around my neck. My hands went around her waist. She whispered into my ears. 'Michael, you're simply the most beautiful thing, the most magical thing that has ever happened to me. I wake up every morning looking forward to seeing your face and hearing your voice. There's a particular magic in your smile. I love everything about you. I've felt different since we met. I know it's because of love. As you said, everyday has been a Valentine's day. Indeed, I agree with you that where there's love, there's magic. Where there's love, there are miracles. You can be sure of one thing I will keep all your secrets. Your honesty is refreshing and rare. I know things are hard for you but I promise to be by your side through everything; when I say everything, I mean everything. I'll stand by you in the rain, the shade, in the sun, in the cold, in the light and in darkness. I'll stand by you through good and bad times, because that's what being in love is all about. You can also be sure of another thing I'll be by your side until the very last breath I take. Michael, I'm all yours from now till eternity.'

Eighteen

Light at the End of the Tunnel

'So when is the wedding?' Dr Asibong asked as we settled down in his flat.

'We've no date yet.'

'What are you waiting for?'

'Why are you in hurry?' Suzanne asked. 'I want a white wedding. You know the type of wedding you see in glossy magazines where the bride wears an expensive white dress and the ceremony takes place in an old castle somewhere in Scotland,' she paused and asked. 'Why are you looking at me like that?'

Dr Asibong was looking at her with his mouth partly open. 'But that'll be very expensive.'

'But I'm not cheap,' she argued nodding her head. 'I'm not cheap at all. I have always dreamt of wearing a custom made designer wedding gown made of French lace and it has to be one of those hand-embroidered with pearls diamante accents. It's very beautiful. On our wedding day you'll see it.'

'Sheikh, did you hear that?'

'I did.'

'But you're going to wear this expensive gown for just a few hours.'

'The dress may be temporary but the memory will be forever. It's a once-in-a-life time experience; something to always look at for the rest of our lives. After the wedding, your son and I will look forward to everything in life together. Are you happy with that?'

'No.'

'Why not?'

'Where are you going to get the money for such a lavish wedding?'

'You want us to get married so you'll pay.'

'You don't have to have an elaborate wedding.'

'Doc,' Suzanne said smiling. 'We want to take things one step at a time.'

'But sometimes you have to fast-track things. Do you need the blessings of your parents?'

'Not really – maybe Michael.'

'I'm his father and have given him my blessings.'

'And his mother?'

'I can vote on her behalf,' he said.

'Why are you in a hurry?' Suzanne asked again.

'I want to see and touch my grandchild,' Dr Asibong started. 'Now that you've found a healthy, handsome young man that is winding up your biological clock don't waste this opportunity. You don't have much time to waste. I can see that you want to have a baby too and as soon as possible.'

'How do you know?'

'I can hear your biological clock ticking. Tick, tick, tick,' Dr Asibong said chuckling. 'You see, I have inbuilt sensors that scans and sends me signals. I can tell exactly what your womb is saying.'

'It's begging *izzit*? My womb is saying, I'm ready to breed.'

'That's correct. You see, I picked the right signals.'

'Anyway Dr Asibong don't worry. We still haven't talk about your position on monogamy.'

'Today is not a good one for me. I've been ill of late but I can summarise my position as this. One man, one wife is complete and utter nonsense.' He began to cough. 'Men are not meant to have one partner.'

Suzanne interjected. 'I cannot agree with you. A musician cannot play more than one violin at the same time so a man cannot have more than one wife.'

'A drummer needs many drums to show how good he is.'

Suzanne laughed. 'So I cannot get you to change your position.'

'You can always try …' Dr Asibong said laughing too. 'The Bible commands us to go forth and procreate…to multiply … to spread our seeds. We cannot carry out this very important commandment with only one wife.'

'Is that how you interpret the Scriptures?'

'The Scriptures are constant. We interpret them the way it suits us.'

'I must say that you're someone with lots of contradictions.'

'We all have our contradictions and I can live with mine. You're right. I talk about polygamy but the truth is I'm not even married. Having said that the truth is one-man, one wife is pure fantasy invented by priests and the state long time ago to control the people. We live in a different era now and need to update the goals of our relationships. The whole idea that one woman is sufficient for one man is a big con. Having said all these, your case is different.'

'How's it different?'

'In English law there's a concept that states that for every rule there's an exception. When you marry Michael I will change my views.'

'Okay. I will prepare a document for you to sign renouncing your views on the day we marry.'

'I would sign anything you give me as long as you marry my son Sheikh.'

'And by signing the marriage certificate he'll not marry another wife.'

'That's correct. That's fine by me. Just fix the date and I'll be there.'

'Instead of drafting a document, I'll get you to be his witness. With your signature on our marriage certificate, you renounce your ancient views that polygamy is the way forward for humanity.'

He nodded. 'Yes, I'm willing to sign the marriage certificate any time.'

'Michael did you hear that?'

I nodded. 'I did.'

'By the way Suzanne,' Dr Asibong started later when we were about to leave. 'There's something I'd like as a present from you on your wedding day.'

'What's it?' she was very excited. 'You want something from South Africa?'

'No. What I want is in your flat,' he revealed smiling and coughing. 'What's it?'

'I want all the contraceptives in your cupboard. From that day onward no more pills.'

Suzanne smiled. 'I didn't realise you were into family planning too.'

That night, just before we went to bed, Suzanne said. 'Michael, I'll choose the date for the wedding. I'd like to have something like this in summer; ideally at the end of June or early July.'

'It's up to you. Once you have the date, please go to the council and do the necessary. Ideally I should have gone there but you know the situation I'm in.'

Suzanne nodded.

'I don't want to any take chances. If they ask you where I am, just make up a story. Don't tell them I'm somewhere abroad because you'll have my passport. You could just tell them that I'm busy working somewhere in Scotland on the oil rigs, for example. Or tell them I'm very sick, you know what I mean. They would trust a white person and wouldn't ask serious questions. A black man with a Nigerian passport would arouse a lot of suspicion. One very important point – please remember my full names. Don't go there and say Michael one minute and Mustapha the next. They are trained to look out for such inconsistencies.'

'It's alright, what's your real name again?' Suzanne asked opening my passport. 'Ah yes, Mustapha. Of course I'm only joking. Don't forget my brother Albert is coming here tomorrow evening.' I looked at her closely. 'Don't worry, he knows about you. I've informed them that I'm engaged. It's not going to be fun but it's a bridge we have to cross.'

'Do you want me to stay away for some time?'

'No! Why? We're too old to play hide and seek. Whoever doesn't like it can stuff it! One thing you can be sure of is that the conversation with Albert will not be rational and grown up.

'Let me tell you a bit about Albert. He's ten years older than me. He went to universities in South Africa before studying in the US. He's got a lot of businesses in southern Africa and here in the UK. He's into mining and real estate. Albert is very rich but is one of the most selfish people you'll ever meet. He's is a real bastard. We never really got along. It's amazing how we came out of the same womb. Having said that, he's got a different father who died when he was very little we were told. Albert lives a few streets from here and this is one of his properties. My other brother is called Alfred Jr. He's okay because he minds his own business – to a point. Also, I can tell him to shut up whenever I want and he'll simply laugh or walk away. He's not like Albert who makes life difficult for me. Alfred Jr doesn't like the fact that I'm going to marry you but he wouldn't say it to my face. It hurts the two of them because I refused to date their mates or business partners. Albert wanted me to marry his close friend called Kenneth years ago. He was a very rich man. I would have been his fourth wife. No wife ever lasted for more than three years. Then he wanted me to marry his golf partner, Alex who was into space engineering. He was very rich too but was well over sixty years old and not my type really. Alfred Jr introduced me to a tall Dutch military officer called Ruud. You see, Alfred Jr was a top officer in the South African army and a member of the elite commando under the apartheid regime. A couple of years ago he left the army to set up a security firm, which guards mines, farms and houses and runs a secret army to protect the interests of rich people in southern Africa. He's too busy chasing money and enemies across Africa to worry about you. As long as I don't ask him for money he'll not say a word. He wouldn't attend the wedding even if it were held in front of his house.'

The next day I heard a man's voice as I entered the flat. The door to the sitting room was partly open. I tried to close the front door quietly and tiptoe into the bedroom. 'Michael, come and meet Albert,' Suzanne said opening the door. I could see she was upset already. His face was red and tight.

'I'm very pleased to meet you, Mr Albert.'

'It's nice to meet you too Mike.'

We shook hands. I walked out of the sitting room. Suzanne followed me. 'There is something in the microwave for you. Just warm it and eat. He won't be long.'

'Please darling,' I whispered. 'Please don't lose your temper.'

'I love you,' she kissed me and went back to the sitting room, leaving the door open. I went to the bedroom and sat down and left the bedroom door open too. I could hear their conversation.

'Suzanne I want you to call this wedding off before you send out the invitations, before it's too late.'

'Too late for what? Who do you think you are Albert?'

'Your brother.'

'Absent brother, I've already agreed to his proposal and am not calling it off.'

'Look for any excuse please. Just tell him something.'

'Why?'

'Simply because this black man is only interested in your money.'

'Who told you? The only thing you see in this world is money and that is why you are always miserable. You know what Albert, you're a poor soul if the only thing you know and have is money. I love Michael because he sees other things in life, not just money.'

'Suzanne, all these black people are the same at the end of the day.'

'There are other things in life besides money and other things that he's interested in.'

'I'm sure he's just biding his time. He'll reveal this true colours later.'

'He's not like you.'

'Of course he's not. He's black for God's sake. How can you trust a black man?'

'Don't you do business with them?'

'Yes I do but marrying a black man is the most stupid thing you can do.'

'Don't insult me Albert.'

'Something is wrong with your sense of judgement. Have the two of you been smoking *dagga* (Afrikaans word for ganja) in Holland?'

'We don't smoke and he's never been to Holland.'

'Do you know the implications of marrying Michael?'

'No I don't, tell me.'

'It will have a serious effect on your inheritance. There is nothing that states you lose your inheritance should you marry Michael but as you know, I'm in charge of the estate and I have the right to take what I would call a commonsense decision.'

'I don't care anymore.'

'Sooner or later you have to make a choice.'

'I've chosen already, in case you've not noticed.'

'You cannot bring that black man into our family. You'll pay the price.'

'You go ahead and do your worst. If you're asking me to choose between love and money, I've already chosen love. You keep the money. There's more to life than money. I've only one life and I want to experience love – to give and to receive love. I'm happy with what I have. What's the point of having money and no love? What's the point of life if you are surrounded by material things but no one to share the basic things in life with, no one to love and no one to love you back? What's the meaning of life then, Albert? Tell me. I'm a human being who's in love with a man that loves me. I feel alive because I'm in love. Albert, why can't you live your life and I live mine? Live and let others live? What's your problem?' She yelled at him.

'He's black and incapable of loving you. This marriage has no future at all.'

'That's rich coming from you. You've had two wives already haven't you? You've had so many girlfriends but I have never judged you. Please respect my feelings and my choice. You gave one of your ex-wives a flat in France and the other one walked away with a house in Cheshire after only ten months of marriage. Yet you have the audacity to deny me my inheritance and tell me that Mike is incapable of loving me and that our marriage has no future,' Suzanne said and started to laugh.

'Why are you laughing?'

'They say if you don't cry, you laugh. I'm certainly not going to cry because of you. I would not give you the pleasure of making me shed a tear because of your stupidity. I wouldn't cry because of the rubbish that comes out of your mouth. Instead I'm laughing at your stupidity.'

'So you're happy to be used as a sex slave and be paraded around as a light-skinned trophy.'

'You're simply jealous I'm enjoying sex. You're begrudging me of what you're not enjoying – what you couldn't have with your ex-wives and girlfriends. One of your ex-wives told me you spent so much time thinking and worrying about money that you completely ignored her.'

There was a moment of silence.

'Listen to me Albert. Do you know that we have black blood running in our family? Aha! Have you ever asked yourself why Alfred Snr left South Africa for Holland? Have you bothered to study the family tree? Why has Mum got curly hair? Look at the photographs of our mother and you will see that she's a shade darker. For your information, I've looked at our family history and the startling revelation is that Alfred Snr's girlfriend – our grandmother was a mixed-race woman. The woman's name was Martha. When she became pregnant with our mother, Alfred Snr was sent into exile in Holland. The church said he had committed an abominable offence. Of course you and I were not told all these things. I saw one photograph in Mum's house and that made me fly to Holland to talk to him. You know that, we were only told about his existence very late. Alfred Snr told me everything that had happened between him and the woman and many other things as well. Take a weekend off and sit down with him and find out more about your ancestors. As for Martha, our grandmother no one knows what happened to her after she gave birth to our mother. She simply disappeared. Mum was brought up by relatives. So Albert, go and do a DNA test. Part of you is black and you cannot deny it and please show a bit of respect, Mr pure white.' She paused. 'Listen Albert, I'm not going to get anything out of this. I want to get something out of my life.'

'I'm not coming to your wedding.'

'You're not on our list of invited guests.'

Albert left.

Suzanne went to the toilet. 'Mike, are you alright?' Suzanne asked in the bedroom. 'Albert is such a pain. It's like this since we were children and to be honest with you, I'm totally *gatvol* ('fed up' in Afrikaans). Changing into her nightgown,' Suzanne continued. 'I hate it when people don't mind their own business. For God's sake, I'll soon be thirty-three. I'm old enough to decide who I want share my life with. I've only one life and I'm determined to have a good shot at it.'

'It's okay! Calm down darling.'

'Mr Nasty as I call him is so ignorant. He talks before he thinks – if he ever thinks. He talks because his mouth is open. He has no concept of shame at all. I've never met anyone so paranoid and gripped by irrational fear. Honestly Michael, I was so angry at one point that I felt like shooting him.'

'Suzanne I hope you haven't got a gun. I understand South Africans like guns a lot.'

'I don't have a gun. If I had, I'd have used it about half an hour ago.'

There was silence. Suzanne was still restless. She tossed and turned restlessly in bed.

'I really need something to calm me down otherwise I cannot sleep. Albert has succeeded in really winding me up. A very difficult man that never understands,' Suzanne said and went to the kitchen. 'This should do,' she said coming in with a two glasses of white wine. 'Michael, it's my turn to ask you a personal question.'

'Can I go to the loo first? I don't want to pee in my pyjamas. They're very expensive you know. I bought them in this posh shop,' I said laughing and showing off the pyjamas she bought for me. Suzanne hit me several times with a pillow, laughing too.

'Okay I'm listening.'

'You know I already say you are the sunshine in my life. I really love you Michael,' she went on her knees. 'Michael, will you marry me?'

'Of course,' I said and kissed her. 'Yes, I'll marry you.' I opened the window and shouted from the ground floor flat. 'YES! I WILL MARRY SUZANNE.'

'So what, fuck off,' someone shouted back.

'Good luck mate,' another voice added.

'Close the window. Don't disturb our neighbours.'

Suzanne slept quietly as usual. I could not. I looked at her in the middle of the night and whispered into her ears. 'Good night and thank you, my sweetheart!'

'What did you dream about?' I asked her at dawn.

'I dreamt about something to do with me and you.'

'Where, South Africa? Crossing the Sahara? Inner or Outer Mongolia?'

'No. The dream was a little bit complicated. I dreamt that you and I had enough of all this troubles and decided to leave. We wanted to go to where nobody knows us so that we can live peacefully together.'

'That's a good romantic story.'

'We ran away from all these problems for good. We decided to start a new life somewhere very far away. First we took the public transport, I remember that very well. Then we took a ship.'

'That's strange, not a plane?'

'Don't interrupt me. It was definitely a ship. I think we were actually stowaways. Nobody saw us when we sneaked onto the ship. When the ship docked in a remote island, we decided to disembark – secretly of course. No one saw us run away from the ship.'

'Has the island got a name?'

'No.'

'Where was it, near Mauritius, South Africa or where about?'

'I think somewhere in the Caribbean.'

'An island without a name?'

'The locals did not tell us initially. It did not matter to us anyway. The most important thing was that we had a place where we could live together in peace.'

'And we lived happily ever after.'

'Exactly.'

'Until the authorities realised we were illegal immigrants.'

Suzanne was quiet for a while. 'Why did you spoil my dream? That's not a good ending.'

'You see you can have all the dreams in the world until you become an illegal immigrant.'

There was a long silence.

'It's time to get up. You've to believe in your dream because they don't have expiry dates.'

'With someone like you by my side I'm beginning to believe in my dreams again. I'm not alone. Suzanne is with me.'

There was a moment of silence.

There were rays of the rising sun piecing through the window. I felt a sense of optimism I have never felt before. It was very powerful. I heard myself saying silently, 'Yes I can live now. Yes, I can love now. Things can only get better from now on…' I left the bed that morning with a big smile. I couldn't help but ask myself, 'is this the light at the end of the tunnel and is the sun at last beginning to come out?'

Days later, Suzanne told me she had registered the marriage and gave me a piece of paper. 'Now we have to inform all our guests. I'll buy the invitation cards and you'll deliver them to you friends. I'll print a short poem by a seventeenth-century Dutch poet on love and marriage on one side and the details of this ceremony, reception and dinner on the other.'

'Tell me, how did it go at the register office? Did they ask you questions?'

'Of course they did but I lied to them. I said my future husband is terminally ill. We want to tie the knot before he dies. I promise to love and marry only this man and I want to fulfil my wish. I wouldn't let my sweetheart go to his grave unmarried.'

'And …?'

'The woman fell for it,' Suzanne said and started imitating her English accent. 'Oh, poor you, I'm so sorry to hear about his ill health and that he is about to leave us all. What a shame but it must be a great feeling to love someone and to marry the one that you love, even though you know he is about to die. That's very romantic you know – a wonderful love story. We rarely come across such stories these days. At least he would go to his grave knowing how much you truly love him. At least you'll be very happy too that you loved your man right to the end. Come to think of it love, tying the knot would probably save his life. Love is very powerful you know.'

We both laughed. I was beginning to be anxious about the story.

'What if they turn up and see a healthy young man?'

'Miracles happen! If they turn up, the healthy, young, handsome man, will have to defend himself on that day. I've done my bit of lying.

You said I should make up a story didn't you?'

'Yes I did, but…'

'Don't panic Michael. You register in one room and this ceremony takes place in a hall somewhere. It's not written down that Michael is about to die. It was a simple conversation. She might not be on duty that day anyway.'

She paused for a while.

'Michael? I hope you didn't register me as Michael.'

'Sorry Mustapha. It's confusing. Don't worry darling, everything will be okay. Now we've got a date let's get on with the preparations.'

Several days later, Bozo's Joint was full when I entered. There were people on the staircase drinking. The music was very loud. I went into the Politburo meeting room.

'Look at this man! You still remember this place?' Jarvo asked laughing.

'Of course I do. Politburo still meets here?'

'We've not voted ourselves out of existence yet. When are you getting married?'

I gave him the invitation cards.

'I can see you're both serious,' he said laughing.

'Why waste time? We are not that young you know.'

'By the way, Stacy, the cockney woman called a few times. She says she really likes you and wanted to invite you over for a weekend. I told her you're very busy and will talk to her when you're free. I'll not close that door yet. You never know.'

'Thanks.'

'So our future Sembéne is settling down,' Taj said later. 'I hope things work out for you.'

'Don't worry Michael, we'll put up a show for you,' Jarvo promised. 'We'll make sure it looks as genuine as possible. If there are Home Office officials there, they'll look at the ceremony and say yes, this is a wedding. I'll invite as many people as possible.'

'I'll try and bring some Hausas. I'll invite Alhaji Sulaiman and his family. I'll get them to wear Hausa clothes so as to make it very colourful.' Taj lit his pipe and told us jokes.

'The president of an African country decided one day to visit the only mental hospital in the capital city of his country. During his tour of one of the wards, one of the chained mental patients waved at him frantically and told him to come. The president was surprised and bemused. He and his entourage stopped and looked at the patient. The patient insisted that the president should come to his bed. The President obliged. 'Who are you?' the patient asked.

'I'm the life president of this country.'

'You know what?' the patient started after a prolonged laughter. 'For many years I used to think that I was the life president of the country and I used to go around telling people this until one day I was brought here and chained to this bed. Welcome, another life president. There are empty beds as you can see. Now I know why there are people behind you, so that you cannot run away. That's exactly how they brought me here. You are welcome Mr life president.'

We laughed.

Taj continued. 'A young man called Charlie had some mental problems in Ghana. He was taken to a well-known mental hospital outside the capital city, Accra, for treatment. The doctors decided that the best thing to do was to remove his brain and examine it in the hospital. They successfully opened his skull, removed his brain and closed it and told him to go away and come back after three months. Charlie returned to Accra but after a few weeks he disappeared. Three months later the doctors went to Accra looking for Charlie but he was nowhere to be found. Several months later, a friend of Charlie's visited a neighbouring country. Whilst travelling on a bus, he saw someone that looked like Charlie in a particular uniform. This friend alighted from the bus and approached the young man.

'Excuse me sir, you look like Charlie from Accra, Ghana.'

'Yes you are correct. That's me.'

'Did doctors remove your brain for examination?'

'Yes, that's me.'

'The doctors are looking for you to put your brain back.'

'I don't need a brain.'

'What?'

'Can't you see I'm in the army? The soldiers in this country don't have brains.'

We laughed again.

Taj continued. 'Long time ago, a well-known German missionary felt he had a duty to convert Africans and spread the gospel. He was particularly incensed by what he called the worst offence against God. He wanted to preach to Africans the essence and value of human life and how cannibalism was against one of the Ten Commandments. He went to a remote African village where he was told that the chief of this village sacrificed one human being a year. The chief welcomed him and listened attentively to his preaching.

'Thank you for your message. Please tell me, missionary, how many people were killed during the First World War?'

The missionary told him, 'About nine million.'

'And how many were killed during the Second World War?'

'No one is absolutely certain of the figures but it's a lot, between forty and seventy million people perished.'

'Why kill all these people if you're not going to eat them?' the chief asked.

Nineteen

The Magic of Love

It was pouring with rain when I entered the flat in late June. 'I hope they get the weather forecast right on our wedding day. To marry on a day like this wouldn't be fun at all,' I struggled to say through the noise of the vacuum cleaner. Suzanne switched it off.

'I've checked the weather forecast and it should be fine,' Suzanne assured me.

'Well, you chose the date.'

'The forecast is that it's going to be very hot tomorrow.'

The phone rang. Jarvo told me that they are building a defensive legal wall, as he put it. 'We do not want to take chances at all. Kofi, a legal expert in immigration law is here with me. He wants to talk to you and your wife to be.'

The man over the phone wanted to talk to Suzanne first. I explained to her what my friends were trying to do. 'It's a precautionary measure, in case immigration officials turn up at the wedding ceremony.' She took the phone and went into the kitchen. I continued to vacuum and clean the flat. When she had finished, she handed the phone to me. 'Mustapha,' Kofi started. 'You'll be okay. I'll be there with all the necessary documents just in case some Home Office officials appear. I'll make sure I stand right behind you before you make your vows. Technically, the moment you make your vows they have no rights to arrest you. The main thing is to make sure we stop them from getting to you before you make your vows. I've assured Suzanne that we'll do our best to make sure you are not touched.'

'Thank you.'

'So young man, relax and take it easy.'

The phone rang again. It was Jamila. 'My children and I can only come for the wedding ceremony at the registry. We cannot do the reception and dinner. I think I've already told you that but I just want to remind you. I'm really sorry about that.'

'I'm going to the hotel where my nephew and her friends are staying. I'll be a bit late. Don't panic. I'm not going to run away on the eve of our wedding,' Suzanne said wearing her shoes.

Jarvo called in the evening. I could immediately tell from his voice that he was a bit nervous. 'Michael, please be very careful tomorrow. As you know Home Office officials are cracking down on sham marriages and are using wedding ceremonies to crackdown on illegal immigrants. In some cases, they position themselves in wedding halls looking for signs that the marriage could be bogus and one mistake, they pounce before the vows are made. A few days ago, a Nigerian was picked up from a wedding hall, handcuffed and taken away in a security van because he couldn't properly pronounce the surname of the bride. She had one of those difficult names from Poland. Their argument was that if he was really in love with her, he should have known how to pronounce her surname.'

'I don't know how to pronounce Suzanne's surname. God help me tomorrow.'

'Also try to make sure you are with her all the time. Make sure you're holding hands, kissing and smiling at each other. Try to do as many things together like welcoming guests.

'Why?'

'You wouldn't believe this. The authorities use CCTV cameras in the halls and corridors to monitor the movements and relationships of the bride and groom where they suspect it's a bogus marriage. We also understand that body language experts are employed to watch how the couples relate. You have to show that you two are madly in love. If it does not meet the requirements of what they think a bride and bridegroom should be, they pounce before the vows are made.'

'Jarvo, this is tough,' I confessed. 'I don't know how I'll be able to sleep tonight.'

'Drink a bit of vodka. It helps to calm the nerves. And don't forget to speak the little bit of Russian language you know while drinking,' he advised laughing.

'I've promised Suzanne that tomorrow is the last day I'll drink alcohol. It's enough.'

'But you've got twenty-four more hours,' he added laughing.

I went to bed a man full of worries. Suzanne had informed them that I was terminally ill and was dying. What if the authorities came around to see the dying bridegroom? What if someone in the register office had contacted the tabloids? This would be a front-page news story. Imagine walking into the council hall and then they say, 'hey, we thought you were about to die, but look he's healthy.' What would be my defence? Will it be enough to tell the world that she was joking? Instead of getting married to the woman I love, on the day that should be one of my memorable days, I'll be on my way to the detention centre. The night was warm and I was wide awake.

In the middle of the night, Suzanne and Joanna returned talking in loud voices and laughing. Suzanne entered the room. 'What's keeping you awake? I told you I wouldn't run away.'

I did not answer. She slept as soon as her head touched the pillow.

'Did you have a good sleep?' Suzanne asked at dawn.

'No! I was too nervous.'

'Michael, it's only a wedding, not a death chamber. Even those condemned to death sleep well before they are executed.'

'Someone going into the death chamber the following day knows that something is coming to an end, a sense of finality anyway. Did you have a good sleep?'

'Yes I did,' she replied yawning. 'Okay off we go. It's time to get out of bed.'

When we were ready to leave the flat, I leaned over and reminded her. 'Darling, please remember my real names, Mustapha Abdullahi. You cannot afford to make a mistake. Whatever you do please don't call me Michael in or around the wedding hall.'

'How many times are you going to tell me that Michael?' she said. 'This is the hundredth time.'

'Please remind your guests that they should call me by the name on the card.'

'You're getting neurotic Michael.'

I told her what Jarvo had told me. 'By the way, how do you pronounce your surname?'

She explained calmly how to pronounce van Anhalt Zerbst.

'Why don't you have a simple surname?'

'To test you on a day like this.'

I stood by the door waiting for her. Will today be my last day as a free person in the UK? Would I be arrested in front of my fiancée, friends and well-wishers? Would Suzanne forget and call me Michael and then some officials would pounce on me?

'Michael,' Suzanne shouted from where she was primping her hair in the mirror. 'Tell me something, how does my hair look?'

'Looks great,' I said without looking at her.

'Okay, does the colour of my hair match my eyebrows?'

'Yes, it does,' I replied without looking at her.

'No it doesn't. You're not looking at me.'

I looked at her.

'Does my bum look big in this?'

'No it doesn't,' I reluctantly answered.

'What do you mean? Are you really sure what you're talking about?'

'Okay, yes it does.'

Suzanne was wearing an unusually tight low-cut top that revealed her cleavage. The tight white dress held her breasts high. I held Suzanne's hand as we alighted from a taxi in front of the council building well ahead of time. I made sure we were holding hands and from time to time we kissed each other. 'Whatever you do, don't call me Michael for the next hour or so,' I reminded her.

Joe was the first to arrive. He and his wife came in a classic 1970 white convertible Mercedes-Benz. His wife Agnes wore colourful African clothes. She gave Suzanne a bunch of flowers.

Joe, who was wearing a three-piece suit, shouted as he climbed the stairs. 'Michael, look even the weather is on your side. You're a lucky man to have 30 degrees on your wedding day. You couldn't have asked for better weather. What a blessing.' He hugged and kissed Suzanne on the cheek and added. 'The English say something like: *Happy is the bride that the sun shines on.*'

I pulled him aside and reminded him that my name was Mustapha.

'Shit! I completely forgot. I'm sorry. I know what you mean. These guys are everywhere looking for illegal immigrants these days. They eavesdrop at weddings. You'll be all right. God is on your side,' Joe patted me on the back.

Bilal and Aisha walked up the stairs smiling at me. I noticed Aisha was pregnant. '*Assalaam Alaikum* Brother Mustapha,' Bilal said with a big smile.

'*Wa'alaikum Salaam*, Brother Bilal and Sister Aisha,' I answered embracing Bilal.

'How are you?'

'*Alhamdullilah*,' I said with a smile.

I could see they were delighted by my reply.

'I'm really sorry brother, we cannot attend the ceremony. We felt we had to come and congratulate you on your big day. We've a very important meeting in the city.'

Aisha was full of smiles. 'So brother, you converted to Islam and kept the name Mustapha. *Masha'Allah!* We were extremely happy when we saw the card.'

'Welcome Brother Mustapha to *Dar-ul-Haq* (House of Truth). Please when you have time bring her to the restaurant and *Insha'Allah* we'll pray together.'

'*Insha'Allah*,' I said smiling.

They left.

Jamila and her children Johanna and Bamidele arrived. Suzanne welcomed them on the stairs. 'I always wanted to know how African women tied this headgear,' she said referring to Jamila's headgear.

'When next you have time, I will show you how we do it,' Jamila said smiling.

Jarvo and members of the Politburo arrived in a bus with their friends. Jarvo was wearing a complex gown made from traditional *kente* cloth. 'You look like a local chief,' I said welcoming him.

'No local chief will attend a bogus marriage,' he replied laughing. 'Don't worry – we'll put on a real show for you.' He pointed at a young man in a suit. 'That's the guy you spoke to yesterday. Kofi has prepared an injunction to stop anyone from interfering with the ceremony just in case. As you know, once the vows are made, technically they cannot arrest you. I'll position him right behind you before the ceremony. Don't worry he's on your side. He is working for you.'

'Thanks.'

Wassa appeared with a broad smile on his face. He was wearing a big white gown and a hand-woven cap. He introduced his wife Fatou. She was wearing a traditional African dress. 'I'm here just for solidarity on the orders of the Politburo,' he whispered smiling.

At quarter to two, an official invited Suzanne and I into her office. My heartbeat increased. I was wondering if she was going to confront us with the secret recording of Suzanne saying I was terminally ill and dying. I could hear her already asking. 'Does this man look like someone who has months left to live?'

The black woman introduced herself. 'My name is Donna Brown and I'm the superintendent.' She looked straight into my eyes and smiled. I began to worry why she paid attention to me. She confirmed our names and dates of birth.

'Can you confirm that at least two people are here with you to witness your marriage?'

'Yes,' Suzanne answered.

'Please confirm that these people are old enough to understand what is taking place.'

'They are,' Suzanne said.

'Could I have a look at the rings please?' she asked smiling. 'You may not believe this but some people turn up without rings.' Donna opened the window. 'It's a bit hot for you,' she said looking at me. She noticed I was sweating profusely.

'What do you do when they come without rings?' Suzanne asked calmly.

'We always keep a supply of surplus rings here,' she laughed and showed us a cupboard. 'We do see all kinds of incidents here.' Donna gave us a piece of a paper. 'I'll leave you two to practise the lines for about five to ten minutes but before that I must say that exchanging rings is not an essential part of the wedding ceremony but your wife, sorry, Suzanne chose to include it. Are you happy with that?'

'Yes,' I said nodding.

'We don't want surprises because I notice from your names that you're from different cultures. What's a priority in Suzanne's culture may not be in yours.'

'That's alright.'

'I'm mentioning it because some couples from different cultural backgrounds don't discuss these sensitive issues before coming here and it becomes a drama during the ceremony.'

The superintendent turned to Suzanne. 'The wedding ring is usually placed on the third finger of the left hand as you make a declaration of commitment to him.'

Suzanne nodded smiling. 'Do we have to mention our middle names?'

'No. Just first and last names will do but the middle names will be on the certificate,' Donna clarified and left us alone in her office.

'So your middle name is Isabella?' I whispered looking at Suzanne.

'Shut up.'

'I didn't know that.'

'You never asked.'

The door opened. A tall bald white man entered with a frown. He had a badge on his coat. He looked at Suzanne and smiled at her. He was silent for a few seconds. My heart began to race again. I thought that was it. I was very relieved when he said. 'I'm the official photographer in the building. I would like your permission to take some photographs during the ceremony. I'll prepare an album. I'm a professional.'

Suzanne gave him the permission and gave him her details. 'Come to think of it …' I could sense Suzanne wanted to say Michael she stopped and giggled. 'Darling,' she finally said, 'that was something we haven't really arranged.' The man was happy. He left us in the office.

'Why are you sweating like this?' Suzanne asked. A dark pool of sweat had appeared under my armpit, spreading across the expensive blue shirt I was wearing. Beads of perspiration dappled my forehead.

'You don't seem to understand what's going on inside me.'

'Relax. You may have to make your vows in a soaked shirt.'

When we were ready, we entered the hall where our guests were already seated. I could see the photographer busy taking photographs. Kofi sat behind me holding a file. He looked very serious and looked around like a trained Secret Service agent. Suzanne sat next to me with her flowers. I sat there with my thoughts: I was very anxious.

'We're ready to start,' Donna Brown announced calling for silence. After welcoming everyone to the marriage ceremony, the superintendent looked at Suzanne and I. 'I would like to remind you of the solemn and binding character of the vows you're about to make.'

Suzanne and I stood in front of the big desk. I brought out the rings. The official ceremony began. I looked around nervously. There were no suspicious people around.

'Please answer this question loud and clear,' the superintendent implored looking at me. 'Mr Mustapha Abdullahi, will you take Suzanne Isabella van Anhalt Zerbst to be your lawfully wedded wife? Will you cherish and respect her and be loving, faithful and loyal to her throughout your marriage?'

'Yes I will.'

She looked at Suzanne and asked her a similar question.

'In order for a marriage to be legal you must make the legal declaration by repeating these words after me,' the superintendent continued.

I cleared my throat and repeated the words. 'I call upon these persons here present to witness that I, Mustapha Abdullahi do take thee Suzanne Isabella van Anhalt Zerbst to be my lawfully wedded wife.'

Suzanne made her declaration.

'Time to exchange the rings,' Donna Brown said. Holding the third finger of my left hand with her left hand, she held the ring with her right hand and declared looking straight into my eyes. 'I, Suzanne Isabella van Anhalt Zerbst give you this ring as a symbol of our marriage. All that I am, I give to you. All that I have, I share with you. All my love I promise you.' She slipped the ring onto my finger.

The superintendent was pleased. She smiled and declared that we were now husband and wife. 'You may now kiss the bride.'

I kissed Suzanne.

'You're free at last,' she whispered.

Dr Asibong stepped forward to sign the marriage certificate as my witness. Suzanne smiled. 'I'm so happy that there are so many people witnessing not only our wedding ceremony but Dr Asibong renouncing his ancient beliefs.' He did not reply. He smiled, signed the certificate and congratulated us. Joanna signed as Suzanne's witness.

We all went and stood on the stairs for the final photo shoot.

'You'll be alright,' Jarvo said. 'We'll be going back now. We've done our best.'

I thanked them.

The reception was set for 4.00 pm in Finsbury Park. Joe rolled out his classic, convertible Mercedes-Benz car which was now open. He and his wife left immediately after we signed the certificate to decorate the car with balloons. JUST MARRIED signs covered the number plates.

The photographer took more pictures.

Suzanne and I entered the decorated open-top Mercedes-Benz. Joe and his wife sat in front in the car. 'Let's cruise around for an hour or so before the refreshments. Lovely weather,' Joe said wearing his sunglasses.

At the traffic lights, I noticed a lot of people looked at us and some cars honked.

'Congrats mate,' a taxi driver said winking.

'Where're you off to on honeymoon?' A truck driver asked.

'Maldives,' I lied.

'I'm jealous,' he said. 'Do me a favour bridegroom. Kiss the bride for me.'

I kissed Suzanne.

He was very happy. He gave a thumb up and honked.

Taj stepped forward with a grin as soon as we arrived in Finsbury Park. 'I want you to meet Farouk. I've mentioned him in earlier conversations but you've both been too busy to meet.'

'*Salaam* Brother Mustapha,' Farouk said and embraced me. 'Congratulations. Taj has spoken about you a lot.' He greeted Suzanne.

'Thank you for coming.'

'Are you going to Mauritius for your honeymoon?'

'I wish,' replied Suzanne. 'Beautiful country and very nice people too.'

'Let me know if you're really going because I'm from Port Louis.'

'Yes I've been there,' Suzanne said. 'I really like Mauritius.'

Suzanne and Farouk spoke in French.

'So what are you doing?' Farouk turned to me. 'This is my card. Call me as soon as you're back from your honeymoon. Taj and I have something in mind for you.'

'*Ango*,' a man in Hausa clothes greeted me. I turned and shook hands with him.

'Is that another name?' Suzanne asked smiling. 'Is that your other name in Nigeria?'

'No. *Ango* means bridegroom in Hausa.'

'What about the bride?'

'*Amarya*,' the man said and introduced himself. 'My name is Alhaji Sulaiman. I'm a linguist. I teach Hausa in London. You mean he has not taught you Hausa words?' he asked smiling.

'Not a single word.'

'*Haba ango*,' he exclaimed looking at me. 'Please don't forget your culture. As we say in Hausa: *Kowa ya bar gida, gida ya bar shi.* Whoever forsakes his culture, his culture will forsake him.'

I joined Farouk who was talking to Frank B.

'Look at the bride,' Frank B commented as Suzanne walked past slowly.

'She's got childbearing hips and can carry two babies at the same time.'

'Blimey! You mean you could only see the childbearing hips? With due respect Mr Farouk,' Frank B said, 'Suzanne has one of the best backsides I've ever seen. Look at it. Well rounded and see how they move as she walks. Young fella, you're a lucky man.'

'Are they real or plastic?

'Her tits are definitely real; they're not plastic,' Frank B said with conviction. 'She does not appear to be a surgically modified babe. She's wholly organic.'

'How do you know?'

'Simple! See natural ones move a bit with any movement of the body. Plastic tits are too well rounded and static. No matter how large or small, a tit must shake a little bit when the woman walks. See what I mean? Look at Suzanne, see how her tits are moving?'

Later in the evening, over twenty of us settled in a special room at Persia restaurant for dinner. Dr Asibong was the first to speak. 'Let me thank you all for coming but especially thank Suzanne for making today one of the most memorable days of my life. Sheikh as you all know came to the UK many years ago with a big dream. What he did not know was that part of the dream would be meeting and marrying Suzanne. We know that he went through a very difficult patch but luckily he met his soul mate in Suzanne. I could say that meeting Suzanne has changed Sheikh. I hope that we'll be invited to a naming ceremony soon.' He looked at Suzanne.

'Why are you looking at me like that?' Suzanne asked laughing.

'The clock is ticking and my scanner is sending me signals.'

'You mean it's time for Suzanne to breed?' Frank B asked loudly.

'She knows what I mean.' He laughed and continued. 'To love is to face dangers and challenges. They've both been able to overcome so many hurdles so far to get to where they are today. Let us not only pray-that they are further sheltered from these dangers of love, but that they should be fearless, courageous, reasonable and lucky when facing them in the future.'

When he stopped talking Suzanne gave him a wrapped packet laughing.

He laughed and thanked her.

'What's going on?' Frank B asked loudly. 'That's very unusual. Hang on, a bride giving her father-in-law a present on her wedding day. Is that the custom in South Africa?'

'Dr Asibong, you tell them what's in there. You asked for them.'

Dr Asibong stood up. 'When they announced their engagement, I made a modest request. I told Suzanne that the best present she could give me as her father-in-law today would be all the contraceptives in her cupboard.'

There was laughter.

'Did he really ask for them?' Joanna asked Suzanne.

Still laughing, Suzanne nodded. 'Yes he did.'

'What's he going to do with them?'

'I don't know. That's his business.'

Suzanne asked Dr Asibong. 'What about our agreement?'

'What agreement?'

'*Pacta sunt servanta*,' Suzanne said.

'I know what it means. It's a Latin phrase. *Agreement must be kept*.'

'It's not enough to know. You must honour the agreement.'

'But *pacta sunt servanta* is a concept in International Relations and refers to agreements between nations. It has nothing to do with the relationship between a bride and her father-in-law.'

'I'll tell everyone about the agreement. We both agreed, and Michael is my witness, that by signing the marriage certificate, you Dr Asibong will renounce your ancient views on polygamy. As from today you will not support polygamy any more.'

'Did I say that? I cannot remember,' he said laughing.

'I've fulfilled my part of the deal. I've married your son Sheikh and I've given you all the contraceptives. Now it's your turn fulfil your part of the deal.'

'As you all know, I've believe that the one man, one wife ideology is a total nonsense.'

'That's right,' Frank B said loudly nodding. 'I'm happy somebody else thinks the way I do.'

'But we have an agreement,' Suzanne insisted.

'Of course we do. In England we say, "For every rule, there's an exception." Suzanne is the exception. I would be the last person to tolerate that from Sheikh. I'll be the first person to say no, Suzanne is sufficient for you because Suzanne is special. She's more than a wife. Suzanne is a companion, a soul mate and such women are rare.'

'Doc, you've not totally renounced your position.'

'Machiavelli once said: *The promise given was a necessity of the past: the word broken is a necessity of the present.* Please raise your glasses and join me in drinking to their everlasting love, good health, success and we hope and pray that this marriage will be blessed with a healthy child soon.'

'Now that the contraceptives have been liberated we're eagerly waiting the next big news,' Frank commented looking at Suzanne.

Dr Asibong sat down. 'Oh yes, we're looking forward to having a baby soon.'

'Who are *we*?'

'I'm your father-in-law now.'

Joanna complained loudly. 'Don't you feel offended being asked to breed?'

'It's alright,' Suzanne said. 'They're just having a laugh.'

Dr Asibong whispered something into Frank B's ears. 'I definitely agree with the Chinese idiom,' Frank B looked at Joanna. 'It's true. A Chinese teapot can fill four teacups and have some left for other side cups.'

Joanna looked puzzled. 'What has a teapot got to do with wedding?'

'It's okay,' Suzanne said smiling. 'They're winding me up. I know what it means.'

'It's a Chinese idiom and can be interpreted in whatever way you want.'

'What Mr Frank B is saying is this, a man can marry four wives and still have the time and energy for concubines; true or false, dirty old man?'

'If that's the way you understand the idiom fine,' he replied laughing.

'Time to order,' Suzanne said looking at the menu. '*Vuil ou man* – that's dirty old man in Afrikaans by the way. What would you like, leg or breast, I mean chicken?' she asked Frank B laughing.

'Oh blimey! Could I have both?'

'No you can't. You have to choose only one.'

'It's better to be a dirty old man than a lousy or nasty old man,' Frank B replied and called for silence and stood up.

'This young fella here is lucky in many respects. He might have one of the biggest smiles on his face and look very happy, but let's not forget that his journey in the UK started very badly. I still remember the first day I saw him at his uncle's flat in Maida Vale. He was full of hope and optimism, full of innocence and energy. Then tragedy struck. His uncle Mo, who was one of my best friends, died suddenly. This terrible incident of course created all kinds of problems for Michael. I notice his wife calls him Michael. I don't know where they got that name from. Anyway, the young man endured and persevered. Very few people go through what he's gone through and are still able to have a big smile on their faces. The remarkable thing is that he's always wearing a beaming smile. Suzanne, I have a confession to make. I teased him many times about going out and having fun, to go out and get a girlfriend. I didn't know he was waiting for you. But after the pain comes the gain and it came to him in the shape of this lovely woman here called Suzanne. It is often said that the best things in life come to those who wait. When life threw him into the deep end this young fella did not sink, instead he floated and swam to the shore and into the arms of a lovely woman. From what I can see, Michael as his wife calls him, is definitely one of the luckiest men because he's married to a woman who sees and appreciates the man in her husband. Very few women see the man in their husbands, Suzanne does. Enjoy each other. Jump on each other and breed like rabbits.'

The food was served and we ate.

Sara and Dara served everyone a glass of pink champagne. Dara the Head Chef called for silence before the dessert was served. He stood up to speak. 'I'll be very brief. I remember clearly the first time Michael and Suzanne came here on their first date. Michael was very nervous.'

Frank B interrupted. 'I'd be nervous if I was taking such a lovely lady out for the first time.'

'It was during their second visit that Michael proposed to her. You wouldn't believe this, he proposed to her again on their third visit.'

'I would propose to her ten times,' Frank B said.

'I've never seen a man propose to a woman twice in the same spot. Michael did it. We are so happy to be witnessing the union of these two. It fills us with joy to just watch them as lovebirds. I hope the next party will be a naming ceremony. May their marriage be blessed by the Almighty with healthy and beautiful children. Let's celebrate and appreciate the love between M & S as we call them here. Shakespeare had Romeo and Juliet. We have Michael and Suzanne.' Dara paused. 'I want to recite a poem by Jalaluddin Rumi, the 13th-century Muslim scholar and philosopher.'

Az mohabbat talkh-hâ shirin shavad
az mohabbat mes-hâ zarrin shavad
az mohabbat dord-hâ sâfi shavad
az mohabbat dard-hâ shâfi shavad …

He then translated it:

By love, the bitter becomes sweet;
by love, copper becomes gold;
by love, dregs become clear;
by love, pains become healing …

After dessert, Dara came around and whispered. 'Don't worry, the champagne as usual is on me.' He pulled up a chair and sat next to Joe. They were chatting and laughing.

'Do you know each other?' Suzanne asked them.

'Dara is one of my best friends.'

'He reserved Rumi's corner for the two of you,' Dara revealed.

'I see. That's how you knew my favourite cake. I always wondered how Michael knew because only one person knew.'

Joe stood up. 'I think you all need a short speech from me. I remember clearly the first day Suzanne came to the institute to work as a general assistant from the agency. During the first short break I didn't know why but I asked to see her palm. I told her that I was a member of a lost tribe of African gypsies and could tell her fortune. It was a lie of course. She looked at me as if I was a murderer. You should have seen the expression on her face that day. I was scared she was going to attack me with the cutlery. To my surprise she put her fork down and reluctantly opened her palm. I looked at her palm closely and pretended to be reading it. I told her something like this. Correct me, Suzanne, if I am wrong. I said, Suzanne whether you left South Africa in search of Mr Right or not, you're going to meet the man of your dreams in London, in this kitchen. He will be tall, dark and handsome. She interrupted and said, "But I'm returning to South Africa soon." I said either things will happen and you won't be able to go or you'll come back because this is where you're destined to meet him. I said something like this: He is the man that will make two of your dreams come true but Suzanne, for your dreams to come true, you will have to make his come true too. This young man will awaken your soul, your spirit, desires and ignite the light inside you and you'll love him to the point of marrying him and only death will part the two of you. But to do that you have to let go of your life plans and accept the ones waiting for you. You will have two children, a boy and a girl – a pigeon pair. Meeting this man will take you to a place you never thought you would end up. But the journey will be worthwhile because fortune, peace and tranquillity await you.'

'Am I right Suzanne?'

'Yes,' she shook her head. I could see tears rolling down her cheeks.

'Suzanne was supposed to work for only one week. On Friday, after she had changed her clothes and collected her signed timesheet, she came to me, arms akimbo and asked with a smile. "So, where's the tall dark handsome young man that'll sweep me off my feet and make my dreams come true, Mr African gypsy?" I told her that the sun has not set yet. Be patient. I reminded her that miracles do happen and that she was still standing in the kitchen. We were still having the conversation, when Leslie our boss walked in and asked if she could come back the following week. Suzanne was to work somewhere but the agency told her to remain at the institute. Within a very short period, so many things happened and Suzanne was made an assistant catering manager. I don't know the details but I know that Suzanne cancelled or postponed her return to South Africa twice. Am I right?'

'Yes you are.'

'Then one Monday morning she came in a bit moody, singing as usual. I told her not to worry, "he'll soon come and your lonely days will be gone." She was irritated and swore at me but I was already used to Suzanne swearing at me. Later, a tall, dark and handsome young man walked into the kitchen smiling. As he walked closer to the manager's office, Suzanne started singing the song being played on the radio. It was Lionel Richie's hit song *Hello, Is It Me You're Looking For?* Just as she came out of the office, singing the song, this tall, dark handsome young man said. "I'm looking for Suzanne." By the way he was wearing a T-shirt that said *I'll Make Your Dreams Come True.*'

'Blimey! I gave him the T-shirt,' Frank B said.

'Suzanne continued singing the song looking at him. I could see something clicked between the two of them as they stood looking at each other for some seconds. You feel these things – the magic of love. You could see the instant fantastic attraction these two had for each other; you could feel that a romantic connection had been made. From that moment on Suzanne was a changed person. When Suzanne showed him the changing room and came back, I told her something like this, correct me if I'm wrong Suzanne. I said, Suzanne, treat this young man well. That's your Mr Right. It's with him that you'll embark on this extraordinary journey; a journey of self-revelation and self-fulfilment. This is the man who will bring the best out in you and you will bring the best out in him. You have met so many men but this is the special one; the chosen one for you. I'll never forget the smile on her face.'

'This is extraordinary,' Joanna said. 'Did he really say that?'

'Yes,' Suzanne replied and nodded.

'I want to thank Suzanne for many things. She listened and reasoned well but, above all, I want to say a big thank you for disappearing without any trace after their first date. Whoa! Michael almost went mad. It was fun watching him. He almost lost it. He wanted to report the case to the police or the Missing Persons helpline. He was desperate. You should have seen him.'

Suzanne was laughing.

'Michael was completely lost without Suzanne. Anyway, after some time Suzanne returned to London and the rest as they say is history. The joy and happiness of Michael and Suzanne makes me happy too. Please join me in raising a glass to toast the health, love and success of M & S.'

'Can you read my palm for me please, African gypsy?' Frank B asked. 'You never know, I might be about to meet my soul mate too.'

'Too late in the day dirty old man,' Suzanne said yawning.

'Good morning, my beloved husband,' Suzanne said as soon as she noticed I was awake in the morning. 'You must be very tired.'

'Morning to my wife,' I struggled to answer. 'Yes, I'm knackered.'

'Let's get up and get ready for our honeymoon,' she said. 'Our train to Cardiff is at 2.00 pm.'

We had a quick breakfast.

'Great! Now my darling husband,' she said when we were ready to go. I looked at her as she approached me hiding something behind her back. 'Close your eyes,' she said smiling. I did. 'Michael, you're certainly not the most stupid person walking on the surface of the earth. Among the qualities I saw and admired in you was your honesty and forthrightness. Open your hand. I've a big surprise for you.'

I opened my hand. She placed something in it.

'Now open your eyes.'

'What!' I shouted the moment I opened my eyes.

'Yes,' she said nodding and smiling.

'An EU passport?'

'Yes,' she said still nodding and smiling.

I opened it. I could see her passport photograph and what I thought was very strange language.

'Is this Dutch?'

'You're a smart cookie.'

'You're Dutch?'

'Yes! I'll explain. It's a long story. That's one of the reasons I've been going to Holland. I'm not doing an MA in sociology. You think you are the only one who can lie? I'll tell you more.' She held me closer. 'So when we come back from Wales, do me one big favour, pick up the telephone and call that friend of yours who said you are the most stupid person walking on the surface of the earth. Tell him you are not stupid but in love. Tell him what you told me on Valentine's Day at Persia restaurant – that where there's love there's magic, where there's love there are miracles.'

It was hard for me to believe what was going on. I looked at Suzanne and the passport again and again. My eyes welled with tears and within seconds started to cascade over my eyelids and down my cheeks. Suzanne wiped away the tears. 'So my wild lion, that's your passport to freedom. Soon you will be free to chase your dream again and apply for your residence permit when we return. First things first, let's have a honeymoon.'

I stood there in tears looking at her in complete shock. I tried to speak but couldn't. Still sobbing I asked, 'What have I done to deserve this?'

'You're my husband and I love you. And you've been honest with me,' she said.

'And I love you Suzanne,' was the only thing I could utter still crying.

'I love you too,' she kissed me passionately.

At Paddington Station, I sat on a bench numb. I could not believe what had just happened to me. Suzanne went to the toilet first and then to buy us sandwiches. I looked at her passport over and over again. I pinched myself several times to be sure it was not a dream. Is this true? Is the passport genuine? Why would she get a fake passport? Is this really it? Am I really beginning to see the light at the end of the tunnel? My eyes started welling up and tears started streaming down my face again. Suzanne returned and sat on the other side of the bench sorting things out in her bag. I remained speechless looking at her. She turned to me. 'Why are you looking at me like that? Do you know me? Have we met before? You want something from me? Can I help you?' she asked looking very serious.

'Excuse me sir, could you please stop harassing this young lady?' A security officer told me. 'Do you have a train to board or are you loitering around here.'

'Oops! I'm sorry,' Suzanne said laughing. 'He's my husband and I'm just winding him up.'

'Sorry boss,' the security man apologised and walked away laughing too.

On the train Suzanne said. 'Listen Michael, I deliberately didn't take any book with me. I wanted us to talk. For God's sake, we're on our honeymoon say something. If you're not going to talk to me, I'll find someone to talk to.'

In Cardiff, Suzanne started. 'I've two confessions to make.'

'Number one.'

'I think I've told you already. I wasn't doing research for an MA course in sociology. I was doing research into my family history. I used the MA course as a smokescreen to hide the fact that I was also applying for my Dutch citizenship and then passport.'

'I see. Confession number two please.'

'Ah!' she started laughing. 'I was very happy when you said I should go and register the marriage. You would have known that I had an EU passport if you had done it. I used the EU passport. There was nothing like a sick and dying groom ready to be married off into his grave. I made that up to confuse you. As an EU citizen, I have the right under certain articles of the Treaty of Rome to marry without being questioned.'

'I was really worried.'

'I'm sorry. I didn't even think of the consequences. The solicitor who called before the wedding knew that I used the EU passport. But I told him not to tell you and your other friend. So it was an elaborate plan to surprise you.'

'I see. I have a lot of confessions to make but first Suzanne please tell me how you got the passport. I'm puzzled.'

'When I went to South Africa after our first date, I went and spent some time with my Mother. She's not with my Dad any more. Normally I stay with my Dad but we had a big row over my future and I went to stay with my Mum, with whom I always had issues. I can tolerate her to a point. She told me to help her clear out some things and with time I became curious and I started looking at other things. Rummaging around her cupboards and old files, I came across many old photographs that aroused my interest. The one that particularly struck me was where my grandfather, Alfred Snr as he is known, was standing on the farm near the house, well-dressed and smiling, with a mixed-race woman. It was a black and white photo but you could see she was a shade darker than him. Then it occurred to me that we were actually never told anything about our grandmother. Who was she? Very little was said about Alfred Snr too. We knew he was in Holland but no one told us why and we were not encouraged to be in touch with him. I desperately wanted to know more about this woman standing with him. How could a mixed-race woman get so close to a Boer man? He was full of smiles. The body language suggested a close relationship. It was obvious she was not his maid. She was smartly dressed too. Who was she? What was she doing in a Boer family? Remember those were the days before apartheid but as you probably know, racial segregation existed long before the 1948 Act. The Boers always felt racially superior. My Mother wouldn't say a word. She said that was my grandmother and that was it. It was a difficult revelation for me. I asked for Alfred Snr's details and called him. He lives in a place called Zeeland in Holland. He was delighted that I called and wanted to see me. To apply for a visa, I asked him to send me all those stupid letters embassies ask for. It was a hassle but I eventually got one. In the end I flew to Holland and met him for the first time. He told me everything. His memory is still sharp. He told me that he had fallen in love with this woman in the Church. In those days white churches were highly segregated but somehow she was allowed in because she was mixed-race probably. Alfred Snr said it was love at first sight. Her name was Martha. He still smiles whenever he pronounces her name. He must have loved her truly. When the relationship became intense the Church told him to stop seeing her. He refused arguing that he was obeying God's commandment to love thy neighbour. Then she became pregnant. That was a big scandal. First, he had a relationship with a mixed-race woman and secondly it was a pregnancy outside wedlock. There was no way the Church would allow him to marry her. His family ostracised him. The Church excommunicated him. Martha was taken away to an unknown place to give birth while Alfred Snr was told to leave South Africa and go back to Holland to live in exile. He wanted to marry her and live with her but the Church and the authorities categorically refused and would not allow him take her to Holland. He was a disgrace to the white race and had to be punished. The information was a shock to my system. I began to see myself in a new light. Then I returned to South Africa and wanted to know what eventually happened to Martha. I wanted to trace her family. It was possible that we would pass each other on the streets without know-ing that we are related. Just as I was about to contact the Church, Alfred Snr called. He wanted to see me again. That was when I called and told your landlord that there was a change of plan and I was not returning to the UK immediately but going to Holland.'

'I see. And did the Church give you access to their records?'

'Of course not! I tried but they refused. No one knew where Martha was or what happened to her after giving birth to our mother. But I'm sure, once this generation of church leaders go, the next generation will open up the archives and I'll be able to do research on Martha. Anyway, going to see Alfred Snr in Holland was another hassle. It was a nightmare getting another visa. When I met him, he wanted to know why there were all these difficulties in getting the visa. I told him I was travelling on a South African passport. A very good friend of his called Jos told me that I could apply for a Dutch citizenship based on ancestry. The fact that Alfred Snr was my grandfather meant I could apply and get Dutch citizenship. Alfred Snr signed the necessary forms and I applied. I returned to the UK and you were still here. By now I strongly suspected you were an illegal immigrant.'

'How?'

'You never talked about going out of the country, about going home, for example. I also thought this guy is too intelligent to be washing dishes. How could someone quote philosophers, read Pushkin and wash plates? I put two and two together but I still wasn't sure and I didn't want to ask. I knew that if I asked you, there was a possibility that you would feel exposed. It might scare you off.'

'I see. I'm too intelligent to wash plates and too handsome to be single.'

'Shut up! Then I went to Holland from the UK to finalise my citizenship. A day before I left South Africa, I was told by Jos that my application for Dutch citizenship was successful. If you remember, as soon as I arrived, you proposed and I accepted knowing that I had EU citizenship already. If you were illegal, I calculated that by the time we get married I would have my EU passport. It would give you the right to remain in the UK as a legal immigrant. If not, it would make my life a lot easier. I could travel without all these hassles. If you remember, Jos called one evening and I went to Holland for one night only.'

'Yes I remember.'

'I went to pick up the passport. So I waited till this morning to surprise you.'

I took a deep breath and looked at her for a long time. 'Suzanne how can I thank you?'

'I love you and I want you to meet your destiny.'

'How's Alfred Snr?'

'He's okay. The remarkable thing is that he's not bitter at all. He said he was madly in love with Martha. He kept saying. "I fell for God's trick by falling in love with Martha."'

'I don't understand.'

'He believes God created human beings in different colours and shapes and sizes. God wanted us to mix as races so as to move forward towards what he called the perfect human being. He was and remains against white supremacy. Alfred Snr believes we feel love towards each other as human beings and that if God did not want us to mix He would have found a way of making it impossible for a white person to fall in love with a black person and vice versa. A human being cannot fall in love with a gorilla he argued. He strongly believes God tricked him into falling in love with Martha and that falling in love with her was God's command. The paradox I still can't resolve is how a sin can help fulfil God's plan. In many ways he reminds me of Dr Asibong and his strange beliefs but we are what we believe. We may not agree with what they say but we have to understand where they are coming from.' She paused. 'Alfred Snr said he died the day the Church took Martha away from him. He managed to write down many things about himself, about Martha and the Church. I have to learn Dutch properly to read and understand them. He never married in Holland. This is a man with a real heart.'

'Does he know about our relationship?'

'Of course, I told him everything about you, especially your laughter. He said it reminded him of Martha who also had a wonderful laugh. I told him the last time I went that you were an illegal immigrant. He laughed and found it hard to understand the concept. "How can a human being be illegal?" he asked me several times.'

'And our wedding?'

'He knows. He actually wanted to come and hand me over to you but he was ill. It would have been great to listen to the conversation between him and Dr Asibong. He said that if I love you I should marry you. I would always remember his words. "My dear Suzanne, follow your heart for you only love once."'

'I look forward to meeting him.'

'Once you're sorted we'll visit him. He would be delighted to meet you too.'

'You only love once,' I repeated.

Twenty

Free at Last

Suzanne exclaimed the moment she stepped into the flat, 'Aha! A card, let's see who sent it.' She opened it and showed it to me. 'It's from Alfred Jr. I'm surprised he had time to write and post the card. He knows that I would have a go at him when next I speak to him. He's not like Albert who talks all the rubbish in the world.'

'Why would he send such photographs on a wedding card?'

'Alfred Jr is not like Alfred Snr. This one is weird. The guns and fast cars on the card show his philosophy. That's his passion. He belongs to a club whose motto is: *live fast die young.*'

The next day I went to the GP surgery in West Hampstead for my prescription.

'Back already,' Jamila said. 'I thought you would go to some faraway romantic places like Barbados, Maldives, Madagascar or Thailand.'

'We went to Wales for a couple of nights where it rained, rained and rained.' I walked closer to her and whispered. 'Can I tell you something in confidence?'

'Of course,' she said and led me into a consulting room and closed the door.

'You know what? Suzanne is a Dutch citizen and has a Dutch passport.'

'What?'

'Yes,' I showed her the passport.

'And you never knew?'

'I knew the day after we were married.'

'*Allahu Akbar*! *Allahu Akbar*! This is unbelievable. This is a miracle. You see. I'm happy I told you to listen to your heart. *Allahu Akbar*! Now hurry up and apply. Quick! Quick! Quick! Don't waste even a minute.'

'We came back only yesterday and I have to see my friends and get a good solicitor this time around.'

'My cousin Bash is a good solicitor. He's got an office in Kilburn. Incidentally he's going home to get married next week. My daughter Johanna is getting married too. Wedding bells ringing all around us,' Jamila started dancing. She was very excited. 'I'm so happy for you.' She went and brought my prescription. 'This is my cousin's card. Call him or go to his office immediately. Off you go. Wonders never end. *Allahu Akbar!*'

'Sheikh! That was a great wedding. I thoroughly enjoyed it,' Dr Asibong said outside his flat on Sumatra Road. 'How was your honeymoon?'

'It went well.'

'And Suzanne?'

'She's fine. Suzanne is a Dutch citizen,' I said and showed him her EU passport.

'*Abasi Kenyon* (Gracious God),' he shouted. 'You don't mean it. Sheikh! How do you explain this? It's like something out of a movie. And of course you never knew all along. Oh my God!'

'I'll tell you more when I have the time. I'm in a hurry to go and see a solicitor.'

'I hope you're not going to use that man again.'

'No. Auntie Jamila has just given me the details of her cousin who is a solicitor.'

'Great. Send me the invoice. I'll pay. Don't let Suzanne pay. She's done more than enough for you. If you don't mind I'll call later and thank her. Thank you very much Sheikh for the good news. I'm so happy.'

I rushed to the Kilburn office of the solicitor. 'Auntie Jamila said you should see me?'

'Yes. She gave me your details.'

'Please sit down. What can I do for you?'

I told him.

'Okay. I need three things as soon as possible – your passport, her passport and the marriage certificate.'

I gave him the documents. He made photocopies. Handing over

the original documents to me he said. 'I'm going to the Home Office right now. I'll put in your application straightaway and fast-track the issuance of a reference number.'

'How much will it cost?'

'It's okay. Actually, Auntie Jamila called to say her adopted son was on his way to see me. It's important we apply as soon as possible. We can talk about money later. Getting a reference number is the best I can do right now. It's as good as a stay permit because you cannot be detained or deported for being illegal while your case is under consideration at the Home Office. My secretary will give you the necessary forms to fill in and the list of documents we'll need from you and your wife in due course. Do you want to know under which EU laws I'll be applying?'

'No thanks.'

He laughed. 'We'll call you as soon as we receive the reference number.'

'Thank you.'

Later in the evening, the phone rang. 'That was Alfred Snr. He wanted us to go to either Galapagos, Curaçao or Aruba for our honeymoon. I told him it would cost a fortune. He promised to send me the money. We'll live on that for a while before you look for work.'

'I was just about to call the agency.'

'Wait for a while.'

A week later I called the solicitor's office. 'Mr Abdullahi, we have just received the reference number. Have you got a pen and paper handy?'

'Yes I have.'

The secretary started dictating the reference number. U408537741.

'Thank you very much.' I put the receiver down and shouted, 'Freedom at last.'

'What's wrong with you?' Suzanne asked from the kitchen.

'I've got my freedom number.' I showed her. 'Let's go to Persia restaurant.'

'Not today. Let's do something local. Let's go to the Bangladeshi restaurant.'

'That's fine. Get ready and let's go.'

When Suzanne went to the toilet after we'd ordered the food, I asked the waiter if there was a mosque in the area. Mohiuddin, as he was called said, 'We've a room upstairs where we pray.'

'Thank you very much. Could you give me the prayer times please?'

Mohiuddin went to the counter and came back with a folded sheet of paper.

'Have you got a compass?'

'When you come next time, I'll give you one.'

That night, I could not sleep. Suzanne noticed it.

'What's bothering you Michael?'

'There are so many things on my mind.'

'Tell me one. Talking is a form of therapy. What's it?'

There was a long moment of silence. 'Go on!' she urged. 'If you can't sleep I cannot sleep either. Let it out and then the two of us can sleep.'

'Suzanne, you probably would not believe this. For the first time since September 1991, I'm going to bed without any fear of arrest, detention and deportation. With the reference number I have cleared that hurdle.'

Suzanne was quiet for some a while. 'That's an awful long time. Over seven years is a long time in the life of any human being to go through such an ordeal. How on earth did you remain sane? I'd have gone mad.'

Stroking her hair, I let out a sigh of relief and said, 'Good night sweetheart.'

'Just the person I was trying to contact,' Farouk said the following day over the phone. 'Taj is away and I haven't got your number.'

'Sorry I should have called you earlier.'

'It's all right. What are you doing now, I mean in terms of work?'

'I'm doing nothing really.'

'There's something coming up in the sales department where I work. My assistant is leaving soon. Send me your CV as soon as possible. The position is an assistant sales manager.'

Suzanne was more excited than me. We drafted the CV and she typed it in Joanna's room and printed two copies. 'We'll post it tomorrow,' Suzanne said smiling. 'Hopefully you'll no longer be washing plates, cleaning tables or working as a security man.'

A week later I received a letter from the company inviting me for an interview.

'I strongly believe you'll get this job,' Suzanne said.

'Why do you think so?'

'Once you've turned the corner, things start to come your way. Your star is on the rise and the best is yet to come. I can feel it. You've weathered the storm and, as they say, after the storm comes the rainbow.'

I called Farouk and explained my immigration status. 'No problem,' he said. 'Hopefully by the time you will be required to travel abroad the Home Office will have granted you the permit to reside and work in the UK. I'll try and protect you before then.'

I went for the interview. I answered all the questions confidently. 'One last question Mr Abdullahi,' said the Personnel Manager. 'Do you have a work permit?'

'Yes I do,' I lied looking straight into her eyes. 'My wife is an EU citizen and I have the permit to reside and work in the UK.'

'Thank you. You'll hear from us soon.'

That evening the phone rang. 'You've got the job. It's a three-day-a-week job. Don't worry I'll train you and the company will send you on various courses. As I said, you will be my assistant and I'm sure it will be fun working together. Don't tell anyone except Suzanne.'

I told Suzanne immediately. 'You see. I told you.'

'I'm going out for about an hour.'

'Where to?'

'To a mosque. I want to pray.'

'You can pray here you know.'

'Thank you. I'll do that later.'

'I understand.'

One evening I decided to walk around the flat blindfolded to know where things were. 'What the hell are you doing?' Suzanne shouted. 'Have you gone mad? What's wrong with you? *Jo*, you gave me a fright.'

'I'm not mad yet.'

'Then what's going on? Why are you walking around blindfolded?'

'I'm practising for one of the tests immigrants are subjected to by Home Office officials.'

'Michael, are you sure you're not neurotic and losing your mind? I'm getting worried. Maybe all this years of being illegal is taking its toll on you.'

'I'm fine darling. I'm sure I'm not mad.' I removed the blindfold. 'I thought the fridge was here but I got it wrong,' I said to myself. 'Listen Suzanne, you think because we have a marriage certificate the Home Office will automatically give me the right to reside in the UK? No way. They do some crazy checks and tests to see if the couples are living together or not and if the immigrant actually knows where things are in the flat. I know it is mind-boggling but what can I do? How do you expect somebody who is blindfolded to know where things are? But if they turn up and say I have to do it, I have to do it. Their visits are often unannounced. I hope they come when I'm not working. Should someone ask if I'm working, please say no.'

'Michael you're making this up.'

'Why should I? They don't make things easy for us. All I need is the stamp in my passport saying I can reside legally in the UK. As long as I haven't got that stamp, I'm at their mercy. Understand?'

She nodded.

'The most ridiculous case I've heard was the one where a young man was denied the right to reside in the UK despite being married to a UK citizen. This young African guy could not tell Home Office officials the colour of his wife's underwear that morning.'

'No! I cannot believe this.'

'Honestly it happened. Suzanne, this guy didn't know it and they said fair enough, no permit. They claimed if he was really married and shared the bed with her he would have paid attention to whatever she was wearing that morning. So darling, do me a big favour. Every morning write the colour on the board there. You never know.'

I returned from work one evening. As soon as I closed the door Suzanne ran towards me shouting. 'Mike my dearest. I've news for you.' I held her closely. I could see in her eyes that she was very happy. 'Give me a kiss first.' I obliged. 'Michael, I'm pregnant,' she said and started crying out of joy. 'I noticed a few signs but I had to wait. I did the test with a home kit and went to the hospital today after work and they confirmed it.'

'I love you Suzanne.'

'So you'll soon be a father.'

'And you'll soon be a mother.'

'Let's go to Persia restaurant.'

'Not today, sometime next week.'

'That's fine.'

We held each other and looked at each other for a long time that evening.

A week later, Suzanne did another pregnancy test. It was positive. In the evening we went to Persia restaurant.

'We're not expecting you,' a surprised Sara said. 'There's a couple in Rumi's corner.'

'It's fine. Anywhere will do,' I said.

'Hang on a minute,' Sara said looking closely at Suzanne. 'You both came here on her birthday. You proposed to her here. You were here on Valentine's Day. You had your wedding dinner here just over four months ago. Wow!' Sara started jumping with excitement. 'Dara please come. Can we really congratulate you?'

Suzanne smiled. Sara hugged her.

'Congratulations. You must be very excited. I must say, you're very lucky.'

'I'm really happy for you,' Dara said. 'If it's a boy his name will be Dara.'

'And if it's a girl her name will be Sara.'

'Could be twins in there; that would be fun wouldn't it?' Dara said with a grin on his face.

'One is enough. I'm going for a scan soon,' Suzanne revealed sitting down.

'How exciting,' Dara said sitting down. 'We are talking babies now. Order anything. It will be a present from us. We've just received a case of very good champagne. I'll open a bottle.'

'No thanks,' I said.

'Why?' he looked bemused.

'She's pregnant,' I argued.

'But you are not. Or are you having morning sickness too?'

'No I gave up drinking on our wedding day.'

'Why?'

'I'm a Muslim and am trying to practise now.'

'*Masha'Allah*! I noticed one of the guests was calling you Sheikh. Are you really a Sheikh?'

'No. My Muslim name is Mustapha Abdullahi but life in London made me become Michael. It's a long story.'

'Tell me about it. What London forces us to do just to survive.'

It had become my daily routine to take time off to go to the mosque in the Bangladeshi restaurant. I would go either on my way back from work or later in the evening. I enjoyed the time I spent just sitting and thinking.

One evening after praying as I entered the flat, Suzanne called me.

'I told you there would be a backlash.'

'You did in fact warn me.'

Albert has given us a three months' notice to vacate his flat. I'm surprised it's that long. He's not going to have you living in his flat. Otherwise he will charge us rent. The initial agreement was for me to pay only the bills and taxes – no rent. Basically he wants you out of my life. He knows we cannot afford the rent he's going to charge us.'

'Now we've got real problems.'

'Do me a favour Michael, please don't read this letter. Three full pages of venom, insults, insinuations, threats and abuse. He could have sent one paragraph telling us to leave his flat without all these insults. What a bastard!'

'Okay, please Suzanne calm down. Don't be upset. I know how you feel but don't hate him. Don't be angry. It'll affect you not him. He wants you to be angry so why fall for it? Let only good words and sentences come out of your mouth. The baby in the womb is listening.'

Suzanne and I were lying in bed, reading a book about pregnancy and childbirth one evening when the telephone rang. 'Hi Mum,' she started. I left the room and closed the door. I went to the sitting room. Moments later, she walked in. 'Bad news. My brother Alfred Jr died a few days ago.'

'What happened?'

'There was an accident, a helicopter crash somewhere in Africa. I have no details. My mother is in a state of shock.' Suzanne sat next to me sobbing.

'I'm really sorry to hear this sad news.'

'He's not the one that should have died. It's the other one.'

'That's enough.'

'He already said he'd die doing what he enjoyed most. My mother just told me that it was to be his last assignment. He was to planning to settle down in Holland. He was quoted as saying "one more job and I'm done." He has played with risk all his life, since he was a kid. It's been guns, fast cars and anything that gave him the thrill. Damn it. This would greatly affect Alfred Snr who was looking forward to having him in Holland. I'm flying out immediately. The pregnancy is six months old. We should be fine.'

Suzanne booked her flight. At the airport, Suzanne said. 'Mr Nasty will be there and he'll wind me up, that you can be sure of. That man will remain immature till he dies.'

'If he wants his flat, just say yes. If he wants more than his flat just let go. Don't argue. You and I and the baby will somehow survive and prosper. Remember that most birds wake up at dawn not knowing when and whether they will have something to eat. Yet they sing beautiful songs before sunrise. And you can be sure that they'll return to their nests at night with a full stomach. This is the beauty of life.'

'You would say that wouldn't you?'

'Either you are angry or happy; the choice is yours.'

'I want to be happy.'

'Have a safe flight.'

'Don't go mad in my absence. I'll be back in two weeks.'

'Speak to you when you arrive.'

'I'll call you.'

Three days later the phone rang in the evening.

'Have you finished your prayers?' Suzanne asked.

'Yes why?'

'I waited for a while before calling. I know the prayer times now.'

'So how's it?'

'Everybody is upset but no drama. The burial will be next week so I may not call you for a few days. By the way, my dad has promised me some money for a deposit on a flat in London. He will credit my account by the end of the month.'

'You see what I mean.'

'Yes, we'll be free from Mr Nasty. He's already looking to take control of Alfred Jr's assets. He's always grabbing. He's never satisfied.'

'Let him have everything.'

'Okay Michael, time to sleep. I miss you. I miss everything about you, your smile, laughter and occasionally your grumpy look – everything. I've had time to take some walks on the farm alone and think. Ever since I was a child I always wished I could meet a man I could love; to marry him and have a child. My dream is about to come true. I always wanted to know what it was like to carry a child. I'm fascinated and excited. I'm enjoying the pregnancy. I hope I'll be a good mother.'

'Love you Suzanne.'

One Saturday afternoon I decided to visit Imam Murad in Maida Vale. I was now praying regularly and was in the right frame of mind. The minicab office was still there. The mosque was still there. I went downstairs and noticed it had been refurbished; there were new carpets and new lighting. I performed my ablution and prayed alone in a corner before the obligatory *Asr* prayer. I sat and could not help but think about how my life had changed since Samad had brought me here several years before. When I first stepped into the mosque on my second day in the UK, I could not have foreseen that I would be in the UK until now.

'Long time Brother Mustapha, *Assalamu Alaikum*,' Imam Murad greeted me after the prayers. 'I'm very happy you came to see us. How's life treating you?'

'*Alhamdullilah.*' I told him briefly what I went through after my uncle died. He listened attentively. I concluded, '*Alhamdullilah*, I'm healthy, happy, married and expecting a baby soon, *Insha'Allah.*'

Twenty-one

Out of the Tunnel

The Filipino ultrasonographer at the Royal Free Hospital explained in the dark room. 'The purpose of this scan is to check the size of the baby, it's position, whether it's growing or not and for possible anomalies.'

She had earlier applied lubricating gel on Suzanne's abdomen. I held Suzanne's hands and fixed my eyes on the monitor. The ultrasonographer continued to scan in silence and asked. 'Do you want to know the sex of your baby?'

'It's not important,' I said.

'No thanks,' Suzanne said.

'See, that's the head there. See the hands and legs. Hey! Look, at that. The baby's waving at us. I think I captured the waving arm on the machine. I'll print copies for you. Everything is fine I didn't see anything unusual or abnormal.'

Just as we were about to step out of the dark room, the Filipino lady asked. 'Is this your first child?' Suzanne nodded. 'Don't worry everything will fine. If you have any problem just come and see me. My name is Yvonne.'

On the bus to Cricklewood, Suzanne complained. 'I didn't realise buying a flat would be this stressful. This is the fifth viewing in two weeks. I'm already fed up. I hope it's not too far from public transport. I cannot afford a car.'

'I don't even know how to drive.'

We arrived late at the property in Cricklewood.

'Are you married?' the Thai lady asked as soon as she opened the door.

'Yes we are,' I showed her my ring.

'Please come in.'

She showed us the flat.

'What do you think?' Suzanne asked.

'Fine but requires a lot of work,' I said.

'Okay we want it,' Suzanne said. 'The baby must be born somewhere.'

'I will discuss with my husband.'

'We'll match the best offer,' Suzanne said looking at her. 'This is exactly what we need; a two-bedroom flat and close to transport and shops.'

'You look very tired,' the Thai lady said. 'I'll discuss this with my husband and let you know.'

The Thai woman called the following day. 'Michael, the baby needs the flat more than everybody that has viewed it. My husband said you can have it.'

'Thank you very much. Suzanne will talk to the estate agents and take things forward.'

Without any confrontation or drama we moved out of Albert's flat in Earls Court to Cricklewood.

'As you know, I'd like to have a girl, and you?' I asked Suzanne.

'A boy of course – always wanted a boy.'

'Let's see who wins.'

'We definitely don't have to wait for long,' Suzanne said stretching her hand. She needed support to stand up. 'Honestly, can't wait for this baby to come out.'

'I really love the anticipation, the suspense, the waiting. Not knowing whether it's a boy or girl until the baby emerges and then yes, it's a girl.'

'Shut up! I better get my bag ready. I'm beginning to feel different; a different kind of sensation.'

'It's getting exciting. We'll soon be going into labour.'

'Who are the *we*? You and who? You can laugh and be excited because you're not the one going to give birth isn't it?'

'But I'll be there watching.'

'Yes, watching and that's it.'

That evening Suzanne felt some contractions. 'The baby is on its way.'

I called a minicab and took her to the Royal Free Hospital. The following day, I rushed to the hospital during the last stages of labour.

'Definitely a girl,' the consultant said in the labour room. 'Look at her hair.'

'Push! Push! Push!' I kept urging Suzanne holding her hands.

Later, a baby emerged. The midwife, a Nigerian woman called Toyin, gave me gloves and a pair of scissors. 'Cut the cord, my brother.' She then wrapped the baby and lay her on Suzanne. After the initial bonding the midwife handed the baby to me. I looked at the wrinkled watery face of the baby as she struggled to open her eyes and hands. I whispered the words of *adhan* – the call to prayers into her right ear. 'I want to welcome you into this world, my princess.'

The Nigerian midwife took her way. 'She's just come out of her mother's womb not yours. You're going to spoil this little girl. I've been here twenty five years and I know fathers who spoil the daughters by the way they welcome them into this world.'

'But she's my princess. I've been waiting for her for a long time.'

'You hear that mummy? Keep working at it. You'll have a boy next time,' she said laughing.

'I want to announce the arrival of the baby to your parents. I suggest we call her Amira Annabel.'

'I've no objection to the names. You can call my mother. She wanted to talk to you anyway but certainly not my father. I will call him and tell him.'

I called Suzanne's mother immediately. 'I'm very happy that you called, Michael. Thank you very much for such wonderful news. My daughter talked a lot about you. I hope you can visit us soon. I hope it wasn't too painful for Suzanne, I mean the birth.'

'No. It wasn't. I was in the labour room to share the pain.'

She laughed. 'Only women feel the pain but thank you for being there with her. I really appreciate it.'

Seven days after Amira's arrival into this world, Alhaji Sulaiman, the London-based linguist, came to offer prayers. 'Has *Ango* taught you more Hausa words?'

'No. I've even forgotten the earlier ones.'

'Okay. *Yarinya*, a girl. *Yaro*, a boy. *Allah Ya raya* (May Allah cause the baby to grow up).

We went to the Persia restaurant. 'Wow! Look at her. What an angel. She's so gorgeous. She looks like her mum,' Sara said as soon as we settled down.

'No,' she looks more like Michael especially from the eyes down,' Dara countered. 'The two of you are blessed with something special; something money cannot buy and death cannot take away. It's a rare gift from the Almighty, be grateful.'

A month later Suzanne returned to work on a part-time basis. It was a perfect arrangement that suited us both. I was allowed to work two-and-half days a week. Suzanne worked on Mondays and Tuesdays and half days on Wednesdays. On Wednesdays, I took Amira to Suzanne's new office in High Holborn and handed the baby over at around mid-day. I then reported to work in Islington. We could not afford to have a childminder.

One Monday afternoon, after I had fed Amira and put her in the baby rocker, I started talking to her. I showed her some pages of my script. 'Mimi, this was what brought me into this country in 1990, that's over eight years ago.' She sat there looking at me, smiling, as if she understood what I was telling her. 'Mimi, then many things happened. I could not finish the course and did not make the film. In the meantime I became an illegal immigrant. You don't know what illegal immigrants look like. They look like Daddy,' Mimi laughed. 'It's not funny. Then I met your mummy and we got married and you see now we have Mimi. As you can see, I've started rewriting the script for the last time, hopefully. I'll take it to the college soon and have it assessed. I'll take you to the college to meet my course tutor, Hilary. She's a very nice woman and she'll play with you and show you the pigeons on her window ledge. You never know, with a bit of luck I'll make the film. If and when I make this film, I will write something like this: *This film is dedicated to my Princess Mimi.'* Mimi laughed again. She found it funny. 'But I still have one big hurdle to cross. I'm still waiting to hear from the Home Office. Until I have the permit to stay and work in this country, I cannot make the film. So I have to wait. I don't know when but soon I hope I'll be allowed to live in the UK legally. Hopefully you wouldn't have such problems in the future like being an illegal immigrant in the UK. You've a Dutch passport already and we'll get you a British passport because you were born here.'

The doorbell rang. I went and opened the door.

'Can I talk to Suzanne please?' a short slim Asian lady asked, showing me a badge.

'She's at work.'

'Are you Mr Abdullahi?'

'Yes I am.'

'Can you let us in please? We're from the Home Office.'

I went and picked Amira up and let them in. 'My name is Taslima,' the lady identified herself and led two others in, a white man and a black woman. 'As I said we're from the Home Office.'

The two others nodded and looked at me.

'You are welcomed. Please sit down,' I said and turned to Amira. 'Mimi say, *Assalaam Alaikum.'* Mimi started crying.

'*Wa'alaikum Salaam,'* Taslima replied.

'Sorry for the mess around the room,' I said sitting down.

'It's okay. Where's Suzanne?' she asked again.

'She's at work.'

'And you Mustapha at home?'

'Yes,' I said smiling. 'I'm a house husband.'

'Are you studying?' the black woman asked smiling.

'Yes, just to keep myself busy.'

'So you look after the house,' Taslima said.

'That's correct. Roles have reversed. Women in modern societies are the breadwinners. Suzanne wears the trousers and suits. I wear the apron in the kitchen and as you can see, the tracksuit,' I joked laughing. The two women laughed too.

I tried to remain calm. I knew this was the last hurdle. I must say the perfect lie.

'Amira say something. Ask them what they want to drink, tea or coffee or water. Don't just sit and look at the guests like that.'

'Is that her name?' Taslima asked looking very excited.

'Yes and Mimi is her nickname.'

'What a beautiful name. Little Princess, *Masha'Allah*! My cousin in Leicester is also called Amira,' Taslima said playing with Amira's toes. 'You're daddy's girl eh? You're enjoying your daddy, lucky girl, you have daddy to yourself all the time. Mimi, you're so cute.'

'How old is she?' the black woman asked.

'Six and half months,' I replied.

'She's at the age where you still count the halves,' said the black woman smiling.

'Can I have her?' Taslima asked.

'In exchange you'll grant me a right of residence. Suzanne and I can produce more.'

We all laughed.

'I'm sure Suzanne would definitely not want to hear that,' the black woman said.

'As you know we're from the Home Office, we came to check to see if yours was a bogus marriage or not,' the Englishman started. 'My name is Steve, by the way.' I met his gaze, steeling myself. 'As you are probably aware Sir, there are a lot of dodgy marriages around and it is our responsibility to check and that's why we're here. I have a few questions to ask you. What's Suzanne's date of birth?'

I told him.

'Where was she born?'

I told him.

'You know how much is in her bank account?'

'No.'

'Why?'

'Suzanne is the boss here and as far as I know you don't check the account of your boss,' I replied smiling. 'I've never asked how much is in her account. It's none of my business.'

The two women were excited. 'Of course, the man should mind his own business,' the black woman said laughing. 'Why should he be nosy if she's the boss?'

'I take it then that you don't have a joint account. As a married couple you ought to have a joint account,' Steve argued.

'No joint account sir …' I said smiling.

'Joint what? You cannot have a joint account with the boss,' the black woman said excitedly.

'I could have a joint account with Suzanne but I've nothing to put in it.'

'But you've a baby with the boss,' he insisted.

The women laughed. 'That's different,' I said laughing too.

'Of course it's different,' Taslima said laughing.

'Having a baby with the boss is alright,' the black woman argued laughing.

'I believe you are working,' Steve continued.

'No I'm not. I'm a house-husband. As you can see, Suzanne has put me under lock and key,' I said looking straight at him. The two women laughed.

'That's exactly what I want to hear, under lock and key,' the black woman said putting her thumb on her forehead. 'That's good. She's got you under control.'

'I don't blame her,' Taslima added laughing too.

I tried to explain. 'Suzanne doesn't earn enough to employ a child-minder so I have to look after our daughter.'

'Which is the best thing for Mimi anyway, she's with daddy all day,' Taslima said and stretched out her hands. Mimi went to her.

'That's all from me,' the Englishman said looking at Taslima who was now holding Amira and stroking her curly hair. Taslima looked at the black woman.

'I've nothing to ask. I'm convinced that it's a genuine marriage. There's evidence in front of us and in your hand. I'm just curious Mr Abdullahi, what are you studying to become?'

'I want to be film director. Actually this is my script there,' I pointed to a pile of papers on the floor. 'I'm working on it hoping that when I get the permit to work in the UK I can take things forward. At the moment there's nothing I can do. My career prospect is languishing.'

'We understand,' Taslima said stroking Amira's hair.

Taslima looked at Amira. 'It's incredible. She gets along with me. Okay Mimi, you like daddy?' Amira pointed at me. Taslima looked at me. 'I feel I should take her with me. I could look at her all day and all night because she's so cute. John Keats once wrote: *A thing of beauty is a joy forever.*' She handed over Amira to me and stood up.

We all stood up. 'Mimi, as from today your daddy is hereby allowed to remain in the UK legally. He can work and earn money and feed you and mummy who can stay at home and have a little brother for you, someone to play and fight with,' Taslima said making faces at her. Mimi laughed as if she understood. 'Mustapha, you will hear from me soon through your solicitor. You've met all the requirements needed for a right of residence as a family member of an EEA national. This will be for an initial period of five years after which if you're still married to *the boss* and if she's still a resident in the UK you can apply for an indefinite leave to remain. I hope that one day you can take Amira to Nigeria to see her grandpa and grandma and all those cousins, aunties and uncles. I'm sure your parents would be delighted to see such an angel, *Masha'Allah!* Please take her to see your parents and if possible get her a little brother to play with.'

'*Insha'Allah!*'

'*Assalaam Alaikum,*' Taslima said and led the others out of the flat.

As soon as I heard the door close I started kissing Amira until she screamed. I started crying too. 'At last I'm free! Did you hear that Mimi? I've been given a right of residence in the UK. Mimi after all these years now I am free.' I tried to explain what it means but Amira slept off.

I called Jarvo immediately. 'We must celebrate,' he said. 'I'm really happy for you. You've served your time, now you're a free man. You've successfully lied your way to the truth. You took a big gamble and it paid off. Now you can live and work honestly. Please thank the Boer woman for us. She has really helped you. I'll inform other Politburo members.'

I hurried to Kilburn underground station and bought a bunch of flowers.

Mimi and I waited by the door. As soon as Suzanne opened the door, I shouted: 'Surprise!' Suzanne was startled. I gave her the flowers.

'What, for me?' she asked with a slightly bemused look.

'Of course, they're for you.'

'Why? It's not my birthday. I know you've gone crazy since you had your Mimi. You probably bought the flowers for her.'

'No they're for you.'

'But why?'

'For loving me.'

'But I love you every day you don't give me flowers every day. I'm getting a bit worried.'

'You don't have to,' I said. 'I've served my time. I'm a free man now. Officials from the Home Office visited us while you're at work.'

'I see.'

'Mimi charmed the team leader.'

'So that's it then.'

'Yes. I'll tell you more. The flowers are my way of saying THANK YOU!

Suzanne rested. Later while breastfeeding Amira, she started. 'I can make it to the graduation ceremony tomorrow. What an achievement. Master of Arts in Political Economy! Tell me something. I've no time for a long answer. What in a sentence or two did you find most interesting?'

I thought for a while. 'It's difficult to summarise what I've learnt in two years in a sentence or two.'

'Okay, a concept that appeals to you most.'

'I think I really like Adam Smith's benign view of self-interest.'

'What did he say?'

'It is not from the benevolence of the butcher, the brewer, or the baker that we expect our dinner, but from their regard to their own interest.'

There was silence in the room.

'It gave me a deeper understanding of how this society works. Of course I enjoyed other economists and the whole course was great. I'm really happy I did the course.'

'And you had to lie to get the admission.'

'Yes I did.'

I took Amira for a walk on Cricklewood Broadway several days after the graduation ceremony. The window of a car wound down just as I was passing. '*Assalaam Alaikum*,' I heard a familiar voice from inside the car. I thought the person was speaking on a mobile phone or greeting someone else. I continued. Then I heard, 'Brother Mustapha, *Assalaam Alaikum*.' I recognised the voice of solicitor Imran. I turned and saw the number plate of the Mercedes-Benz – IMR 786. Imran climbed out of the car and greeted me. 'I wasn't sure if you were the one. I was at the Wembley Conference Centre some days ago for the graduation ceremony of one of my cousins and I thought I saw someone like you wearing an academic gown with a certificate. Not sure because you were with a white woman who was holding a little girl.'

'How are you?' I asked.

He laughed. 'I'm fine. I'm into real finance now, making a lot of money in a hedge fund in the city, buying properties here and in the Middle East. I didn't realise you were still in the UK. I thought the Home Office had nicked and deported you a long time ago.'

I looked at him. I was not sure if he was joking or not.

'Do you still support Arsenal?'

'Of course I still do.'

'And who is this beautiful girl here?'

'This is Amira.'

'Is your wife Muslim?'

'No.'

'Why did you marry a non-Muslim?'

I did not answer.

'You should get her to convert.'

I ignored him and walked away.

That evening we went to the Persia restaurant.

'Is another baby on its way?' Sara asked as we entered. 'Please tell me it's another baby. Please!' she pleaded.

'Do you think we're rabbits or what?'

'Just one more please, look at how beautiful Amira is.'

'Who's going to feed them?'

'That's not a problem,' Dara said laughing. 'You can come here every day. So what are you celebrating? You just don't come here...'

'Graduation, I graduated with an MA degree.'

'Yes! I saw the picture of three of you in my local paper.' He stood up and brought a copy of the *Brent & Kilburn Times*. He opened the page. 'See the three of you? See Amira smiling at her proud daddy in his academic gown? Isn't it lovely?'

'That's the more reason why you should have one more,' Sara said.

'We celebrate every day because we are grateful and happy,' I said.

'I'm not convinced,' Dara insisted laughing. 'I'll know one day.'

On a Tuesday, I was about to go to work when the phone rang. Suzanne had been unwell and had taken a week off work. I picked up the phone. It was the secretary of my solicitor. 'We have something for you Mr Abdullahi,' she said. I went to the office in Kilburn. As soon as I entered, the lady who was on the phone gave me an envelope. I opened it and looked at my passport. I leafed through it and saw the stamp.

'Thank you,' I said.

'You're welcome,' she said and waived at me. She continued with her telephone conversation.

Halfway down the stairs, I stopped and looked at the passport again.

'*The right of residence in the UK as a family member of an EEA national Suzanne ...*' I stopped reading. Tears began to roll down my cheeks. I looked at the date. 7th September 1999. There was the stamp of the Home Office, Immigration Department. I waited for the tears to stop. I started to read the letter. "*I am returning your passport which has been endorsed to show that you have been issued with a residence document to enable you to remain here with your spouse who is a European community national exercising a right under the Treaty of Rome... You are free to take employment or engage in business or a profession during the currency of your leave to remain here...*" I took a deep breath and wiped away my tears and walked out of the building. As I stepped onto Kilburn High Road, I collided with a young woman pushing a baby in a pushchair.

'Are you fucking blind?' she asked me.

'I'm sorry.'

'You have to fucking look at where you're fucking going, you fucking arsehole.'

'Thank you,' I said and apologised again, smiling.

'Why are you fucking smiling at me? Why are you fucking thanking me? You're so fucking ignorant. You don't fucking understand anything.'

I walked away. From time to time I stopped on the Kilburn High Road and looked at the passport, especially the page with the stamp of the Immigration Department of the Home Office. I looked at my passport several times on the train.

'I like talking to your wife Suzanne,' Farouk said in the office.

'Why?' I asked.

'She speaks French with a South African accent. I called earlier and she said you had left a long time ago. We've urgent things to discuss. I'm flying out to Mauritius within the next few days. I want to go and see my Mum. She's very ill. I want you to look after the sales department in my absence. The most important thing is I want you to represent the company at the Frankfurt Book Fair. Is that okay?'

'Yes it is.'

'Great.' I could see he was relieved. 'I've arranged appointments to meet publishers and distributors. I'll give you all the information later. But first you must apply for a visa to Germany immediately.'

'No problem.' I called the German Embassy to find out what documents were required. 'Of course, I have a right of residence in the UK,' I shouted so that the whole office could hear me. I brought out my passport and showed Farouk the stamp of the Home Office.

'By the way, the Board has agreed to increase your number of working days to five days a week when you return from Frankfurt. You deserve it.'

I thanked him.

'Is this what happens when a dream comes true?' Suzanne asked me in the evening.

'What do you mean?'

'You've been so quiet since you came back. I expected you to be so happy and excited.'

'I don't know how to put it. I'm very happy inside, probably the happiest man on earth today. I've a loving wife and a beautiful daughter. We're all healthy and have a roof over our heads. We've clothes to wear and food to eat. I've a decent job and I have permission to remain in this country. I'm definitely happy but I think the experiences of the past eight years have drained me emotionally.'

'They've taken their toll on your soul…'

'Suzanne how do you explain this. I got my passport this morning and in the afternoon the company asked me to represent them at the Frankfurt Book Fair next month. Imagine if they had told me to fly out last week or last month, what would I have done? I'm happy that I can travel and hopefully with time I can go and see my parents.'

After the book fair, Suzanne and I visited Dr Asibong. 'The little princess will be one soon. I hope you are making plans for her to have someone to the play with.'

Suzanne replied. 'She's got lots of toys to play with.'

'Toys are not enough.'

'What else do you want her to play with?'

'Not *what* but *who* to play with, a little brother or sister.'

'So you're still into family planning.'

'Have you bought contraceptives from the chemist?'

'It's none of your business.'

'You see, it would be very boring for the little princess. It's important that children have siblings you know.'

'Doc, according to Malthus, overpopulation will destroy the world. Look at our world today, there's famine, hunger and diseases. Why bring another human being into this world? Why? The problem we have in the world is overpopulation. I strongly believe that one more child into this world will lead to more catastrophes. We have reached that tipping point. As they say, the last drop makes the cup run over. I'm afraid another child from us will bring this world to a state of chaos. So to save the world and ensure there are enough resources to go round, I'm not going to have another child.'

'Rubbish,' Dr Asibong interjected. 'Greed is the problem facing us not overpopulation. There are enough resources for all but some people are so greedy that they take more than they need. What we need is an equitable distribution of wealth, not a one-child policy. There'll be no chaos because the little princess has a sibling. The world might be a better place because of such beauty. There's nothing like a tipping point. It's a con. If anything Malthus' gloomy prediction of universal miseration might come to fruition in centuries to come due to contradictions in the system and not the addition of one more child in London now.'

'At the end of the day, it all adds up. One child here and another somewhere and that's it; the world becomes overpopulated. I agree with the one-child policy of China,' Suzanne insisted.

'But you're not Chinese,' he argued further.

'I thought you once said you had inbuilt sensors that could read what's going on in my womb.'

'That's correct.'

'Can you hear anything now?'

'The batteries are low, very low.'

'You see, I got you there. I'm pleased to announce that another baby is on its away.'

'*Abasi Kenyon*! God Gracious! That's good news. You really got me there. Thank you very much for such delightful news. I'm so happy the little princess will have someone to play with. Don't worry about Malthus he got it wrong all along.'

I booked my flight to Nigeria. Suzanne made arrangements to go to Holland.

'Michael,' she started one evening. 'I've resigned from my work with immediate effect. It's becoming too stressful.'

'I was just wondering how you'll be able to cope.'

'Alfred Snr has promised to help us. I told him about the second baby and he was so delighted. I told him how tired and stressed out we both are. He wanted to know why and I said we've got a mortgage to pay. He asked how much. I told him and he sent me the money. So as from this month we've only the bills and taxes to pay. He wants us to relax and enjoy the kids.'

'I'm speechless. Please thank him for me.'

'He looks forward to meeting you soon.'

'Once I'm back from Nigeria we'll go to Holland.'

'I've a feeling I'll spend more time in Holland visiting Alfred Snr. He needs help.'

'That's fine. It makes sense doesn't it? Since you don't have to work and he needs someone to help him. He has paid for the time and company by a paying off the mortgage of the flat.'

Suzanne and Amira left for Holland.

I got ready for my trip to Nigeria.

Twenty-two

Home Sweet Home

My father was where I expected him to be around that time of the day, under the tree reciting verses from the Quran. When he saw me alight from the car, my father stood up. I looked at him from the distance. He had hardly changed. He had more grey hair. He was wearing a long white rope and red cap as he always did. He was as calm and relaxed as I had always known him. I went down on my knees and greeted him. He told me to stand up. 'Go and greet your mother, she's been worried sick about you.'

My mother was by the door of the courtyard waiting. I ran and embraced her. She noticed I was crying and led me to her room. The two of us sat there in total silence for about ten minutes. She started talking but I did not hear what she was saying. I had just the dizzying sensation of looking into her eyes. I did not know what was going through her mind. She was delighted to see me. She would from time to time wipe away her tears and continued to stare at me. 'Is it you I'm touching Mustapha?' I nodded. She thanked Almighty Allah for sparing her life to witness my return. 'I thought we had lost you forever but your father, being who he is, believed you would come back one day. He always said you would be all right. I honestly thought you had gone the way your uncle went. I'm the happiest woman – happiest mother in the world today.' She touched me just to be sure I am there in the flesh. For the first time she smiled. 'Yes this is my son, Mustapha.'

The next day my father said, 'I can see and feel you've gone through a lot over the years. I know life was not easy for you after your uncle's death and it must have been terrible when your scholarship was stopped. These things happen. But as a Muslim I continued to pray to Almighty Allah to give you the strength and wisdom to pass through that difficult period. I never had any illusions that things would always be fine. I am not going to ask you the details. If you want me to know, tell me. In a way, it's good. There's always value in suffering. It's through suffering that we do become wise. I'm sure you've learnt something valuable from what you went through. For me, it's better to be wise and content with life than to be rich, anxious and stupid. I hope that what you have gone through will provide you with the wisdom and patience to raise my grandchildren very well.

'As a father I've forgiven you even before you ask for forgiveness. It's my duty. You went out on a journey and it's normal to encounter hardships on journeys. It's also normal that people do things they would not have done if they had never embarked on journeys. Unforeseen circumstances do force us to make some painful adjustments while on a journey. The important thing is to be able to get back on track and continue with a clear head towards our destination. That's why journeys are important. I am happy you have emerged from your hardship in good health and that you were able to come home. Be assured, Mustapha that I will always remember you and your family in my prayers. I'll always forgive you too. I'm saying this in case we don't meet again.'

'Why did you marry a *Baturiya*?' (white woman) my sister Hadiza asked, trying to make a scene in the courtyard. She repeated the question. 'There are so many black women, so many Muslim women who are single and you ignored them all and went and looked for a white woman and married her. I hear white women prefer black men because they treat black men as slaves. Is that true? Here you men will not touch one plate but in Europe I hear African men do everything for white women. They wash their clothes. They cook for them. And you cannot marry more than one wife.'

Our mother intervened. 'Leave him alone. You should be grateful to Almighty Allah that your brother is alive and well, that's the most important thing... Do you know some go to Europe and don't return? Remember your uncle who died there? At least your brother is here in front of you and he is well. Only he knows what he went through and why he married the woman he eventually did. It's not for you to judge. I've forgiven him for everything. He has probably done things I wouldn't approve of but in life things change and we must change too. Have you seen the photographs of his daughter Amira?' my mother asked and called her. 'See one of the wonders of the world. Have you ever seen such a beautiful girl in your life? Is this not a blessing? Is this not a precious gift from Almighty Allah? Would you then not respect and speak well of the woman who carried this child? If I met the mother I'd bow down in gratitude. Please, Hadiza don't open your mouth and say one bad word against my daughter-in-law.'

'I'm sorry,' Hadiza apologised.

'It's okay. My wife is pregnant,' I announced.

'*Allahu Akbar*! My mother exclaimed with joy and happiness. 'I'll remember all of you in my prayers as I always do. I hope and pray that she and the baby will be of good health, that's the most important thing. Please, Mustapha treat your wife well because she's your support.'

'I hope you get a baby boy,' my sister said.

'Whatever Allah gives, please receive it with both hands in gratitude.' She paused. 'It doesn't matter to me any more if she's a Christian. I can see that she likes you and you like her and Allah has blessed the two of you with Amira. Christians are people of the book. The Prophet (SAW) we were told married a Christian. She quoted a line from the Quran: *Unto you your religion and unto me mine.* Mustapha, as long as she doesn't interfere with your faith, that's fine by me.'

'She doesn't.'

'So many things have changed in the district in your absence. What has been particularly worrying is the high rate of divorce which is very disturbing. No one has patience these days any more. If my son is happy with the Christian who is patient with him and he's patient with her, so be it. If she can tolerate Mustapha and if can tolerate her, good luck to both of you. Please take good care of your wife for me. Remember you're happy because she's happy and if you want your children to be happy make sure your wife is happy.'

Standing with my sister in the courtyard later, I asked. 'Do you know a girl called Zainab Zubairu Bakaro?'

'I know her very well,' my sister answered. 'She's one of my best friends.'

I knew I had to lie. 'Someone told me that he met her in London.'

'It's true. She was in London so many years ago. I told her you were there and that she should look out for you. We did not know where you were when she left for the UK. We didn't have any contact details. That was after our uncle died and no one was answering the telephone in his flat. I know her very well. We went to the same secondary school.'

'I see. Where's she now?'

'She's working with a big multinational company in Abuja. She was here last week and plaited my hair for me.'

I nodded.

'She told me long time ago that she saw someone who looked like you but it was a case of a mistaken identity. She's married to a business man in Abuja.'

'I see.' I said and changed the topic. 'What happened to Alhaji Tanko?'

'He died about six months after he stopped your scholarship.'

'*Inna lillahi wa inna illahi rajiuun.*' (Surely we belong to Allah and to Him shall we return.)

'He died after a short illness.' She paused. 'Your friend Ibrahim and our father went to see him when he stopped your scholarship. They pleaded with him. They told him that his actions would bring untold hardships but he wouldn't listen. I'm sure you know the type of person he was – very stubborn. He said you must be punished and you must suffer.'

'He was always like that.'

'Our father said we shouldn't worry too much, that Allah knows best. Our father reminded him of a Hausa saying: *Idan kaine yau, ba kaine gobe ba*! (If you are in charge today, you will not be in charge tomorrow!). Anyway, after he passed away the new secretary of the scholarship board tried to contact you but you had moved from the address we had. Even the college didn't know where you were. Is it possible to live like that? No one knew where you were?'

'Yes it is.'

The next day I went to the scholarship board. The new secretary told me that they had paid the balance to the college but could not contact me. 'Go and finish your course, it has been paid for.'

On my last day in Bauchi town, my father asked just before *Zuhr*- the afternoon prayer, 'Do you know how to call prayers?'

'Yes I do. You don't forget these things.'

'The reason why am I asking is that it's time for prayers and I cannot see Danbala. He usually calls the prayers. If you are not comfortable please don't. I can get somebody else.'

'I'm fine. I've performed ablution already,' I told him and went and stood on the plinth where Danbala usually called for prayers. Facing the direction of Makkah, I cleared my throat and silently declared my intention to call the prayers. I lifted my hands, opened my palms and put my fingers in my ears and recited the *adhan* in a melodious voice. I said the silent prayers afterwards and came down.

I could see my father was impressed. We all formed a line behind him and he led us in prayer.

After the prayers, my father told me that some of his friends would be visiting before sunset. He would appreciate it if I could spend some time with them.

A dozen of my father's friends came. We chatted. They asked me questions about life in the UK. They prayed for my success and good health for my wife and children. When it was time for *Maghrib* – the evening prayer, Danbala called the prayers. One of my father's friends, Alhaji Yusuf, stepped forward and loudly suggested that I should lead the prayers. My father cast a glance at me. I nodded. 'Are you comfortable? If not I can say no. It would be an honour to follow my son in prayers even if it's only once.'

They all lined up. I stood in front of them, in the place reserved for the Imam. I was nervous. It was a strange feeling to be asked to lead prayers, especially knowing that my father was part of the congregation. After Danbala recited the *Iqamat* (second call to prayers said immediately before the prayer begins) I took a deep breath and loudly said: *Salli kaannaha akhir salaatik* (Pray as if it's your last prayer) now with greater meaning. Making sure my face and body were facing the Makkah, I silently declared my intention to say the obligatory *Maghrib* prayer. '*Allahu Akbar,*' I started, my voice echoed around the houses in Kobi district. I continued loudly to recite *Fatiha* (the first verse of the Quran). I was composed throughout the prayers. When the prayer was over, my father almost hugged me. I could see the relief in his eyes.

The next day I left Nigeria.

Weeks later Suzanne reminded me. 'Don't forget the second scan is tomorrow afternoon. You don't have to come.'

'I'll be there to see another baby girl wave at us,' I wound her up.

Suzanne did not pay attention. 'I think I've probably told you this already, with your permission, Senior wants us to spend more time in Holland. He's completely a different person when Amira is in the house. He's full of joy and happiness, with lots of energy and laughter. She likes him too. He almost cried when we were about to leave. She was crying too. He said he can afford to keep us for as long as we want in Holland.'

'That's fine by me.'

At the antenatal clinic at Royal Free Hospital, a black woman in green uniform called Suzanne's name in the waiting hall. Suzanne was surprised. She looked at me. 'Someone at last got my surname right,' she said.

'She's probably South African.'

'Good afternoon to you two,' the woman welcomed us into the room with a abroad smile. She looked at the file again and started speaking to me in Afrikaans. I told her I didn't understand the language. Suzanne replied in Afrikaans. The two women spoke and laughed looking at me.

When she was about to finish, the South African sonographer told me in English. 'Everything is fine except for the position he's in. The boy is in a breech position. That means if he does not change his position he will come out feet first. Do you understand?'

I nodded.

'I suggest you come back in two weeks' time. If he's still in this position we will try and turn him. It's nothing to worry about. An obstetrician will try and turn the baby into a head-down position by applying pressure on Suzanne's abdomen. It's a safe procedure but uncomfortable. Normally these babies know that it's time to come out and they change their position so that they can come out head first. Some can be very stubborn though. All I can say is that the boy inside is fine. I hope you are happy sir,' she concluded smiling.

I nodded and thanked her. Suzanne smiled and said something in Afrikaans. The two women laughed and high-fiving they looked me.

We thanked her and walked out of the room. Suzanne pinched me hard in the corridor. 'It's a boy! Hurrah! It's a boy!'

'Wait! Don't get too excited.'

'Hahaha! You're jealous it's a boy. You feel threatened already.'

'They get these things wrong you know.'

'You wait and see how I'm going to treat my little prince.'

Suzanne was happy.

Several weeks later when she went into labour I was with her in the dimly lit labour room. 'Push! Push! Push!' I urged. The baby came out and was lifted onto Suzanne. It was a boy. The cord was clamped. I wore gloves and picked up the scissors and cut the umbilical cord. The crying baby was dried and wrapped and placed on Suzanne again. After a few minutes, the baby was handed to me. I whispered the *adhan* (call to prayers) into his right ear.

The next day I was approaching the maternity ward with Amira in one hand and bunch of flowers in the other, when someone said. 'Mr Abdullahi, I remember you. Do you remember me?'

'Of course I do. You delivered Amira.'

'That's correct. I see your wife has a boy. Congratulations,' said the Nigerian midwife. 'You're a lucky man. Your wife has had two straightforward pregnancies and births. Count your blessings,' she said and led us to Suzanne's bed in the ward. 'When I see a daddy's girl, I know one. When I see a mummy's boy I also know. What a family.

Complete and compact. May you all be blessed. I'm happy for you all. Now everyone is happy. Daddy has his princess and mummy has her prince. God bless all.'

I thanked her.

Suzanne looked very tired. 'Mimi you have a brother, come and sit next to your *boetie*, as we say in Afrikaans.' Mimi was looking strangely at the newborn.

'I'll call your mum and informed her about the arrival of Alfred Jr.'

'Yes go ahead.'

Several days later Suzanne was breastfeeding Alfred Ahmed, as he was called, when she asked me, 'What am I going to do now?' It was as if she was frightened of something.

'What's wrong?'

'Look Michael, this is what I've always wanted in life. Ever since I was a small girl, I always wanted to know what it was like to be a mother, to have children, especially a boy. When I met you I look forward to having mixed-race kids. I really adored the honey colour skin and the curly hair. They are just different and that's what fascinates me.'

'So what's the problem now?'

'Nothing, you see, my mum never spent time with us. She never knew her mother. I'm determined to break that cycle. I'm trying to enjoy every minute with the kids and I *am* enjoying every minute. Motherhood is the best thing that has ever happened to me. I knew I'd love it but never knew how much.' She took a deep breath and looked at me. 'Michael, please tell me, what happens when your dream comes true?'

I did not answer.

'Mimi, kiss daddy to make mummy jealous.' Amira kissed me.

'I'll kiss my little prince to make you jealous.' She kissed Alfred.

'As soon as this boy can walk, I'm going to kick him out of this flat. Two cocks cannot crow in the same compound.'

Suzanne laughed. 'You'd think two birds can share the same nest?'

'Oh blast!' Suzanne swore at Liverpool Street station. 'I'm losing the plot, too many things on my mind.'

'What have you forgotten?'

'I bought a return ticket for you too.'

'In that case I might as well enjoy the free ride to Harwich and back.' On the train Suzanne confided. 'Maybe I should tell you more about Alfred Jr, my late brother. We heard from some sources that he was hired by a foreign power and some foreign companies to organise and overthrow the government of a small African country. No one told us which country but it's believed the country is very rich in mineral resources. This foreign power and companies wanted to install a puppet regime and his security firm was to execute the overthrow of the regime.

'According to our sources, on his way to the jungle to meet members of this secret army and some rebel fighters they had managed to organise, his helicopter crashed. There were no survivors. Some people said it was due to bad weather, others said the helicopter was shot down by government troops acting on a tip-off. It's a bit complicated. My mother does not understand all these things. No one knows the truth. Almost everything is shrouded in secrecy.

'Alfred Jr, as I told you earlier, was supposed to give up all these adventures and settle down. He chose Holland because he had some friends there. He also got in touch with Alfred Snr and it was agreed he should be the person around for Alfred Snr. That was the arrangement. Everything had been planned down to where he was going to stay. One more adventure and that was it. It's so sad, so tragic. Albert will be in Zeeland too. I'm telling you all this now because at some point some arrangements are going to have to change.'

I nodded. 'I understand.'

'I never had plans to live in Holland but I can see that circumstances might force me to consider moving there, probably on a temporary basis. Someone in the family will have to be there for senior. Albert wants senior to move into old people's home. He wants to transfer his assets into some crazy financial schemes. Of course, Alfred Snr is not keen. He's happy with where he is and thank God he's not senile yet. Basically, he wants me to spend more time there if you're not against it. For me, I know it's a tough decision. Very tough because I know how much it's going to affect all of us. But it's also personal,' she paused, looked at me and continued with a firm voice. 'I don't want Albert to have his way on this.'

'I understand,' I responded shaking my head in agreement. 'Whatever happens please be patient and don't let Albert wind you up. Life is too damn short to quarrel over material things. You've some wonderful things to be proud of. Things money can't buy.'

'Two beautiful, healthy and happy children,' she said smiling.

'And a husband too … I'm still here,' I protested.

'Oh yes! These kids didn't just drop from the sky or delivered by post. Yes, I've a husband and he's here with me.'

The journey to Harwich continued in silence. 'Michael, you've not told me what it feels like to be a legal citizen. Is there any difference?'

I did not reply immediately. 'You don't have to talk about it if you don't want to. I do understand that some memories can be very painful.'

'It's all right,' I started. 'It's very difficult to explain. I'm going through a very strange phase. I think I've not come out of the mindset yet. I suppose it takes a while to get used to the new environment, the new feeling. I was so used to being an illegal immigrant that I still think I am one now. I still wake up feeling like a fraud not sure if I should be where I am. I am not at ease when I see the police, for example, although I no longer cross the road when I see them coming. I haven't got the feeling that I have the right to remain in this country yet. I still wake up in the morning thinking it's my last day. Then I constantly remind myself that I've got the permit now. I still have panic attacks out of fear of arrest. It was a lot easier to slide into illegal immigration than to get out of it.'

'What a surprise! What a pleasant surprise,' Hilary Rogers said as soon as I stepped into her office, after I had knocked twice. 'Just the person I was looking for. If there's one person I was hoping would walk through this door, it was you and look who's here. You know what, I was thinking about you last Friday and even this morning somehow I remembered your smiling face. I saw a young man on the train and I said to myself, I wonder where Mustapha is.'

Hilary was as smiley and jovial as usual. She sat down and continued. 'A film company contacted us early last year. They were looking for a good script from Africa. I sent them a copy of yours and they came back saying they would like to contact you. But I had no contact details for you. Anyway, how are you?'

'I'm fine and you?'

'I'm fine too. You look well.'

'How are the pigeons?'

'They're okay. You still remember them?'

'Yes because I've got two kids – a boy and a girl.'

Hilary laughed. 'Just like a pigeon.'

I showed her the photos of the kids. I brought out a folder. 'This is my revised script.'

'The script is delivered almost a decade late,' she received it laughing.

'Better late than never,' I said smiling.

'That's true.'

'In the meantime, I studied philosophy and political economy. I think it's in even better shape now. With hindsight, I agree with your earlier criticisms and comments. I am grateful you drew my attention to those weaknesses. I've completely revised it. I'm sure you will enjoy reading this version.'

'I'm sure I shall. Give me some time and I'll get back to you. I will definitely read it. I hope you're not going to disappear again?'

'No. So many things in my life have been sorted. Above all, I've got a family.'

'Good. The only problem I think we'll have is with funding. The companies and organisations that supported the series have pulled the plug. Not doing it when you first came to this country was a big opportunity missed. I can only read and recommend.'

'I understand. I just thought I should finish this project once and for all.'

'The production company that asked for your script might have some ideas. The first thing to do now is to give me time to read your script and then we'll see what happens. I'm very pleased you're back. I kept thinking what a shame that such a wonderful script was just literally gathering dust in my office. You'll soon hear from me. Oh! Before I forget, you don't have to pay. After you'd disappeared the scholarship board sent us some money.'

That evening, Suzanne called from Zeeland. 'Alfred Snr says he's the happiest man in the world. He's been smiling, whistling and singing all day. He sits there and looks at Alfred Jnr for hours. You should see the joy on his face, in his eyes. I thought Amira made him happy but Alfred Jnr made him ... He's in another world. He told me this morning. "You should have had such beautiful children long time ago when I was younger and stronger." It's amazing, Alfred Snr tells them stories in Dutch language and they just sit there and listen.'

Frank B called one evening several weeks later. 'I know you're very busy with your family but I think we should do something to remember Mo. You know something, his first girlfriend called Maureen, I think I told you about her, is back in the UK. She said it would be good to have a dinner. She wants to meet you and your family. I'll give you the details of the restaurant once she gives them to me. I really look forward to meeting Suzanne again she's such a lovely woman, and those cute children of yours.'

I put the phone down and minutes later it rang again.

'You're a star,' Hilary started. 'I've just finished reading the script, excellent. You've really reworked it. It reads well and it seems to have matured now. Certainly one of the best scripts I've ever read. It's very original. I'll contact the film production company on your behalf. Congratulations for producing such a masterpiece.'

I thanked her.

When Suzanne and the children returned, we went to a restaurant in Putney to meet Frank B and Maureen. Maureen was a tall, slim and elegant woman. She had short grey hair. She sat next to me saying, 'I'm going deaf in my left ear and I somehow misplaced my hearing aid.'

'I thought you want to chat him up. You've passed your display by date you know,' Frank B said laughing.

'Shut up Frank,' Maureen shouted at him and cast him a very stern look. 'His wife is here for God's sake.' She looked at Suzanne and apologised. 'He's getting worse by the day. I've known him for over 40 years and he's not changed a bit.'

'What do you want me to change to, an angel? I'm one already.'

'Anyway,' she turned to me. 'I was around 20 when I first met your late uncle Mo. It was love at first sight. I was madly in love with him. As it happened, someone from my family was working in the Native Authority office of the colonial administration in Kaduna then. So I seized the opportunity to visit Nigeria. I went to Jos and spent a week there. Then I went to Bauchi town where you came from. I was in Wunti and Kobi. After one month I came back to London and you wouldn't believe it, I found Mo with another girl. I was devastated. I was too young and too much in love. I felt betrayed. I became depressed and dropped out of university. Luckily my father was posted to India, then to South Africa. I followed him. Leaving the UK sort of helped me recover. I came back and resumed my studies. I later got married. I have three grown up children and six grandchildren. My husband died last year.'

'So you're in the market now … back in the game,' Frank B said casually.

'Shut up Frank,' Maureen said. 'I'm really sorry Suzanne you have to hear all this.'

'She knows me very well. You don't have to apologise or introduce her to me.'

Suzanne smiled at Maureen. 'He's right. We've met many times before. He's a dirty old man. *Vuil ou man* as we say in Afrikaans.'

Maureen agreed. 'That's correct. *Vuil ou man.*'

Frank B laughed. 'It's better to be a dirty old man than a nasty, stupid or angry old man. You know what Maureen, I told Suzanne she's got one of the best backsides I've ever seen. I told her that a woman's identity is defined by her backside. Show me your backside and I'll tell you who you are. Suzanne can sit on my face any time.'

'And I said that men who talk about women's backside usually die off earlier than the women.'

'I'd have been dead more than fifty years ago.'

'Listen to this, I was told that in days not that long ago when a man meets a woman he squeezes her tits as a form of greeting and the women enjoyed it and accepted the act as a form of compliment. If one did something like that these days I suppose it would be called sexual harassment. I think I was born in the wrong age. Maybe men pinched or squeezed the backside of women to say goodbye. That would have been very exciting period indeed.'

'Anyway,' Maureen continued talking to me. 'Mo wasn't meant for me. Time healed the wound but I have a surprise for you.'

'What is it?' Frank asked laughing.

'Mind your own business,' Maureen said and opened her bag. She brought out an envelope and pulled out some photographs. 'I was going through my photos last week and guess what I found.' She showed me a black and white photograph. In it she was wearing a dress with flowers and holding and infant. I recognised the photograph immediately and started laughing. 'Who is this new born in my arms?'

'That's me.'

'That's right. It was taken at your naming ceremony. You were one week old. I pleaded with your mother to let me take you. She said no. You see we meet again.'

'So let's toast,' Frank B. said. 'Blimey! This young fella still doesn't drink?'

'No alcohol for us,' I said.

'Good for you,' Maureen said. 'See what it did to your uncle. I'm also happy you're married and have settled down. Mo just couldn't settle down.'

Dinner was served.

After eating, Maureen brought out more photographs of Mo in

London. 'Look at Mo on a London bus. Here he is holding a microphone while singing in Hyde Park. It was a sell out and I was there to hear him sing. This is my favourite,' she said. 'Mo with his Afro hair, thick sideburns, a cigarette in his mouth, holding a bottle of whisky. You can have them all. My son scanned all of them for me.' She showed me a picture of where she was standing with my parents. 'I still remember the following Hausa words: *Amarya. Mata. Miji. Yarinya. Baturiya.*'

Maureen changed seats and sat next to Suzanne. 'You probably don't know this but my late husband was half South African. I was in Jo'burg and Cape Town for many years.' They talked about life in South Africa.

'What are you doing with yourself?' Maureen asked me.

I told her about what I had done and that the script of the film was now ready.

'How timely, it's good that we met. I'm on the board of an art organisation. One of the things we do is help young African writers and filmmakers make the breakthrough. We don't really give them the money. We help raise funds for them. We contact funders like Arts Council England and other organisations on their behalf.'

Maureen gave me her business card. Let's meet as soon as possible. We might be able to help you. It's difficult but we can only try.'

'Why is it difficult?' Frank asked.

'These organisations support projects that are in line with their ideology. They wouldn't support all applications. A lot of them are not Pan African for example so they will not support materials or projects that aim to propagate Pan African ideas. I haven't seen his script yet so I cannot comment. But I think Mustapha has done his bit and I'm very happy for him. I'm really happy he has come this far. I'm particularly happy because you have succeeded where Mo didn't.'

Mr Frank B raised his glass. 'Let me start by recognising the fact that you have done what many people couldn't do: you've lived, survived and succeeded in London. You've suffered but you persevered and I wholeheartedly commend you. Allow me to acknowledge the rock and support of your life in the person of Suzanne. I'm so happy to see all these beautiful faces. Look at these lovely grandchildren of mine. I want to thank Suzanne for all the help and support. To all of you.'

Maureen raised her glass too. 'I'm proud of you, Mustapha. It's obvious you've worked hard. You have a lovely family. You've rewritten your script. You have an MA. Congratulations! To your health and success.'

Twenty-three

Daring to Dream Again

'Baker Street station is closed due to a security alert. Please alight here and use alternative routes to continue your journey,' the train driver announced on the Jubilee Line. I was in St John's Wood station that morning. I hurried out of the station. I was already late for an appointment in the Marylebone area. I jumped onto a bus. Two stops later there was a traffic jam. Everything came to a standstill. I looked at my watch, it was exactly 10.00 am. I should have been doing the presentation of my script to the board members of the art organisation. I asked the bus driver what had happened. 'There's an accident. A HGV ran over a cyclist,' he explained.

'Thank you very much,' I said and alighted from the bus. I went to a nearby telephone booth and called Maureen. 'It's okay Mustapha two board members are also late. Don't worry we'll wait for you.'

'You don't have to run,' Maureen said as I entered the conference room panting. 'What would you like, tea, coffee or water?'

'Water please.'

When all the members were ready Maureen introduced me and asked me to take them through the idea of the project. After about an hour, the executive director started. 'Let's congratulate you for such a wonderful idea. I'm impressed by the depth of your knowledge of Africa. I like the idea very much. It's fantastic and we would very much like to support you. We're going to make all the necessary applications on your behalf. This is what we're here for. I'm not trying to be a pessimist, but you know very well that most people and organisations support projects that concur with their own ideologies. I thought I should let you know this fact. Going through your script, I must confess that it will be very difficult for us to get generous funding because your ideas are very brave and critical of the status quo in Africa. You know that most sponsors have interests in Africa.'

When he stopped, I responded. 'I do understand but as an artist I think that sooner or later I've got to take a stand. All I'm trying to do is to use film to show what is happening on the ground. All I'm trying to do, as an artist, is to hold up a mirror so that Africans can see themselves. The reflection in the mirror is not of my own making and I think it would be dishonest in this day and age to try and distort the reality.'

'Don't get me wrong, Mr Abdullahi,' the executive director cut in. 'I'm not in any way saying you're wrong or should change the way you present the issues, far from it. Your script presents the problems facing Africa from a completely new perspective, something we are not used to in the Western world. Most funders – if not all the sponsors – are based here in the West. I commend you for the maturity and intelligence displayed in the script. I assure you that we are going to do our best. Maureen will be in touch.'

I thanked them.

Three months later, Maureen called. 'Mustapha, I've good news and bad news. I'll give you the bad news first. Just as we feared, all the funders we approached said no to your application. I'm really sorry.'

'And the good news?'

'I've just spoken to a Dutch philanthropist called Jessica. I met her several years ago in Zimbabwe. She's into development projects in Africa. Last week, we were talking about something else and I told her about your project and she was excited. I faxed her some documents and some pages of the script. She rang today to say she'd definitely support the project but cannot pay for everything. So at least you've now got someone who has pledged to meet half the costs.'

'I'm really grateful. As they say, have a loaf is better than none.'

'That's true. But we have to get the other half from somewhere, otherwise the project will not take off.' She paused. 'You know what, let's try all the African embassies in the UK. I've a template that we could use to write to all of them. Come over when you have the time and let's fill in the dots together. I'll get the secretary to compile a list of all African high commissions.'

Maureen and I drafted a letter. The package to the African high commissions included a synopsis and a detailed budget, including costs from the production company and other expenses. When she was ready to send the package she said, 'I want you to succeed in doing something Mo couldn't. He was such an intelligent young man.'

Three months later, Maureen called. 'Mustapha, you wouldn't believe this. We have received nothing, not a single reply, not even a letter of acknowledgement from any of the high commissions in the UK.' I could sense she was upset. 'These people spend so much money on arms to kill their own people and wouldn't even put some money aside, a fraction of what it would cost to buy a tank, to make or support of film. What a disgrace! Shame on these leaders.' When she calmed down, she continued. 'I'm really sorry Mustapha. I've tried everybody on our database. I desperately wanted to succeed. You've gone too far to stop now. Let's try all embassies of Muslim and Arab countries. Maybe your name will help here. I've all their details. These Arab sheikhs spent a fortune in casinos, on horses and fast cars. Maybe one of them will look at the application and say instead of gambling one weekend I'll use the money to sponsor a film written by a Muslim. Maybe another one will say, instead of buying another car that I'll hardly drive, I'll sponsor this young Muslim filmmaker. You never know.'

Maureen and I waited for three months. Not a single reply.

'Let's give up,' I said deflated.

'You men never remember anniversaries,' Suzanne reproached me one morning in the summer. I noticed she had smiled at me at dawn and given me a passionate kiss. 'I thought only my father forgets anniversaries.'

'What are you talking about?'

'Today is our wedding anniversary.'

'Oh my God, I'm terribly sorry! I completely forgot. I'm getting old.'

'That's not an excuse.'

'I'm not upset. My father didn't even remember our birthdays. Let's celebrate at the Greek restaurant in Willesden Green. I want to try something there.'

In the evening we walked to the restaurant.

'What's wrong with you Michael?' Suzanne asked after we've settled down in the restaurant. 'You've been unusually quiet of late.'

'I really don't know. I think I'm giving up on this film project. Maybe it's the thyroid again. Look Suzanne, not a single African High Commission even bothered to acknowledge receipt of my application. Neither did a single Muslim or Arab High Commission. Maureen sent the applications to all of them including a lot of these Arab sheikhs. Where else can I get the money to make this film? Maybe that's why I'm a bit down. I'm fed up.'

'Come on Michael, you can't jump half a hurdle and give up? You've jumped so many hurdles. What has happened to the Michael I knew and fell in love with? Where is the wild lion that was so magnificent in the chase? What happened to the Michael with a dream? What happened to the Michael that was chasing his dream with such vigour, vitality and spirit? I really liked the way you were chasing your dream with passion like a lion chasing his prey.'

'I don't eat well, sleep well and I'm always irritated,' I admitted. 'It's a bit of concern for me because I know it's affecting you and the kids.'

Suzanne held my hand across the table looking straight into my eyes. Amira removed her hand. 'Mimi first,' she said laughing.

'Mimi, don't start winding me up again,' Suzanne shouted at her.

Mimi insisted, 'Mimi first.'

'Mimi, he was my husband first before he became your daddy.'

Mimi shook her head in disagreement. 'Mimi first.'

'Okay. I give up. You can have your daddy.'

Amira sat on my lap and pulled my hand from the table so that Suzanne could not touch it. 'Mike you always said I should be patient in life. You always convinced me that what is mine will eventually come my way. Patience (I remember you told me before my trip to South Africa) brings that which is very far near. You told me that no one could take my luck away from me. Mr Preacher practise what you preach.' Suzanne put her hand on mine across the table again. Amira removed it again.

'Mimi first,' she insisted.

'Mimi, how many times am I going to tell you that daddy married me first before we had Mimi?'

I did not intervene.

'I suppose you are enjoying the fight for your attention aren't you?'

'I'm not,' I said laughing.

'Freddy, where's daddy?'

Alfred pointed at me.

'Where's grandpa?' Alfred pointed to the sky. 'He means a plane.'

'You see Michael, when we first met at the institute did you know that one day you'd be sitting in a restaurant celebrating a wedding anniversary with your two beautiful kids? That you would have a residence permit? That you would have rewritten your script and even travelled home to see your parents?'

'No.'

'So, as you always said, there is a time for everything. Its time will come. Relax. Enjoy the moment. Never give up until it's all over. And it's not over yet.'

'You're right.'

'That's correct. I think you need a break somewhere. Maybe we should go to South Africa and spend at least a week in the Kruger National Park. It's time you met my mother who has always wanted to meet her grandchildren. Maybe a trip like that would reboot you and give you more energy to think positively. Maybe seeing wild animals in their natural habitat will give you the necessary inspiration.'

'Do you think it's the right time to go to South Africa?'

'Yes but there are a few things I want to sort out before I take you all there.'

'It's up to you.'

Several months later, on a Sunday morning, I was in the sitting room with Alfred who was playing with some of his toys. I switched on the television. I changed the channels but nothing interested me. Alfred gave me one of his toys to play with. It was a model of a racing car. I thanked him and played with it on the floor. Just as I was about to change the channel I noticed that similar cars were racing on a circuit. I was not interested. Alfred was by now playing with the remote control. He ran away with it. Before I could chase him and collect it, I saw a familiar face on the screen. 'Yes!' I shouted with excitement. 'He's the one. That's Danny.'

'Are you okay?' Suzanne asked. 'Arsenal scored a goal?'

'No. I've just seen the son of Rosemary on television.'

'Who's Rosemary?'

'The old woman I once told you about. The one I used to read newspapers to in the care home and then in Teddington.'

'The woman that gave you the African name?'

'Yes. Her son Danny is into Formula One.'

'So? Why are you so excited, because he's on television?'

'No. You know what, Danny told me that he doesn't just do fast cars. He said that he does charity too. When he called to inform me about his mother's death, I told him I was rewriting my script. He said that I should contact him if I needed any help. And he said if he could not help me he would link me up with people who could. Look, there he is again.' Danny was shown smiling in the paddock with a headphone on looking at the screens in front of him.

'And you're sure he's the one?'

'Of course, I went to his office and there were models of racing cars, posters and everything to do with Formula One. I'm definitely sure. He told me he's into Formula One.'

'Someone on a F1 racing track with headphones on a race day must know someone somewhere who can help you. Are you're sure he said he was going to help you?'

'I'm very sure. He said something about a foundation he was setting up and that he knows people in the film and entertainment industry. He was very nice to me, I must say. He had very little time for his mother though.'

'If he had time for his mother he wouldn't have invited you to read the newspaper to her.'

I called the house in Teddington.

'Victor doesn't work here anymore. My name is Andrei and I'm also from Ukraine.' After the initial conversation Andrei refused to give me the office number for Danny. He would not even book an appointment for me to meet Danny in Teddington. He refused to take down my number and pass it onto Danny.

'Michael, someone like Danny must be in the BT directory. His office must be listed for sure,' Suzanne said and called BT. Minutes later she came in and gave me the number.

On Monday I called Danny's office. 'Is he expecting your call?'

'Yes.'

'What's it about?'

'I was the carer of his deceased mother and he said I should call him when the project I was working on was ready.'

'But she died long time ago.'

'That's correct. But I started the project just before she died and he said I should contact him when the project is finished.'

'Is it business? I mean something to do with F1?'

'It's not but the moment you mention my name to him he'll remember.'

'What's your name again?'

'Michael Kimani.'

'What's it about?'

'Application for funding.'

'Okay. I'll discuss it with him and call you back. You're lucky he's just arrived back in the UK.'

The secretary called back after about an hour. 'Mr Kimani, Danny does remember you very well,' she started. 'He said that you should put in the application and that he would look at it when he's in the office.'

I called Maureen immediately. 'Leave the rest with me. I'll prepare a very good application and send them to him by courier in the next hour or two. Great Mustapha! We're getting somewhere. Fingers crossed.'

Suzanne called me at the office the following day to say Danny's secretary had called. He wanted to see me on Thursday afternoon around 2.00 pm. He is scheduled to travel out of the country that evening.

I took Thursday off work. Suzanne, the kids and I arrived in the area half an hour before our scheduled appointment. 'This is the building. Apart from the scaffolding, everything remains the same.'

When it was time, I pressed the buzzer. 'Michael Kimani here for Danny.'

'Pull the door please.'

As we waited for the lift I blurted. 'Shit.'

'Sssh, Don't swear. What have you forgotten?'

'Nothing, he knows me as Michael Kimani. The application is in the name of Mustapha Abdullahi. Damn it.'

'Damn it!' Amira repeated several times laughing in the lift.

'If he'll help you the name doesn't matter as long as he recognises you.'

'My past is catching up with me.'

'You still have a long way to go Michael,' Suzanne said as we walked out of the lift.

'I still remember you,' the secretary said as we entered the office.

'I remember you too.' I noticed she still wore bright lipstick.

'You came here with Rosemary in your white overalls.'

'Yes I did.'

'Danny is very busy.'

'I know. We're not in a hurry. We can wait.'

When she entered Danny's office Suzanne whispered, 'You're right, even the office celebrates the glamour, glory and global business of motor racing.'

There was racing on TV screens. There were models of F1 cars, enlarged photographs of F1 drivers, sample of engines and names and logos of sponsors.

Moments later Danny emerged from his office. 'What a surprise Michael! Thank you very much for keeping in touch,' he said shaking my hand firmly. 'I very much appreciate it. Please come in,' he said and ushered us into his office. 'Is this your family?'

'Yes. Please meet my wife Suzanne and our kids Mimi and Freddy.'

Danny greeted them. 'Look at what he's holding,' Danny laughed. 'An old model of a Formula One car. So you're into F1 too are you? That's my business you know. When I was a kid I used to hold toys like this. The problem was I never grew out of it.' He joked and asked Freddy, 'Do you want to drive F1 car?' Freddy said no. 'Do you want to design F1 car?' No. 'Do you want to be a team engineer?' No. 'Do you want to be a test driver of F1 car?' No. Anyway, you'll grow out of F1 – I can't,' Danny joked again and looked at me. 'Michael, I envy you. I mean positive envy.'

'Why?'

'You've time to spend with your family,' he said sitting down. 'I'm always busy. I saw an application but I haven't had time to read it. Tell me what you are applying for. I vaguely remember you told me something about your script. Am I right, was it you?'

'Yes you are right Danny.' I told him that I had rewritten the script and that it had been approved by the film college.

'Ah! I know the director very well. Robin is a very nice man.'

'A production company is ready to commence filming in Dakar, Senegal, sometime next year, but they need some money. The total sum needed is in the application. A Dutch philanthropist called JCT Foundation has pledged to give me half the amount. I would like to know if you could help me with the other half. If you can't, could you please direct me to someone who could help? You once told me that you don't just do cars.'

'Yes you're right. I remember telling you that.'

There was a moment of silence.

'Tell me about the film.' He dropped his pen on the table and leaned back to listen to me.

I told him a summary.

'That's fascinating. My brother Pete who is a professor would definitely like it. He's into all these political issues.' Danny opened the file in front of him. 'Hang on, there's only one application on my table. I'm not sure if it's yours. Is Mustapha your name?'

'Yes.'

'Oh my God,' he shouted and dropped his pen. 'Oh my God!' he repeated. 'This is weird. This is unbelievable.'

'Is that a problem?'

'No! Not at all. So you're a Muslim?'

'Yes I am.'

'That's really interesting, really interesting. I must call my brother and tell him immediately. This is a very significant piece of information. You've confirmed something very important. You see Michael, our late mother told Pete and I that you were a Muslim. She actually told him the first day you were with her at the care home. When he called her that evening, she told him that she had met someone who claimed to be what he was not. She told me that Michael was not your real name the day you took her to my house in Teddington. We thought she was senile. Thank you very much Michael. You made my day. We shall forever be grateful that you came into our lives. Our minds are at rest now.'

Danny opened the file. He looked at it again. 'Mustapha,' he said laughing. 'Where is the total amount again Michael? Sorry Mustapha.' I showed him. 'Is that all?'

'Half of it.'

'Okay, I will approve half of this amount plus something for the little ones, these wonderful kids that are such a delight to watch. Michael, if JCT or whatever their name is decides for some reason not to support the project, please come back to me. I know someone who will help you. I know more than one person who'll chip in to make this dream come true. As I said a long time ago, it is one thing to have ideas but another thing to have the money to put those ideas into the real world.' Danny stood up laughing. 'How do you live with two names? It must be complicated. Don't you get confused? What does your wife call you, Michael or the other name?'

'Darling,' I said laughing.

Danny laughed. 'I suppose that makes it easier even.'

'No, she calls me Michael. That was my name when we met.'

'If I may ask, where did you meet?'

'We met somewhere in central London. I was working as a kitchen porter and she was my boss.'

'Amazing isn't it? From a kitchen porter to a film director! What a life. I'm really inspired. I like to hear such stories. My brother would be delighted to hear this news. He always wanted to meet you to find out the truth about your identity, just out of curiosity, nothing else.'

Danny called his secretary. 'Louise, I've approved this amount which should come from The Rosemary Foundation. Please discuss with Michael what would be the best way to remit it to him. I leave the rest to the two of you to sort out.' Danny walked to me smiling. He shook my hand firmly. 'Well done! I still remember you in your overalls when you brought my mother here. It was a crazy day for me. Lawyers were chasing me for this and that. I was going through a divorce then. Silverstone was coming up and there were many logistical problems. It was madness. You must have thought I was going mad. That's my life. But I was lucky on that day you took care of my mother. She got along very well with you. She loved your voice. Just before she died, she looked at me and said call my Mohammedan friend and say thank you. Congratulations Mike. I like seeing people who achieve something in life. Life is too short to be wasted. You have a beautiful family too. See how calm they are. My kids would have turned this office upside down. Good luck with the film and please, please and again please do invite me to the premiere. I would love to be there for you. Unless there's a F1 race on the day of your premiere, or I am too far away on the other side of the world, I promise, Michael, I promise that I will be there for you. I have a private jet that can fly me in and out for it.'

Danny picked up Freddy. 'Your daddy was very close to my mummy. We all called him Michael. My mummy called him something else. I cannot remember. We didn't know he had another name. I'll train you to be a Formula One driver.'

'No mummy.'

'He's a real mummy's boy,' Danny said and gave Freddy a miniature F1 helmet and a model F1 car. He gave the kids F1 caps and key holders. He opened his drawer and brought out a small box. 'This is for the filmmaker. I hope you'll wear it on the day your film is shown,' he said handing it to me.

I took it and opened it. It was a wristwatch. I thanked him.

'Wow!' Suzanne screamed looking at the wristwatch in the box. 'This is one of the best-loved motor sport watches, definitely one of the most expensive watches around. I read about it somewhere. Oh my God, what a present. It's very special indeed.'

'Your husband deserves it. Sorry I've nothing special for mummy,' he said looking at Suzanne.

'What you've given us is more than enough! We're very grateful. I was about to buy him a wristwatch.'

'You still have to buy him one I'm afraid because this is not a watch you wear every day; not something you wear in a crowded bus or train in some parts of London. Even our racing drivers wear them only on special occasions.' Danny thought for a while. 'You know what, I have something special for mummy,' he said and opened another cupboard and brought out a medium-sized bottle of champagne from a bag. Handing it to her he said, 'Don't do what those crazy F1 drivers do on the podium. Don't shake it and spray it on Michael on the day of his premiere. Enjoy it.'

Suzanne and I were speechless in the lift. Outside she looked at me and shook her head. 'Wow, congratulations,' she eventually managed to say. 'Let's go to Hyde Park. I haven't been there for ages,' Suzanne suggested.

'Let's go.' We walked slowly towards the park. We looked for a bench under a tree and sat down. 'I'm a bit dazed,' I admitted closing my eyes. I was feeling dizzy.

'I would have fainted. I'm not in the thick of things yet I feel the emotions. It's very nerve wracking. I don't know how you were able to cope, Michael.'

Suzanne continued to talk but I did not hear what she was saying. She tapped me. 'Here,' she said giving me a bottle of water. 'This might help.'

I shook my head and gestured that I didn't want it.

'Sorry, I forgot you're fasting.'

My mind went back to the two nights I had spent in Hyde Park. The bench I slept on had been removed but I could see the spot from where we were sitting. I remembered how I had walked into the park that evening in a state of confusion. I remembered vividly the clothes I was wearing. I remembered saying to myself when I entered the park that I needed a few hours to think. I never for one moment thought that I would sleep there. I remembered the moment Mark appeared and how startled I was. I remembered the security man who gave us food. I remembered the darkness in the park and how scared I was that night. I remembered the distant voices that sometimes felt very close. I remembered the drunken voices and the fear that any minute someone would attack me. I remembered the thick clouds that formed on my second day in the park and how I hoped and prayed that it wouldn't rain. I remembered the thunder and lightning and then the sharp rain that followed. I had nowhere to run other than to the public toilets. I remembered the brief period I spent there sheltering from the September storm. I remembered the old man with two bags who stood next to me.

Suzanne shook me. 'Are you are okay?' she asked. 'Have you fainted?'

'I'm fine. I'll be all right.' I thought for a while whether or not I should tell Suzanne about my experiences in the park. Something in me said no. This was not the best time.

'Let's go home. I'm fine.'

Suzanne looked at me. 'Michael, you need rest. I don't mean a weekend in Holland as planned. Once everything is sorted, I would like us to go to South Africa.'

'But first we have to go back to Cricklewood,' I said laughing.

We took the number 16 bus home.

I called Maureen that evening. 'Mustapha,' she started. 'I'm really happy for you. I also spoke to Jessica in The Hague. She's expecting you any time you are in Holland. We're in business now.'

A week later we boarded the plane. 'Are you sure you have the energy for all these things?' Suzanne asked as we sat down on the plane. 'I know its Ramadan and you have been fasting. You're tired and hardly slept all night.'

'I'll do my best.'

'I want you to spend only a couple of hours with Alfred Snr.'

'Why?'

'First you need to return to The Hague and break your fast there. But more importantly, I'm trying to be very cautious here. I don't know him very well. He could be my grandfather but I don't know how he would react if you were there for a long time. Human beings are very complicated you know. I could not handle a quarrel between the two of you. I know that. I know you both respect each other but I don't want to take any chances. I would rather keep the two of you apart than to be forced to choose.'

'I understand and agree with you.' I paused. 'Are there any forbidden topics?'

'No but I suggest you let him do the talking.'

'Just tell me when you want me to leave for The Hague.'

'I'll do that.'

We arrived at his house on the outskirts of Zeeland. There were about a dozen cows and three horses grazing on a farm nearby. There was a garage next to the building with a tractor outside.

We entered the huge living room. It was loaded with beautiful works of art, lovely furniture and carpeting. In the perfectly tendered garden adorned with roses, Suzanne introduced me to Alfred Snr. He stood up from his chair and shook my hand. He was delighted to see me. I could see it in his warm eyes and delicate smile. He sat down but before this said, 'Please sit down. I'm really happy to meet you at last,' he said nodding his head several times. 'You have beautiful children. Well behaved and intelligent. I like them and they liked me. I'm sure

Suzanne must have told you that already. There's chemistry between me and your children.' He looked calm and relaxed. He looked at me and smiled slightly.

I let him do the talking. He told me about the problem that changed his life several decades ago.

'I did something I was not supposed to do with somebody I was not supposed to do it with,' he started as a form of introduction. He paused for a while and looked at me. 'I was young and I listened to my heart. We're all human beings. Maybe I was naive but who in love is not naive? I didn't like what they did to us. I didn't expect the church to do what they did. It was very difficult. I have feelings too. I suffered a lot but I think they had to do what they thought was the best at the time. Somehow we are all victims of circumstances in one way or the other. That's the way things are in this world. I did not believe in the superiority of one race over another. For many reasons, one race does have an advantage over others but I strongly oppose the notion of superiority. It's a matter of principle. It was a position I took when I was a teenager and I still hold that principle today.

'Look at South Africa today. Completely different from the time they sent me here into exile. Now you have the African National Congress in power. Whoever would have thought it was possible, even ten years ago, that the ANC would be in power? So the world your children will live in will be different from the world you are familiar with, completely different. I told Suzanne many times that despite the way I was treated I am not angry or bitter. Human beings can be irrational and we must learn to deal with that. I don't want to go to my grave an angry man.

'Suzanne told me that you're into films. I'm very glad that you have a good vocation. It's important for the intellect of a man to have a vocation. We're happiest when we do things – when we create. I wish I could live long enough to see your film. I must thank you for allowing Suzanne to visit me quite regularly. It has been very good to see her and to talk to her.'

'No, I should thank you for all the support.'

'There's nothing that can replace the company of a human being. Maybe Suzanne told you but when your family are here I am very happy. I know of course it means you are lonely in London. I'm sorry. I feel guilty but as you can see I don't think I have many years left.'

'It's okay. I'm busy at work and with my film. You can have them for the time being,' I said laughing.

He laughed too. 'Thank you.'

The doorbell rang. Suzanne opened the door. A tall, lanky man walked in smiling. 'You must be Michael,' he said shaking my hand. 'My name is Jos.'

'Nice to meet you.'

'I'm delighted to meet you at last. I've heard a lot about you.'

'Jos is a publisher and a teacher. He's a very good friend of Alfred's. He helped me with all the paperwork needed for my visas, my Dutch citizen and my Dutch passport,' Suzanne said.

'I thank you very much for all the assistance you've provided my family.'

'It's okay. It's her right. She's entitled to it. What about the kids?'

'They are Dutch too.'

Senior showed me Amira chasing the chickens and ducks. 'She likes it here. I only wish I was younger to play with them, to show them around.' He paused. 'You know Michael, I can only be grateful. Life has taught me many things. Never worry about the future because it will come one day and you will have to confront it the way you have confronted the past and the present. For example, I never in my dreams thought I would one day live with my granddaughter and great-grandchildren in the same house, never. I always thought, until some years ago, that I'd die alone.' He paused. 'Sorry if I talk too much but Suzanne said you have other things to do and would be leaving soon. I understand that you are going to meet the sponsor for your film in The Hague.'

'That's correct.'

'Yes it's time to go I'm afraid,' Suzanne said standing up. 'Jos will drop you at the station.'

I stood up. I was happy our meeting had ended on a happy and grateful note. I could see from his eyes that Alfred Snr was happy too.

'Please try and switch off after the meeting. You need rest. Just relax and enjoy Holland for three days.' I started laughing. 'Why are you laughing?'

'I'll go to the coffee shops to see why they don't serve coffee.'

'You're crazy. Leave the coffee shops alone. Remember you're fasting.'

'But what if I want to drink coffee in the evening?'

'You go to the cafes not coffee shops.'

'Alright then, I'll avoid the coffee shops,' I promised. I picked up my bag. 'Where are the kids?'

'Alfred is playing with them in the back garden.'

'*Oppas!*' I heard Alfred Snr saying to Amira. '*Bokkie, pas op!*'

'What does it mean?' I asked Suzanne.

'Sweetheart, watch out. Be careful.'

'I see, in Afrikaans?'

She nodded.

'I look forward to seeing you again. Maybe I'll see your film,' Alfred said and waved goodbye.

I stood in front of the ticket office at The Hague train station. At the agreed time, a tall man wearing a red scarf approached me with a broad smile. 'Mustapha?' he asked.

'Yes,' I said and smiled too.

We shook hands. 'Hubert is my name. I'm Jessica's husband. Jessica and the kids are in a restaurant nearby. Please follow me.'

Hubert was whistling as we walked out of the station. 'So tell me about your film.'

I told him what it was all about.

'Interesting,' he said as he listened attentively.

Hubert opened the door of the restaurant. 'After you,' he said.

I entered. 'Follow me please,' Hubert said and led me to the first floor, which was full. 'This is Jessica,' he said removing his jacket and pointing out a woman sitting with two teenagers.

'Nice to meet you at last,' Jessica said shaking my hand.

'It's a pleasure meeting you too.'

Still standing, she asked, 'Is this your first visit to Holland?'

'Yes.'

'Please sit down.'

We sat down. 'Meet Joost and Tessa,' she introduced their children. Jessica gave me the menu and explained. 'I chose this restaurant because they have a good variety of vegetarian dishes. I know we are in the month of Ramadan and I wasn't sure if you're fasting. Is it time to break your fast already?'

I look at my watch. 'Five more minutes,' I said yawning.

'Sorry, I had no time to see if there are any *halal* restaurants around here. I thought it would be safe for you to eat vegetarian. You like fish?'

'Yes I do.'

When it was time, I silently broke my fast.

We ordered our meal.

'First of all, I want to thank you very much for the pledge you have made to contribute towards the making of my film. I'm happy and grateful.'

'When I agreed to pay half of the total cost of production, to be honest with you I had read only the synopsis. I've now had time to read the entire script. I hope you'll succeed as a director in capturing the spirit of the script. I can't wait to see it on the big screen. It's very imaginative. I'm very proud to be associated with such a wonderful project.' She paused. 'By the way, I'm not going to the office tomorrow but the administrator will be there. I told her you would be there in the morning. She'll sort you out. I look forward to meeting your family soon and, of course, I look forward to seeing the film.'

After the meal, I thanked them and left.

I returned to London and started making preparations to shoot the film. I took time off work to travel to Dakar, Senegal to direct the film.

Twenty-four

My Dream Comes True

Five months later I returned from Dakar to the UK.

'I'm back,' I said as soon as Suzanne picked up the phone. 'I didn't realise it would be such fun and hard work. Everything went well.'

'I'm glad to hear your voice again. The feeling must be great. You must tell me more. So what's next?'

'I've got one month before I return to work and I intend to spend it editing the film at the studios in Kingston.'

'Can we come for a week?'

'Of course.'

Months later the phone rang. 'Hi, this is Andy here. I work for a PR company responsible for the marketing and publicity of your film. I just want to inform you that we have booked a hall in the South Bank for the premiere of your film. We've dispatched over a hundred short clips and other marketing and publicity materials of the film to many outlets, including newspapers, magazines, leading critics and other media outlets. We're expecting very positive reviews. I'll courier fifty free tickets you're entitled to straightaway. Please note the date in your diary. I'll put my number on the complimentary slip and feel free to call me. Do you have any questions?'

'No I haven't.'

'Now Suzanne, close your eyes and open your hands.' She closed her eyes. I placed the ticket for the premiere in her hand. 'Now open your eyes.'

'Michael! This is extraordinary. Wow! It's good to dream. Nothing succeeds like success. I'm really proud of you.'

'I thank you. I am grateful for everything you have done for me.'

I started singing the song, (*Everything I do*), *I do it for you.*

'Do it for Mimi,' Amira sang.

'Did you hear what she said?' Suzanne asked. 'Everything I do, do it for Mimi.'

Mimi laughed and hugged me. 'Thank you Mimi, wind mummy up for me.'

'Hmmm Michael, I still remember that evening in Pall Mall when we were doing silver service together. I remember the grumpy face that said, "I want to be a film director." And here we are, after all these years, we are all set!

'I really want to see your face after the film. You know the moment when the film comes to an end and something appears on the screen WRITTEN & DIRECTED BY MICHAEL.

'… by Mustapha.'

'You know who I mean. That moment you're officially christened a film director. Wow! The feeling must be great.'

Suzanne changed the topic. 'I'll be moving more things to Holland. The kids have settled down nicely there. They've made so many friends. And I'm happy about it. It's important to socialise. Mimi's friends are from Morocco, Sri Lanka and Guyana. I understand your worries and anxieties. There are kids from all backgrounds.'

'What about the prince?'

Suzanne laughed. 'You know that everybody calls him Prince Alfred of Zeeland. His best friend is a girl from Zeeland whose mother is my friend but no one calls her Princess. What a shame. By the way I've been offered a part-time job at the school.'

'That's good. I was worried you'd be bored at home. As they say, an idle mind is the devil's workshop. As one of your favourite French philosophers Voltaire once said: *Work spares us from three evils: boredom, vice and need.*'

'Don't worry! Senior and the kids keep me busy. I've also made a few friends there. I can't complain about boredom. Taking care of two kids is a full-time job already. I have everything I need there, I'm happy and contented.'

The phone rang. It was Andy. 'I want to keep you up-to-date with what's happening. We'd like you to come in for a photo shoot ASAP. After that we'll be putting out posters across the capital about the film and we want your photo on it. I'd like to speak to your wife if that's possible.'

I gave Suzanne the phone and went to pray in another room.

Imam Murad's eyes lit up with excitement when I gave him the invitation to the premiere. '*Masha'Allah!*' he shouted several times. 'You did it! Brother Mustapha, congratulations. He hugged me several times in the mosque. He turned to other worshippers and explained to them in Urdu, 'Let's make *dua* for Brother Mustapha for successfully completing his project.' He sat down and crossed his legs and cupped his hands. Imam Murad recited verses of the Quran. He prayed that Almighty Allah shower blessings on my family and that the film should be a success. After the prayers, he said, 'Please remember that every success comes from Almighty Allah alone. Remember that simplicity and modesty are part of the *deen*. So do not let the success of making the film go to your head and make you pompous, arrogant and boastful and take you away from the right path. Please be grateful to Almighty Allah. Remember that it's very easy to deal with failure. When you fail, you struggle to succeed. But it's very difficult to deal with success. It's a huge challenge. May Almighty Allah give you the humility and modesty to handle this success because humility is important,' he emphasised and paused. 'Unfortunately I cannot be at the premiere. I'll get Samad and Asghar to be there. I'm so happy for you and I'm happy that you remembered us here in Maida Vale.'

Andy called a day before the premiere. 'We've got some fantastic reviews in already. He read one. "If you want to understand the problems of Africa in general and Nigeria in particular in 120 minutes – watch this film." There's another one by a well-known film critic. "Mustapha must be considered as a pioneer of postcolonial realism … He has successfully followed the footsteps of Ousmane Sembène in producing a very progressive and illuminating film." Andy paused. "Fresh and brilliant debut. A film of its time and the future. A director whose time has arrived. Thrilling, spectacular and brave."'

'Thanks Andy.'

'We have a file full of reviews and will give you the file tomorrow. We're expecting a full hall and at least twenty people from the media. Your request to arrive ten minutes before the premiere has been granted. We have moved photo shoots and other activities till after viewing. So see you tomorrow evening.'

Suzanne called. 'I'll give you the bad news first. Senior has been rushed to the hospital again. I have this feeling that this is the last time he'll be taken to hospital. It's that bad.' She paused.

'What's the good news?'

'Jos came this morning terribly excited, waving a newspaper at us in the school. He repeatedly punched the air. "Michael has made it," he shouted several times. There was a big article in a national newspaper about you and your film. The article was by a well-known journalist and film critic. And you know what? Mimi was to have a session of *Show and Tell* in her class. She went around and proudly showed every pupil your photograph. She pointed at it telling them proudly: *"Dit is mijn papa"* (*This is my daddy*). The title of the article was: *An Extraordinarily Raw Talent is Born*. It says "something new always comes out of Africa. A talented filmmaker has appeared on the radar. Watch this man."' Suzanne paused. 'My partner in crime, my magnificent wild lion, I'm terribly proud of you. You've made it at last. See you tomorrow. By the way, I've paid for the refreshments.'

It was a very difficult night. I could not sleep immediately.

I woke up at dawn and said my prayers. Suzanne called. 'I was just wondering whether you were able to sleep.'

'I slept well,' I said.

'I don't believe you. I know the type of person you are.'

'All right then, I slept for only three hours. I'll be all right just a bit nervous but I'll see you at the airport later.'

On the train to Heathrow Airport, an elderly couple sitting opposite me were reading a national newspaper. It was a broadsheet. The woman looked up at me and at a page. She looked at me again and at the page again. She nudged the old man and whispered into his ears. He looked at me and at the paper. Then again they looked at me and at the paper. 'That's right,' I heard him say. 'He's the one.' They smiled at me. I nodded and smiled back. I stood up and looked at the photograph.

'You're right. It's me.'

'Well done,' the man said and shook my hand. 'It's not every day you meet a film director on the train. You've made our day.'

At the airport, I bought a copy of the newspaper. There was a half-page review. I did not read it all. I looked at the photograph and read the last paragraph. 'For anyone wanting to understand the much misunderstood issues of governance in Africa, there is no better place to start than this magnificent, penetrating and dramatic film.'

'Bravo daddy,' I heard Mimi shout.

'Can I kiss mummy today?'

Mimi nodded.

'Michael, you are a star,' Suzanne said hugging me. 'How do you feel?'

'I feel tense, excited and happy.'

'I bet you're thrilled.'

'Suzanne,' I looked into her eyes, 'I'm tense.'

'Relax, everything will be fine.'

'How's Senior?'

'Very bad,' she replied shaking her head. 'He's drifting in and out of consciousness. I'll rent a car,' she said walking toward one of the counters.

Driving out of Heathrow Airport, Suzanne continued. 'Senior is in bad shape but I insisted us that we will be here for you. He would have approved of it anyway. There's nothing I can do apart from visiting him from time to time and sitting by his bedside for a while. The kids must witness this historic day too. At least Senior lived long enough to see a grandchild and a great grandchild named after him. To be honest with you, he was happy towards the end of his life and that's the most important thing. He is ever so grateful to you for letting us be with him.'

'I should thank him. Imagine if Senior had never come into our lives. I'll probably still be an illegal immigrant washing plates and dreaming of my film or I would have been arrested and deported a long time ago. I am grateful for what he has done for all of us.'

Suzanne changed the topic. 'As I said, I've got someone to provide light refreshment before and after the premiere. I spoke to Andy when he called to ask a few questions about your background. He told me you wanted people to go straight into the hall, watch the film and go home after the film.'

'What else do they want?'

'You're always crazy. Anyway, guess who will provide soft drinks before and after your premiere?'

'MKJ?'

'No.'

'Joe.'

'No.'

'Dara and Sara?'

'No.'

'I give up.'

'Your former boss, Ms Katsy Robertson.'

'Oh my God, how come?'

'I searched the Internet for a catering company and so many of them came up. I then narrowed the search by adding her name. It was an exercise initially to find the best at most competitive prices and I was surprised when the search flagged this website. I looked at it and it was hers. So I called her and placed an order. I did not tell her it was your big day. I did not say a word about you. I thought I should organise an awkward reunion for you. See if she'll remember you.'

'Yes I remember her very well. I wonder if she'll remember what she told me on that Wednesday afternoon in the canteen.'

'What did she say?'

'She said, "You're only a kitchen porter." It was not what she said it was the way she looked at me too. I'm your boss type of look. She threatened to sack me, I remember that.'

'Do you want to remind her?'

'No. Let bygones be bygones.'

'Maybe just tell her that I've graduated from being a kitchen porter to a film director.'

'Nah! Silence sometimes speaks louder than words.'

At a traffic light, Suzanne inserted a CD. 'This is the song I want to dedicate to you, Mr Film Director.' She changed the track. It was Jimmy Cliff's song: *You Can Get It If You Really Want.*

'Now sing along,' Suzanne said. We both sang along.

Dara and Sara welcomed us with open arms and smiles at the Persia restaurant.

'Look at these kids. Suzanne what are you feeding them?' Dara asked.

'They've really grown up,' Sara said, playing with Amira's hair.

'*Masha'Allah*! It's such a joy to see them grow like this.' Dara said.

Suzanne and Sara sat some tables away.

Dara and I sat down. He looked at me. 'Amazing isn't it?'

I nodded.

'I saw a review in one of the papers this morning but before that I heard someone talk about it on the radio when I was driving to work. I said to myself, what a man and what a journey! From Mustapha to Michael to Sheikh, from a kitchen porter to a filmmaker, what a remarkable journey!

'I still remember the day Joe called to book Rumi's corner for a new kitchen porter, as he said, called Michael. "Take care of him," he said. "He's a nice guy but a bit shy." See life? How's Suzanne?'

'She and the kids have settled down in Holland. They like it there. The old man gave her his house and the farm.'

'Hafiz of Persia once said: *For I have learned that every heart will get what it prays for most.* I'm happy for you especially with the film.'

'Making it took so many years and a lot of tears. I left my country and came here with this script in 1990. All these years of pain and hardships to do a film that will run for 120 minutes.'

Dara interrupted. 'Michael, you should be grateful. There's a Persian saying: *The longer the journey, the bigger the treasure.* Look at the result of leaving your country. You have these beautiful kids, Suzanne and now the film. These are things money can't buy you know.'

'*Alhamdullilah*, I'm not complaining. It was really hard.'

'What about us? What about me as a chef? I spend so many hours preparing the meal and people come in, sit down and just gobble everything down in thirty minutes. Six hours later the food is out of their bodies. Most people cannot even remember what they ate the next day. You're leaving a legacy that'll educate and inspire people. Long after you're gone, people will remember you and the film. You are blessed and must be very grateful.'

'I am.'

We ate in silence.

'Here's a designer suit for you.' Suzanne said after the meal. 'We should all change here. What about the watch Danny gave you?'

I showed her and went into the gents to change.

'What should I wear? I brought two dresses and cannot decide which to wear, green or black?' Suzanne said and showed me the dresses.

I brought out a coin and showed her the green side and the black side. I tossed the coin three times and green came up twice.

'That was easy in the end. Thank you,' she said and led the kids to the Ladies to change.

Suzanne changed into her thigh-skimming emerald green dress.

'Look at our princess,' Sara said admiring Amira who had changed and was wearing a designer navy cat-print party dress under a navy cardigan. 'You like cats?'

Amira nodded. 'We've got two in our house in Zeeland.'

'Almost every dress you wear suits you,' Sara said to Suzanne.

Dara looked at Amira. 'Soon someone will be competing and will probably outdo their mum on the fashion circuit.' No one answered. 'I can see everyone is dressed up,' Dara added looking at me smiling. He sprayed perfume on me murmuring prayers. 'I hope everything goes well. Good luck.'

Outside the restaurant, I told Suzanne, 'I'll find my way there. I want to arrive at the hall only about ten minutes or so before the lights go out.'

'You coward,' she said smiling. 'I didn't realise you're a *moegoe* (coward) as we say in Afrikaans. I thought your nerves were made of steel.'

'I'm not a coward. I'm just a bit nervous. I'm not sure how I'll behave in front of my friends and well-wishers before the lights go off. By the way, the bravest lion has its moment of fear too.'

Suzanne led the kids into the car. She called me. 'Michael, I hope you won't be too nervous and decide not to turn up.'

'I'll be fine.'

I arrived at Waterloo Station at 4.00 pm. I had one hour before the premiere. From where I was standing, I could see the hall. I had enough time to wander around the area before going into the hall.

I walked into the empty foyer ten minutes before five. Everyone was inside the hall. I opened the door and entered. Andy, who was on the stage, gave me a thumbs-up and showed me to a seat marked RESERVED next to Suzanne.

'Here you are. I was worried you wouldn't turn up,' Suzanne said. 'Anyway I told everyone that you were fine and you'd see them after the film. Everybody is looking forward to it. I bet you're nervous.'

I nodded.

'You'll be all right,' Suzanne assured me.

According to the programme, Hilary Rogers was to introduce the film. She was talking about it. 'There are many things special about this film. It explains, in a subtle way, why Africa has been sliding backwards … it offers a rare and fresh perspective into the reasons why Africa is where it is today … I must praise Mustapha for his extraordinary ability to capture reality and preserve it for posterity … it takes a lot of creativity, courage and imagination to do this and very few filmmakers have successfully done something like this in the past … for this and other reasons, it's bound to be a classic. Hopefully, in generations to come, the world will be a changed place and this film will serve as a historical record of a long-suffering era. On a personal note, it has been a great pleasure working with Mustapha on this project. Mustapha is lively, vibrant and hardworking and I'm happy that at last we are all sitting here today waiting to watch this film.'

'Any news from Zeeland?'

'Yes. I've just received a text message from the hospital. The news is not good at all. His health has deteriorated seriously. We shall return to Holland tonight,' she said looking at her mobile phone that beeped. I looked at the stage. Hilary and Andy were leaving the stage.

'So, here comes the biggest moment of your life so far,' Suzanne said holding my hand. I was shaking. The lights were switched off. There was a moment of silence. It was dark. Then suddenly there was light on the screen and the opening credits started with the name of the production company, then the title of the film *They Turned Day to Night* by Mustapha Abdullahi. Suzanne pinched me.

I took a deep breath. The film started with the cock crowing. Minutes later Suzanne released my hand to check her mobile for more messages from Zeeland. I tiptoed out of the hall. Amira followed me. Outside the hall I felt a lot better. 'I want to go to the toilet,' Mimi said. I took her there and afterwards we walked to the banks of the Thames. I found a spot and sat down.

'Daddy why are you crying?' Mimi asked.

It was only then that I realised tears had been flowing down my cheeks.

'Nothing, I'm very happy.'

'Why?'

'Because I've got you, prince, mummy and now I have a film.'

'Bravo!' she said and hugged me.

I looked at my watch later. Fifteen minutes left. 'Let's go Mimi.'

We entered the dark hall. 'I thought you had run away,' Suzanne whispered as we sat down. 'I didn't realise I was married to such a genius. I thoroughly enjoyed your film. As from now on you're no longer my partner in crime. You've graduated to something else. Wow! Well done! A very good quality film with very deep insights and meaning.'

I knew from the action on the screen that there was only a few minutes left. I closed my eyes until I heard the very last sentence of the film: *This is what happens to a people and a country when the leaders have no vision, when they have no shame – they turn day into night.*

The film ended. I looked up. The credit lines followed

Special thanks to JCT Foundation (The Netherlands) and Rosemary Foundation (UK) for their generous support.

I want to thank my wife, Suzanne van Anhalt Zerbst, and our children Amira Annabel and Alfred Ahmed.

WRITTEN AND DIRECTED
By Mustapha Abdullahi

THE END

There was a huge applause. The lights were switched on. I felt ecstatic, nervous but somehow complete. I took a deep breath and let out a sigh of relief. I stood up and climbed onto the stage. According to the programme I was to speak for two minutes. Someone gave me a microphone. I cleared my throat. 'Good evening ladies and gentlemen, I'll be brief. I want to thank you all for honouring the invitation to be here today. It's such a historic day for me. I hope you all enjoyed the film. Making such a film would not have been possible without the help and support of so many people, most of who are in this hall today. These are friends, neighbours and colleagues. I'm sorry I'm not going to start mentioning names because I'm afraid I will leave someone out. Having said that, please join me in thanking my wife, Suzanne, for her unconditional love and support over the years. To be honest with you, without Suzanne I wouldn't be standing in front of you today.'

There was a huge applause.

'I hope I'll have the time to go around and thank you all individually.'

Suzanne was the first to climb onto the stage. She hugged me. 'I love you Michael. Congratulations and we're terribly proud of you!' Amira followed with a bunch of flowers. Alfred gave me a big card. BRAVO DADDY! I thanked them all and opened the card. There were photographs of animals, including a big photograph of a South African lion. I read out what was written in the card. *Now we are going on holidays to South Africa. We're going to see the real wild lions.* Suzanne whispered smiling, 'Just tell me when you are free. My parents are looking forward to meeting you and the kids. Anyway, we are off to Holland. Enjoy your big day or what's left of it. I'll talk to you tomorrow.' She stopped and looked at me. 'Tell me Michael what happens when your dream comes true?'

I smiled. 'I'll tell you tomorrow.'

'I love you,' she said smiling and left with the kids.

Danny climbed onto the stage smiling. He hugged me. 'Michael, I'm impressed, absolutely brilliant, top-class. Nothing beats quality. I'm really happy I met you.' He turned. 'Meet my brother Pete.'

'Gosh! What an achievement!' Peter said. 'We must meet and talk. This is my card.' Danny stood there smiling. He tapped me on my shoulder several times.

'This is what life is all about – achievement, hard work, self-belief and endurance. I give you ten out of ten for commitment, effort and determination. Well done, wonderful! I'm inspired now. As it is often said, the cream always rises to the top. Somehow you've risen to where you belong, at the top. If you can survive the hardships of London you can survive everywhere; if you can succeed in London, you can succeed everywhere. Well done Michael. As usual I'm in a rush. When you've got time let's meet somewhere, preferably when there are no Formula One races. Let's meet in Monaco. I've got a flat and a yacht there. I want to know your future plans. I had the opportunity of meeting your wife and children again before the film. By the way, if you and your family want to see any Formula One races just call my secretary, she'll arrange everything on me. You deserve it.'

Pete said. 'You know what Michael our late mother Rosemary told me that you would be famous. That was the very first day she met you at the care home. She said we should treat you well because you would be famous one day. Gosh. You and I must sit down and have a good chat.'

Dr Asibong was next. 'Sheikh, I'm really proud of you. You're a great man, a great film director. Ousmane Sembène would be proud of you. What a great film, fantastic to watch! I enjoyed every minute of it.'

Jessica and Hubert walked towards me smiling. 'I didn't know you were coming. I thought you said you were very busy,' I said.

'We wanted to surprise you,' Jessica said smiling. 'We thoroughly enjoyed your film and are very proud to be associated with such a good work of art. By the way, we met your wife and kids. Your kids speak Dutch fluently. You must bring them over to our place for a weekend.'

I thank them for all the generous support.

'It's okay. Maureen and I will discuss how to get the film into Africa but I want you to turn the script into a book. If you don't have the time and money, let me know. We could employ someone to do it for you. I'd gladly get it published here and in Africa. It's something that must be read by as many Africans as possible.'

'I'm really grateful for all the support you've given me.'

'It's all right. I want to reserve your place in history. I want to be your sponsor – someone to plead your case. I have the money, you have the ideas.'

'Start working on the next project,' Hubert said tapping my shoulder.

Hilary hugged me. 'You did it at last! As they say, better late than never. Congratulations! I'm really happy for you. I give you full marks for directing, excellent stuff. I saw your wife and two kids. Tell me, why did you come late?'

I did not answer.

'Brother Mustapha,' Bilal started and hugged me. '*Assalaam Alaikum*. Thank you for such a wonderful film. It's so different from what we see every day. I enjoyed the spiritual message in it. You used reason to explain revelation. Very educative and it encourages self-reflection. I wish you good luck.'

Aisha, who was holding their daughter Imani, added. 'Brother, as you know it's said in our glorious religion that: *Allah loves those who excel in every task*. This is one of the best films I have ever watched. *Masha'Allah*. We're all happy for you.'

Bilal put his hand on my shoulder. 'I was telling Aisha before the film that I remember the first time I met you. You came to work as a kitchen porter in the bank. I told her how I introduced you to Marina who, as it turned out, saved you from the Home Office officials who raided the building on a day she was not supposed to be working.'

I nodded in agreement. 'And you disabled the alarm at the backdoor which enabled me get out of the building without being noticed.'

'*Allah Kareem*,' he said nodding too.

'Almighty Allah works in mysterious ways,' Aisha said smiling at me. 'Now here we are, an accomplished film director. May Almighty Allah reward you for such an inspiring and wonderful film. We'll always remember you in our prayers.' Aisha was excited.

Samad, now a bright-eyed thirty something approached me with a huge smile on his face. '*Assalaam Alaikum*, Brother Mustapha. Congratulations,' he said and hugged me. 'We're all happy for you.' He was wearing a two-piece suit and had grown a beard. Asghar, wearing a three-piece suit and a colourful tie stepped forward and hugged me. He was clean-shaven. I greeted Safia and Fajr who were wearing *salwar kameez* (colourful Pakistani clothes).

'No henna today?' I joked.

'You still remember henna?' Safia asked.

'Of course I do.'

They showed me their hands, full of new henna designs.

Fajr stepped closer. 'We saw your wife and children. They're very cute. *Masha'Allah*. Bring them to our house. We want to play with them.'

'Come and visit us. I want to sit down and eat with you as we did when you first came into the country,' Samad said and gave me his business card.

Farouk smiled and hugged me. 'Now you can go to Mauritius on holidays. You deserve a good break. You can take time off work, that's not a problem at all. Suzanne and the kids are looking very well. Congratulations.'

Jamila walked to me very excited. 'So, my son is now a film director. We thank God. Now that your film has been screened, please try and take my grandchildren to Nigeria. It's important for them to know and see where you come from and meet your real parents.'

Bash the solicitor shook my hand firmly. 'Well done!'

'Sorry! I cannot remember if I paid you the legal fees. I was so excited.'

He laughed. 'Don't worry,' he said smiling. 'We're all happy and proud of you.'

Frank B laughed, 'Young fella! What a remarkable achievement! We have to celebrate. Your lovely Suzanne gave me this present.' He showed me a bottle of single malt whisky in a bag. 'She brought it from Holland. I'm so happy for you all. You have to come and have at least one shot of whisky to celebrate. I enjoyed your film.'

Maureen hugged me and introduced her son Andrew and granddaughter Nancy. 'We must meet and talk. I'm really delighted that you made it at last and we thoroughly enjoyed the film. It's very compelling and compassionate. You've done so well. Mo would be so proud of you. I've a few ideas on how to get the film out there. Call me when you're free and come over for dinner.'

Ama hugged me. 'Comrade, I truly commend you for the revolutionary spirit you've shown in your life and in your film. It was a magnificent film. A true example of not giving up until victory is achieved. I admire your patience, courage, perseverance and willpower. To be able to rise from where you were and produce this wonderful film is just extraordinary. I spoke to Taj this morning and he sends his salutations from Kampala.'

'*Tovarish,*' Jarvo said with a broad smile when Ama had walked away. 'I honestly don't know where to start. I'm really impressed and happy. We have to celebrate big-time. The decision to remain in this country and marry the Boer woman paid off. What an achievement! You deserve an award. It's a lovely film, straight to the point. No messing around at all. I'll convene a special plenum of the Politburo to discuss this. I spoke to your wife before the film. She looks very happy and relaxed. It's just amazing how things turned out. Let's meet at Bozo's Joint soon. We're going to get the real Russian vodka for you.'

'Michael,' Joe shouted and hugged me. 'This is incredible. It's your life that should be a film and I'm sure I'll be there somewhere. I was telling my missus before the film that I vividly remember the day you came in as table cleaner and how your boss, Ms Robertson, hated you and wanted to sack you. She's here you know serving drinks.'

I nodded.

'Did you ensure she came and served the drinks as a form of revenge?'

'No. Suzanne organised the drinks.'

'Anyway, I reminded Ms Robertson just after the film about the incident and said to her look at him now, a film director.' He hugged me again. 'I saw Suzanne and the lovely kids. She's settled down in Holland and she seems to be blissfully happy there. I'm really happy for both of you.'

As he spoke I noticed there was a woman in Hausa clothes speaking to Bilal and Aisha. I could not see her face.

Someone hugged me. It was tight and I was groaning. I could smell a familiar tobacco. 'My African brother,' Leroy started in his lyrical Jamaican accent looking at me. 'I'm really happy to know you. I'm so happy to have met you. I feel so special that I spent days with you in my flat and on the streets of London. You and I struggled together. I told people when I saw the poster of your film with your photograph on a billboard in Brixton that, look this man rented a room in my flat when his missus sent him to the doghouse. Melody misses you too. Remember Bob Marley once said: *In this bright future you can't forget your past.* Tell me Kimani, you still remember our song? You still remember how we used to sing in the nightclub, in front of Brixton and Piccadilly Circus underground stations? Kimani, please come and visit us and drink rum with me, eat jerk chicken and let us dance with you wearing the rasta wig.' Leroy laughed. 'I want to remember those days. I see you have a white missus and really beautiful children. Give thanks.

'Kimani, when you write a book about your life in London, don't forget your Brixton days. Don't forget to write about that room you rented on Cold Harbour Lane when your missus sent you to the doghouse. Don't forget your Jamaican brother who always wanted to take you to Montego Bay to find you a woman. Don't forget our song; *War is Business.*' Leroy grabbed me with two hands. 'Yah man. As I always say when I look at you, I see only the truth. Now I see your film and I see only the truth. Give thanks. Give thanks. Jah Love.' Leroy hugged me for a long time.

When Leroy released me I was a bit dazed. I looked left and there she was standing in front of me, Zainab Zubairu Bakaro. The Hausa woman was standing, not too close and not directly looking at me, just as she had many years before in the canteen. She seemed not to have changed. She was as beautiful, modest and simple as she had been many years before. She looked at me again. Our eyes met. I did not feel anything.

'*Assalaam Alaikum* Mustapha, *yaya kake?*' Her voice was the same.

'*Amin Alaikum Wa'asalaam* Zainab, nice to meet you again,' I stammered.

'How are you?' she asked looking at me.

'*Alhamdullilah,*' I answered avoiding eye contact.

Zainab gestured to a young man in suit. He stepped forward. 'Meet my husband Murtala.' We shook hands. 'I'm really happy we meet again,' Zainab continued. 'You've made all of us very proud of your astonishing achievement. You've written and directed one of the best films I've ever seen. It really touched my heart. Bilal and Aisha told me about you and gave me the invitation. We went to their restaurant to eat some days ago. They said you worked for them many years ago.'

'Yes, I worked as their kitchen porter,' I replied nodding.

'I can only imagine what you went through to get to where you are today. But as we say in Hausa: *Bawan damina, tajirin rani* (A slave to the wet season is a rich man of the harvest season).

I nodded.

As she spoke, Ms Kathy Robertson approached us with a tray of drinks. I looked at her closely. She had put on weight. I wondered if she recognised us. I wondered if she remembered that on a particular Wednesday afternoon, in the month of September, almost fourteen years before she had reprimanded me for talking to Zainab for a couple of minutes in the canteen at the London Institute of International Finance and Business.

'Water for us please,' Zainab said and took two glasses of water for herself and her husband. I noticed Ms Robertson looked closely at me. She did not say a word. I took a glass of water and thanked her.

'Mustapha,' the soft voice of Zainab floated into my ears as we walked out of the hall into the crowded foyer. '*Sannu da kokari, Allah Ya kara rufin asiri* (May Allah make you more successful). You must tell us how you made it.'

THE END

Lightning Source UK Ltd.
Milton Keynes UK
UKOW01f0507300617
304366UK00001B/27/P